M000316912

Beneath the Stars

Stars

J.L. Jackson

NEW YORK TIMES BESTSELLING AUTHOR

Copyright © 2020 A.L. Jackson Books Inc.
First Edition

All rights reserved. Except as permitted under the U.S. Copyright Act
of 1976, no part of this publication may be reproduced, distributed,
transmitted in any form or by any means, or stored in a database or
retrieval system, without prior permission of the publisher. Please
protect this art form by not pirating.

A.L. Jackson
www.aljacksonauthor.com
Cover Design by Silver at Bitter Sage Designs
Editing by Susan Staudinger
Proofreading by Julia Griffis, The Romance Bibliophile
Formatting by Mesquite Business Services

The characters and events in this book are fictitious. Names, characters,
places, and plots are a product of the author's imagination. Any
similarity to real persons, living or dead, is coincidental and not
intended by the author.

Print ISBN: 978-1-946420-64-0
eBook ISBN: 978-1-946420-53-4

Beneath the Stars

More from A.L. Jackson

prologue

Rhys
Six Months Earlier

*H*ave you ever experienced a moment in your life that should have been commonplace?

Seemingly inconsequential?

No big deal?

Yet you couldn't shake the feelin' that it might change everything? That you were on some path you shouldn't have been traveling, but you couldn't stop yourself from doing it, anyway?

I guessed that was the way I was feeling when I sat tucked into a booth at the back of the rowdy, dank bar in my hometown of Dalton, South Carolina, sipping at a beer while I watched Maggie Fitzgerald, the baby sister of one of my closest friends, guzzle the last dregs of her margarita from the straw pursed between her lips.

The girl grinned around it in some kind of drunken ecstasy

while I tried to pretend like I didn't notice how fuckin' gorgeous she was.

"Ahh, look at you, little miss drunkey drunk. You better watch yourself there, sweetness. You're looking way too happy right about now," I told her, voice rough with the tease and the assault of lust that took me over just looking at her. "Don't want to have to carry you out of here."

"Mmhmmmm..." Maggie hummed around the straw, barely loud enough that I could hear over the din. "I think I'm in love."

I itched in my seat, dying to reach out and touch a girl who was so off-limits that just sitting there felt like committing a mortal sin.

See, I wasn't exactly the type who got an A+ for good behavior.

I loved playing with fire.

But this?

It was different.

This was dancing into treachery. Treading into perilous waters.

It wasn't like we were doin' anything illegal.

Okay, at least we hadn't been until the girl had gotten up to go to the restroom and had somehow managed to return with a full pitcher of margarita and a five-thousand-watt smile on her face.

Way too pleased with herself for being able to swindle some unknowing sucker into buying it for her, but not yet quite as pleased as she was right then.

She groaned around the straw as she slurped up the last bit. "Oh my goodness ...why does this taste so good? This is the nectar of the gods," she sang-slurred as she fumbled to pour the last of the pitcher into her glass.

I stretched my arms out on the back of the booth and pointed at her where she sat across from me. "Come tomorrow mornin', you're gonna realize tequila is actually the devil's poison. Pretty sure you're gonna be rockin' a hangover like nobody's business."

"Will you hold my hair if I get sick?" She seemed way too eager by the prospect.

A rough chuckle climbed my throat. "You're really tryin' to get me in hot water, aren't you, Mag Pie? Your brother finds out where you're at tonight, and he's gonna chop off my dick, and then what am I supposed to do with my life?"

I tried not to grin at the way her eyes bugged out when I brought attention to my cock.

"That would be bad," she whispered the scandal before her expression shifted to something fierce. "But don't you think it's time I started thinking for myself? Started doing what I want to do?"

I knew Royce, Maggie's older brother, wanted to keep her in a gilded cage, especially in light of the horrible shit that had gone down in her life.

On some level, I got it. I had this crazy need to protect her, too.

The other half of me?

He wanted to open the latch and set her free.

There was no question this girl was itchin' to fly. Spread her wings, step off the ledge, and soar.

My gaze devoured her where she sat across the table.

Black waves cascaded over her delicate shoulders and ran like a river of seduction down her back.

Her charcoal eyes were big and round, the unique color like the dusting of a pencil across a page, soft and shadowed and somehow piercing at the same damned time.

Maggie Fitzgerald always looked both curious and shy.

But the thing that stood out most about her was she seemed furiously real, which considering I was nothing but a sham and a fake, only amplified the fact that I most definitely shouldn't be there.

Her nose was sharp, almost as sharp as the defined angle of her jaw, but her cheeks were somehow full and forever pinked, the lips of her sweet mouth three shades darker and verging on red.

There was a tiny dimple in her left cheek that had already driven me halfway to mad.

She was like looking at something magical.

Ethereal.

A siren who had no fuckin' clue just how dangerous she could be.

She kept staring at me like she actually wanted the answer to the question she'd asked.

"I think you should do anything and everything that brings you joy," I finally answered, straight-up honest. I took a swig from my bottle, watching her over the top.

The way those eyes traced my movements.

Like maybe she wanted to memorize them.

Maybe become a part of them.

"What if I'm just figuring out what that might mean?" she asked.

"Then you have to trust yourself to make a few mistakes along the way."

My stomach twisted in a knot of need that I refused to acknowledge. I sure as fuck wasn't gonna be one of them.

Truth be told?

Tonight's mission was all kinds of covert and most definitely unauthorized.

Just because the concert was dubbed 18+ didn't mean this little excursion wasn't one-hundred-percent illicit. No question in my mind that Royce would have my ass if he found out where I'd taken his baby sister.

His baby sister who was twenty.

His baby sister who was twelve years younger than me.

His baby sister who, since the second she'd come into town to help prepare for Royce's wedding to the lead singer of my band, had captured me in a way that I couldn't let her.

"Not sure how I let you talk me into this," I grumbled the tease.

Her brows lifted in the cutest way. Dark, dark eyes flashed something so sweet that it panged through the middle of me. "What, you don't want to make a few of those mistakes with me? And here I thought we were friends," she razzed.

That was exactly how she talked me into this.

That smile that took up the entirety of her sweet face, the one tool in this world that held the power to put a chink in my armor.

Right that second, I knew any ass-kickin' comin' my way would be a small price to pay to get to see her expression shine like that.

"Yeah, Mags, we are definitely friends."

She stretched her margarita glass across the table and clinked

4

it against my bottle. "To making a few mistakes," she murmured.

Energy zinged through the air. A bolt of lightning. Same feeling she exuded every time she got into my space.

Girl was a jolt of electricity that both soothed and sparked.

Shadows from the bar played across her face. She smiled beneath the flashin' lights, making that dimple dance and play.

Fuuuuuuck.

I wanted to reach out and touch it.

Taste it.

Gave myself a harsh shake of the head to break me out of the trance that this girl lulled me into with a glance.

Might already be on my way to Hell, but touching her? That would earn me a first-class ticket on a direct flight.

Being around her felt like balancing on a high-wire without a net underneath to catch me when I slipped.

Exhilarating and dangerous.

So forbidden I might as well have been watching her through bulletproof glass.

She sucked at that straw, and for a moment, her eyes flashed their sorrow.

Danced their demons.

I got the distinct sense that she had an unobstructed view of mine, too. Like she could see straight into me and find all the things I couldn't allow her to see.

"How are you doin', Mags?" She'd been through some shit.

Crazy shit. The culmination going down just this last week that had sent us all reeling. Maybe that was part of the reason I'd brought her here. Feeling like maybe I could step in and be something for her. A reprieve. A distraction.

Maggie pulled back from the straw, and her teeth clamped down on her bottom lip as her head pitched to the side, taken by a swell of grief.

"You want to know how I really feel, Rhys?"

I swallowed the lump that grew in my throat. "Yeah. Think I do."

She glanced away before she was staring me down with those charcoal eyes. "I feel broken. I feel freed. I feel this huge amount of relief that the chains are actually gone and now I can finally live, and at the same time, terrified that I don't know how. But I'm ready to try." She kept her gaze locked on me.

So real. So genuine. So different.

There was no missing the agony that burned from her spirit or the hope that shined from her eyes.

"I'm sorry, Maggie," I told her. "So fuckin' sorry."

Her brow pinched just a fraction. "Don't be because I'm not."

"You're kinda amazing, you know?"

Shyness crept over her face, and she fiddled with her empty glass. "You don't even know me."

I edged forward. "How's that, I thought we were friends?"

I let the ribbing wind into my tone, lovin' the way redness splashed on her cheeks.

She shrugged a little, peeking my way. "You know what I mean. But...I want us to be. Friends. Good friends. For you to know me."

She rushed the last like a secret.

Like she might regret the words later.

If she got too close, she would.

I drained the rest of my beer and set it on the table before I eased out of the booth, pushing to my full height. I moved over to her side.

My shadow eclipsed this petite girl where she looked so tiny tucked in the booth.

Wondered if she could sense the danger. Way she saw deeper. If there was some kind of warnin' going off in her mind to keep her distance and something that lured her to me at the same time.

I extended my hand. "C'mere, Sweet Thing." She stared at it before she set hers in mine.

Energy crackled.

A snap in the air.

Motherfuckin' flames.

Shit.

This girl.

She tipped her chin up my way as she climbed out to stand, and there was something playful that took to her expression. "You wanna dance with me, Cowboy?"

"Cowboy?" I said it like I was offended. "I thought I made it clear it's Stallion…Stallion, baby."

She giggled, and she tipped back her head, smiling that smile that nearly dropped me to my knees. "I think I'm gonna find me one of those, Rhys. I'm gonna find me a cowboy and move here to Dalton, have about five babies and own about ten horses. Buy a big old house that always needs work. Get away from LA forever. Leave it all behind. Doesn't it sound nice?" It was a hum and a slur and the whisper of a dream.

Chuckling a rough sound, I curled an arm around her waist. "That so? Sounds like you're gearing up for one of those mistakes."

"Or maybe it would be the best thing I could do."

I pressed my nose to her temple.

Fire.

I was no longer playing with it, I was dancing in it barefoot.

I led her to the dance floor, anyway. Like I said, I wasn't so good at making prudent choices.

I was all about the greed and gluttony.

Around us, couples two-stepped, a crush of bodies sliding and twirling and grinding.

I pulled Maggie into my arms.

That fire was doused in gasoline.

My insides went raw with a brand of need I'd never experienced before.

Like a fool, I ignored it. Pretended that it didn't matter.

That my fucking heart didn't flutter when she laughed.

That I wasn't grinning right back when her smile grew wide.

I dipped her and she squealed, girl laughing and laughing while I continued to spin her round and round.

"You're a natural, you know. You've got country in your soul, darlin'. Think we need to run out and get you some boots."

She grinned up at me. "And one of those cowboys, too?"

I chuckled even though I couldn't stomach the idea of passing her off to one of these pricks.

Thought of someone else's hands on her made my vision turn

red.

So I danced with her instead like that was what I was meant to do.

When the band shifted into a slow song, Maggie didn't hesitate to loop her arms around my neck. She rested her cheek against my chest. "What do you want in this life, Rhys?"

We were barely moving, just swaying from side-to-side. "For my band to make it. Nothin' else matters but that."

It's what we'd been working toward for what felt like our entire lives.

"Well, that and for my mama to be happy," I said on a bout of wistful laughter. "I'm gonna bulldoze her old house and build a big one in its place. That's my goal."

Maybe set fire to it and torch all the horrible memories hidden inside.

Maggie rumbled a sound of affectionate disbelief. "Haven't you realized yet that your band has already made it? Six months from now, you'll be heading to Savannah to record your big album. Everyone's going to know your name, Rhys Manning."

She stared at me like she was proud.

"That's the plan. I mean, who could forget me?" I let one of those smirks take to my face.

Redness pinked those cheeks, but she didn't look away when she whispered, "Impossible. You're unforgettable." Then she grinned, mischief winding into her tone. "Have you seen these women eyeing you? Hell, I'm probably going to have to walk home with all these girls who want to get with you. I think three or four of them are currently trying to figure out how to lure me into the bathroom so they can shank me. Get me out of the way so they can get close to you."

I pulled her closer. "You really think I'd ditch you?"

"Um…let's see…your friend's little sister who begged to tag along, or one of these gorgeous women who would know how to handle a man like you?"

Uneasiness flooded her expression, even though she kept her tone light when she asked it.

Trying to play and pretend like it didn't matter and hating the idea of it, too.

I felt it.

Knew it.

Two of us were treading those treacherous waters.

Reaching out, I let my fingertips flutter along the angle of her cheek, right over that dimple that I'd been dying to touch.

Playing that reckless, greedy game.

"No contest, Mags. No contest." I forced some levity into my words before I went and said something I couldn't take back. "Besides, haven't you heard it said, friends before fucks?"

I gave her a big, waggish grin.

Maggie laughed and blushed and grinned, and shit, she was so fuckin' cute.

"No...no, I've never heard that said before. I guess I must be a *really good friend*." She let something flirty infiltrate her voice.

I wanted to sink into it.

Slip inside.

Get lost.

Fuck.

I needed to rein myself in.

Hold myself back.

I was losin' footing.

That high-wire I was balancing on was fraying fast.

I spun her again. Slowly this time, so out of time with the music, Maggie and I moving to our own beat. Pulling her back, I slipped an arm around her waist and murmured, "Good, good friends," close to her cheek, wonderin' if there was any point in hiding what she was doin' to me.

What I was wanting.

This energy that quietly boomed. A thunder that grew.

I knew I couldn't go there.

She was sweet and good and innocent and had been hurt enough, and the last fuckin' thing I wanted was to be responsible for injuring her in any way.

Even if she was only looking for a good time, which was the one thing I was good for, I doubted very much the prudence of her having it with me.

Six months from now, we'd all be on Tybee Island to record. Royce would be there because he was married to our lead singer, Emily, and we were in talks with his band, A Riot of Roses, about doing some kind of collaboration, so they likely would be there, too.

Bottom line? Maggie would certainly be there, and gettin' naked was probably the type of debris we didn't need strewn between us.

Besides…fun didn't make you feel like this.

Because she sighed and rested her cheek back on my chest. Though she curled her arms so tight around me there was no space left to separate us, like she was trying to find her way inside.

I didn't think I could really hear the questions, I just felt the words that she muttered against my heart that was battering at my chest. "What do you really want, Rhys? Under it all? After the fame? After the music? After the money?"

I want to take it back.

I want to erase the pain.

I want to make it right.

Impossible.

So I gave her the next best thing. "I just want to enjoy each day. Make it better for the people around me."

She tightened her hold, and she shifted to look up at me, her body tucked against mine.

So tight and hot.

All wrong and undeniably right.

And God, I was such a dirty fuck because my dick was hard and my breaths had gone shallow, fingers itchin' to explore.

Feeling myself being drawn, I leaned closer.

Our noses touched.

Her sweet, seductive mouth parted, and her pulse ran wild.

Those eyes flared with a desire and an innocence that made me sure she was not to be toyed with.

Fuck.

I wanted to kiss her.

Devour her.

Show her that she was beautiful.

That she was to be cherished.

But I knew better than to go playin' these games.

Knew better than touchin' a treasure. One that the only thing I would ever do was turn around and taint.

Forcing myself from the haze of lust, I peeled myself from her sweet body and pinned on a casual smirk that was nothing but feigned. "Gotta piss."

Classy.

But it was best if she took me for a thickheaded fuckwit who didn't have any manners. There were probably about a thousand women scattered around the world who would attest to the fact, anyway.

Maggie frowned.

Yeah.

Felt like frowning, too.

I squeezed her shoulder like I was talking to a kid. "Why don't you head back to the booth? I'll be right back to settle the tab. Think we'd better call it a night. Get you tucked in."

Awesome, Rhys. Lay it on thick.

"Sure. Yeah. Okay," she mumbled, confused by the shift.

She went to chewin' at her lip again, dropping her attention to her feet, and shit, I hated that she even thought for a second that I might want to reject whatever the hell this was, but I was doing her a favor.

"Be right back." Before I went and did somethin' stupid, I angled through the crowd and down the hall into the men's restroom. Trying to get myself together.

To reiterate the five-fuckin'-thousand reasons I couldn't touch her.

No, douchewad, a one-night stand with your friend's little sister is not a brilliant idea. Might be the worst one you've ever had.

And believe me, I'd had plenty enough stupid ideas to last me a lifetime.

In the restroom, I went straight to the sink and splashed cold water onto my face, dragging in deep, steadying breaths. When I finally managed to get the raging need in check, I headed back out and down the hall.

I shouldered through the crowd that had grown tenfold since I'd gone to the restroom.

Bodies packed.

Greedy and wild.

A disorder on which I normally thrived but tonight suddenly had me feeling all wrong.

My chest grew tight.

My hands tingled.

I needed to get her out of there.

Away from me.

I should have listened to those warnings that had lit in my mind in the first place.

I pushed through the mob back toward the booth.

Nearly tripped when I broke through the crush and found some jagoff salivating all over her at our booth.

The girl sat there in the shadows while he leaned over the table and probably fed her some seedy line.

Rage hit me from out of nowhere.

A kick to the gut.

A twisted possession I had no right to feel.

That connection shivered and glittered and closed in at the edges of my sight.

I tried to swallow it down.

Wasn't like she was a child. Wasn't like she couldn't make her own decisions.

But I couldn't shake the sensation screaming at me that somethin' just wasn't right.

I scrubbed a hand over my face to curb the disorder that took to my spirit.

Relief filled Maggie's expression when she saw me come up behind the prick who was still leering over her.

"Hey, baby, you ready to get out of here?" I let the claim bleed free like it was real. A demand for him to get lost and to do it fast.

I managed to keep my cool.

That was until I caught a glimpse of his profile.

Ice streaked down my spine.

Heart stalling.

Spirit sinking.

Fear.

Fury.

Agony.

All it took was one second for every fucking one of my ghosts to catch up to me.

Howling their warning of destruction.

Rage came bounding in behind it. No space for anythin' rational when the only thing I wanted to do was choke him out and keep going until he had no chance of ever coming back up for air.

In the flash of a second, I had a hand locked at the back of his neck, my voice whispering murder up close to his ear, "What the fuck are you doin' here?"

He shifted to look at me, just enough that I could see the smug smirk on his face, promising this little encounter wasn't close to being by chance. "Just asking a pretty girl to dance. You got a problem with that?"

Knew he knew I'd broken the rules.

That I'd overstepped a boundary.

That he was there, searching for any way to make me pay. To tighten the chains that would forever bind me.

My teeth grated, and I fought the bile that rushed as memories surged. I struggled to beat it back, to take on the persona that I wore best, just an easy-go-lucky guy who didn't give a fuck.

But right then, that guy didn't exist.

"Get the fuck out," I seethed, fighting the rush of dizziness that spun my head.

Her face flashed.

Sickness churned.

I was sure I'd been sucked under water, so deep I couldn't tell up from down.

Drowning.

He laughed a morbid sound and swiveled to fully face me. Asshole with hatred writhing on his smug face that I wanted to break. "Wow. So overbearing. Don't you think we should let the lady decide? Or are you all about defiling her, too?"

Tormented fury clouded my sight.

I fisted a hand in the collar of his shirt.

"I said to get the fuck out. Get the fuck out of this town." I choked over the words, every one of them jagged, broken glass.

Maggie was suddenly standing at my side.

A soft hand landed on my arm.

A balm tugging me from the daze.

"Rhys…" Her voice was soft. Calming. Like the girl could touch me in the darkness. "I was just telling him I was here with someone. It's okay. Let's just go, okay? It's okay."

My brow pinched, and I sucked in a breath, and I shoved him off while I warred with the need to go for him.

To end this now.

Keeping one eye on the asshole, I dug into my wallet and pulled out a few bills to cover the tab. I tossed them onto the table then jammed a finger in his direction. "Stay the fuck away from us."

"Funny, I could say the same."

It was a flat-out threat.

I fought to ignore the weight of it, and instead, sent his pompous ass a parting glare as I grabbed Maggie's hand to haul her out.

I didn't make it a foot before his words struck me from behind, "Who is she, Rhys? Tonight's fuck or does she have a name? Hmmm…I think she has a name, doesn't she? I saw her getting out of your car. What would she think if she knew?"

I was on him before I realized I'd even made the move.

Blinded.

A boiling fury that covered all reason.

A rage that extinguished all sight.

He was wearing that superior smile when I grabbed him by the back of the head and slammed his face against the tabletop.

I should have taken that expression as a warning, but I was feeling too much satisfaction in the sound of his nose crunching on the wood.

The table shook, and our empties toppled and crashed to the floor.

Glass shattered as I gave in to the intent of shattering the bastard's face. Fisting two hands in the back of his shirt, I flipped him over.

Blood spurted from his nose, streamed down around his mouth, and dripped from his chin.

"She's no one. No one." The harrowed words rasped from my throat as I threw another punch.

Fist after fist.

Each blow harder than the last.

I devolved into incoherency.

Fell into insanity.

Like I could pound Maggie's face from his brain.

Spare her from the misery of who I was.

The fucker just grinned beneath the blows.

His white teeth smeared with blood.

I could almost feel the stakes of what I'd said impale her.

But I had to do it.

Couldn't risk it.

Couldn't afford it.

Hadn't I already known what being around her was gonna do?

On a groan, the prick slumped to the ground. But he was still grinning, already sure of the result.

He'd achieved exactly what he'd set out to do.

I dropped to my knees, gasping for a breath that I couldn't find. The music was dead, and every person in the place had gathered around to get a firsthand peek at the carnage of *happy-go-lucky* me.

Rhys-motherfucking-Manning.

Most of them were recording or snapping pictures.

Fuck. My eyes raced for the girl.

The girl who was twenty feet away where she'd been dragged back by a bouncer. He had his hands on her shoulders to keep her out of the fray. My wary gaze tangled with those charcoal eyes that were etched in hurt and confusion.

"I'm sorry," I mouthed.

Two more bouncers broke through.

"Don't fuckin' move."

One of them grabbed me from behind and dragged me back.

I didn't fight it.

Just let him push me facedown to the sticky floor with my arms pinned behind my back.

Didn't know how long he held me there until sirens could be heard from outside. The sea parted when officers and paramedics descended on the scene.

They put me in cuffs and yanked me to my feet.

Maggie stared at me.

Hurt and helpless.

Regret lanced through my chest.

I wanted to go to her.

Tell her I was sorry.

That I didn't mean what I'd said.

But it was for the best.

It was for the best.

I didn't even know why I'd wondered it.

It was inevitable.

I destroyed the good.

Broke the beautiful.

I'd known it from the beginning, hadn't I?

Except *I* was the road that shouldn't be traveled. I was the dead end. I was the disaster waiting up ahead, and she was the one who didn't have the first clue.

And I refused to be the downfall of Maggie Penelope.

Maggie
Six Months Later

*O*nce a bad boy, always a bad boy?

It would seem so for Rhys Manning, the bassist of Carolina George, record giant *Stone Industries'* latest musical lovechild. Manning is scheduled to be in court late next month on charges of assault and disorderly conduct against a patron at a local bar in his hometown of Dalton, South Carolina.

It seems Manning, known for his charismatic stage presence and his penchant for leaving behind a superhighway of dropped panties and broken hearts, also loves to leave behind a trail of brawls and barfights.

Celebrity Spread has learned the country-rocker has a record almost as long as the notches in his belt. After five arrests and two minor convictions, Manning now stands to serve up to six months in jail.

Earlier this year, Carolina George announced its first major-label album, backed by Stone Industries, will be released this winter, though sources close to the band have been tight-lipped about when they are scheduled to be in the studio.

When a storm of speculation about Manning leaving the band hit the social media airwaves after he disappeared from the spotlight, Carolina George offered this official statement: "Our band is family, blood or not, and that includes Rhys Manning. We can't do what we do without him. We believe the fight occurred in self-defense, and we stand behind him one-hundred-percent."

Yet at his arrest, Rhys Manning showed no signs of injuries.

The band stole millions of hearts during their stunning performance at last year's ACB Awards, and now adoring fans are desperate for more.

But will this chronic bad behavior derail Carolina George's skyrocketing rise to superstardom or will the turmoil only feed the band's creative force? Only time will tell.

Throat thick, I reread the article that had been published last week as I sat in the backseat of the black SUV that sped toward our destination on Tybee Island.

Nerves fired through my body.

A chaos of excitement and dread that toiled and pled from the depths of me.

I guessed I finally understood why they called it a *crush*.

It might have been the first one I'd ever had, but I recognized the heaviness that sat like a ton of bricks at the center of my chest. Recognized the way my heart pinched and squeezed and made it feel like it was difficult to breathe.

Constricting and compressing.

Part of me felt desperate to see his face. To get the affirmation that he was fine and whole, while the other half still felt raw and broken by what he'd done.

It wasn't like we were a couple or anything.

I wasn't delusional.

But I swore there'd been something there.

Something that was bigger than the two of us.

Something unfound that had begged to be acknowledged.

And then he'd just...freaked out.

Beat the hell out of that guy for no reason.

All while he spewed words against me.

Words that had slayed and stung.

After that?

Nothing.

Not a word.

I hadn't heard from Rhys Manning in six months.

Radio silence.

So I'd resorted to this—stalking him on the internet.

Devouring any articles I could find. Searching his hashtags for a glimpse. Gorging myself on his music night and day.

Pathetic.

But it was like he'd disappeared from the face of the earth.

Only a few pictures had popped up of him in all that time— one of him with his mama in his hometown and a few others with women who were reposting from times before.

And I worried. Worried for him.

That he wasn't okay.

That whatever demons had possessed him that night had completely infiltrated his heart and mind.

Taken over.

And I had no way to call him out of it.

I shifted in my seat, trying to pull myself together.

I needed to remind myself it wasn't my job.

We were barely even friends.

Besides, I had enough of my own mess to deal with, didn't I? Only God knew the kind of trouble I'd brought into my life.

I reached into the top pocket of my purse and ran my fingers over the little origami duck that was tucked inside.

Feeling its worn edges.

I'd made it in my group therapy class. It was meant to be an illustration that we had the power to reshape our circumstances. Form them into what we wanted them to be. That we might have been dealt a bad card, but we had the power to fashion that card into a new shape.

At the time, I'd picked a duck since it was easy to make. But there'd been something to it, and I'd kept the duck all this time, carrying it around with me as a reminder that I was in control.

Yeah.

My own demons might be on the hunt, but I was going to do whatever it took to pull this off.

It would be worth it in the end.

From where he sat in the middle row in front of me, my older brother Royce released a strained sigh. "Still not sure about all of this," he grumbled as he roughed his tattooed fingers through his shock of black hair.

A rush of his anxiety slammed me. Palpable. As if it were a part of my consciousness.

I guessed that was the hardest part about being me.

It always seemed as if I felt too much, and the moods of people could be overwhelming.

The feel of it was wonderful and horrible, and everything in between.

"And just what aren't you sure about?" his wife Emily questioned, voice wry and filled with a shot of southern amusement.

She sat on the opposite side of him, their sweet newborn Amelia nestled in her car seat in between.

"Dragging Maggie all the way out here." He didn't hesitate to say what was on his mind.

I frowned. "Is that your subtle way of saying you're sick of your baby sister tagging along everywhere you go?"

From over his shoulder, Royce trained his dark gaze on me, the smile that graced his face close to a sneer. "Nah. It's my way of sayin' I hate that I'm always exposing you to douchebags."

There was no missing the guilt that flashed in his eyes.

My head barely shook. "That's untrue, Royce."

A grunt escaped his throat. "Untrue? Seems to me every time I turn around, you're getting hurt by someone I introduced you to."

Suffice it to say Royce had been pissed over the whole Rhys debacle.

He'd been terrified when I'd called him in the middle of the night, drunk and crying and asking him to pick me up.

Finding the bassist of Carolina George cuffed and being dragged to a cruiser had only made it worse.

Royce had been irate.

Demanding to know what the hell I'd been doing with him. Hardly willing to believe we were only friends. "I wasn't in any danger."

"Bullshit," he refuted.

Emily sent him a warning glare.

He cringed. "Fuck...I just hate that every time I turn around, seems like there's something I can't stop or control when it comes to you."

"That's because it's not your job," I told him, my tone going soft. Laden with the affection that I felt for him.

My brother might look bad, made of stone and printed in mayhem, but I'd learned long ago that it was what was on the inside that mattered.

Royce had been my savior. My hope. My liberator when I hadn't been strong enough to stand or speak for myself. Now that I could? Now that I'd found my freedom and my strength?

He was having a hard time letting go.

The fact I seemed to be a magnet for disaster didn't help things.

"And then your goddamned condo caught fire..." he gruffed

21

out.

You know, like that.

"I wasn't even home, and I'm completely fine," I finished for him.

I beat back the guilt for leaving out the rest.

The sense I'd gotten that it hadn't been an accident when I'd gotten back to my complex and had found a fleet of firetrucks and ambulances in front of my building.

The fact I'd thought someone might have been in my car earlier, searching for something I made sure no one could find.

But that was the problem when you'd lived most of your life in fear. Paranoia took hold, and you no longer could discern when that danger was real or conjured in the darkest places of your mind.

So, I shoved it all back down into that bottomless pit where it belonged. Refused to remain a prisoner to it.

I would no longer be chained by my past.

Emily touched Royce's arm. "And since we're lookin' at the bright side…let's remember that means Maggie is spending the summer with us and we have someone we can fully trust to take care of Amelia. Love her the way we do."

She glanced back at me, her blonde braid swishing over her shoulder, her sweet face filled with the adoration she had for me.

Love pulsed.

I couldn't be more grateful that after what I'd cost Royce earlier in his life that he'd found this…

The greatest joy.

A wife filled with grace and strength and loyalty.

A new baby girl.

He was also reconnecting and establishing a relationship with his older daughter who he'd lost years ago.

Not to mention the fact he'd reunited with his band.

"I couldn't imagine a better way to spend my summer than with all of you…watching Amelia…spending time with the rest of the band and their families. They've all become that to me…family," I told them.

The original plan had been that I would spend the summer in LA at my own place. Continue working. Continue figuring out what I wanted to do with my life.

But the fire had displaced me, so I'd asked to come along. Offered to watch Amelia in exchange for a place to stay.

It wasn't like Royce would leave me homeless, anyway. But I was tired of him having to rescue me.

A tender smile pulled at the edge of Emily's mouth, her joy full and real. I inhaled it, held onto the hope of it.

"Then maybe this was exactly the way it was supposed to be." She reached out so she could squeeze my hand.

Before she had a chance to glimpse at what was on my screen, I flipped my phone over. The last thing I wanted was for her to discover my little obsession with the bassist of her band.

I reached for her and squeezed back. "I think you're right."

Royce grunted. "Just stay away from handsy assholes, yeah?"

"You mean that as in one particular asshole?" I pushed.

He shrugged. "If it fits."

"Says the guy who has his whole wild, unruly band comin' to record with us in a couple weeks?" Emily asked, a tease lilting her voice.

So A Riot of Roses was known as being exactly that—a riot. Royce's three oldest friends were untamed and a little unhinged.

But I'd never gotten a malicious vibe from them.

They were good guys who'd done some dumb things.

"Awesome. Now you're really tryin' to give me a heart attack," he said with a feigned scowl.

"Just tellin' it like it is."

"And let's not forget that I'm not twelve," I told him, not sure if I wanted to laugh or if I was actually annoyed.

But that was the thing when you were twenty and had never even been kissed.

Your naivety and vulnerability showed.

My heart lurched as the memory assaulted me. Rhys so close. Those big, big hands on my body. His mouth a breath away. His spirit surrounding me. His need palpable.

I'd been sure.

So sure.

I swallowed the lump in my throat.

Royce smirked. "You might not be twelve anymore, but you'll always be my baby sister."

"You know, I will meet a man one day." No harm in taunting my overprotective big brother a little.

"And he'll meet all the criteria." Royce lifted a hand in the air and started ticking off his fingers. "One, he's gotta be a nerd. The awkward type. Pose no threat. Two…he needs to be smart. A professor or a doctor or some shit like that. Three…he's never been in trouble—not even a ticket. Slow and safe. Four…he has to love his mama." He lifted his thumb on the last. "Oh…and a virgin. Let's not forget that."

I rolled my eyes. "I am quite sure that man does not exist."

Besides, he wasn't *the* man. The man who made me shiver and shake. The one who currently had my insides twisted in a fist. At least he had one thing going for him—there was no question he loved his *mama*.

"Fine by me."

Emily swatted him on the side of the arm. "You stop it. And would you watch your mouth. Our Amelia here has sensitive ears."

His brow lifted toward the sky. "She's six weeks old."

"And you think she doesn't hear you? Look at her little mouth twisting every time she hears your voice."

"Fine. I'll find better things to do with my mouth." He leaned over and started running kisses along Emily's neck.

I ducked my gaze and tried not to blush when I felt the roll of need and love billow through the air.

It was beautiful, but I definitely didn't need to bear witness to it.

Emily giggled and Royce rumbled something I couldn't make out before he pulled away, still angled to the side but twisting his attention so he was facing me.

Any playfulness had been wiped from his face. "I respect you, Maggie. Know you're grown and you've got to do your own thing. But promise me one thing…promise you'll keep your distance from Rhys. He's trouble…the kind of trouble you don't need."

Worry heaved from his spirit.

And I knew he was right.

Rhys was trouble.

A danger to my soul. A threat to my heart that was barely mending. The scars so deep.

"I promise," I forced out, not sure if it was a lie.

Royce nodded. "Good."

He sat back in his seat, and Emily sent me a covert glance.

Her green eyes full of knowing concern.

Like she held a secret of mine.

Meeting her gaze, I attempted an indifferent smile. The one she returned was sympathetic.

Royce shifted around and sat forward.

Emily's voice was soft though running with an undercurrent of fortitude. "And I need you to remember something, too, Royce...Rhys is one of my best friends. Like a brother to me. I know up until a few months ago, you'd come to feel the same way."

Royce sighed. "I know that, Emily. But my sister will always be my first concern. You gotta respect that."

"I do. I'm just askin' you to respect mine and Rhys' relationship, too. I truly believe he would never want to put her in danger. Sure, he's made mistakes, but he is a good man."

His nod was tight.

The two of them settled as we continued down the highway.

I stared at the back of his head.

The man was so rough and fiercely protective.

I knew it would take time for him to let go of all that had happened to me. What had happened to him. His single drive for so many years had been taking out the ones who had hurt us.

Now that they were gone, I sometimes wondered if he weren't a little lost.

Floundering.

Like he was no longer quite sure of his purpose.

Thing was, I was sure there would always be a piece of me who would cling to him, too.

The part that would never forget what he'd sacrificed.

What he'd done.

I would forever be grateful.

Indebted.

I turned to gaze out the window at the passing marshlands that flashed by with each mile that brought us closer to the sea.

It suddenly felt like the moment was fluid.

Liquid.

A shaken concoction from the normal as we raced for the house that would be our home for the summer.

It felt as far away from Los Angeles as could be.

Our driver slowed as we got into town.

A town that whispered of peace and quiet and faith.

Like Dalton.

Warmth spread through my veins and my spirit shivered in anticipation.

The stampeding of my heart only intensified when the ocean suddenly came into view.

Crisp, blue waters fronted by white, smooth sand.

High grasses grew along the dunes, and the road curved so that we were following along rows of houses, condos, and apartments that faced the beach.

The houses here seemed older, not close to boasting of riches and luxury, but more a testament to that slowed, relaxed pace. Downtown, people strolled the sidewalks fronting bars, restaurants, and hotels in their beach attire.

Casually.

Relaxed and without a care.

We made it from one end to the other in what seemed a blip since the town was so tiny.

The driver made a left and started to inch down a narrow road.

Hurt and confusion fluttered and pulled at my insides, all mixed up with a flurry of excitement that had my breaths going short and shallow.

Here, the homes became increasingly larger and more luxurious. They were mostly concealed by palms and spindly trees, giving privacy to the beachfront properties.

I inhaled a shaky breath, taking in the sultry scent of the sea.

The driver took two more quick turns before he pulled through a gate and into a private driveway that made a big circle in front of an even larger house.

The Stone Industries mansion that housed its artists while they recorded.

Anxiety and need crawled over me when it came into view.

A shiver that raced across my flesh.

Not because I was impressed by lavish things. I'd seen plenty of that growing up the daughter of a crooked, wicked music mogul who's worth was only found in the wealth that he controlled.

I learned quickly those things meant little to me.

I knew firsthand what greed could do. The lengths that people would go to in order to build and protect it.

But this…this was for a man who'd turned me inside out and hadn't had the first clue.

The one who didn't know he'd been the first to make me feel.

The first to make me want.

I inhaled a sharp breath when that anticipation turned to a burn.

A boil in my blood that had sweat slicking across my skin.

The SUV came to a stop in the round drive in front of the five massive steps leading to the front door.

I tried to convince myself the physical reaction was only because I was getting ready to witness history being made. Two bands at completely different spectrums of the music industry, one country and the other metal, preparing to converge in the same spot.

Carolina George and A Riot of Roses.

A confluence of differences and like-minds that together I was sure sheer magic would be made.

Or maybe it was the fire.

The truth that I was displaced from my first home.

Or maybe…maybe I should just be real.

Accept it.

Acknowledge it was entirely, one-hundred-percent, due to that *crush*.

That mad, unrelenting crush that made me feel like I was going to get pulverized.

Smashed into oblivion. Because standing at the top of the steps was Rhys Manning.

Thick and tall and intimidating.

Since the last time I'd seen him, he'd grown a full beard.

He wore jeans and a tee that stretched across his wide, wide shoulders.

The playfulness he wore like a brand barely covered the outright strength that blistered from underneath, and I could see the layer of rigid worry tighten his corded muscles.

But what he was known for was all there—the fame he'd gained for himself that had women dropping to their knees—the tease of sex that seeped from his skin and his smirking, delicious mouth.

Those blue eyes were warm and dancing and oh so sweet.

From where he stood staring down at us, I was sure my chest was caving in. My heart beating wild for a man who was twelve years older than me.

So off-limits it wasn't even funny.

So out of reach he might as well have been a poster tacked on my wall.

In an instant, I was both terrified and ensnared.

And I knew Royce was right.

I had to stay away because Rhys Manning would bring me the type of trouble I couldn't afford.

Rhys

"Here...let me get that." I tugged at the suitcase Maggie had dragged out of the back of the SUV.

Rays of sunlight speared through the heated sky, the air sticky and hot. The severity of it was eased just a fraction by the light breeze that gathered over the ocean and billowed through the trees.

Paying us no mind, the rest of her family scrambled around to gather the mountain of shit they had brought along. When they'd first rolled up, I'd gone directly to Emily and pulled her into a big, welcoming hug, not close to bein' faked considering I'd missed her so damned much, then my poor heart had gotten all mushed up when I got a peek at her new baby girl who was the sweetest, tiniest thing.

Then I'd moved over to Royce and had shaken his stiff hand.

Suffice it to say the guy hadn't been as excited to see me as Emily had been.

I'd convinced myself the only thing I was gonna give Maggie was a harmless, indifferent wave. You know, keep my distance like a wise man would do. Then I'd found myself standing in front of her two seconds later.

But since I was only trying to help her with her bag, I figured that at least earned me a C- for behavior.

Look at me—I wasn't totally failing.

"It's fine," Maggie muttered as she tightened her hold on the handle.

I set my hand over hers.

Ah.

There we go.

I'd call it an F+.

Because both of us froze.

Taken by that flash of fire that neither of us should be feelin'.

"Please." The word came out rough and like an apology and didn't have a fuckin' thing to do with the bag.

The girl had barely dared to look at me since she'd climbed out of the backseat in all her sweet, soft, siren glory.

Wearin' these high-waisted black fitted jeans and a cropped tee that showed off a swath of silky skin, high-top white Chucks on her feet, the river of black cascading over her shoulders in the softest waves.

My fingers itched.

I'd prayed it would have evaporated over the last six months, or maybe that I'd just have become immune to it—that aura that surrounded her.

The warmth.

The heat.

That unsettled peace I wanted to dip my fingers into and pull into my mouth. Taste it on my tongue.

No such luck.

The force of it had hit me like a shockwave the second she'd set her feet on the ground. In the second she'd risked a peek at me with those charcoal eyes before jerking her attention away.

So sweet and sexy I could hardly breathe.

In reluctance, Maggie sighed. "If it'll make you happy."

"Think it's the other way around, Sweet Thing."

She barely shook her head, like she didn't know what to make of me. "Go for it. I have plenty of other things to bring in."

She ducked back into the SUV and pulled out three giant duffle bags and a couple smaller totes, dropping them to the ground with an *oomph*.

"Crap," she muttered, looking at all her stuff.

I reached down to grab a couple of those duffles.

"I'll get them," she rushed.

I swiveled away when she tried to grab them. "Nah, I've got it."

She wavered. God, she really didn't want me to help out, did she?

Was gonna do it anyway.

I slung one on either shoulder.

Was a good thing I'd been hittin' the gym, because holy fuck, she must have packed bricks in these bags. "Good lord, woman, what do you have in here?"

Her face twisted up in a way I didn't get before her brother was interrupting again.

"Need help, Mag Pie?" Royce's voice was gruff. No question, it was meant for me because it sounded a whole hell of a lot more like a warnin'.

"I got it," I told him. "Looks to me like you and my Em-Girl have plenty to keep you busy."

He grunted.

Maggie just ignored him and started for the massive house.

I followed behind. Trying to give her space and not wantin' to at the same time.

The urge to apologize was overwhelming. To explain what couldn't be explained.

I knew it'd hurt her. Not returning a single one of her calls. I'd heard it clear in her honeyed voice that had whispered her worry through the line when she'd left a handful of messages over the last six months, her concern stark, all mixed up with this fear and confusion of who I was.

Like she'd known she should stay away but didn't know how.

Might have been a dick move, but I figured the least I could do was dodge that bullet for her.

Hell, I was the one who'd fired it in the first place.

I'd known from the get-go I never should have taken her there. Never should have put her in that position. Not when she'd made me feel the way she had.

We climbed the five steps, and our feet echoed on the marble tile as we stepped inside. The house was this rambling, white gleaming show of extravagance.

Maggie paused in the middle of the foyer that was half the size of my mama's house back home, the girl taking in the two-story wall of windows that overlooked the Atlantic Ocean.

Over the mesmerizing ebb and flow of the waves that could barely be heard from where we stood.

"It's beautiful." Her voice was filled with all the awe that surrounded the girl.

Her peace.

Her beauty.

My insides shook.

I just kept lookin' at the stunning line of her profile where I stood three feet behind her and off to the side. "Yeah."

She peeked over her shoulder. Charcoal eyes flashed. Like they were sketching me. Soft, soft pencil-strokes that wanted to write their own story.

"Isn't it funny how looking at the sea makes you feel so small? Like how all your problems suddenly seem insignificant in the grand scheme of things?"

There was something knowing in the way she said it. In the tilt of her head that took me in like she was readin' me. Like her spirit had direct access to mine and there wasn't a fuckin' thing I could hide.

Before I could respond, she turned away and heaved her bags back onto her shoulders. "Do you know which room is mine?"

I shook myself from the stupor. Pulled my shit together because I couldn't be losin' control again. "Yep. I got you covered,

Sweet Thing. Right this way. Hope you're okay with spending the next three months bunked right next to me. Sharin' a bathroom, too."

Shea Stone had made the suggestion to put all the families with children on one wing and those without on the other.

I should have complained.

Found a way to explain why it was a bad idea.

Maybe told a tale or two about how I actually loved the idea of being woken up every night by crying babies.

Supes fun.

I hadn't.

Those eyes flared.

Concern and attraction.

She seemed to steel herself and lifted her chin. "I guess I'm going to have to be, aren't I?"

"Good." Angling around her sweet body, I headed for the grand staircase that curved as it made its way for the second floor, my heavy boots echoing loud against the shiny floors. I hoisted the ridiculously heavy bags higher onto my shoulders and lifted the wheeled suitcase so I could carry it. I tossed a glance at her as she started up behind me. "You need any help?"

Maggie all but rolled her eyes. "I think I'm plenty capable of carrying a couple bags upstairs. You and my brother are going to have to give it up."

A grin pulled at the corner of my mouth. "And what are we supposed to give up?"

"Treating me like a child."

Against my better judgment, which clearly was lackin', my eyes raked her. Head to toe.

"Don't look much like a child to me. Besides, my mama would have my ass if I didn't act like a gentleman." I let the tease wind into the last.

She edged farther up the staircase, and I guess I didn't really realize all that beauty had brought me to a complete standstill until she was right there, in front of me, brushing by with a whisper of that seductive voice as she passed, "And just exactly how does a gentleman treat a woman, Rhys Manning?"

It rang of shy seduction.

A surge of that energy erupted in the air.

A silent boom that held enough power to blast through my insides.

Something that wrapped me whole and thudded my heart in an errant beat.

Fuck me.

I was pretty sure Maggie Fitzgerald had been sent to torture me.

A penalty.

Punishment.

She'd made it to the top landing by the time I finally regained coherency from the spell she had me under. I forced myself into action, hurrying behind her like a panting dog with his tongue hangin' out.

Hell, was pretty sure my tail was waggin', too.

When she got to the top, I called, "To the right, Sweet Thing…and then you're gonna be the second door on the right."

She headed that way, and I'd caught up to her by the time she made it to her room. Before she had the chance to step inside, I let loose the grumble of a confession. "That's what I was tryin' to do, you know?"

She paused at the threshold to look back.

Girl slaying me with a glance.

A riot broke out in my guts. This war of regret and guilt at odds with the hope and need she sparked.

Bad, bad combination.

What the fuck was she doin' to me?

"What?" she asked.

"Respect you."

Disbelief filled her expression before she turned and moved into her room, the disappointment in her mumbled words echoing off the walls as she dropped her bags and took in her surroundings, "Is that how friends show respect? Ignoring them for months?"

Shutting the door behind me, I set her things on the floor, and then I gave into that bit of bad behavior by easing up behind her where she'd gone to stand in front of the flowy, translucent drapes that covered the balcony doors. She'd nudged them open a fraction to look out at the view of the ocean below.

Rays of glittering light streaked through.

Illuminating the girl like a dream.

Lust jumped into my bloodstream and seeped all the way to my bones.

I had to suppress a groan. It didn't matter that my mind hadn't strayed from her for the last six months, that she'd affected me in a way she couldn't, knew full well taking of this sweet, shy, innocent girl would be nothing short of savage gluttony.

My dick needed to simmer the fuck down.

Still, I was inching forward. Drawn into her space. Filling my senses with that sweet, sweet scent.

Jasmine and vanilla.

My voice was gruff when I leaned in and whispered at her ear, "I didn't want to hurt you."

A chill rolled down her spine and that tight body trembled.

Took my all not to press my front to her back. Not to reach out and trace the path of that shiver with my fingertips.

"But you did," she whispered.

Girl shocked me by turning around to face me.

Stealing my breath and a bit of that sanity, too.

"But you did," she repeated. "I was worried about you."

"Didn't want you to be."

She scoffed out something that sounded like frustration. "You can't just make that decision for me. Whether I care about you or not."

My head barely shook. "You and I both know that whatever went down on that dance floor was crossing a line that can't be crossed. I'm not the kind of guy you should care about. I'll only end up hurting you. That night should have been proof enough. Only thing I'm good for is a good time."

I forced a smirk when I said the last.

Maggie didn't smile.

"I'm not scared." Except when she said it, she shook. Words scraping her throat as she pushed them out.

My chuckle was rough and full of a disdain that was fully directed at myself, and I was easing in closer, so fuckin' close because I was the fool who just couldn't seem to stay away.

Beggin' for trouble.

Everything about her was shy. But it was a *knowing* kind of naivety.

She had experienced things no one should ever have to.

Innocent except for something profound that radiated from her soul.

This girl who could do me in.

Greed consumed me, and I reached out to let a knuckle trace along the delicate angle of her jaw.

Need crackled in the air. That *thing* there was no chance we could acknowledge.

Maggie released a ragged, stuttered breath.

My words were gravel. "You should be."

Before I let myself slip any farther, I ripped myself away and forced myself to head for the Jack and Jill bathroom that adjoined our rooms.

I needed to put about a thousand miles between us. I'd say between here and Dalton would do, except for the fact I hadn't been able to purge her from my mind in all the months she'd been in LA.

A fuckin' continent between us, and still I was achin' for something I couldn't have.

Her voice speared me to the spot when she whispered at my back, "You're right. I am scared, Rhys. I'm scared of the way you make me feel. Of the way you make me feel something I don't understand."

I swung a glance at her from over my shoulder, taking in the girl where she stood in front of the balcony.

Beautiful in a way that shouldn't be real.

"Believe me, darlin', I feel the same. But you and I can't go there."

For a second, we stared.

Just fuckin'…caught.

"Friends?" she finally forced.

"Yeah, Sweet Thing. Friends."

Maggie gave me a tight nod, and then I pushed into the bathroom, shutting the door to her room before I crossed to mine and shut that one, too, because shit, we needed some barriers between us.

I heaved out a sigh of relief that we'd actually made it through that encounter halfway unscathed, and then I sucked in a startled breath when I noticed the dark figure lurking across my room.

In an instant, the storm gathered.

My insides clotted with fury, and a shock of rage curled my hands into fists.

Took me a flash of a second to come to realize who was standing there. That it hadn't been the type of threat I'd been anticipating, though I shouldn't have been surprised by this one, either.

Blowing out the strain that nearly had caused me an aneurysm and forcing myself to play it cool, I smacked an overexaggerated hand over my chest. "Scared the shit outta me, bro. You tryin' to give a poor boy a heart attack? For a second there, I thought the Grim Reaper had come to pay a visit. I mean, shit, look at you." I let all the razzing I could muster rise to the surface.

Royce grunted.

Not amused.

He was leaned against the massive carved black dresser that took up one wall of my room, wearing a dark-gray suit, tats leaking out from under his shirt onto his neck and hands, all black hair and blacker eyes.

Funny that his sister favored him so much when she was an angel and the dude looked like the devil.

"Want a word with you."

Shocker.

I grinned, smug as fuck. "All ears."

He pushed from the dresser. All kinds of intimidation. Royce Reed might be a badass motherfucker, but he had no clue that the demons I was dealing with were way bigger than him.

Besides, I was about twice as thick. Could take him.

Lickity split.

Not a problem.

But I wasn't about throwing blows with my Em-Girl's man. With Maggie's brother.

Besides, dude was just doin' his damned job.

Could feel it…the protectiveness that radiated from his pores. The old fears that haunted him.

Recognized it well.

"Want you to keep away from my sister." His voice was low.

My laugh was boisterous. "Ah…come now…playing the overprotective card? I think your sister can make her own decisions about who she's hanging around."

So maybe there was a slight warning there. I respected him. Liked him. But he needed to get somethin' straight. "You need to give her a little space. Let her figure out who she wants to be."

Darkness clouded his expression, animosity dripping from the kind of wounds that just weren't gonna heal. "That's fine. Just not with you."

I cracked a grin, fighting the part of me that wanted to be pissed at what he was insinuating.

He knew I would hurt his sister.

I knew it just as well.

I forced as much lightness into my response as I could, patting his cheek condescendingly. Basically being me. "No need to worry your emo-heart, rocker boy. Your sister and I are only friends. That's all."

He made a sound that promised he didn't trust me.

Yeah, me neither, asshole.

"She shouldn't have been with you at that bar."

Obviously.

"Girl wanted to go see a live band. I took her. Not a big deal."

"And she ended up drunk."

My brows lifted. "She's twenty. Not fourteen."

Royce angled in closer, fear and anger breaking free. "You should have been watching over her. Taking care of her. And instead, your pathetic, selfish ass who only cares about having a good time got into a barfight and got yourself arrested. Left her vulnerable."

Should have let it go.

Grinned and bore it.

Didn't know how to do it when it came to Maggie Fitzgerald. I moved on him before I could stop myself, cocking my head down to glare at him, fighting the urge to fist my hands in his suit jacket. "You think I wasn't lookin' out for her?" I grated, my teeth grinding so hard that I thought they were gonna turn to dust. "You think I wouldn't stand in front of a fucking speeding train for her?"

That's what I'd done.

A fucking train I couldn't stop that ushered my destruction.

Sought it.

And I refused to let Maggie stand in its path.

Royce's voice cracked with the care he had for his sister. "She's been hurt, man."

"Know that."

Before he could respond, my door banged open and a burst of wild energy came bounding in ahead of a clatter of excited footsteps. "Oh, Uncle Rhys, Uncle Rhys! Did you hears it? My baby cousin Amelia is here, and she's soooooooo cute."

Royce and I separated to find Daisy standing there with her hands pressed together like they were issuing a prayer, the child giggling and sighing and clearly enamored.

Daisy was nothin' but adorable pigtails and earthshattering smiles, this wee little girl who'd gone and obliterated my heart.

She was the daughter of my oldest, closest friend, Richard Ramsey, lead guitarist of our band, and his wife, Violet.

Immediately, I knelt in front of her, brought to my knees.

Thing was, looking at her was pure pain and outright joy. My chest in knots every time her tinkling voice filled my ears.

"She is precious, isn't she? Just like my Daisy Mae." No fakin' the smile that spread across my face.

Redness splashed her chubby cheeks. "You really thinks so or are you just givin' me the teases?"

"Think so? Heck no," I said, acting as offended as I could. "Scout's honest truth."

She beamed at me and then turned course, scampering over to

Royce and throwing her arms around his knees. "Uncle Royce! I missed you. Your baby is the cutest, cutest. I hope you want to stay forever in South Carolina at our new house. Maybe you could build a house right next door. What do you thinks of that? I thinks it is a really smart idea. And I am the smartest. Just ask my papa."

She rambled the words so fast she could make a man's head spin.

But apparently, she had the exact same effect on Royce as she did me because he scooped her up into his arms and squeezed her tight. "Wow...that's quite the plan. Who have you been scheming with?"

"Anna, of course." Daisy shrugged like it should have been obvious. "She is my bestest friend in the whole wilds world and my cousin. Did you know Anna is my cousin? And now I get to have a baby brover so soon. I got so's much family and all the amor, amor, amor."

She lifted her arms out wide.

Affection pulsed.

Dense and thick.

My lungs squeezed.

Anna was Royce's little girl from a previous marriage. Child shy and quiet. Basically, Daisy's polar opposite.

Royce chuckled as he dropped a kiss to her temple. "Well, since she's my daughter and you're my niece, I think I might have had a suspicion she might be your cousin."

Daisy frowned. "A suspicion? Suspicions are bad, bad things. Papa had a suspicions I ates all the oatmeal cookies." She dropped her voice to a quieted confession. "And I did."

I couldn't cover my laugh as I pushed to standing. "Yeah, your uncle Royce is nothin' but suspicions, isn't he?"

I let it drop like the ones he was having about me were outrageous.

He shot me a glare as he set her onto her feet.

"Come on, Uncle Royce...we gotta go see your baby. Auntie Ems said I can even holds her!" She grabbed his hand and tried to tug him toward the door.

Royce started behind her only to pause to look back at me in

40

the doorway. "Just…keep your distance from my sister and we won't have a problem, yeah?"

I gave him a salute and a wild, unhinged smile. Nothin' but the dull, thickheaded fuckwit. "Yes, sir."

Like it didn't matter a bit.

When in reality, the man was speaking wisdom, and I was giving him what I prayed to God was the utmost truth.

Three

Rhys

*I*t was just after eight-thirty when I slipped out my bedroom door and into the hall. It was lit in a dim, golden glow by the sconces that hung on the wall between each room.

Conversations and laughter carried over the dull hum of music that played from below, echoing against the sleek marble floors and pulsing a little charge of excitement into my veins.

The kick-off party was in full swing.

I was chalking my lateness up to the fact that I was sharin' a bathroom and had made sure to let Maggie go first.

You know, ever the upstanding gentleman.

If only that wasn't a complete and utter fallacy.

What had really gone down was I'd spent the entire thirty minutes Maggie had been in the shower tryin' not to imagine her on the other side of the door. Clothes discarded on the floor.

Shower pounding over her sweet, tight body. Rivulets running her curves and splashing to the ground.

Once she'd gotten out and the lock had clicked, giving me the green light that it was my turn, I'd spent an inordinate amount of time in that exact spot trying to rein the need that was burning far too hot.

To bridle my cock and corral the fantasies.

I started down the hall, only to stall for a beat when I sensed the movement from behind her bedroom door. I was impaled by the need to press my ear to the wood. Get a little closer.

There I went again.

Such a sick, twisted fuck.

Friends.

Before my thoughts went spiraling again, I scrubbed a hand over my face and hit the main stairway, hand riding the curved railing as I bounded down into the mass of bodies that had gathered to celebrate the start of recording Carolina George's first major-label album.

A welcome to the family, of sorts.

Considering the place was crawling with the faces of Sunder, the band who'd started it all, it left no doubt that's exactly what this was.

I'd made it about three-quarters of the way down to the main floor when a raucous voice rose above the others. "Ahhh...there he is. About time, brother. Here I thought I was gonna have to step in for you and show these poor assholes how a real man plays bass."

Ash Evans, Sunder's bassist, was all cocky smiles as he lifted his arms out to the sides where he stood near the massive island in the kitchen. His wife, Willow, was tucked to his side, and he had his arm slung over her shoulder.

Two of them were awesome. Tied at the hip. Complete opposites yet completing each other in a way that no one else could.

"Pssh...you were just hopin' I'd up and disappeared so I wouldn't come in and show up your ass," I razzed as I ambled the rest of the way into the fray.

He and I had become friends when I'd gotten the opportunity to play with him during Royce and Emily's wedding back in Dalton.

Might give him shit, but the dude was probably the best bassist that ever lived. Someone I'd looked up to for years. Admired for his art.

Now he was basically in my arena.

A part of my crew.

Blew my small country mind, that was for sure. Fact we'd really made it. That Carolina George was getting ready to step into a greatness that I didn't think any of us had quite yet grasped.

"You wish, man. We all know who the master is around here," he said.

"Yeah…me." I sent him a smirk.

"Cocky son of a bitch," he grumbled with a laugh as he stepped away from Willow and pulled me into a hug, clapping me on the back. "Good to see ya, man."

"Obviously."

Willow giggled as she gave me a quick hug. "Lord…I don't know which of you two has a bigger head."

Before Ash had a chance to crack a joke about the size of his head, which he clearly was gettin' ready to do, she pointed at him. "Don't you dare go there."

Ash curled his arms back around her waist and pulled her tight, leaning down so he could nuzzle his face into her throat. "Oh, Peaches, I'm always already there, darlin'."

Sebastian Stone moved through the crowd and stretched out his hand. "Rhys. How's it goin'?"

Sebastian, or Baz like everyone called him, was the owner of Stone Industries. The former lead singer of Sunder had retired from the stage in favor of staying close to his family here in Savannah, but he hadn't wanted to get too far from the music, either.

I shook his hand. "Doubt things get much better than this."

I sent an indulgent wave over my head because truly this house was out of control. "I might get used to this and start squattin'. You're going to have to drag my ass out of here to get rid of me."

He slung an arm over my shoulder, turning me a fraction to look out over the luxury, lifting his drink out to the room like he was offering a gift. "Nah, man…after this album, you'll be able to afford two or three of these yourself. No squatting required."

"Don't tease me, dude."

"No teasing to it. Carolina George is about to become a household name," he proclaimed.

Sure, Carolina George had picked up a faithful following through years of touring and paying to have our albums made in back door studios, but I knew it wasn't close to the stardom we were gettin' ready to touch.

Was it considered stumbling onto greatness when you'd strived and hungered and clawed your way to the top?

Funny how it lost part of its luster when you kept losing the people you wanted it for most. When the cheers no longer quite touched your ears. When the music no longer quite touched your soul.

My gaze jumped over the faces in the room. Some I knew and others I didn't recognize.

All of Sunder was there with their wives.

Local friends and family.

The production crew.

Party private but packed.

It wasn't close to resembling the ragers I was used to, since almost everyone here was married and had families.

My eyes roamed to find the rest of my band where they had gathered on the far side of the living room.

Our drummer Leif and his wife Mia stood wrapped up in each other, laughing, smiling, and chatting with Royce and my Em-Girl who was grinning with so much joy that she was just glowin' with it. My best friend Richard and his wife Violet, who was expectin' their first son, Daisy's baby brother, in three short months, were with them, too.

Each of them were finally whole in their freedom.

They'd all been through so much bullshit to get to this place.

My chest clutched.

I wanted it. Wanted it for them. That group of amazing people deserved success and joy more than anyone else I knew.

Hell, I had to admit I wanted it for my mama, too. I wanted it so she could look at me and maybe not see the greatest mistake of her life.

I shook off the gloom because I was so not about moping in my misery.

Problem was, I'd sunk into it over the last six months, considerin' it'd been the longest stint I'd spent in that house with my mama.

Unable to leave because I was terrified that prick might show again. Sick that he'd been there. My sanity teetering on a razor-sharp edge.

Bein' on the road made it easier. Easier to forget. Easier to pretend.

But when I could feel it all catchin' up to me? This feelin' that something was about to snap? It left me...*afraid*.

I sucked that bullshit down before it spiraled and swung a grin at Baz. "Well, we definitely intend on makin' you proud."

"Make me proud? Hell, I'm the one who's proud," Baz said. "Honestly, couldn't get those contracts drawn fast enough when I found out it was a possibility that Stone Industries was going to have the opportunity to represent Carolina George."

"Guess you do have good taste, after all." I let a smirk ride to my face.

"Fuck yeah, I do. You think I got here tone deaf?"

His wife, Shea, was suddenly wrapping her arms around his waist from the side, girl so tiny she was basically pressing her cheek to his stomach as she grinned over at me. "Hi, Rhys! How's your room?"

Hell.

Torture.

Blissful agony.

"Perfect."

"Awesome. Well, you just let me know if you need anythin' at all. We want to make sure our artists are cozy while they're here. We wouldn't want your inspiration fizzlin' because of a lumpy pillow."

A low chuckle rumbled out. "Uh…not even close. Stayed at some pretty ritzy places in the last few years, and I promise you, this takes the cake."

"That's what we want to hear."

She beamed, then turned it up at her husband who dropped the peck of a kiss to her mouth.

"Thank you, baby. You run a tight ship," he said.

She winked and then strutted away.

Baz followed her with his eyes, and when he turned back to me, he looked a little dazed. I almost laughed when he finally blinked, coming to.

"Whipped, man." He just gave a little shrug when he admitted it. Zero shame. Then he reached out and squeezed my shoulder. "Come on…time to get this party started."

I rubbed my palms together. "I'm game."

I needed the reprieve.

To slip into oblivion. To forget a certain somebody who'd become a naggin' itch in my mind.

Hell, what I really needed was to get laid.

Out of sight. Out of mind. Out of reach.

Permanently.

I followed Baz through the crush toward the opposite side of the island in the kitchen. He grabbed a bottle of Jager from the bar on the way, along with some shot glasses. He lined them up on the island and poured the liquid out over them.

I quirked a brow. "Looks like someone wants to get rowdy."

Lyrik West, Sunder's lead guitarist, broke away from the conversation he was having and planted his hands on the island, dude as dark and menacing as the drink. "Don't question it, brother. It's tradition. You want in?" he asked as he lifted his glass.

"You know I do."

This was exactly what I needed. That and a warm body that wanted a nice, hard fuck.

I swiped up the glass Baz offered. I was feeling one-hundred-fifty-percent better until I felt the air stir.

My gaze drawn.

It darted directly for the stairs where the woman was

descending from the second floor.

Sight of her hitched my breath and set a bomb off in my senses.

Eyes racing to take in every delicious inch.

Fingers itching to touch.

Girl wore a slinky white dress that looked like silk and clung to her curves.

Strappy heels and all that curious innocence on her face.

Stunning.

That's exactly what I was—stunned.

Frozen and staring.

Baz broke me out of the haze when he shouted over the din, "All right, everyone, bring it in…I'd like to officially kick off tonight's party by recognizing those we are here to celebrate."

Conversations trailed off and someone turned down the music.

Everyone crowded in toward the kitchen.

Maggie hit the landing and edged into the fray. But she was looking at me when she did, wearing a soft, coy smile that looked like she had a secret dancing on her lips.

Baz and Lyrik passed out shot glasses to those partaking, while two servers moved through the crowd refilling champagne flutes.

I kept trying not to steal peeks of Maggie while the rest of my band moved in closer, huddling around me where I stood next to Baz.

Baz lifted his glass over his head. "Just wanted to say a couple things. Emily, Richard, Rhys, Leif…" He gestured to each of us as he went. "Having been in a band for many years myself—"

The rest of Sunder chanted, "Sunder, Sunder, Sunder!" drumming their hands on the island.

Baz grinned. "Alright, assholes, let's try not to steal someone else's thunder, yeah?"

"We are the thunder," Ash cracked.

"Not today, bro, a new storm is in town, and this one rolled in from the country. A little tornado, anyone?" I tossed right back, gesturing at myself as I let my gaze jump over the smiling faces.

Of course, it went straight for one.

Redness flushed her cheeks.

So damned pretty.

Baz chuckled. "Have no doubt you're going to bring on a storm, Rhys. Betting the bank on it, actually. Bettin' on all of you." He pointed at each of us with the hand he had wrapped around his glass.

"I know firsthand the work it takes to be standing in the spot you are today. The sacrifices that are made. The loves that are lost and some of the dreams you have to let go in order to have the strength to chase down another. But I knew years ago that Carolina George was something special when I first heard you play at Charlie's right here in Savannah. There was no question you had what it took. There was a quality to your music that stilled hearts and quieted people's souls. It was clear you had a message that needed to be told."

He cleared his throat, still looking between each of us. "Never could have imagined the turn of events that would lead us here today, that I would actually have the honor of getting to represent you, to come along beside you to help you become everything you are destined to be. But I can say I am grateful for it, and that I'm going to do everything in my power to guarantee your success."

I glanced around at my crew.

Could physically feel the excitement stirring through their spirits.

Baz lifted his glass higher. "To Carolina George, on this day that marks a new beginning…may the music pour from your souls, may your inspiration never run dry, and may you never stop until you touch the stars."

Shouts and cheers and clinking glasses erupted, and I was grinning like mad as I toasted my bandmates and they toasted me.

Because this…this was what I was supposed to be working toward. What I was purposed for. There had to be a reason.

I tossed back the sweet liquor. It burned as it raced down my throat. I breathed out heavily at the impact of it, as it coated my belly in a soothing, calming fire.

Instantly, my eyes were back to seeking hers.

Charcoal was staring back. Sketching again.

Cautiously, Maggie tipped me her glass in a silent cheer that somehow felt a little sad.

Girl looking at me in a way that touched me from across the space.

Innocent but knowing.

Unfound but familiar.

Impossible but real.

I jumped when my phone buzzed in my pocket.

Thankful for the distraction, I dragged my attention from the trance and pulled out my phone so I could read the text.

My blood went cold.

It was the same number he always contacted me from, when he'd mete demands and tighten the fist he had wrapped around my throat.

Though this was different.

This was a picture…a picture of my mama…out in her garden tending to her tomatoes. It had been taken from a bit of a distance, clear as day that she had no clue that she was being photographed.

Being tracked.

Rage exploded in the middle of me.

My hand shot out to the island to keep me from dropping to my knees. Or maybe it was to keep me from flying out of there to go on a rampage.

Violence on my fingers. It buzzed again and a message blipped through.

You want to play with fire? Let's play.

Dread curled down my spine.

Fuck.

The motherfucker knew.

I tried to swallow, but my throat felt sticky. Too tight.

Anger and guilt gushed, a thunder that raced through my veins. Sweat slicked my skin, and I could feel myself burning up from the inside out.

Barely able to stand, I muttered a quiet, "Excuse me." I ducked out of the circle of my band who'd struck up a conversation with Lyrik and Baz, and I wound through the crush packed in the kitchen.

I snagged the half-empty bottle of Jager, and the second I cleared the crowd, I rushed for the back door, refusing to look back.

I stumbled outside into the darkness like a fool clutching that bottle and that phone.

I ran smack into the smell of salt and the sea and humidity, my ears full of the pounding of the waves that pummeled the beach on the shore.

Wind whipped through, battering my face, and I sucked for more of that air I couldn't find as I treaded across the elevated deck and down the boardwalk toward the darkened beach.

I never slowed as my feet hit the sand.

Emotion crashed.

Fear overwhelming.

My breaths were coming in jagged pants.

A million thoughts zipped in and out.

Wanted to get up and go.

Fight.

Protect.

But to Dalton or Tennessee, I wasn't sure.

I sank to one of the high banks of sand, balanced the bottle between my knees, and tapped out a message.

Stay the fuck away from her. You know the deal.

I unscrewed the cap on the bottle and tossed it back while I waited for the response.

Sucked it down.

Relished the promise of oblivion while sickness churned in my guts.

A second later, my phone buzzed again.

Exactly. We had a deal.

Fuck, fuck, fuck.

I roughed a shaking hand through my hair, realizing I was rocking.

Rocking with rage.

I buried the bottom of the bottle in the sand to keep it from tipping over and let my fingers fumble over the screen.

I needed to verify that she is okay.

I'd needed to check on her.
See her with my own eyes.
Tell her I was sorry.
Genny.
I'm sorry.
I'm sorry.
I'm so fuckin' sorry.
Except I'd been saying it for years, and it didn't change a fucking thing.

Two seconds later, the phone blipped again.

Your mom looks happy.

I choked over a sob that formed at the base of my throat. A knot of fury and desperation.

She doesn't have anything to do with this. You do anything to her, and I will destroy you. End you. I promise you that.

I meant it in the most literal way.
My phone pinged again.

You don't make rules. You suffer the consequences. I warned you I didn't ever want to see your face again.

Yet he had no issues accepting the money I sent month after month.

Agony clawed across my flesh.
Pain.
Regret.

A ghost I was never gonna outrun.

Just stay away from my mom. I'll give you anything you want.

I could almost taste the bitterness through the miles.
The hatred.

You haven't even begun to pay for what you did.

Motherfucker.

Torment screamed, and I wondered if he could feel my hatred radiatin' back.

Way it curled around my consciousness and seeped into my spirit.

Didn't matter…I owed it. Would give it all.

Take care of her.

Both of them.

I reached over and gulped down more of the fire from the bottle like it could be a balm.

Medicine.

A cure.

It tore up my throat like a slosh of lava and landed in a pool of fury that boiled over in my belly and spilled into my bloodstream.

I could feel it speeding through my veins. Taking over. Filling up the void.

My sight came in and out of focus.

Delirium so close to taking hold.

I slugged back the rest of the bottle, and I welcomed the way consciousness ebbed and flowed. Darkness pressed into my mind and threatened to take me hostage.

It crawled over me like the waves crawling the beach.

Heavy and corrupt and foreboding.

Taking me under and swamping me in my regrets.

I wished I could go back.

Change it.

Stop all of it before it happened.

I slumped back onto the sand and let the darkness take me.

Knowing no matter where I went, how much money I had, how much success I had tacked to my name, that was where I was always gonna be.

Rhys
Six Years Old

"Richard, Emily, Rhys, it's supper time," Mrs. Ramsey called from somewhere downstairs, her voice echoing up to Richard's room.

All three of them scrambled to their feet from where they were building a fort. They went racing out the door to the staircase, each trying to get ahead of the other, their feet pounding on the hardwood as they trampled downstairs.

Way out front, Rhys jumped from the third step. He landed it without toppling over. He threw a fist in the air. "Heck, yes! Did y'all see that? I just nailed it."

"You're lucky you didn't fall and ruin your face," Emily scolded. She constantly was naggin' at him and Richard that they weren't followin' the rules and were gonna get hurt.

"Pssh. Not a chance. I'm the strongest man in the world."

"No, you're not. My daddy is," she retorted.

"Heck no, my daddy is," he returned, just a tad louder.

She stuck out her tongue and stomped off to the kitchen.

He figured that meant he won, not that he didn't think Mr. Ramsey was really cool and strong. But his daddy was just way taller and way bigger and he had about fifteen thousand muscles puffed out all over the place.

Richard laughed. "She's nothin' but a sass attack."

Rhys shook his head. "Girls."

Richard curled up his nose in disgust, and Rhys almost did the same, except Emily was his best friend, too, and his mama was his favorite person in the world, and he was figurin' he liked girls just right and fine so he'd better treat 'em with respect like his daddy told him he was supposed to do.

Mrs. Ramsey appeared in the doorway to the kitchen, drying her hands on a towel. "You need to get washed up, Richard, and help your sister set the table. And you better run on home, Rhys…your mama is going to be wondering what you've gotten up to."

"Yes, ma'am," he told her before he waved at Richard. "See ya tomorrow."

"Later, Rhys' Pieces."

"Bye, Richie-Poo-Poo."

Cracking up, he hustled out the front door and across the deck, and by the time he was taking the five wooden steps down to the gravel to head in the direction of his house that was on the next property over, he could see the plume of dust rising up behind his daddy's truck that bounced up the one-lane dirt road.

Rhys took off, racing something fierce up the drive. Without slowing, he ducked down and slipped between the planks of the wooden fence that separated their properties.

His daddy came to a rumbling stop in front of their house, and Rhys pushed his legs as fast as they could go.

His mouth stretched in a wide grin and excitement bumbled in his stomach.

This was his favorite part of the day.

"Dad! Dad! You're home!"

His daddy cranked open the door and stepped out, his own grin sliding over his sun-weathered face. His work clothes were worn and covered in dirt, his hands stained with years of oil and grease when he swept Rhys right off his feet.

"There's my rough and tumble." He ruffled a hand through Rhys' hair. "Let's see those muscles."

Rhys lifted both his arms out to the sides and curled his fists, showing off his biceps. His dad gave 'em a squeeze. "Strong as a horse, my boy."

"Yep! You won't even be able to hold me soon I'm getting so big."

So maybe he was probably already a little bit big. At least that's what his mama would giggle and say, but Rhys didn't care.

"Not a chance of that. You're never gonna get so big that your daddy can't pick you up and squeeze ya."

"Even when I'm twenty-five?"

His daddy chuckled. "Okay, fine. You'll probably be carrying me around by then…takin' care of me and your mama."

Pride puffed out Rhys' chest at the thought. "I'll always take care of you."

"That's because my son is the best son around."

Rhys nodded like crazy, and his daddy ducked back into his truck and grabbed the silver lunch box he took to work every mornin'.

His daddy didn't even set him down, and instead he carried him up the two steps to the front of their house. He opened the door, shouting when he did, "Where's my woman?"

A giggle floated from off toward the kitchen where Rhys' mama was at the stove cooking something in a big pot that made Rhys' mouth water.

Their house was kinda smaller than Richard's, no steps or stairs, and there was a big room in the middle with the TV and couch and the kitchen on the other side.

His mama arched a brow at his daddy. "Your woman, huh?"

His daddy waltzed into the kitchen, setting Rhys on his feet before he whisked up behind her and wrapped an arm around her waist. He hugged her back to his chest.

"Mmmhmm." He hummed into her hair. "My woman."

Rhys' cheeks always got all red and hot when his mom and dad got like this, which was pretty much all the time.

"Missed you," his daddy rumbled.

His mama got all gooey and soft. "I missed you, too. But you stink. Go get yourself cleaned up before we eat."

"Bossy. I know who holds the reins around here."

"Well, someone around here's gotta make sure my wild boys behave."

"I thought you liked it when I misbehaved?" He kissed the back of her neck.

"I got news, Dad, Ma hates it when we misbehave. Don't know what you're talkin' about. Think I already spent half of my whole life in time-out."

He stretched his arms out to the sides.

His daddy chuckled, his blue eyes twinkling, and Rhys felt like his heart was gonna bust right out of his chest.

Love, love, love.

His mama said this house was built on it.

That it was the foundation of a family.

And without it, everything would collapse.

His daddy moved toward Rhys and brushed his fingers through his hair. "You're a good boy, Rhys. A good, good boy."

Maggie

I hovered at the edge of the kitchen, trying to keep myself together and not do something foolish like chase him out the door. Rhys had slipped out a second before without another soul noticing, and it felt almost impossible to remain standing beneath the stunning shockwave of turmoil that had pierced the air.

So violent I felt as if my chest had been impaled.

Around me, the party grew rowdy. The shots that had gone up to toast Carolina George were clearly hitting bloodstreams, the alcohol now flowing freely. The music had been turned back up, and a clamor of voices and laughter lifted above it to be heard.

I could physically feel the mood sliding into revelry.

And there I stood in the middle of it, caught in his wake. Feeling like I was being taken under. Lured into waters I couldn't tread.

Deep, dark, and dangerous.

I swore, the man was a glittering, shiny stone at the bottom of the sea that I would drown trying to recover.

I wondered if I'd have sensed it so intensely if I hadn't already been watching. If there'd been a single chance in the world that I could tear my eyes from the gorgeous man as he'd toasted with his band.

For a moment, I'd witnessed it—the true joy that had set so deeply in those blue eyes as he'd looked at his bandmates, at the people I knew were closest to him. That was until he'd looked at something on his phone, and he'd been stricken by panic.

My stomach twisted in a knot of worry, and I shivered with the prickles of unease that crept across my flesh.

I should look away.

Mind my own business.

But I wasn't quite sure how to turn a blind eye on his suffering.

That's what that man did to me, though, wasn't it?

Confused me.

Conflicted me.

Made me want things I knew I certainly shouldn't want.

Things I knew full well were going to hurt in the end.

Off to my left, a riot of laughter broke out in the kitchen. I was close enough to hear but far enough away not to be caught in the middle of it.

Ash Evans gave a lighthearted shove to Richard's shoulder and then stumbled back, smacking his hands together. "It's on. A thousand bucks, baby." The gesture he made at himself was playfully arrogant. "Prepare to be schooled, oh young one."

Ash hopped onto the middle of the island. Shoes and all.

Ash's wife, Willow, groaned as she pressed the heel of her hand to her forehead. "Don't you think you're gettin' too old for this?"

He sent her a waggish grin. "Too old? Come now, Peaches. This boy right here is in his prime."

"Just don't break a hip." This from Zee, Sunder's drummer, the guy nursing a beer where he was leaned up against the opposite counter.

Richard hopped up beside Ash, all smiles and cockiness. "I'll try not to show you up too badly, old man. Don't want you to have to suffer the embarrassment."

Lyrik stepped to the bar, pulled out his wallet, and made a big show of slapping a bill onto the granite. "Got a Benjamin this newbie can't make a fool outta my boy."

Leif came up beside him and tossed two bills onto the pile. "I'll see you and double it."

Music thrummed, the lights dim, everyone's faces full of their smiles and laughter. Some moved in to pay attention to the commotion in the kitchen while others paid no mind, clearly accustomed to the antics.

Lyrik took out a wad of cash, tattooed fingers fanning it out. "Easy money, baby. Bring it."

Lyrik's wife, Tamar, grinned behind her champagne flute. She was all leather and sex and red-slicked lips. Covered in ink. She looked like a modern-day pin-up. Gorgeous to the extreme.

"The balls on these boys," she teased above the mayhem, angling up to slip her arm around her husband's waist from behind. "Someone run and get the measuring stick...I feel what's coming next."

Lyrik shifted to drape an arm around her shoulders, dropping a kiss to the top of her head. "Now why would I go and embarrass my friends like that? No competition, Baby Blue."

Her smirk was even bigger than his when she tipped her face up to look at him. "Maybe I just need a little reminder."

"Ahh...there's my Red. I do think that can be arranged."

"All right...time to prove it," Baz said. "You two ready?"

"Yup. Let's do this."

"Hells yeah!"

"Go," Baz shouted, and Richard and Ash flipped into handstands. Everyone cheered and started throwing in their own bets.

They were having a blast.

Me?

I couldn't settle into it.

Into the festivity.

I felt like an outsider. Like I was floating around the perimeter witnessing it all through a fuzzy pane of glass.

My conscience wouldn't allow me to look away, to pretend like everything was just fine, when things clearly weren't for Rhys.

A buzz of nerves rippling through my body, I slipped through the fray and wound toward the back doors.

Feeling like I was on a covert mission.

A forbidden endeavor.

I was almost there when someone grabbed my hand.

Suppressing a yelp, I whirled around to find my brother staring back. I heaved out a breath of relief. "Royce."

He gave my hand a gentle squeeze. "Hey...you good, Mag Pie?"

He looked like he was regretting bringing me here all over again.

"Sorry. Yeah. You just startled me."

He frowned, his dark eyes flashing severity. "Someone make you uncomfortable?"

There he was.

My overprotector.

If he only knew what I'd gotten myself into, he'd lose his mind. Would probably pack me in bubble wrap and lock me in a padded safe.

I smiled at him, half in affection, half in annoyance. "I'm fine, Royce. There's just a lot of people in here, and I thought I'd get some fresh air. I think the ocean might be calling to me."

"You want company?"

No doubt, he'd ditch the party without a thought.

With my free hand, I reached out and squeezed his upper arm. "No. I'm great. Honest. Go. Be with your wife. You're supposed to be celebrating her."

He glanced back into the room where Emily was with Violet. The two of them were sharing some kind of sweet secret. Smiles stretched across their faces.

Love pulsed, my heart squeezing in a deep, adoring beat. I was overcome with the happiness I felt for these two women who had become sisters to me.

"You sure?" Royce asked.

"I promise."

A sigh pilfered from his nose. "Just...be careful."

I rolled my eyes and let the tease glide free. "I'm fine. It's not like Baz doesn't have everyone's name signed in blood here."

Every person involved in the making of this album had been required to sign an NDA, including me.

The artists and timing secret.

It offered a little privacy, even though these things often got leaked, considering the house was a legacy in itself.

The bands who'd recorded here were legends.

Royce squeezed my hand again, the man so rough and tender in his care. "Okay...just...call me if you need me."

"Thank you," I told him.

He hesitated for a second. I angled my head, urging him to go. Then he spun on his heel and started for his wife, glancing back at me once. I gave him a small, reassuring wave, and then he seemed to fully give, his demeanor shifting as he moved across the room to edge in behind Emily. He wrapped her in his arms and smothered her neck with kisses from behind.

Before I lost my nerve, I ducked out the doors and into the night. Outside, the thick, unrelenting heat of the Georgia summer was in full swing.

The only relief was the slight breeze that gathered on the sea and billowed across the sand.

Above, the sky was a blackened canvas that seemed to be painted into forever, the stars infinite, the stretch of the ocean just as black where it glittered and churned beneath.

I could almost hear the dark waters calling out their claim.

It was like they whispered seduction. Temptation. Enticing me to dip in my toes when I was sure of the danger.

That great big ocean would swallow me whole as I searched for a shimmery, shiny stone fascinating me from the abyss of its depths.

Sweat beaded my nape.

I felt flushed.

Hot.

Fear and uncertainty knocked my knees and the thunder in my

heart propelled me forward.

I eased deeper into the darkness, and from the edge of the deck, I peered out onto the shore that I could barely make out beneath the nearly nonexistent moon.

When I saw nothing, I moved down the steps and onto the boardwalk that led to the beach. My heels clicked on the wood, and I bent over to work them free of my feet. I nudged them aside, and then crept to the end of the wood and stepped onto the cool sand.

"Rhys?" I realized I whispered it. Calling to him silently.

The wind echoed back.

I started in the direction of the ocean, my feet sinking deep as I trudged toward the shore.

Slowly.

Carefully.

A shiver of something moved through the air.

I froze, held in apprehension. Warily, I peered over my shoulder as I was hit with an unwarranted rush of foreboding.

Alarm compressed my ribs, and my pulse slugged harder.

I squinted into the nothingness.

God.

I had to get over this.

Stop imagining someone was watching me at every turn.

Something sinister.

Something vile.

I gathered myself and moved closer to the water.

"Rhys?" I called, this time louder, searching the line of the sea.

Why was I doing this? Trying to hunt down a man who clearly didn't want to be found?

"Rhys!" I shouted again. The sound barely broke over the crashing waves.

Shit.

I turned, my attention moving for the house lit up in the distance.

This was crazy.

I needed to stop getting myself into situations where I didn't belong. Blowing out a sigh, I started back in the direction of the house, deciding I needed to give him space. He'd slinked out to find it, hadn't he?

A smart girl would respect that.

I lumbered up the soft sand on my bare feet. I was halfway to the boardwalk when a sound stopped me in my tracks. A shiver tumbled down my spine. But this? It was a different sort of apprehension. A different kind of fear.

Shifting course, I moved up along the dunes that ran the high side of the beach.

Tall grasses grew over them, waving and thrashing in the night. I kicked up sand as I stumbled over one and then another.

With each step, a desperation grew.

A panic seeded in the reminder of what had been in his expression before he'd slipped out.

Horror.

Hurt.

I fumbled over another dune, and then I gasped when I came upon a dark silhouette lying in the sand.

Facedown.

Worry slammed me.

I couldn't tell if he'd been knocked out or had passed out.

All I knew was his big, intimidating body was shaking.

Shaking and shaking.

Bone deep.

I saw the bottle he'd snagged from the kitchen was tipped on its side.

Empty.

Clearly, it had found its home in the pit of his belly.

Definitely passed out.

"Rhys."

A moan reverberated from his being.

Beside him, I sank to my knees. My hand was quivering like mad when I tentatively reached out and ran my fingers through the longer pieces of his hair.

Energy crackled.

Sparked and shivered.

Crap. Why did he have to affect me this way?

This man wasn't close to being safe.

It didn't matter because I leaned closer, my words softened like I could offer reprieve from whatever hell he'd descended to.

"Rhys...hey...are you okay?"

Another moan rumbled from him.

Deep and guttural.

Laden with pain.

"Hey, I'm right here. It's okay. It's okay."

With the way the words tumbled in desperation, I thought maybe the only one I was trying to convince was myself. The way I wanted to lie down beside him and take on some of the hurt I could feel seeping from his pores.

Soothe the pain I could feel gushing from the well of a broken spirit he clearly wanted to hide.

I wanted to confess to him that mine was broken, too.

That I'd been hurt.

Brutalized.

That I was terrified of letting it go and desperate for its surrender at the same time.

The biggest problem was I couldn't help but wonder if maybe this man felt mine the same way as I felt his.

That maybe...maybe together we could hold some of the fractured pieces for the other.

Crazy.

Of course, I knew even thinking it was insane.

Reckless to the extreme.

But I wanted it...wanted to hold what he couldn't. Soothe it from his soul.

Be his balm like I was aching for him to be mine.

Rhys groaned.

"Let me get Royce. He can help get you inside."

I started to push to standing when a massive hand reached out and clamped me by the wrist. "No."

A shock raced my arm.

Heat.

Flames.

It stoked a fire I'd never felt before.

I heaved out a shuddered breath.

Oh God.

I searched him through the lapping shadows as he turned his head enough to look at me.

Stark blue eyes stared out from behind the wild pieces of hair that had fallen in his face.

Disoriented but sharp.

"No," he rasped. "Just you."

My chest squeezed, and I was such a fool, reaching in to brush the hair back from his handsome face. "What happened?"

"Got in a tussle with a bottle of Jager. Clearly, I was outperformed." One side of his bearded mouth tipped in a meager smirk.

My stomach fisted and a bolt of attraction streaked through my veins.

"That's not what I meant, and you know it," I told him, keeping my voice hushed, just loud enough to be heard over the whipping of the wind. "I…saw you."

On a grunt, Rhys managed to flop onto his back. His eyes were squinted but still focused on me.

"Believe me, Sweet Thing, you don't wanna go there," he slurred, trying to sit up and then collapsing back down.

"What if I do?" Throat tight, I moved to lean over him.

Compelled.

Drawn.

A fool.

I couldn't help it.

Captured, I stared down at the beautifully brutal lines of his face.

"What if I've been worried about you all these months?" I murmured. "What if I spent too many nights wondering what happened that night? What made you snap? What if I wanted to be there for you?"

That blue gaze flashed.

A white strike of lightning.

Without answering, he reached out and twisted a lock of my hair around his finger.

The air whooshed from my lungs.

When he spoke, his rumbled words were like prods of desire raking across my skin. "Look at that…a goddess beneath the stars looking down over me."

"Are you sure you didn't fall and hit your head?" I asked him, giving it my all to keep cool and calm. Knowing he was only teasing me.

Flirting a little.

Such a liar, Maggie.

I was positively shaking, and the man was messing with my mind.

"Must've died and went to heaven." The knuckle wound in my hair brushed my chin. "Goddess Girl."

Oh god. There he went.

Doing me in.

Tempting me into imagining all the things I knew better than to imagine.

"Rhys." It was a murmur.

Confusion.

A plea.

Intensity crackled.

Fired and flashed.

For the longest time, we stared.

Held.

Entranced.

Found in a single moment together.

Then he seemed to think better of it, shook his head, and pushed to sitting. The movement of his big body jostled me back.

Or maybe it gave me access to my senses, and my self-preservation kicked in.

A clear, distinct warning that if I got too close, I was going to get lost in his destruction.

Then he was back to flaunting that ridiculous grin.

Whiplash.

"Just how strong are ya, Mag Pie? Think you can sling me on that back and carry me inside?" He managed to only half slur the words.

Droplets of giddiness dripped into my chest. A well gathering fast. "You're asking me if I can lift a Mack truck?"

"Hell, no. Just if you can tackle a stallion."

He waggled his brows, though it was sloppy and goofy and kind of adorable, and god, how easily I could fall for this man.

Like slipping into quicksand.

"What would you say if I wanted to try?" I whispered, throat so tight it was difficult to speak.

He grunted. "I'd say that sounds like a mistake."

"I thought you said I needed to make a few mistakes along the way?" I lifted my chin, my eyes searching his face in the darkness.

He forced a grin that felt wholly faked. "Ahhh…a few mistakes are called for. But believe me, baby, you don't want this kind of tragedy."

"Rhys—"

He shook his head to cut me off. "Don't."

I glanced back at the house. "I really should get Royce. He can help me get you inside."

Rhys huffed out a laugh, shoving off the darkness that had gathered around him like a violent storm. He cocked a playful grin. "Think I've received my full allotment of death threats from your brother today, thank you very much. I can make it just fine."

"Death threats?"

"Let's just say he made our boundaries very clear." He gestured at the bare space between us. "Just so you know, we're already crossin' them."

I scowled. "When?"

"Doesn't matter."

I huffed a sigh.

Freaking Royce.

"Richard?" I offered instead.

"Nope. Good as new. Can't keep a good man down." His words were all slurry and mushed together.

He hopped up like he was going to prove the point.

Only he stumbled three feet to the side.

A goliath who swayed.

I jumped up and rushed to his side. "Whoa there, cowboy. You keep it up, and you're definitely going down."

He leaned against me, slinging his arm over my shoulders.

The man heavy and hard and pure masculinity.

He staggered a bit, and I struggled to keep him upright, because holy crap, he was made of brick.

Suddenly, his nose was in my hair. "Why you gotta smell so good, Mags? And this dress."

My brain was short-circuiting with him this close.

With the words that slipped from his mouth so errantly.

With the way his fingertips grazed over the silky fabric in the barest brush.

Wildfire.

It consumed my flesh.

But it was my heart that was at risk.

Because there was no missing the most glaring truth—I felt no fear when Rhys Manning was pressed up against me.

For the first time since I was fifteen, a man touching me didn't send me into a tailspin. Even the barest brush would leave me with the sense of fight or flight, something that usually pitched me into a panic attack.

With Rhys? It was nonexistent.

The same way as it'd been that night all those months ago when he'd had me on the dance floor. When I'd sworn there was something swirling around us. An intensity that shimmered and shined and glowed in the space.

It was something he'd acknowledged today.

What I needed to remember was in the same second, he'd shot it down. Said it couldn't happen.

No question, he was right.

"Let's get you inside, big guy," I muttered while I internally chastised myself for itching to run my hands all over his body.

"You're too good. Too good," he mumbled, close to incoherent. There was something in his tone. Something weaved in remorse.

"No, Rhys," I told him. "I'm not."

Somehow, I managed to grab the empty bottle and keep him upright at the same time.

"So good," he slurred at the side of my head. "So pretty. Oh, you could fuck me up, Sweet Thing."

I gulped down the need and focused on getting him back to the house because clearly, he was saying things he was going to regret in the morning.

I managed to guide him to the boardwalk, and the sounds of the house became more distinct.

Music thrumming.

Laughter ringing.

Hardly any time had passed, but it felt like hours.

He clung to me as we slowly moved up the planks, my feet bare, his footsteps clomping in his boots.

I left my shoes because there was no chance I could balance those, too.

"Up you go," I said when we made it to the steps that led onto the deck.

He lumbered up.

"I've got you," I promised.

"Course you do," he rumbled.

I started for the back door.

"Side door."

Right. I probably didn't need the headache of explaining away my helping a drunk Rhys through the door.

Not that I wouldn't gladly do it.

But it was more that Rhys didn't need an audience. He didn't need the questions when it was clear he'd fallen apart.

We wound around the side of the house, keeping quiet as we let ourselves into the side door that opened into a hall lined with bedrooms and offices.

There was a narrow set of stairs that led to the second floor, hidden from view of the party that still echoed from the living area.

"Are you doing okay?" I asked as we climbed.

"Got you." It was a grunt.

Did he have the first clue what he was doing to me?

The stairway dumped us out on the second floor across from our rooms. My room was closest, so I led him through the door and toward the Jack and Jill bathroom that connected our rooms.

"Bet you never 'magined when you agreed to share a bathroom durin' this little adventure it would mean you were gonna have to take care of an asshole like me, did you?" It was the mumble of a tease, words lumbered as he tried to form them on his drunken tongue.

"I don't mind," I said, so quiet as I flicked on the bathroom light.

We both blinked against the intrusiveness of it, the white marble gleaming beneath the stark light.

The bathroom was every bit as lavish as the rest of the rooms. The quartz and granite were accented by gold finishes and navy-blue touches, the walls done in a textured, gilded wallpaper.

I eased him down onto the side of the massive jet bathtub. He canted to the side, and I rushed to keep him steady.

Blue eyes peered up at me. I saw the devastation in their depths. He reached out and fluttered his fingertips down my cheek.

I struggled to breathe.

"You should mind, Maggie. You shouldn't have to deal with the likes of me. Guys like us? We're no good. No good. You're too good. Too pretty. Too real."

I tried to ignore the garbled, incoherent confession.

But my spirit shivered, and my fingers twitched.

I looked at the door in contemplation, wondering if he needed someone with a little more experience than I possessed, which was basically zero.

As if he knew exactly what I was thinking, a big hand clamped down on the outside of my bare thigh. Right through the slit of my clingy dress.

Holy crap.

Shivers raced as I was slammed with a flood of need.

My hands shot out for support.

The problem was I found myself clinging to Rhys' shoulders.

More, my body whispered.

I wanted it, for him to let his hand slip higher.

To find that achy spot that throbbed between my thighs.

Desperate to know what it might be like.

I had to suppress a moan.

That ocean of blue stared up at me. Sad and filled with something I couldn't quite decipher. "Stay with me, Goddess Girl. You make it better. How do you make it better?"

Then his eyes went wide. "Gotta puke."

He pushed to standing and flew for the little alcove that housed the toilet.

He dropped to his knees and started heaving like mad, while I stood there fidgeting, caught in the tornado that was Rhys Manning.

Okay.

I could handle this.

I went to the linen closet, grabbed a cloth, and ran it under warm water. I rushed back to him, knelt behind him, and brushed back his hair, trying not to be grossed out while he puked up his guts. I let loose soft laughter while I whispered at his ear, "I guess the tables have turned, and now I have to hold your hair."

Rhys grunted and flushed the toilet, and then he turned around and slumped onto his butt.

Leaning against the wall, his head tipped up to look at me where I knelt high on my knees.

And he was looking at me the way he had out on the beach.

Like maybe I was his guardian angel who'd come to rescue him.

The thing was, I was one-hundred-percent certain it wasn't his body that was in need of saving.

The man's heart was bleeding all over the floor.

His defenses down.

That unending smile dipped in a frown.

Carefully, I dabbed the cloth around his mouth.

"There we go." The encouragement trembled from my tongue, and he kept watching me with those blue, blue eyes.

He slanted me a wayward grin. "Some kinda cowboy I am. Can't even hold my liquor. Embarrassin'. Richey-Poo's gonna have my man card for this."

My insides nearly splintered apart.

I dabbed the cool cloth across his forehead, glancing down at him, the man watching me the whole time.

"And here I thought I'd heard it said you were a stallion," I murmured.

A light chuckle left him. "You gonna rein me?"

My stomach fisted.

Truth was, I wasn't equipped. I knew he would tear me apart.

I focused on running the cloth over his forehead like it was some sort of mission, fighting the flush that spread across my chest and climbed my neck.

So hot I was sure it lit up my cheeks.

I had no clue how to navigate this.

Friends.

A hand cinched down on one side of my waist. "Just playin', Mags. Wouldn't dream of it."

I wanted to whisper in his ear that I did.

That I dreamed of it again and again.

I wanted to confess I didn't think I was ever going to stop.

Before I did, I pushed to standing and held out my hand. "Let's get you into bed."

I helped him up, which was a feat in itself, getting the giant of a man upright.

He rose to his hulking height.

Imposing.

Powerful.

All bristling muscle and wide shoulders and endless temptation. He made a pit stop at the sink and rinsed his mouth with mouthwash, and then he let me help him into his darkened room.

Even without any light, I could tell it was a wild mess. A bull unleashed. The man untamed.

"Just wanna lie down. Can you help me?" he muttered as we stumbled toward his bed.

He started tugging for his shirt. What in the world? Was he going to strip right there?

"Rhys." I hesitated. At a loss for protocol.

He cracked a crooked grin. "Most women don't have so many reservations about helpin' me into bed."

"In case you hadn't noticed, I'm not like most women."

"Believe me, Sweet Thing, I noticed then I keep noticing all over again."

Slay. Slay. Slay.

The man was wrecking me.

I managed to help him sit on the edge of the mattress. "There we go, big guy."

"Old guy, you mean," he ribbed, his words garbled as I knelt to unlace his boots.

Beautiful guy, I wanted to say. Or maybe I wanted to show it, the way I felt the urge to set my hands on his knees and run them up his muscular thighs.

Explore the way I'd never explored before.

Heat blistered through the air.

Could he feel it?

The crush of emotion?

I dropped my head and forced myself to pay attention to the task, made myself a promise that I would get him into bed and get the heck out of there before I made a complete fool of myself.

I tugged his shoes from his feet, one and then the other, the bulk of them thumping onto the floor when I got them free.

Rhys moaned, though this time it was throaty, something that sounded a whole lot like pleasure.

Damn.

My hands were shaking when I eased up higher and grabbed the hem of his shirt so I could help him get it over his head.

Our proximity was far too close for comfort.

I could taste each of his ragged breaths.

The Jager he had drank and something headier. The country boy that was all man invading the space. That energy snapped.

Wrapped me like chains.

My insides twisted and my heart battered against my ribs.

Carefully, I peeled the fabric up.

Oh god, was the man pretty.

Massive arms and wide, wide chest.

Abdomen this work of art, divine divots and masculine lines.

The whole of him was covered in ink, and I had the urge to

trace the lines with my fingers. Maybe follow the designs with my tongue.

Standing up, I shifted his legs around and managed to get him mostly onto the bed.

"Jeans," he grumbled low.

Anxiety held me before I sucked in a steeling breath then climbed onto the mattress because apparently, I'd lost all self-control.

Self-preservation gone *poof* with a flash of that smile.

Straddling his legs, I ticked through the buttons of his fly.

I tried not to die right there when I started to drag them down.

If I thought the top half of him was pretty...

I averted my gaze because *Jesus, Mags, when did you become a pervert?*

That was so not my speed.

I managed to get his jeans the rest of the way off without stealing another peek.

Like I might catch fire, I fumbled off the bed, rushing for safer ground.

I looked down at him. The man's gorgeous chest rose and fell in spastic quakes.

He was already asleep.

Guess he hadn't been affected, after all.

I started to slip from his room, then froze with the gruffness of his voice. "Stay."

"Rhys."

"Please."

Crap.

I chewed my lip, contemplating this craziness. I made the quick decision and acted on it before I could talk any sense into myself.

"I'll be right back."

I was already tossing my dress to the floor by the time I'd cut through the bathroom and into my room. I pulled open the top drawer of the dresser, and I quickly changed into sleep pants and a t-shirt, careful to make sure everything was covered.

I darted back into his room. I left the bathroom door open a crack so a sliver of light could shine through.

My way back to sanity.

Then I was back to standing at the edge of the opulent bed.

The humungous bed covered in rich linens and silky sheets.

But it was the man lying in the middle of it that stole the show.

Country to the core. Rough and raw. Tough and rugged.

It was clear the man was no stranger to working with his hands.

And I liked it…liked that unbridled intensity. The fact he was so different from the men in LA.

Or maybe it was just that I liked him.

Shit.

I liked him.

And that was bad news for me.

Butterflies fluttering chaotically, I peeled back the sheet so I could crawl in beside him. I hesitated when I was again faced with the fact the man was only wearing briefs.

I shuddered a breath.

So much skin.

I got brave.

Bold.

I curled up close to him, leaving two inches of space between us. Still, I was close enough that I could feel the rhythm of his breaths. Close enough I could sense the beat of his heart.

The raging rhythm battering his chest calmed as the seconds passed.

I would stay right there and make sure he was fine, sound asleep, and then I'd sneak out.

He wouldn't even know I was gone.

I'd slip into my own bed where I could fall into the horrible abyss of sleep.

Where my demons waited to consume.

Where I got lost each night, and I had to claw my way out each time I woke to find myself all over again.

It seemed like a solid plan until one of those massive arms curled around my back and tucked me against his hard, rigid body. Right up to where I could feel every deliriously delicious line of him.

Our chests were pressed together, and our hearts beat

manically in time.

And his nose was in my hair, his mouth at my temple, the mumbled whisper seeping way down deep where it didn't belong. "Died and went to heaven." His nose burrowed deeper. "Goddess Girl."

Rhys

*T*orment ripped me from sleep, shooting me upright in bed.

Alcohol still slogged through my veins, walls spinning and my stomach sour. Disoriented as fuck, I scrubbed a palm over my face, trying to see through the darkness and make sense of what was goin' down.

Legs flailed and sheets ripped and short, rapid gasps panted into the air. All of it was comin' from the girl who'd been tucked to my side.

Now, she writhed.

Fear leached from her skin as whimpers tumbled from her mouth.

That sweet, sweet thing that I knew better than touchin'. One who sure as fuck shouldn't have been in my bed.

But that didn't matter a thing.

My arms were wrapping around her, like a rope lassoing a wild calf, except the last thing I wanted was to hold this girl down.

Still chained to her dream, she yelped at the contact, her skin so hot she might as well have been a thousand degrees. The feel of her was like reaching out and touching the sun.

Blinding, sparking light.

My insides charred, nothing but ash.

Because she thrashed and whimpered, "No, don't, please."

And my lips were at her temple, whispering, "I've got you, Sweet Thing. Mags, shhh…baby…I've got you. Not gonna hurt you."

I attempted to rein the rage that blistered beneath my flesh. Torched me to the soul.

Because I knew. I fucking knew, and I'd never wanted to slaughter anything like I wanted to slaughter the man who'd harmed her. All I could think as I pulled her trembling body closer was that bastard Cory Douglas was one lucky motherfucker that he was already dead.

Whoever had choked the life out of him in prison had done him a mercy.

I pressed my lips to her forehead that was drenched in sweat. "I have you."

The tiniest whimper slipped between her lips before she began to settle, the tension that stretched her body taut with agony seeping out, girl letting go, submitting into the comfort I had no right to be offering.

Her fingernails scraped into my chest, and her nose nuzzled into my beard.

"Wanna be free," she murmured from the depths of sleep.

My arms curled tighter, wishing when she did, I might be the one worthy of watching her fly.

I awoke to the welcome of her soft sigh. Warmth curled around me like some kinda drug.

Both hauntin' and mesmerizing.

Hypnotizing.

Like I'd slipped into her dream and soothed her while I was there.

For a moment, I clung to it, felt like I was floating somewhere in the clouds, even with the pounding in my brain from the remnants of the Jager.

I got selfish and hugged her tighter, that sweet, sweet body tucked close to mine.

Died and went to heaven.

So yeah.

Maybe a flash of guilt slapped me across the face because holy shit, it was damned near painful how hard she had me.

Lying there like this.

Tangled.

Problem was, after last night? I was torn between feelin' like this girl might need me, like maybe she got a little bit of that peace from me, too. All while feeling like a straight douche-nugget for knowing I was crossin' a line that shouldn't be crossed and being just greedy enough to two-step straight into forbidden territory, anyway.

Dancing in a few fires as I went.

Because this story already had failure stamped all over it.

Red pen scribbling out the lines.

Because I could physically feel myself already hurtin' her. This creaking ache in the middle of my chest. Knowing I had nothin' to give and wanting to dig around inside myself to find some scraps to offer.

Then what?

A shock of old grief welled fast.

A flashflood.

I ground my teeth, trying to hold it back, to beat it down where it belonged.

This girl had no idea about the monster lyin' next to her.

Girl nuzzled closer, her nose in my bare chest, a whisper from her mouth, "Rhys."

Like she'd just gone and sensed the torment, tapped into my

agony, and it'd drawn her from the dream.

"Goddess Girl," I rumbled back.

She pulled back just a fraction. Charcoal eyes blinked in confusion.

I shifted so I could peer down at her better.

At this sweet siren lying in my arms who had no clue what she was doin' to me.

Those eyes went wide when she realized she was lying on me, my dick hard and my chest bare. A grin stretched my mouth because she was just so goddamn cute.

"Oh my god." She scrambled back. She was on her hands and knees, so much guilt on her face she might as well have committed armed robbery. "Oh. I didn't mean to fall asleep."

My brow quirked. "Tell me you aren't apologizin'?"

Slipping the rest of the way off the mattress, she fumbled to standing on the side. "I didn't mean…"

She gestured to the bed as if she thought just sleeping beside me had been a salacious act.

My gaze took her in where the bare mornin' light flooded in through the drapes, the girl lit up like a goddess in the glittering, golden rays.

How she made sleep pants and a tee look like negligee, I didn't know.

But the girl was sexy as fuck.

Enticing.

Kinda amusin', too, with the way she danced around on her toes and shook out her hands like she'd been caught committing a few more of those crimes.

I sat up farther, slanting my fingers through the disaster that was undoubtedly my hair. I canted her a grin as I peered over at all that adorable fluster. "Let's be clear about one thing, gorgeous…"

Her brows lifted in confusion. "What's that?"

"You don't ever have to apologize for climbin' into my bed. Kinda like you there, if I'm being honest." I let it play out like a tease. It was a shame I wasn't joking.

She released a tiny gasp, and shit, my cock twitched, and I

wondered if she'd actually felt it because those eyes were raking over me where I was sitting up with just the sheet covering my poor throbbing dick that was thinking this whole situation was totally unfair.

Far too interested in how she looked standing right there.

Delicious.

Decadent.

Forbidden fuckin' fruit I wanted to pluck from a tree.

When she looked back at my face, her cheeks were bright red, and she went to chewing at that bottom lip, nervous and shy and still wholly concerned about me. "How are you feeling?"

This girl.

I gruffed out a disbelieving laugh and scrubbed a palm over my face, getting all spun up in who she was. "You're askin' me how I'm feeling?"

"Well, you did puke your guts up last night." She almost managed a smile.

A chuckle rumbled free, and then my tone shifted back to serious again. "Well, I'm feelin' like I puked my guts up last night. But I think the real question we should be asking is how you're feelin'?"

She blanched. Her expression going dim. Like maybe she'd thought I was gonna ignore what I'd woken up to last night.

"I'm just fine."

"Don't lie to me." Demand was out before I could think it through.

There was no stanching the rage that blistered across my skin when I thought of what'd happened to her.

Maggie's father had been a piece of shit. Karl Fitzgerald had been the CEO of Mylton Records, a label Carolina George was set to sign with before all kinds of shit went down.

Came down to the fact the fucker had run one seedy empire.

Sex, drugs & rock 'n' roll.

Except the sex and drugs had been coercion. The artists videotaped and photographed, their illicit activities used as blackmail so the prick could siphon more from their royalties.

The real kicker? It'd been discovered women and men had

been held in a house in LA. They'd been tricked, manipulated, some straight-up abducted and forced into servitude to feed the bullshit he was playin'.

Fucking disgusting.

Razors scraped my throat.

Maggie had gotten caught in it. One of the sick, twisted artists had hurt her.

Cory Douglas.

It'd been covered up until the lid had been blown off the whole thing thanks to Royce going after his stepfather.

Toppling him from his throne.

Maggie had been set to testify against them both until they had ended up dead in their jail cells six months ago, permanently silenced. It'd gone down right before I'd taken her to that bar because I'd wanted to give her a moment's distraction from that bullshit.

Still didn't know if she considered it a blessing or a tragedy. That it'd come to a violent, gory end.

Only thing I was certain of, the ghosts of it were still haunting her dreams.

"It was nothing," she muttered, though pain slashed through her expression. Unable to stand still beneath the weight of it, I was on my feet, and Maggie was makin' a shocked little sound, her eyes going astray as she dragged her attention down my torso before she snapped her focus back to my face.

She backed away as I edged her direction. "It's something, Maggie."

A trembling hand fluttered to her mouth, and she blinked, gesturing behind her. "I...I should go."

I grabbed her by the wrist to stop her.

Gentle but fierce.

Heat pulsed, and shit, the girl looked so confused.

Yeah, sweetness. I'm fuckin' confused, too.

"Please...don't pretend with me." The words grated from my throat.

I was so sick of the make believe.

Pretending like everything was fine and dandy. All rainbows

and flowers and unicorns shittin' glitter.

Maggie searched me.

Frantically, almost.

Her heart banged against her ribs.

Palpable.

A shiver of need rippled across my bare flesh.

"Don't you know sometimes the only thing we can do is pretend?" she whispered.

"Not with you." It was out before I realized what I was asking of her.

Something else I couldn't give.

"Rhys." It was a whimper, and I was right there, the girl pinned against the wall with me towering over her.

Her chest heaved with her strained breaths.

Her eyes wide.

Like she didn't know if she should be terrified or lean in.

"You don't want to pretend? Then who are you really, Rhys Manning?" She set her palm over the thunder of my chest. "Who's this sad boy wearing that grin who's hurting so deeply inside?"

There she was. This girl who could see right through me. Like she had a tap. All she had to do was pull the handle and all that dark bitterness would come gushing out.

I swallowed hard. "You're right, Sweet Thing. You should go."

Before I begged her to stay.

Before we crossed a line we couldn't uncross.

Before I repeated every mistake I'd already made and dragged her down a road I knew better than to ask her to travel.

A dead end.

Because mixed up in me was a place she couldn't afford to be.

seven

Maggie

*M*y feet pounded the cracked pavement as I jogged along the side of the narrow, desolate lane. There were few better ways to clear your head than a good morning run.

My lungs strained with my panted, hardened breaths, and with each one, I inhaled the distinct scents of the sea.

After spending the night in Rhys Manning's bed doing not so salacious things that still had felt erotic, I had to get out of that house.

Regroup and reclaim a little clarity because I was concerned the man was clouding sound mind.

Skewing judgement.

I could still feel it. The way it'd felt in the safety of his arms.

Every sensation dark and decadent.

Rife with the promise of pleasure that had been just out of

reach, dangled over my head like a tease.

It'd left me so needy that I'd worried I would start begging for it.

Reckless girl.

It didn't matter if I'd never experienced it before, there was no mistaking what he was igniting in me.

I needed to fight it.

Ignore it.

This feeling I wanted to disappear into.

I needed to hold onto the truth that the man was nothing but a threat to my heart that was just beginning to heal.

This man who was chaos.

Rough and playful.

Aloof and caring.

So glaringly broken yet I wondered if anyone else could recognize it the way that I did.

And then he'd gone and held me when I'd been the one breaking apart. The way I did most nights. I'd woken up not sure if I wanted to hide it, pretend some more, or offer that part of myself to be held by those big, capable hands.

The biggest issue with all of this?

There was absolutely no question those capable hands had the power to crush.

And I needed to focus more on healing rather than setting myself up to get hurt again.

The air was hot and muggy, and the sun beat down on my skin where the rays speared through the leaves of the sprawling, gangly oaks that were interspersed with leafy palms that grew in front of the properties that lined the road.

The Earth's beauty all around.

The rhythm of my steps and the steady thrum of the music pulsing from my earbuds lulled me into a peace.

Pound. Pound. Pound.

It called me to a place where the fears and the worries melted away.

When I ran, it felt like my spirit and body were in sync.

At one.

It was as if I could physically feel some of those internal scars healing. The ones that had been buried deep.

Ones I'd had to cover for so many years and pretend like they didn't exist.

The ones Cory Douglas had inflicted.

I'd almost come to accept their presence as normal.

As a permanent, ordinary part of me.

Outrage flashed.

A blaze that singed my blood and a sickness that crawled beneath the surface of my skin.

A permanent ache.

Being brutalized the way I had was a far cry from what should be considered *ordinary*.

It made me sick that it almost was.

That it occurred so often, affected so many, that it'd become the everyday.

I refused to accept it.

Wanted to change it.

I knew the scars would forever remain. That they had played a part in shaping who I was today.

But I could feel them shifting. Transforming. As if when the wounds callused over, those fragile spots had become stronger.

The brittle fractures hardening.

The weakness strengthening.

That's the way I felt.

Stronger.

I was terrified, but I was ready.

The ugly duckling that grew into a swan, but it didn't have a thing to do with the exterior.

Pound. Pound. Pound.

I felt the rhythm in my ears.

My feet and my heart rate and the bass from the song that blasted through my earbuds.

When I'd made it about two miles from the house, I decided I'd better get back before I let myself drift too far.

Carolina George was scheduled for their first practice at ten, and I needed to grab a shower before I was due to watch Amelia.

It was auntie duty time.

My heart fluttered.

Now that was one label I was all too eager to accept.

I glanced over my shoulder to check that the road was clear.

Lush branches swayed beneath the bright, glaring sun, and birds flitted through the morning air. Other than that, there wasn't a soul afoot.

The neighborhood was quiet and overflowing with the tranquility I'd felt the moment we'd crossed onto the island.

I made a U onto the other side of the road and started in the opposite direction.

My playlist changed to a faster, rowdier song, and my strides grew longer.

Stronger and faster.

Pound. Pound. Pound.

Drenched in sweat, I hooked a left when I got to the intersecting street. It led through an older neighborhood that cut through the middle of the island. The houses here were more modest and without a beach view.

Here, the trees grew thicker, the foliage dense and green.

With the back of my hand, I swiped the sweat dripping across my forehead, feeling the burn in my muscles and exhilarated at the same time.

An expectation gathered at the far corners of my senses.

I felt like I was on the cusp of…something.

Something great.

Something big.

Something that might change everything.

An elderly woman who was tending to her flower garden waved as I passed, and I waved back, a smile on my face and flickers of joy sparking all around.

I gave myself over to it.

The exertion.

The freedom.

I guessed I was about halfway down the street when that free feeling shifted.

When it curled and twisted and mangled into a prickling of

dread.

I tried to ignore it.

Shake it off.

I was so tired of it—so tired of being a prisoner to the fear.

So tired of the paranoia that had stolen so many of my days.

Crippling.

Making me question what was real and what should cause me concern.

But that disquiet only intensified. It slithered down my spine in a sticky awareness.

I whipped my head around.

Nothing.

Trying to shake it off, I took the next right and increased my pace.

But I couldn't outrun the feeling.

Panic built.

Violent.

Vehement.

I looked behind me again.

There was a car a bit back in the distance.

A silver car that I could chalk up to being a rental. Innocuous and plain.

Most likely a tourist.

Trying to claim it, I faced ahead and tried to get it together.

I was fine.

I was letting the ghosts haunt.

The demons invade.

The paranoia cripple.

On top of it was the worry that I might not be able to pull this off. That I was going to be found out before I had the chance to make it right.

Pound. Pound. Pound.

My feet thudded the ground.

But the thunder was coming louder. A wild drumming in my ears that spread to my chest.

Out of sync with the music.

Drumming out of time.

Faster and fiercer.

My breaths grew harsh. Short, haggard pants as I pushed myself into the panic. Trying to flee.

And then a wave of it crashed over me.

Terror.

A surge of it nearly knocked me from my feet as I whipped my head around to see the car suddenly accelerate. It screamed up the street in my direction.

From harmless to sinister in a second flat.

I veered farther off the side of the road in hopes of getting out of the way.

I was being crazy. I was allowing fear to dictate.

Only I swore the car swerved in my direction.

Every nerve in my body fired.

Fight or flight.

I dove.

Pound. Pound. Pound.

I flailed through the air as the car raced by.

The ferocity of its energy burst in the air.

So close.

So close.

I slammed against the ground.

Hard.

A tangle of limbs and ripping skin as the momentum sent me tumbling.

Tumbling and tumbling.

Grunts and jagged cries ripped from my mouth.

I finally came to a stop.

Facedown.

Disoriented.

Shocked.

But alive.

For the flash of a moment, I lay there trying to process what had happened. As the paranoia tried to possess me the way it always did.

To convince me it was purposed, and the car had tried to run me down.

Memories of coming home to find flames devouring my condo that night invaded my mind.

Old fears screamed this wasn't by chance.

It wasn't by accident.

But how many times had I done this? How many years did I spend hiding at the back of my closet, shivering in terror? How much life had I missed because of it?

Both pain and relief suddenly splintered through my body as the adrenaline drained free of my pores and my nerves took over. A wail erupted from my raw, aching throat.

Disoriented and shaking, I pushed myself up enough to see the car skidding around the corner at the four-way stop up ahead. It disappeared behind a hedge of shrubbery the second it made the turn.

Choking out a cry, I slumped back down. Tears blinded my eyes and gasps ripped from my throat as dread hooked like splintery barbs into my spirit.

You're fine. You're fine. You're fine, I silently chanted in an attempt to stave off the fear.

A shriek tore from my lungs when a hand suddenly landed on my shoulder.

I jerked that way to find an older man wearing baggy swim trunks and a stained tee hunched over me.

His mouth was moving frantically.

Shouting.

Worry came off him in waves.

Overwhelming.

I braced myself against it, and I managed to shift around to sitting, groaning with the pangs that already were screaming from my muscles.

I ripped the earbuds free.

The second I did, his distress poured into my ears. "Can you hear me, girl? Are you okay?"

I blinked. My mind tilting from one direction to another. Panic and relief.

Before I could figure out how to respond, he lifted both my arms away to inspect me.

He whistled low. "Lord have mercy. You are busted up good. Leakin' blood like a sieve."

Slowly, my gaze traveled to where he was looking. In slow motion. My thoughts so muddled, I was having trouble processing.

The sight of blood dripping down my leg and arms triggered another rush of pain.

My right knee was split open in about a three-inch gash, and my palms were shredded, pebbled with tiny rocks and sand.

"I'll get an ambulance out here. Dontcha worry, girl. We'll get you patched up quick."

Alarm raced, and the word sprang free on a shout, "No."

My tongue darted out to wet my dried lips, and I forced myself to get it together. "No. I think I'm fine. I'm fine."

"Don't look so fine to me. I see some stitches in your future."

"I really don't think it's necessary. I just…need to make a call."

Dread glimmered. Different this time. Royce was going to lose it.

"That car nearly hit you," the man rambled. "Thought they were gonna run you plumb over. Damn tourists. Probably partied all night, got liquored up, and decided to use our neighborhood as a playground. No one's got any respect no more…not for property or human life."

I barely nodded, fully agreeing with him and feeling awful that I wished in this instance his speculations were right.

That it was someone out for a joyride.

Swallowing the horror, I attempted a smile that was nothing more than a tremble of my lips. "It's okay. I don't think they saw me until the last minute. I should have been paying attention. Shouldn't have had my music playing so loud. I didn't even hear them until they were right there."

I did my best to convince the guy that it was no big deal.

That it was my fault.

It wasn't.

It wasn't my fault.

For so many years, I'd questioned if it had been. If I'd done something wrong. Said something that invited it.

I'd let my mind toil with *I should have done this,* or *I shouldn't have said that.*

I knew better now.

It didn't matter what I'd said or done.

It wasn't my fault.

But the guilty always wanted to make the innocent pay.

Not this time.

My paranoia and fear would no longer rule, and I was going to do this, no matter what it took.

I was determined to take back a little of what was owed.

To make a difference.

To make a change.

Even if it cost me my life.

Rhys

"*Y*ou are my sunshine…my only sunshine! You makes me happy, when skies is gray…"

Daisy belted out the song where she sat on a stool coloring with markers on blank pieces of white paper at the island.

Pouring myself a fat cup of coffee, I joined in on the next line, singing it loud and raucous…because how could I not?

Not when the little thing grinned and giggled and mashed up my heart all over again.

I actually croaked over one of the words.

So what if I wasn't feeling top-notch this morning.

I could blame it on the bottle of Jager I'd drowned myself in. Or maybe I could pin it on the anger and the fear I'd felt when I'd gotten that fuckin' picture of my mama last night that was nothing but blackmail and bribery.

A knife stabbed straight into my greatest regret, that motherfucker giving it a good, hard twist.

But I knew the disorder I felt right then was a direct result of the girl who was toyin' with my logic and rationale.

She was a storm currently wagin' war on my insides.

It was rare that my head, spirit, and dick were at odds.

Usually, we were a one-track mind.

Get in. Get out. Get gone.

And that girl had me itching for all kinds of irresponsible, delusional things.

Daisy shook her head like she felt sorry for me, breaking me from the thoughts, the child still coloring away when she said, "You sings it so bad, Uncles Rhys. You ain't got the pipes like my auntie Ems and my daddy and me."

Overdramatic, I smacked a hand onto my chest. "Now how could you go and be so cruel, oh, young one? Five years old, and already breakin' hearts."

Daisy ho-hummed and sighed. "I gotta tell the truth because the lies are bad. And I'm almost six. Get it straight."

"Well, okay then, almost six-year-old sassy pants."

Emily shuffled into the kitchen, looking like she was lacking about a week's sleep, hair a disaster and bags under her eyes. She hip-checked me to get me out of the way of the coffee pot. "Scoot."

I hopped out of her way. "Well, good morning to you, too. Sheesh. I'm surrounded by nothin' but a bunch of bossy pants and sassy pants. Way to hold a good man down."

"No way. I'll hold you up, Uncle Rhys' Pieces!"

"Oh, and how are you gonna do that…build me an altar on all those truths?" I teased.

Daisy gave me a resolute nod. "Yup. And I gots the most important truth—all the amor, amor, amor, and I gots lots and lots of it for you."

Damn.

There went my mangled heart.

Setting my coffee on the counter, I moved around the island and swung her up from her stool and into my arms. I spun us in a circle, singing off-key and just as loud as could be. "Amor, amor, amor. Give me some more. Don't drop Little Miss Daisy on the floor."

I fumbled, pretending like she was slipping from my hands. I caught her a second later, just as she screeched, and I swept her back upright. Daisy scrambled to get even closer, locking her tiny arms around my neck. "Don't drop me, Uncle!"

A light chuckle rumbled out, and I kept swaying her, hugging her tight. "Never."

"And stop with all the teases."

"Never."

I could feel her grin pressed to the side of my face. "Okay, fines. I like your teases alright."

Amor. Amor. Amor.

Love, love, love.
Rhys' mama said this house was built on it.
That it was the foundation of a family.
And without it, everything would collapse.

My heart clutched in old agony, and I squeezed Daisy just a little tighter.

Royce strolled in holding Amelia. At the sound of his footsteps, Daisy pulled back. "Ooh…look it! My baby cousin is here!" she squealed. "She's soooos the cutest!"

She wiggled, and I set her down so she could go scamperin' that way.

Emily beamed at her little family. She lifted the carafe in her husband's direction with that adoring expression on her face. "Coffee?"

"Please," Royce grumbled, shifting down onto a knee so Daisy could *ooh* and *aah* over the tiny infant.

"Ah, I see how it is, Em-Girl. Offer him coffee but ignore little ol' me," I taunted.

Emily rolled her eyes.

Some might not know the difference, but I knew it was filled with affection. "Um…if you wanna start gettin' up for three a.m.

feedings, I'll be happy to pour you a cup of coffee in the mornin', too."

My hands shot up in surrender. "Hey now, let's not get crazy."

Her eyes rolled again, and she was shaking her head, looking at me the way she did. The girl one of my oldest friends. Family. Her joy mine because it was the only thing that mattered.

Truth was, I'd step in for every feeding if that's what she needed of me.

Royce's cell rang from his pocket, and he seemed to waver, unsure, like he was contemplating juggling our poor little Amelia.

"Here," I said as I ambled that way.

It was almost a scowl scrawled across his brow when I offered assistance, but he straightened and passed her over. "Careful."

"I've got her."

All chubby, pinked cheeks and pursed, adorable lips.

She weighed next to nothing.

I held her against my chest, bouncing her soft.

Yeah.

Definitely *ooh*-worthy.

"Hey there, gorgeous girl," I murmured when she made a tiny, squeaking cry. "Look at that, another one that's gonna be breakin' all the hearts."

Daisy grinned up at me. "I don't think so, Uncle Rhys' Pieces. I heard my mommy tellin' my daddy you is the one who is nothin' but a heartbreaker."

I forced a smile.

Heartbreaker.

Heartbroken.

Same dif, right?

"She did, did she?"

"Yup…and she said you is a catch." Daisy's dark eyes lit, and her voice switched to a squeal. "Hey, do you wanna play catch with me on the beach? I brought some balls with me! And we can go swimmin'! Can we go swimmin'?"

She tugged at my pant leg when she asked it, and light laughter tumbled out. That smile didn't feel so forced as I looked down on the little girl that turned me to mush. "Sounds like a good plan to me, Daisy Mae. Right after practice, yeah?"

Only, I could feel that smile slippin' when Royce answered the phone, his casual, "Hey, Mag Pie, what's up?" shifting to alarm when he stopped talking to hear whatever his sister was saying.

I couldn't make it out.

Didn't need to in order to feel it.

To get dragged right into the undertow of worry.

The current this raging toil I could feel crashing against my feet.

Had no idea what was up, but I was ready to go flyin' out the door.

"What? Are you okay?… Fuck… Are you sure?"

His eyes were wild as he glanced at Emily who'd stepped away from the counter in concern.

"Okay. I'll be there in a second," he said before he dropped his phone to his side. Man looked like he was about to crack. Was it fucked up it felt like he was gonna take me right along with him, too? "Maggie tripped on her run. I have to go pick her up."

I was already moving before he finished talking, handing Amelia off to Emily. Without missing a beat, she accepted her, bouncing her as she rushed to ask, "Is she hurt?"

Royce roughed an agitated hand over the top of his head. "Hurt enough that she called…so knowing my sister, I'm going to say, yeah." He started for the door before he whirled around. "Shit. Our rental isn't being delivered until eleven."

I was already halfway to the door, dragging the keys to my baby from my pocket. "I've got you covered."

Dude actually tried to snag the keys from my hand. Like I was gonna let him go without me? Like I could abandon the fear that burst in my blood?

Shit.

This was stupid.

Stupid bad.

Didn't matter.

I snatched the keys out of his reach.

"You think I'm gonna let you drive my baby?" I drew it out like the idea was ludicrous as I whirled around, walking backward with my arms stretched wide.

Good excuse.

Everyone knew the love I had for my car.

Royce didn't argue. "Then hurry up, asshole."

He angled around me, and I turned at the same time, following him out into the heat of the day.

Sun obnoxious as the rays blazed down.

Daggers of fire.

Or maybe it was just the worry.

The antsy irritation that slicked my skin in an instant sheen of sweat.

We raced for where my car was parked in the circular drive, car bleeping as I pushed the fob to unlock it. We both jumped in, and I had the engine turned over and was peeling out of the drive before either of our doors were shut.

Zero to sixty in a blink.

The powerful engine roared as I gunned it the second we hit the street.

Royce gave me quick directions as I flew around the corners.

Normally, driving was my freedom form. Where I felt like I could outrun my ghosts. Where nothin' could catch up to me.

It was pure fuckin' fun.

Not today.

"She's fine. She's fine," Royce rumbled in the seat next to me. "Talked to her myself."

"Yeah. Sure she's good, man. She's good. Would have gotten a call from the hospital if it were something significant."

Think both of us needed to see it to believe it, though.

Because saying it out loud didn't seem to soothe a thing.

I took a sharp right, the tires squealing as I fishtailed around the corner. The wheels caught, and the car righted, and we shot down the road.

"There."

I was already coming to a screeching stop when Royce sat forward to point to where Maggie sat off to the left side of the road with some old dude hovering over her.

Royce was out of the car and rounding the front before I could put it in park.

"Maggie," he shouted.

The guy was all fury and darkness, and I think I got it then, his devotion to this girl.

His fear.

The truth that he would do absolutely anything to protect his sister.

Could feel it coming off him in staggering waves as he knelt in front of her.

Didn't mean I didn't want to push him out of the way so I could get to her when I climbed out from the driver's side.

My own shout of protectiveness rose to fill my chest.

My damned hands twitched with the urge to run them over her. Search out every injury.

Had to physically restrain myself from busting through to toss her over my shoulder and carry her away to safety like some kinda fatheaded dolt.

The blotches of blood staining her light-blue running shirt and the webs streaking from her knee sure weren't helpin' things.

My bad behavior was about to get worse.

Charcoal eyes found me from over his shoulder.

"Mags." It was an exhale from my lips.

The hair knotted on her head was sprinkled with dried grass, and a little scrape was starting to swell on her chin.

But what got me most was the girl was clearly wired.

Shaken and agitated.

"Hey, Rhys," she answered, breathing heavily.

"You good?"

She forced a brittle smile. "Yeah."

Shit.

Wanted to gather her up and promise that she was okay. That I wouldn't let anything happen to her. That I'd take the brunt of any injury or harm comin' her way.

I had to remind myself fifteen thousand times that danger was me.

"What the fuck happened?" Royce demanded.

"It was nothing. I just tripped," she told him.

"Fuck," he hissed, but in it was torment. Like the guy was just waiting on their peace to be stripped away. "You tripped? How? Look at you...you're a mess. Maggie. Shit."

"I wasn't paying attention and must have—"

The ratty guy who'd been standing by her cut her off, "I was in my yard right over there and this car came speedin' up the road like some kinda maniac. Got this close."

He pinched his finger and thumb, leaving a sliver of space. "Sure thought we were gonna have us a tragedy right here on our quiet street. Damn kids. She's lucky she's only banged up a bit...though she scared me right and good with all that blood."

Slack-jawed, I realized I was just staring at the dude.

Mortified.

I pried my attention from him and slowly turned it to Maggie, trying not to freak the fuck out.

Royce wasn't doing such a good job of it. "What the fuck? Someone almost hit you? Who was it? Who did this?" His voice rose with each demand he issued.

Maggie huffed out a nonchalant laugh, shaking her head, acting like it was no big deal when I could hear each of the words trembling from her tongue. "It was an accident, Royce. Calm down. I got lost in my music again, and I...I think I must have drifted out into the road. I wasn't paying attention, and then I looked to the side and saw a car was right there. I got spooked, panicked, and I tripped."

"You got spooked?" The words grated from his mouth.

She nodded.

Resolute.

"Yep."

I was ninety-nine-point-nine-percent certain it was a lie.

Like maybe I had one of those taps, too.

Royce grunted, angling away to run his shaking hand through his hair, trying to keep calm. "Told you I didn't want you out jogging by yourself. You don't know what kinda psychos are lurking about."

I punched a fist into my opposite fist. Needin' to do something with the sudden aggression. "Yup. Sounds to me like someone needs an ass whoopin'.'"

Maggie scowled at me, one of those brows arching for the sky in her annoyance.

God, why'd she have to be so fuckin' cute?

"I do hope you aren't talking about me."

Horror took me over at the thought, my eyes going wide, before I realized she was cracking a joke.

More than likely trying to distract her brother from his worry.

I gave her a grin that was absolutely forced. "Hells no, baby cakes." I stretched my arms out wide. "I'm talkin' about the psychos out drivin' like maniacs. Stirrin' up a ruckus."

"Don't think you have much room to talk." This from the scruffy old dude. "Come blazing down here like a bat outta Hell. All you tourists are alike."

Wow, dude, wow.

I swiveled my attention to him. "No need to worry, Sir. I'm a professional."

Professional bullshitter, of course.

But the guy didn't need to know that.

"That so?"

"Trained by Ford's great-grandson himself." I gestured to my car.

"Huh." Old guy actually looked impressed.

I was pretty impressed with the lie, too.

Maggie giggled.

Shit, she giggled, and my heart did that wayward thing, beating that extra beat that never should exist.

"Let's get you to the hospital." Royce pushed to standing and stretched out a hand.

Wanted to be the one doing it.

Maggie accepted it, though she was rolling her eyes when she did. "I'm fine, Royce. It's only a couple scrapes. You think I need to go to the hospital when what I need is a Band-Aid or two."

"Don't like it."

"I just want to go home."

"No more jogging alone," he grumbled as he looped an arm around her waist. "Treadmills were created for a reason."

Maggie shook her head as she leaned against him. He started to lead her around the car, while I followed, wanting to tell him she could make her own *mistakes* all while fighting the urge to jump in and agree.

"I think I can go out for a run when I feel like it." Clearly, she didn't need me to do the talking for her.

"Can you?" he bit out.

"Wow. Thanks." It was pure affront. She pulled away an inch to throw a frown in his direction. "Twenty, not twelve, remember? You have to quit tossing rules at me, Royce. I'm not a child."

"Fuck. I'm sorry. I just...can't..."

There was no missing the implication when he trailed off.

Fact he couldn't handle the idea of losing her.

In it was this old agony.

The kind that was distinct.

The kind that I recognized all too well.

They made it around to the other side of the car when Maggie stopped and turned to look at him, her expression fierce and soft and a fucking wrecking ball to my senses.

She reached out and touched his chest. "Hey, I'm okay. I'm right here."

Girl was so real and genuine. Both wise and naïve.

"But what if you weren't?" His voice cracked.

"We can't live life on what if's, Royce. You know that. I can't live my life in fear any longer. We have to embrace every day. Cherish them. *Use* them because each day is a gift that's been given, and I refuse to waste any more of them because I've already wasted enough."

Royce's face pinched and he spread his hand over hers and pressed it tighter to his chest. "And it's my job to make sure you have a hundred years of them."

Her smile was soft.

Understanding.

"No, Royce, it's not. But the fact that you want to? It means everything to me."

His tatted throat bobbed hard, and he pulled away to open the passenger door, unable to give her a response. "I'll get in the back."

She gave a nod.

The second he wedged into the miniature backseat, I was right there, taking his spot, slippin' my arm around her waist so I could help her the rest of the way in.

Turned out, it was me who needed assistance. The way my knees almost buckled at the connection. At the furnace inside that someone had turned to a thousand degrees.

Maggie tried to swallow her gasp.

Shocked, too.

What in the actual fuck?

"You good?" I played it off like I was asking her the same question as her brother.

She gulped. "Yep."

Another one of those lies.

I angled her into the seat. "In you go, Sweet Thing."

Royce all but growled from the back seat.

Right then, he could fuck off.

I dipped my head in, watching her as I grabbed the seat belt and dragged it across her body.

Girl right there.

Invading my space.

Infatuating my senses.

Makin' me weak.

The lock snapped into place, and Maggie heaved a breath.

I froze for a second, just staring at her, trying to rein the direction my heart was thumping. "You good?" I asked again.

"Yeah. Thank you."

"You sure we can't take you to the ER to get checked out?"

"I'm sure."

"Stubborn," Royce grumbled.

Finally, I gave her a slight nod and dipped back out. I rushed around the front, waving at the guy who was still standing there watching us. "Thanks for your help."

He chuckled, something gleaming in his eye. "Play it cool, young man."

Dude actually tipped his head toward where Maggie sat.

Tell me I wasn't that fuckin' obvious?

I just let my brow curl, and I moved the rest of the way around to slip into the driver's seat.

And there it was—I was slammed by her aura all over again.

Vanilla and jasmine.

Sweet, sweet, sweet.

I scrubbed a palm over my face like it could break it up, then I looked over at her and she was looking at me.

Soft.

Tender.

But there was more lingering in that charcoal gaze.

Strokes of pencil that shrouded and shadowed.

I'd bet my left nut she was keeping a secret.

One she didn't want to tell.

Had to respect that because I knew that feeling all too well.

"You want to go home...I'll get you home." I cracked a playful smirk and gave her a little salute before I shifted into gear.

I gunned it down the street.

And I just barely registered the sight of the silver car sitting off to the side of the intersecting road through my rearview mirror.

Maggie

"See, I knew that cut was deep."

"It is not deep." I sent a scowl at my brother who hovered behind Emily where she knelt to clean my knee.

I sat on the edge of the massive tub in my bathroom, pretty much in the same spot where I'd been tending to Rhys last night.

I hadn't talked to him in months, and now I couldn't escape him.

The lure and the trap.

I was still dealing with the after-effects of the car ride home.

The man so big where he'd taken up the space. The muscles of his hulking arm flexing as he'd driven.

Aggressively.

Almost violently.

Glancing at me every second or two.

Seeing that I was safe. But it was more than that. The way he was looking at me.

This man who could so easily destroy me.

Decimate.

Annihilate.

Sitting there, I still wore my running shorts and tank. Drenched in sweat. Covered in dirt and blood and most likely a sheen of fear.

Probably not my best look.

I flinched when Emily dabbed at the cut. She sent me an apologetic glance. "Sorry. Does that sting?"

"Just a little," I said as I sucked in a steeling breath, trying to put on a brave face.

Emily cringed when she worked the Q-tip a little deeper.

"Ouch." I couldn't help it. I could deny it all I wanted, but it freaking hurt. Still, I had to thank my lucky stars this was the worst of it.

"Dang it. There is a tiny piece of gravel stuck in there that I can't quite get," she whispered below her breath, trying to focus as she leaned in closer to get a better look.

"See...we need to go to the ER." Royce was right there again, pushing his face into her space.

Emily shoved at him. Playful and one-hundred-percent serious. "Would you scoot?"

He straightened, crossing his arms with a huff.

She shifted around to look at him, gesturing at the door. "All the way out, mister. Go on. Maggie needs to get out of these clothes, and she doesn't need you loiterin' around, gettin' in her way."

Royce grumbled.

Emily sent him a silent look that I was betting said so many things.

Because he blew out a sigh and roughed a hand over his face. "Fine." Then he shifted his attention to me. "Are you sure you're good?"

"I promise."

Reluctantly, he finally eased out the bathroom door and softly clicked it shut behind him.

Taking in one more worried glance before he went, of course.

On a soft giggle, Emily shook her head as she went back to cleaning my knee. Pure affection. "That man. He is about as overbearin' as they come. Thinks he has to save the whole dang world."

"Yeah."

She peeked up at me. "That's what sets him apart, though, you know. What makes him great. The fact he would lay down everythin' for the ones he loves. For ones he doesn't know, too."

My smile was soft. "He's probably the best man I know."

Her smile turned wry, her green eyes sparking with playfulness. "But he's still drivin' you crazy."

I giggled. "Completely."

"He thinks he was meant to be your protector."

"Obviously." Playfulness rolled out, and for a flash, Emily's expression was filled with it, too, before she sobered, her tongue swiping out to lick her lips as she looked at the floor. Worry seeped from her. Care and kindness. She finally looked at me. "Just…neither of us could handle it if somethin' happened to you. We love you so much."

I reached out and touched her cheek. "I love you, too. Both of you. You've given me more than I could ask for. I don't think I can ever truly express what that means."

Emily heaved out a choked laugh. "Us? I believe it's the other way around. Our family is complete because of you, Maggie. Because you were brave enough to come to me and lay it all out." She squeezed my uninjured knee. "Brave enough to share your story. Brave enough to step out and take a chance to make me see what was really going on with your brother. I hope you know that I will forever be grateful for that."

Joy pressed full.

Overflowing my spirit.

Adoration spinning and spinning.

Emily and Royce had overcome huge obstacles finding their way to each other. It was an honor that I got to be a part of their story. That I played a small part in bringing them together in the end.

"That gratefulness will always go both ways," I told her. "I am so thankful you took the chance. That you trusted enough in what I told you to go after what you wanted. To chase down what was right. And more than anything else, I'm grateful that you love my brother the way he deserves to be loved."

Moisture filled Emily's green, green eyes. "I hope you take that same advice, too. I hope you always go after what you want. After what you need. *After what is right.* That you believe when your heart is tellin' you it's the right thing to do. That you put yourself out there, take every opportunity, even when it might be scary. That you chase down your own joy."

Mischief sparked in her gaze. "Even when your brother might throw a fit about it."

A soft smile tugged at the edges of my mouth. "I intend to."

Tenderness flooded the room as she puffed air from her nose, and she started to go back to work on my knee. I reached out and stopped her. "Honestly, I think what I really need right now is to get these clothes off and get a shower. I'm sure Amelia is needing you by now, anyway."

With a frown, she sat back on her knees. "Are you sure?"

"Completely. I feel gross and just want to wash the day from my body."

Exhaling, she pushed to her feet. "Alright, then. I'll give you some privacy. Supplies are on the counter. If you think there is still something lodged in there when you get out, give me a holler and I'll come dig it out."

I smirked at her. "That's what I'm afraid of."

A light chuckle rippled from her, and she dipped down and placed a kiss to the top of my head. "I'm so glad you weren't hurt, my sweet sister. I was really worried when Royce got that call."

I squeezed her hand as she pulled away, and she squeezed back before she turned and headed for the door, leaving the same way as her husband had done.

The second the door clicked shut, I huffed out in relief. In confusion.

I was still reeling.

Trying to process.

Wondering if I was being paranoid or if I wasn't being cautious enough.

That was a fine line, wasn't it?

Embracing life without being reckless?

Doing what was right without being foolish?

I pushed to standing, and I groaned.

Stiffness was already setting in. Oh man, was I going to be sore in the morning. I toed off my running shoes and socks, and then I peeled the tight tank over my head and started to go for the sports bra when I froze.

When I felt the shift in the air.

The worry.

Different than my brother's, though.

This was raw.

Potent.

Lined with passion.

Maybe need.

I was barely breathing by the time I heard the taps at the door that separated the bathroom and his bedroom.

My heart accelerated into chaos.

I grabbed the shirt I'd just dropped to the floor and balled it against my chest.

Like I could shield myself from him all while wanting to beg him to come closer.

Talk about foolish.

"Come in," I rasped, turning that way.

The hinges creaked and the door cracked open.

Intensity surged.

Coating my flesh.

A slick of heat and a tumble of that awareness.

Rhys poked his head through, blue, blue eyes devouring me from where he stood.

An ocean.

A torrent.

My sanity's demise.

His powerful gaze swept over my body.

I knew he was just checking on me.

It didn't matter.

That rush of heat amped to an inferno.

Burning me up.

"Rhys," I managed.

The smirk that took to his sexy lips was soft, twitching around his beard. "Thought they were never gonna leave. Was going crazy out there."

"I told you I was fine."

"Yeah," he said, shouldering the rest of the way through. "But that was with your brother squawkin' around you like a mother hen."

He hit me with a full-fledged grin.

Oh damn.

I gulped and took a step back.

If I remained standing too close, I was afraid my hands were going to get unruly. Straight ignore all social cues and reach for him.

Touch his chest as a reminder of how it'd felt to be tucked against it last night.

Trace the tattoos on his arms.

Discover each one.

Or if I let myself get really carried away, maybe I'd let my itching fingers take a ride up his thick throat and into his beard, all the way until I was caressing the angles and lines of that beautifully rugged face.

Chills raced. Lifting on my skin. I trembled.

"You cold?" he asked, tipping his head to the side. I didn't know if he was being serious or messing with me.

"A little. I was just getting ready to get into the shower." I still had my bloodied shirt clutched against my chest.

"Sorry to interrupt." I was thinking he wasn't sorry at all because he edged in another inch.

Rigid severity hit the air. His burly, lumbering body overflowed the room.

I sucked in a staggered breath. "It's okay."

"Is it?" he asked. "Is any of this okay?"

"I told you it was just a little stumble."

He took two big steps closer. "Not what I'm talkin' about, Maggie."

Memories swam.

Being in his arms.

The way he'd had me against the wall in his room this morning. His nose brushing mine. Our need palpable.

Before he'd gotten scared and asked me to leave.

I'd felt it like a blow.

Experienced it as his truth.

"I want to know why you lied to your brother."

My brow curled. Surprised. Shocked that he'd recognized it.

I just hoped my reaction came across as denial. "I don't know what you're talking about."

He chuckled a rough sound. Frustration and a plea. "You were scared out there."

"Of course, I was scared. I almost got hit by a car. It freaked me out."

His head shook, refusing the excuse. "You might be able to pull the wool over your brother's eyes, but you and I know better than that, don't we, darlin'?"

A shiver wracked through me. I was accustomed to sensing people. To being overwhelmed by their emotions. What I wasn't used to? Them sensing me back.

Sharing a connection that made me feel so incredibly alive. One I knew would devastate me if I fell into the false safety of it.

I could feel it shimmering around him like a forcefield.

Heartbreak.

It didn't matter. I pressed forward. Lifted my chin and turned the tables on him. "Why were you scared this morning?"

Disbelief filled his huff, and he angled his head, the longer pieces of his hair flopping to the side. "Goin' there would be a mistake."

"Maybe it feels like I'm already there, whether you want me to be or not."

And maybe I wanted to make a thousand mistakes with him.

There I stood in the middle of the bathroom wearing nothing but a sports bra and shorts.

Skin torn up.

Body aching.

But this was an ache that started from the inside.

Bubbling up from some unfound spring that I hadn't known existed.

A place Rhys Manning had uncovered.

The man slowly stalked the rest of the way in. Step by monstrous step.

My head tilted farther back as he came closer.

Hot.

Heat.

Fire.

Fumbling beneath the intensity of him, I stumbled back until I gently knocked into the wall.

Until the mountain of him had me pinned.

Delicately, though.

Like the mass of him knew I might be fragile.

He rested his left forearm on the wall above my head and slowly...so slowly...he reached out and dragged the knuckle of his right index finger down the angle of my jaw. "Goddess Girl."

My spirit leapt at his tone.

At the affection.

Blue eyes toiled like the sea that crashed against the beach outside.

Their depths unfounded.

Uncharted and undiscovered.

I swore I could hear the hammer of his heart.

Pound. Pound. Pound.

Blood sloshed through my veins, trying to keep time.

"And I feel like I'm *right here*, too," he rumbled as his fingertips fluttered down my jaw. A wave of chills scattered in their wake. The man was so close. His lips right there. "No matter how fuckin' hard I'm trying to stay away."

I blinked up at him. "Isn't it okay for us to take care of each other?"

"Oh darlin', I think it's plenty clear it was me who was reapin' all the benefits last night." His words came out riddled with lust.

I was certain of that.

I felt it like a rake across my flesh.

Hooks deep enough I thought they might sink into my soul.

"That's funny. I thought it was you who came racing up to save me with my brother this morning."

He let that finger trail down my trembling neck.

Tentatively.

Carefully.

"Couldn't have kept me away."

And I was distinctly aware that I was a mess. Sweaty and bloody. But Rhys somehow chased my insecurities away.

I tipped my chin up farther. My words whispered with his mouth an inch from mine. "Isn't that what friends do? Take care of each other?"

Rhys traced his rough fingertips lower. Until he was tickling across my collarbone, over the thunder of my heart, nudging the shirt I was clinging to out of the way.

It dropped to the floor.

My breaths turned ragged. Shallow and needy.

He managed to get even closer, and his nose brushed mine.

"Is that what we are, Maggie? Friends?" It was another warning.

"Rhys." His name came on a moan, and my back hitched to the wall, my spine arching my chest toward him.

An unsung plea.

So unlike me.

Or maybe…maybe this was me.

Maybe for the first time, I was courageous enough to explore it. To chase it, like Emily had said. Even when it terrified me.

Blue eyes flared.

His fingers dipped even lower, his touch not quite making contact with the scar forever marked on my chest.

Like he'd gone on the hunt for it.

"Sweet Thing," he grated.

I could almost taste the rage that seeped from his spirit. The way it tightened his muscles.

His teeth clenched.

He knew of the scar's existence.

Hell, the whole world was aware of the calling card Cory Douglas had left on his victims. The way he'd signed himself on our skin as if we were possessions.

Half of it had been exposed when I'd worn my bridesmaids' dress for Emily and Royce's wedding six months ago. On the night this man had danced and danced with me and made me fall a little bit for him right then.

It was an X just above and off to the side of my right breast.

That scar was something I had been working on overcoming.

Learning not to cover or hide like I was written in shame.

It was a reminder of why I was doing what I was doing. The reason I would risk it all.

My chest jutted out.

"I'm not afraid," I whispered.

He would be the first who had touched it other than the doctor who'd patched it up. The one my father had paid to write in my hospital chart that I'd cut myself on broken glass after I'd fallen down the stairs when really Cory had done it after he'd violated me.

Rhys groaned.

It was a pained sound.

Needy, deep, and wholly conflicted.

A shudder ripped through me when he carefully flattened his massive palm over the scar. "Goddess Girl."

He whispered it, and his nose ran up my jaw and lingered on my cheek.

Inhale.

Exhale.

Me breathing him. Him breathing me.

He brushed the pad of his thumb over the spot.

"Rhys." A jagged whimper left me.

"Maggie." Caution danced on his lips. I got the sense the man was trying not to snap.

"I'm not afraid."

It was a lie, but I wanted it to be our truth.

To give into this.

Grief flashed across his face.

A streak of the pain that was so clear to me.

"You should be."

I didn't get to argue before the shrill ring of my phone lit up the room, even more obnoxious than normal where it echoed off the stark marble counter.

Rhys went stumbling back like he'd been caught red-handed in the most treacherous of acts.

I struggled to swallow around the moment. Around the need that had me in a fist. My stomach in knots of greed, and my thighs trembling with desire.

I didn't know whether to curse the call or be thankful for the interruption.

Before I could orient myself, Rhys had shot clear across the bathroom. Both his hands were braced on his doorframe like they were the only things holding him back from coming for me again.

The man panted like a beast.

So unbearably gorgeous it hurt looking at him.

Clearing the discomfort from my throat, I moved over to my phone.

Disgust and fear staked through my being when I saw the name on the screen.

Definitely, definitely cursing the call.

But I had to answer it.

I couldn't shrink or cower.

I had to play it cool.

Pretend.

Still, I wished Rhys wasn't there to witness it.

Pretending was the one thing he'd asked me not to do with him, but that was going to prove hard to do.

"Mom," I answered, turning my back on Rhys and doing my best to keep it together. For my voice not to tremble.

"Maggie, darling, how are you?"

She asked it casually and with all the feigned haughtiness she'd perfected. She was great at acting like she'd been raised in that mansion in the Hills instead of a trailer park in San Jose.

The suspicions I'd been fighting all morning flared. The feeling that she was digging. Prying. Knew more than she would ever let on.

"I'm great." I tacked on all the faked enthusiasm I could muster.

"Oh, that's wonderful." She couldn't even cover her disappointment. She was most likely hoping I was dead in a ditch somewhere. "Where are you?"

Not in a ditch.

I had to keep myself from spitting the words. Had to ignore the rash of anger that slithered beneath the surface of my skin.

If she was playing me, then I had to play right back. Pretend as if I had no clue what she was after.

"Don't you remember?" I almost sang it. Like I was in some magical place. I was, but she definitely didn't get that part of me. Not anymore. Not ever again. "I'm nannying for Royce and Emily this summer."

You know, since my condo had gone up in flames.

"And where might that be?"

"It's at an undisclosed location. I had to sign an NDA promising I wouldn't let anyone know. I'm sorry."

"Well, wherever you've run off to, it's time for you to come home to LA." She snipped it. A clear demand.

My head shook, and I whispered the words in a rush, "That's not going to happen."

"That's fantastic, Maggie. Abandon your mother in her greatest time of need."

Now this? I doubted very much that she was faking.

My mother had been absolutely devastated over the death of my father six months ago.

Devastated by the loss—the loss of the millions of dollars that no longer resided in her bank account to be precise. I doubted she was missing that money as much as the secret stash that had gone missing.

My *daddy's* stockpile that the feds had never known about.

My sigh was bitter. "That's funny, Mom, considering you ignored mine for years."

She had gladly gone along with my father, pretended as if Cory

Douglas hadn't brutalized me. Hadn't stolen my innocence. My faith and my hope and my belief and mangled it into a ball of terror that had sat on my chest for years.

All those years until Royce had gotten free and then had freed me.

It had all been in favor of keeping her luxurious lifestyle intact.

"That accusation was fabricated, and you know it." She tsked like I was silly. "You fell down the stairs, remember?"

Pain staked through my heart.

I hated that I still felt it. That I still expected something better from her.

"I was fifteen." I whimpered it on a shallow breath, my head dropping as low as my voice. "*Fifteen*. And you dismissed it, *denied it*, to keep the money rolling in."

From behind, a shockwave of rage reverberated through the room. Banged against the walls. A harsh growl was intertwined with the ferocity of it.

No question, Rhys was picking up on the bits I didn't want him to hear.

"Well, whatever happened, it doesn't matter any longer. It's behind us now."

I battled to guard myself against her blatant disregard.

Still, I stumbled a step forward, unable to process the cruelty.

"Now, it's time to stop this nonsense and come home where you belong. There are matters to attend to."

The warning was there. Clear and present. All contained in the hoity pride she wore like a brand.

Disbelieving laughter escaped from my tongue. "No, Mother, there is nothing left. Nothing left to say. Nothing left to do."

I could almost hear her teeth grinding to dust before the venom came pouring out. "Your pathetic brother put you up to this, didn't he? Convinced you into holding onto your morbid little lies to keep us apart? All of this is his fault. None of this would have happened if he hadn't stolen your father's position at Mylton Records. Your father was innocent. Royce framed him. Was jealous your father wasn't his father, too. He's responsible for it all."

"No, Mom. Dad was responsible." My father had been the CEO of Mylton Records. He had also been a major player in an international crime ring. He just hadn't been *quite high enough* and had been killed in prison while awaiting trial.

A clear strike to keep him silent.

The same as had been done to Cory Douglas.

As much as I'd hated them both, I still couldn't fathom their fate, then I'd been destroyed all over again when the depths of their depravity had been brought to light.

When it'd been exposed how violently evil they really were when that house had been discovered that was nothing less than a prison.

"He was good to us," she argued.

Agony clutched my spirit, and tears blurred my eyes. "No. He wasn't. You can cut the act because you and I both know it."

I could feel her physically snap.

"Where is it, Maggie? Where *is* it?" she seethed, her voice slipping into malice, no longer trying to hide her true intentions.

"I have no idea what you're talking about."

"Now who's acting? I won't let you take what's rightfully mine, you little bitch."

I ended the call before she had a chance to say anything else.

I slumped forward, gasping out a breath.

A hand touched my bare shoulder.

I didn't jump.

I already knew he was there.

Awareness shimmered and pulsed against the walls.

"Maggie." His voice was gruff.

As hard as I tried to stop them, tears streaked free of my eyes.

His hand curled tighter. "Mags."

"I need you to go. Please."

He hesitated.

"Please...I just need some air. Some privacy to clear my thoughts."

"Okay," he said, even though I could tell he didn't want to agree.

He'd wrap me up and promise me it was okay if that's what I

needed.

The problem was, this wasn't okay.

Reluctantly, he slipped out, and I moved over and turned the shower on as hot as it would go. Let the steam fill the room as I peeled the rest of the way out of my clothes.

I stepped in, and I shivered under the spray that was hot enough to burn.

I dropped my head in the fall of water, and one of my hands shot out to the wall to keep myself standing while the other went to my mouth to cover the sob that wrenched free.

My body bent in two as the tears came and came.

As I wept with the reality of my life.

My mother knew and I had no idea what she would do or the lengths she would go to feed her greed.

Fear rolled and toiled and climbed out through my mouth.

I expelled it in choking, writhing gasps.

Then I lifted my chin to the spray. Let it wash it all away.

My mother could threaten me all she wanted.

I would do this.

I would.

No matter the cost.

Like Emily had said, I had to go after what was right, even when I was terrified.

Even when it might cost me everything.

Ten

Rhys

"Spill it." The grated voice hit me from behind where I'd just snagged a beer from the industrial-sized refrigerator in the kitchen.

Heart rate doublin' time, I whirled around, a scowl on my face.

"Dude, what the hell? You scared the piss outta me."

I rubbed at my chest to calm the raging. Damn, she was a sneaky little mouse.

Melanie stood there, the band's manager and basically the bane of my existence, with her scowl five times bigger than mine.

Ahh shit.

I was in trouble.

"The daggers," I told her, holding a hand up between us like it was a shield before I cracked the beer cap and gave her a wry shake of my head. "Put 'em away before someone gets hurt, lovie humps."

On top of that whole bane of my existence thing? She was also one of my closest friends. Other than Richard and Emily, she was the only one who *knew*. Mostly because she was in the business of getting me out of the disasters I got myself into.

Diving into hot water to drag my pathetic, drowning ass out.

"Don't *lovie humps* me," she growled, those hands perched on her hips. "Tell me what's goin' on in that warped little mind of yours."

She pointed her finger at my head like she might be pointing at a crusty pair of underwear stuck to the rug in the corner of her bedroom, and she wasn't quite sure how they'd gotten there.

"Knew the second I saw you that somethin' was up."

She'd shown up this morning right before what turned out to be our first practice since we'd delayed yesterday's after Maggie had taken that tumble. Melanie had come in a few days after the rest of us because she'd been in Vegas for her sister's bachelorette party.

As per her usual M.O., the second she'd walked through the door, she'd started flinging demands left and right. Had done my best to keep any wayward emotions under the radar, but those beady hawk eyes had been watching me the whole damn time.

Still, I shrugged and said, "Don't know what you're talkin' about."

Tipping the beer up, I gave it a good guzzle.

"Yeah, right. I see those dodgy eyes, and believe me, I've seen those dodgy-ass eyes enough times to know when you've gone and gotten yourself into a load of trouble. Now what did you do?"

Wasn't really the question of if I'd gotten myself into somethin'. It was which somethin' I was gonna fess up to.

In this case, I was going for deflection.

"Um… you were here for the whole showdown. Thanks to Leif and Richey-Poo, I now have to write an epic song that goes on the album or I have to ditch my hashtag that I've built up with nothing but years of TLC. The pressure," I whined, playin' it up.

During practice, my online 'antics' had once again been called into question.

I had a little tradition that after each show, I'd do the crowd a solid and strip off my shirt and toss the sweaty mess out into the mayhem. Girls would go nuts. Clamoring to get it, fighting over it like it was their own personal version of MMA.

Tradition had it that whoever finally managed to take it home would take a picture of themselves in it and post it with the hashtag, #IGotWetWithRhys. Usually, they didn't have anything on underneath.

Most of the time, I'd be waitin' on the sidelines. Doing another honor of helping them out of said shirt.

It made for a great distraction.

Easy sex. Easy smiles. Easy fun.

Both parties more than satisfied.

For a little while, it kept my mind from wandering to places I didn't want it to go and let the tension I carried around bleed free.

For a moment, that lonely, vacant space didn't gape so wide.

Turns out, the rest of the band didn't like it all that much, and they thought it'd become unfitting for the type of music we were putting out into the world. They'd gone and challenged me to write a song that would blow Sebastian Stone's rock 'n' roll mind.

It would be the first time a song I had personally written would be included on an album.

If I failed? I had to put that whole hashtag biz to rest.

Unease squeezed my rib cage.

Thing was, I wasn't so sure I liked the whole hashtag thing all that much these days, either.

Tried to snuff my thoughts from racing toward the reason for that.

The girl who was gettin' under my skin.

Far too deep.

"Bullshit. You think I don't know you're salivatin' all over that challenge? A chance to show how great you are? Come on." Ponytail swishing around her shoulders, Mel rolled her light-brown eyes before they sharpened again. "Now fess up."

I blew out a sigh. Might as well go for gold. "So, I might have gone back to Tennessee and snuck in to see her." I hem-hawed the confession out, like maybe there was a chance I hadn't *actually* done it and I was contemplating the viridity of the statement, head bobbing before I was chugging the second half of the beer.

I turned my back on her and went for another.

I might as well have opened the freezer side with the artic chill that suddenly iced over the room.

"You did what?" she hissed.

Shutting the door, I moved over a fraction and leaned against the counter. "Went to see her."

Mel sighed. It was sympathy and disbelief. "Jesus, Rhys. Do you have a death wish?"

Looking to the ceiling, I blew out a strained breath before I dropped my attention back to her. "I know."

Her head barely shook. "You're just askin' for it. He finds out and—"

"He already did." I cut her off before she could finish the thought. I sipped the beer and then crossed my arms over my chest, still clutching the bottle in one hand.

Her eyes snapped to mine. "What do you mean?"

"Got a text...a picture of my mama. Someone was in Dalton...watching her in the distance."

Worry filled her expression, and she inched closer. Her voice dropped to a whisper, even though there wasn't a soul around to hear her. "What did it say?"

I shrugged. "Same shit as always. More money. More threats."

And he wouldn't stop until he had my head on a plate.

"Rhys...you've got to let it go. Stop goin' there. He seems content to swindle you out of your money, but one day, I'm afraid he's gonna take it farther. He hates you."

I tipped up the beer and sucked it down like I could suck the regrets down with it. Erase the anger and the grief. Make it better.

But it never was gonna be.

"Doesn't matter."

Melanie shook her head. "Seriously? All this blackmailin' is just fine?"

"Owe her," I grated, barely able to force out the words.

She touched my arm, and her voice slipped into a plea. "You've got to take back control. You don't know the lengths he might go to when he realizes you're willing to give into whatever he demands."

"Like I said, it doesn't matter."

She squeezed my arm tighter, her words a whisp of terror. "You matter. You matter and you keep forgettin' that."

"I'll take whatever's comin' to me."

Disbelief twisted her features, and Mel pushed farther into my space. Like maybe she wanted to reach inside and shake me. "What's coming to you?" she hissed, words nothin' but razors.

"It was my fault. What the hell do you want me to do?" I finally asked, helpless.

"I want you to stay away. Every single time you go there, he has something else to hang over your head. Pretty soon, he's gonna own you."

"He already does." The words were shards.

Visions flashed.

The lights.

The screams.

The pain.

My heart seized around the images.

My throat so damned tight I could barely breathe. "How am I just supposed to turn a blind eye? Fuckin' how?"

"I don't know, Rhys. But you have to. For you and your mama."

Agony crushed me, and I dropped my head.

Only for the world to tilt when I felt the shift in the air.

A pulse of intensity went slicing through the room. A warm chaos that soothed and stoked.

This girl, who against my better judgment, I'd left trembling and crumbling after whatever fuckin' thing had gone down between us in that bathroom yesterday.

I hadn't seen her come out since.

She'd had me pacing the floors all night.

I'd even gone to the lengths of pressing my ear to her door like some kind of creeper.

Worried.

Listening for any intonation that she wasn't all right and listening harder when I couldn't hear her make a sound.

This girl who was wrecking me bit by bit.

Blowing up walls and demolishing sanity.

Wasn't like I was all that known for playing it smart.

I lived large in the limelight to keep the rest in the dark.

But this girl threatened to draw it all out.

I looked over Mel's head at Maggie who stood on the other side of the island just inside the room.

Frozen like she thought she'd walked in on somethin' that she shouldn't have walked in on. Something salacious. Something private.

Which it was, but not close to the way that she was imagining.

Looking at her nearly dropped me to my knees.

She was wearing a floral sleeveless blouse with spaghetti straps. She'd paired it with a sleek pair of black jeans and sandals, the girl making casual look queen.

I was bettin' those jeans were to cover up where she'd been hurt.

My fingers itched.

Ached, really.

Desperate to fist around that high ponytail, so long that it still swished down her back in these lush waves.

Charcoal eyes slashes of dark, stormy secrets.

Lightning strikes.

Each flare created a crater that opened up to depths that I knew better than to go diving into.

Body a beacon.

A treasure that couldn't be touched, and there I stood, the fool who was salivating to do it anyway.

Maybe I really was insane.

Unstable.

Prone to all sorts of treacherous things.

F-fuckin'-minus.

Mel slowly peeled herself from me and turned around, and Maggie jerked her attention from where it'd been locked on me and turned all of it on Melanie.

"Hey, hi, Melanie."

"Hi, Maggie," Mel returned, voice way too bright. "It's so good to see you. It's been way too long."

Maggie looked at her as if she were worried. Taking her in. Searching deeper. Glancing at me for the hottest second in all of history. "I'm really sorry to interrupt. I was just going to grab some waters to take to Emily's room. They're almost out."

"Oh, no worries. Come right in." Another high-pitched peep from Mel. "How is that baby?"

"Beautiful." Maggie answered it with a rush of awe. Like she couldn't possibly answer any other way.

"Gah. I can't wait to get some Auntie Mel snuggles," Mel gushed and drawled. And they called me the exaggerator. "It's been three whole weeks since I've seen her and I'm havin' withdrawals."

"I'm sure they're both going to be excited to see you," Maggie told her. "Honestly, I think Emily is still having some adjustment issues living in Los Angeles."

"Well, that's because she went and let your brother steal her away from where she belongs." It was all a tease from Mel, and Maggie was smiling softly, fully understanding.

"I'm sure it's really hard for all of you."

When I couldn't stand the way she was trying not to look at me for a second longer, I said, "Hey, Sweet Thing."

I mean, fuck, I hadn't seen her since she'd been falling apart in her bathroom, after I'd been zero-point-five seconds from giving in and kissin' her like some kind of selfish wanker.

This time, it was Maggie's smile that was faked.

It was kind of grim and tugging at the side in discomfort.

That attraction that constantly sparked between us washed in something ugly.

Like it was dirty and she was standin' there thinking it was something wrong or illicit.

It was. Definitely. But not in the way she was thinking.

Apparently, all my flirting with Mel in the past, which was nothing but an act for us both, hadn't gone unnoticed.

"Hey, Rhys." Vulnerability filled her voice.

No doubt, I'd overheard somethin' yesterday that she definitely had not wanted me to hear.

It'd only stoked my worry.

Made me all the more certain she'd been lying to her brother.

"How are you feelin'?"

"Not too bad. A little sore."

Melanie moved forward. "I heard what happened. That is crazy scary. I'm sorry."

Maggie trembled a half smile. "Luckily, I wasn't hurt."

"Absolutely."

Could feel Mel glancing between us.

Couldn't make myself look her way. My attention locked on this girl who was doin' me in.

"Guess what?" Damn it. I couldn't help myself.

Maggie's brow twisted. "What?"

"I'm gonna write a song. Best damn song that's ever been written. Band plans to put it on the album if it's good enough."

Wow.

I was really layin' it on thick. Trying to impress a girl I really shouldn't be impressing. What I should have been doing was encouraging her to run for the hills in the opposite direction.

The real fucked up part was I worried I might follow her into them.

"Oh." A true smile pulled at her mouth, and that charcoal dimmed and danced. Like she was contemplating somethin'. "I don't doubt that. I have faith in you."

I suddenly got pushed on the shoulder, nothing but sarcasm rolling from Mel when she tried to steal the attention. "He better. Otherwise he has to ditch the whole bad boy player reputation. Hashtag and all."

Maggie's eyes shifted again. Surprise and curiosity before they fell into something painfully sweet. "He doesn't seem so bad to me."

Well fuck.

Then Melanie howled. "Have you met him?"

I slammed my hand over my heart. "Well, thanks a lot, Mells Bells. Way to go throwing all this deliciousness under the bus."

Mel shoved me again. "You wish."

I laughed and Maggie giggled.

And shit.

I loved the way that sounded.

And I realized I was back to staring at her. Was that a dopey smile I was wearing?

Yup.

Definitely a dopey smile.

Couldn't help that shit.

Not when that redness streaked across Maggie's flesh. Something palpable and real.

Ready to burn both of us.

Maggie finally snapped out of the tether holding us hostage. "Oh, let me get out of your way. Just going to pop in and out really quick." It was her turn for her voice to be about five times too high.

She moved in the direction of the huge butler's kitchen and pantry off the back of the main kitchen, tossing out the question as she moved that way, "So, why are you sitting around here? Shouldn't you be working on that song?"

Her tone was playful, genuine as she ducked through the door.

I was still stuck, standing there staring at where she disappeared before she came back out.

I might have heaved out in relief.

Like missing out on those five seconds she'd been in there had been too much.

She stepped back into the main kitchen with a case of water.

"Not, yet. Working out some ideas with Mells Bells here."

Mel coughed a *bullshit*.

Maggie just smiled soft, standing there, balancing that water on the front of her thigh.

Her gaze went tender. Filled with her soft, sweet belief. "Well, wherever you find your inspiration, I know it's going to ruin some hearts."

"Hope so."

She nodded then hefted the case.

And I realized I was standing there like a douche.

"Damn it, where is my mama to whip me into shape when I forget to be a gentleman?" I forced it out like a tease.

Clearly, I was distracted by the very thing I should be showing respect to. Suffice it to say my thoughts right then weren't all that gentlemanly.

"Let me help you with that."

She backed away. "No, I'm good, honest. Emily is taking a nap, and Royce has the baby, so it'd be better if I slipped in and slipped out."

"Are you sure?"

"Absolutely."

In reluctance, I gave her a small nod. "Okay then."

"See you later. Glad you made it into town safely, Melanie."

"Thanks, Maggie. Let's catch up tonight over dinner."

"Sounds good," Maggie called as she dipped out through the archway and down the hall that led to the smaller staircase that I'd sneaked in with her just a couple nights before.

Silently, Mel and I watched her go, and when she disappeared out of earshot, Mel whirled on me. She was already pointing before she'd turned all the way around. "Don't you dare, Cowboy."

"Cowboy? How many times do I have to tell you, it's Sta—"

She jabbed me in the chest with that stabby finger.

Hard.

Cutting me off.

"Oww," I whined, clutching the spot.

She kept pointing at me, jabbing that finger into my sternum.

"I will cut your balls off if you even think about it," she warned under her breath, glancing around once before looking back at me. "And Royce will literally kill you." Her voice dropped lower. "Like, we will find your literal rotted, decayed body buried in a shallow grave. You think you've got trouble now?"

I lifted my hands in a placating fashion. "Don't know what you're—"

"Don't bullshit me, Rhys Manning." Her voice was venom. She was most definitely not playin'. "I think I've seen you in action enough times to know when you're undressin' someone with your eyes, and you already had her clothes strewn across the room. Maggie is special. Different. Off-limits. Do you hear me?"

Melanie was right on all accounts.

She'd seen me in action more times than I could count.

More than that, she was right about Maggie.

She was special.

Different.

One-hundred-fucking-percent off-limits.

I lifted my hands higher. This time in surrender. "I hear you. Loud and clear."

Loud and clear.

Rhys

With the crash of the waves on the beach below, I sat out on the balcony plucking the strings of my guitar. It made it so I barely heard the timid tapping against the inside wall of my room.

That didn't mean I didn't feel it.

That didn't mean the ground didn't tremble and the air didn't shift.

I gave myself a beat to pull my shit together. To remember the warning Mel had dished out earlier today. Rein in the direction my thoughts immediately went stampeding.

Night pressed down, time set to slow.

The canopy of stars hung like ripe fruit waitin' to be plucked where they were strewn over the horizon.

Like each was holding a wish waitin' to be granted.

Faint sounds of the house echoed through the walls and drifted through the opened windows, my crew, my family, settling in for the night.

I sat propped against the wall, the French doors to my bedroom wide open, sheer curtains dancing in the breeze and lulling me into some kinda dream as I tried to find the melody for the song I needed to write.

Dream took a sharp turn when I angled around to peer into the darkened shadows of my room.

Maggie stood just inside the bathroom door.

Unsure.

Wary.

Bold.

She edged in a step farther like she was worried she was ignoring a sign that read *danger*.

With what she was wearing? It made that endeavor all the riskier considerin' she was wearing the tiniest sleep shorts I'd ever seen and a skin-tight tank.

Every muscle in my body took note.

That river of black was coiled on her head, a little wild and untamed, a few errant pieces dripping down around her slender shoulders like all those stars.

Girl nothing but a motherfuckin' wish.

The impossible kind that I knew better than longing for.

Didn't matter.

Longing smacked me right across the face. Something that just came fiercer each time she stepped into my space.

"Hey there, Sweet Thing. Whatcha up to?"

I went for casual when my heart was thrashing a riot in the middle of my chest.

"Hey. I hope I'm not interrupting."

I chuckled. "I think we already established there is nothin' to interrupt."

So what if I couldn't help bring attention to the awkwardness downstairs earlier. Needing to clear up any runaway thoughts about me and Mel she might be having. Which was fucked in itself.

Maggie laughed a small sound, her gaze enchanting me in the night. "I did just walk into your room without an invitation."

"Well then, Sweet Thing, consider yourself *invited*. Seems to me we might be crossin' paths a bit this summer, yeah?" I said it as playfully as I could, doing my best not to imagine all the types of *crossin' paths* I was aching to do. "No need for us to tiptoe. You good with that?"

Maggie gnawed at that plump bottom lip. "Yeah. I think I'm good with that."

My fingers continued to move across the frets, the melody barely breakin' the dense atmosphere. Couldn't look away as she came closer.

The girl was a sculpture written in the shadows.

Art hung on the wall.

Place was decked in luxury. Extravagance and wealth. No doubt, she was the most precious, priceless piece.

I kept plucking at the strings, and she kept moving across my room like the bare-boned song had her enraptured.

Tendrils of it wrapping her in that same dream.

She stepped all the way out onto the balcony on bare feet.

I gulped, staring up at her where she stood.

Beneath the stars.

Beneath the darkness.

Beauty.

That's what this girl was.

The raw, untarnished version of it.

My gaze got stuck on her, wondering how the hell to wade through this.

How to ignore the energy that crackled in the sea breeze. To ignore the lure that I couldn't understand.

She slipped onto the ground to sit opposite me. She rested her back on the half wall, and she stretched out her feet.

Shit.

Even those were cute.

She rocked her heels where they rested about an inch from mine.

Like we were drawn again.

Needing to get closer in any way.

For a bit, we just rested in the song I was weaving.

Way too comfortable.

Finally, she whispered, "Then why does it feel like we're tiptoeing, Rhys?"

I blew out a sigh. Since I was going gold with the foolhardy confessions today, I might as well break the record. "Probably because I've been thinking all sorts of things I shouldn't be thinking about you."

Attraction flashed.

A shockwave of it.

Fuck.

This girl.

"And why's that? Why can't you be thinking those things?" There wasn't a hint of timidity in her voice. Vulnerability? Sure. Want? A fuck ton of it.

A rough chuckle tumbled out, and I paused my playing to scratch at my beard. "Think you know the answer to that, gorgeous."

"Do I?" she challenged, charcoal eyes flashing beneath the moonlight. "Because of Melanie?"

Apparently, I wasn't clear enough.

"God no. Might give the girl hell and mess with her every chance I get, but Mel and I are nothin' but friends, Maggie."

And not the kinda friends that Maggie and I seemed to be, either.

Rejection radiated from her. "Is this that whole age gap thing? Because you think I'm too young?"

"Maggie." Air heaved through my nose.

How was I supposed to answer that? Because yeah. She was fuckin' too young for me. Had her whole damned life ahead of her and she didn't need the likes of me makin' her trip or stumble.

"I'm sorry I'm being so blunt. I just..." Nervously, her tongue swept across her bottom lip, and her gaze darted to the side as she whispered, "Yesterday..."

Yesterday she'd almost been hit by a car.

Yesterday I'd almost kissed her.

Yesterday I'd touched her in a way that had been both innocent and obscene.

After that, I'd forced myself into accepting that was something I couldn't do again, which had been reiterated times a thousand by Melanie in the kitchen this afternoon.

Maggie brought that penetrating gaze back to me. "I need you to know something, Rhys. I need you to know that yesterday meant something to me."

At that, her voice trembled. Emotion warbled through the mind-bending beats.

My heart clenched.

"How's that?" I was almost scared to ask.

"It meant something because I realized that I trust you in a way I've trusted very few people in my life."

There she was...just layin' her heart at my feet for me to stomp all over with my boots.

The girl flawless in her brokenness.

Fearless in her vulnerabilities.

Old sorrow spun. Rising up from the depths where my grief lived. "That is exactly what I'm afraid of, darlin'."

My grin was brittle.

"Why would you be afraid of that? Trust is a rare and precious thing."

Agony clutched me by the throat.

God.

This girl got right to it.

I roughed an agitated hand through my hair. "Maybe we should go back to that tiptoein', yeah?"

She shook her head softly. "I don't know how to ignore this, Rhys. The way you make me feel. The fact you've made me want something—someone—for the first time since I was fifteen."

Fifteen.

Fifteen.

Fifteen.

Nausea curled through my stomach. Thinking about it made me want to puke my guts up in front of her all over again.

I couldn't fathom someone hurting her that way. My palm still burned with the imprint that bastard had made on her. Like the shape of her scar had been seared onto my flesh.

A fuckin' tattoo stamped on my soul.

"Damn good reason right there."

Touching her would be a travesty.

Straight blasphemy.

Hope and sorrow pulsed across her face. "No, Rhys, it's all the more reason to pay attention to what it's saying."

"Only thing I'm good for is a good time, Sweet Thing, and I'm pretty sure that's not what you're lookin' for."

"And how do you know what I'm looking for?" Shy seduction filled her voice.

"You think I don't feel you, too?" I was moving before I thought better of it, setting my guitar aside and shifting around onto my knees so I could crawl up close to the temptation of her tight, sweet body.

Girl magnetic.

A delicious treat dangled in front of me. Except if I took a taste? Knew I would want more. Forever crave it.

Worst of it?

Thought I might fuckin' fall, and I couldn't shoulder another betrayal.

But there I was, planting my hands on the ground on either side of her legs.

She gasped a small breath.

I inhaled it where I hovered over her, and she leaned farther back against the wall. My words were grit. "I feel you, too, Maggie. And the last fuckin' thing I want to do is hurt you, and I have a really bad habit of hurtin' the ones I love most."

She blinked up at me with those eyes.

Thunderbolts.

Beautiful, awe-inspiring destruction.

"I don't believe you'd hurt me."

I twisted a lock of that shiny black hair around my finger, leaning in closer and murmuring at her ear, "You're right. I won't. Won't let it go that far."

She pulled back enough so she could meet my gaze. "And that's what makes you amazing, Rhys Manning, the fact that you actually care. That's the reason I trust you. That…and you can feel me, too."

With a trembling hand, she reached up and splayed her hand out over the thunder of my heart.

A moan locked in my throat.

Shit.

How was it she could turn the tables on me in a second flat? I had to take control. Turn the focus on this girl and whatever was going on with her.

"Why'd you lie to your brother yesterday?"

Her entire body seized in discomfort.

I eased back a fraction to give her some space.

"I don't know what—"

"Maggie, you do know."

Her head shook, and she shifted to stare off through the iron slats on the far end of the balcony. Moonlight spilled onto the beach, reflecting on the waves, making them glisten and shimmer.

Warily, she turned back to look at me, hesitation firing in every molecule. "Have you ever been willing to do something right for someone else, so desperately, that you are willing to risk it all? Whatever the cost?"

Visions flashed.

Blood.

Screams.

Agony.

Horror.

I gulped it down.

"Yeah." The word was a grunt.

She met my gaze.

Hers held a reservoir of fear and an ocean of resolution. "That's why."

Terror slicked down my spine.

Ice-cold dread.

What the fuck was she in?

I'd immediately known she wasn't bein' straight. Add in the bits of that fuckery I'd overheard with her mother on the phone yesterday and things were not sittin' well.

"What are you sayin', Maggie?"

"Rhys…" She blinked a couple times and then gave a harsh shake of her head. "It's nothing. I didn't want Royce to worry. I mean, have you met him?"

"Maggie." Didn't even try to hide the pleading. "If you're in trouble…"

A pained smile fluttered all over her lips. "It's nothing. Just some family stuff I can't involve him in, and I don't want him to worry."

"Your mother," I settled on.

The crusty bitch on the phone who I'd be more than happy to shove my boot up her ass. I'd barely caught onto a word or two on her side, but it was more than enough.

Maggie choked a pained laugh. "Is a horrible person. Simple as that."

Those fingertips found my face, girl searching me in the lapping night. "And you, Rhys…what are you running from?"

My head barely shook. "I'm not runnin', Maggie. I'm standing still."

Because I couldn't go back, and I couldn't move forward.

Not when I'd ruined the one true, good thing I've been given.

And I was stuck there.

In that moment.

In their eyes.

In the devastation.

In my regret.

Grief flashed. It slicked my skin in a sheen of sweat.

Those fingertips traced over it, like this girl was experiencing me, tapping into my energy and reading every last fuckin' thing written on my soul.

"Friends, Sweet Thing." It was caution.

She lifted those charcoal eyes.

Fierce.

A black bolt of lightning.

Bright and blinding.

I swore, I felt her like a shockwave.

A blow that hammered through my body like a storm.

The urge to rub at the achy spot in the middle of my chest was unbearable.

"I think you're a liar, Rhys Manning."

I forced a grin and some lightness into my tone. "I've been called way worse things, Mag Pie."

And a thief of this girl's beauty wasn't gonna be one of them.

I forced myself to edge back. But I couldn't go far. I flopped onto my ass next to her, our shoulders pressed together.

Our breaths long.

Nothin' but sighs and whispers.

Didn't matter if I tried to fight it. I wasn't sure I had the power to stop it. What I felt building. Gaining strength.

I should ask her to go back to her room, but I got the feelin' it wouldn't change a thing.

There were some connections that were just inevitable. No matter how fuckin' bad they might hurt in the end.

Under the weight of it, I forced myself to say, "There's some lucky motherfucker out there who's gonna steal your amazing heart, Sweet Thing."

I threaded my fingers through hers where she had her hand rested between us.

Fire flashed.

Awesome.

Really helping things.

"One of those cowboys you've been dreamin' of. You'll settle down in a small town and have yourself a brood of kids, just like you wanted." My words were a gentle tease imagining it.

Something simple and right.

Hopefully after she allowed herself to have a million experiences and decided that was what she really wanted.

"Want you to have it all." I squeezed her hand.

She squeezed back.

Energy spun around us.

A blanket of warmth.

Could feel her smilin' next to me. This brilliant, sweet smile that made that achy place glow.

She tipped her head toward the sky. Her eyes dropped closed.

"Don't forget the horses," she murmured, imagining it, too.

I squeezed her hand a little tighter. "Never, ever forget the horses."

A soft giggle fluttered from her, and she began to whisper, "Maybe it's because of my past. The way my parents treated me. But that's what I want, Rhys. My soul's hope. A family. Someone to share this love that's been burning up inside of me for so many years, aching for someone to give it to."

And there I sat, wanting to dip my fingers into the well of her sweetness.

Take for myself.

A savage who fed from her grace.

Something playful and sad stole across her expression when she shifted to look at me. "Maybe someone to dance with me to whatever beautiful song you'd been writing over there."

My thumb ran circles on the back of her hand. "You think it's beautiful, huh?"

"Incredibly."

"Hey, I take bets seriously. I have something really important to achieve," I said, grin sliding to my face.

"I have no doubt you'll win that wager. Then you'll get to keep the hashtag and all the women."

I grimaced, knowing I'd ditch that persona in a heartbeat if it were right. If I had something left to give.

All while that attraction pulled and compelled.

A riddle of lust and something bigger.

I shifted around and pushed to my feet, not letting go of her hand.

I gave her a little tug. "You wanna dance, Goddess Girl?"

Blinking up at me, she gave me a slight nod, and I pulled her to her feet.

I curled an arm around her waist and tucked her close. Tried not to moan out loud with the need that went sliding down my spine and landed like a thousand bricks in my stomach.

"You have to stop calling me that," she whispered. "You're liable to fill my head with the illusion that I might have a chance with you."

Nah. I was the one who didn't stand a chance.

I tightened my hold and pressed my mouth to the top of her head. "Maggie. Wish I was that guy."

For the longest time, she didn't say anything while we swayed in the summer breeze with the scent and the sounds of the sea surrounding us.

Maggie curled those arms around me, her head on my chest.

"Did you ever fall in love with one of those girls?" she finally whispered into the roaring silence. Got the sense that she already knew the answer.

I blew out a heavy sigh. "Yeah. I did once."

She nodded softly.

Gettin' me in a way that she shouldn't.

"What happened to her?"

I pulled her closer, my lips murmuring the confession at the top of her head, "She was one of the people I loved most."

Sadness pulsed from her, and she locked herself to me, like she could hold what was pouring out of me.

Stand for me.

Bear it.

Had the intense urge to weep.

"I'm so sorry, Rhys," she whispered.

She pressed her hand to my thrashin' heart. Like she could feel the cracks. The fractures. What was bleeding out. She peeked up at me. "Who else did you love most?"

Grief gushed, breaking through the gaps, and I couldn't hold back the words. "My daddy. Failed him when the only thing I'd ever wanted to do was make him proud." Sadness tugged at every edge of my mouth and a grieved chuckle rumbled out. "Guy was my hero."

Maggie gazed up at me. "What happened to him?"

"Seven years gone."

She hugged me fiercely. "I bet he was incredibly proud of you, Rhys. How could he not be?"

The fingers of my left hand wound up in the mass of her hair. "I wish that were the truth."

She hugged me tighter, like she wasn't afraid.

"Sing to me," she murmured. "Sing the song you were playing

143

that called to me from my room."

My arms wrapped tighter around her slight body, and I exhaled, the lyrics barely breaking over the wind.

Didn't know what was comin'
Didn't know where I was goin'
Fallin' faster
Comin' slower
Lookin' for a lover
To get lost under covers
In my whispers
In my ear
Wishing on a star
Hoping on a heart
And then you were there
You caught me in a dream

I think I heard you in my sleep
I think I found you in my dreams
I think I felt you in the daylight
Give me one minute, sweetheart
I'll ruin everything

I hummed the last line because I couldn't bring myself to sing it aloud.

Rhys
Seven Years Old

"Just like that," his daddy murmured as Rhys cranked on the wrench so he could get the nut tight.

They were workin' on a big piece of machinery out in the field where his daddy had been called to work on a broken tractor.

Day hot, sun bright and gleaming against the blue, blue sky.

Rhys was sure he'd never felt so right.

He grinned back at his daddy who was watching him from over his shoulder. "I think I got it real tight!"

His daddy chuckled, and he leaned over and placed his hand over Rhys', helping him cinch it down. He grunted when it barely budged any more. "Wow. Look at that. You sure did. You're strong as a horse."

Rhys grinned.

So big.

"Does that mean I can work with you every single day?" Excitement spilled from his words.

His daddy chuckled some more. "Not sure what your mama would say about that. I'm bettin' she'd think you should be in school."

Rhys frowned. "Why I gotta go to school when I'm gonna work with you one day?"

Hopefully right then.

School was not Rhys' favorite.

Not even close.

A loud laugh burst from his daddy, and he scooped Rhys up and tossed him over his shoulder. Rhys howled and squealed and giggled, and his daddy let him slide down a little bit, giving him a tight hug before he set him on his feet. Still, his hand was on the top of Rhys' head.

Brushing through the blond strands.

"You gotta go to school because you have to learn all the important things. Then you get to decide what you want to do with your life. What job you wanna have. Sound good?"

Rhys almost pouted. "Fine."

Another chuckle, and his daddy gestured to the things they had spread out on the ground. "Now let's get this cleaned up and get home. Your mama is gonna be wonderin' where we got off to."

Rhys scrunched up his nose. "I bet you're missin' those kisses. Gross."

All his mama and daddy did was kiss all the time.

His daddy rumbled a laugh. "You just wait."

They went to picking up their things. When they finished, Rhys climbed into his daddy's big old truck and buckled in the passenger seat.

The engine rumbled to life, and his daddy put it in drive and headed back down the dirt lane that wound through the fields. The truck bounced as the wheels ground over the bumpy road that went up a hill and then down another before they hit the paved road.

The engine roared as they went faster, the windows down and

the wind whipping on Rhys' face. He grinned over at his daddy who was grinning at him. His daddy slowed as they came to a four-way stop where there was a little store with gas out front.

"Shit," his daddy muttered under his breath.

Rhys didn't like the tone of it.

Way he felt all his daddy's big, puffed muscles get rigid and tight.

His daddy pulled to the side of the road real quick, tossed the truck in park, and flew out the door without turning off the engine. "Stay right there," he ordered, pointing at Rhys.

Fear tumbled in Rhys' belly, and he unbuckled and climbed to his knees so he could see out the opened window.

There was the old man who talked and walked funny but who was real nice over on the side of the store. He seemed upset because his backpack he carried everywhere had been dumped out on the ground.

There were three more guys there, younger than his daddy, hooting and laughing.

Words were gettin' shouted.

"I'd think twice about what you're up to, Brady. Don't make me call your father," Rhys' daddy warned.

"Fuck off, old man."

"I'd suggest you get back in your truck, drive away, and mind your own fuckin' business," one of the other boys said.

That fear got bigger.

So big in his stomach that Rhys thought he was gonna throw up because the words got meaner and louder.

He gripped the windowsill.

Fighting tears that stung his eyes. But they started falling, anyway, because there were all kinds of shouts.

Yells and bad words.

Then one of the guys picked up a board and swung it at his daddy.

And then his daddy got real, real mad.

Everything was a blur.

Hits and groans and people fallin' on the ground.

Then the three guys went runnin'.

And then his daddy was helping the old man pick up his stuff, saying something that Rhys couldn't hear, his daddy giving him some dollars, and Rhys started cryin' harder because he didn't know if he should be scared or happy and everything felt so wrong.

Finally, his daddy made his way back to the truck. He was quiet when he slipped inside, his knuckles all bloody and torn, and he had a streak of it running down the corner of his mouth.

His daddy watched through the windshield as the old man walked slow down the side of the road.

Rhys was still crying.

Tears hot on his cheeks.

His daddy finally shifted to look at him. "There are lots of different types of people in this world, Rhys."

Rhys nodded through his tears, even though he didn't understand what he was tryin' to say.

His daddy swiped at the blood that was comin' from the split in his lip.

"All different colors and sizes and shapes. All of them are important. All of them deserve respect. And then every once in a while, God makes someone extra special. Someone who is more vulnerable than others, and it's our job to protect them. To take care of them. Even when it ain't pretty. You understand what I'm tellin' you?"

Rhys nodded frantically because his mama had told him the old man was extra special before, too, and she'd always bring him food and clothes and stuff.

"Yes, Sir."

His daddy reached over and squeezed his shoulder. "You gotta have a tough outside and a soft inside."

"Like Mama's apple pies?" Rhys asked.

His daddy chuckled. "Well, kinda like that, but maybe not so sweet."

Pointing out the window, his daddy sighed. "Them boys that just went runnin'? They think they're tough. That they're men. But they ain't nothin' but mean. You understand the difference?"

"Yes, Sir," he answered again. "You gotta be strong and kind."

"That's right." He squeezed Rhys' shoulder tighter. "And my

boy's strong as a horse and real good inside. Want you to remember to always be that way."

"Strong and fast like that painted stallion over on Harper's ranch? I wanna ride 'em, but Mama said he'll buck me right off. Probably trample me, too."

"Yeah…like that stallion over on Harper's ranch," his daddy said through a rumbly laugh. "Only you might wanna tame it a bit." He winked.

And right then, Rhys felt just fine.

Fear sliding off.

His daddy's expression changed again, and he touched the middle of Rhys' chest, tapping there with his calloused fingers. "You take that with you your whole life. You stand up for people who need standin' up for. And when you get a wife and kids? You remember you're strong as a stallion, you protect 'em with all you've got, and you love 'em like a treasure. And you never, ever break them."

Rhys sat up a little higher. "I will, Daddy. I promise. Now how am I gonna find me a wife?"

A laugh rumbled through the cab. "You'll just know, son. When I met your mama? Everything else faded away and she became the most important thing in my life. One day, you'll find yourself a girl like that."

"She gonna be pretty?"

His daddy ruffled his fingers through his hair. "Oh, I'm sure she'll be. I promise, though, no matter what she looks like, once you feel it right here…" He tapped his fingers over the beatin' of Rhys' heart again. "She'll be the only thing you can see. Just like your mama always says…it'll be love, love, love."

Rhys

I shot upright in bed. Disoriented. Confused. Feelin' like I was gonna come out of my skin.

Took only a second to realize my soul had been awakened by the panic I could feel emanating into my room.

It pulsed against the walls and crashed through the air.

Fear.

Dread.

A sickness that I felt like my own.

Tossing off the covers, I kicked my legs over the side of the bed and scrubbed a hand over my face like it could break up the disorder that ricocheted through my senses.

The girl.

The girl.

Could feel her physically callin' to me. Like she was lost in the darkest ocean. Floundering in the waters. Desperate for anyone to find her.

A wise man would forget it. Ignore the call.

Refuse to get involved any farther because I could feel the destruction hovering all around.

None of those things mattered, though.

I felt her spirit like a hook in my heart.

My daddy's voice still resonated in my ear.

A call I couldn't do anything but heed.

Pushing to standing, I eased across my room, trying to keep my footsteps quiet as I edged up to the bathroom that attached our rooms.

The tide rolled in the distance, an echo that infiltrated the darkened, sleeping house.

I inclined my ear, listened to the silenced chaos that shouted in the night.

Darkness reverberated back.

Whipping shadows and haunting ghosts.

Could feel them crawling over my skin.

Confusion and fear.

A whimper filled my ears, and there was nothing I could do, no hesitation when I moved through the bathroom, tile cold on my bare feet, my flesh sticky and hot as I made it to her door.

It was open just a crack.

I peered in.

Darkness held fast.

The barest silhouettes and shadows defined the lines and angles of her room.

I didn't need any light to illuminate the torment banging against the walls and bleeding from her spirit.

Maggie flailed and moaned.

Almost silently.

Like she had to keep it a secret.

Everything ached.

This girl.

This girl.

I couldn't do anything but move the rest of the way into her room. I slipped to the edge of her bed where the girl toiled on the mattress.

Sheets twisted around her, and her body pooled in sweat.

Torment sliced me right in half.

The minimal light coming from the moon that poured in from the balcony doors cast that precious face in shadows.

Only tonight, it was pinched and pained.

Maybe I should have thought twice about it, but I didn't.

I had zero fuckin' hesitation as I was slipping my arms under her thrashin' limbs and pulling her flush to my bare chest like I could bear every ounce of her pain.

I wanted to allow it to seep into me.

Wanted to hold it for her.

Heated flesh burned against mine.

"Mags," I murmured. I tucked her close, pressed my lips to her temple as I whispered, "I've got you, Goddess Girl. I heard you...I heard you in my dreams."

As if she could hear me, too, the tension drained from her body.

A rushing wave.

Relief.

Relief.

She looped those slender arms around my neck.

Comfort and peace wrapped us in a shroud of warmth.

In everything I would never have but felt desperate to give her.

Pressing her nose to my neck, Maggie inhaled, shivering as my name trembled from her tongue. "Rhys."

"I know, Sweet Thing. I know. I've got you. You don't have to be afraid. I've got you."

She nodded in her sleep, burrowing farther into my hold, and I carried her back through the darkness and into my room.

I managed to pull back the covers while still holding onto her, and I laid her in the middle of my bed.

So beautiful where she sighed and relaxed.

Her muscles unwinding.

I hadn't realized she'd been holding anything in her fist until her fingers loosened, and I got a glimpse of what she clutched like a lifeline.

I leaned in to get a better look.

A duck.

A worn origami duck.

Guessed it was confusion and sadness that trickled through me.

This girl so strong.

Hanging on to something I didn't quite understand and understanding it the same.

I leaned in and gently curled her fingers back around it, tucked it to her chest.

On a sigh, she whispered, "Stay with me."

And there was nothin' I could do.

Nothing I could do but crawl in beside her.

Wholly reckless.

Completely irresponsible.

I wrapped her in my arms like that was where she belonged.

All that sweet against all my brash.

"I've got you, Sweet Thing. I've got you."

Yeah.

I knew better.

Clearly.

But right then, I didn't fuckin' care.

Maggie

*D*ay broke at the edge of the world. The slightest hue of it rose over the ocean and bled through the sheer drapes that covered the balcony doors. It cast the room in darkened shadows that danced and flickered over the walls.

The room might have been blanketed in a slow glow of warmth, but my body—my body was drenched in heat.

Strong, strong arms were wrapped around me. In them, I felt no fear.

No need to cower. No need to hide. No need to fight.

My spirit was lulled into peace, though in the middle of that peace, everything raced.

Hope shouted so loudly in my ears, you'd think it'd wake the entire house.

But that silence held fast, and I barely dared to move in worry that it might break the enchantment.

Still, I got brave and let my fingertips curl a little farther into the skin of his shoulder, and I inhaled a little deeper where my nose was burrowed in the wide width of his massive chest.

His heart beat this steady thrum, thrum, thrum, and his even breaths covered me like a dream.

Beneath the sheets, we were tangled.

Souls and bodies.

Nerves fluttered and sped when I realized the full extent of that tangling.

My stomach was in knots, and my fingers kept twitching in a way I couldn't control.

My spirit was held in a moment that felt momentous. Like I was on the cusp of a new understanding. Of discovering a part of me that had been absent for too long.

The man only wore his underwear, and I was in the same tank and sleep shorts I'd had on last night.

Sometime during the night, I'd wedged my leg between both of his.

Now, the rigid length of him was pressed to the top of my thigh.

Hard and huge.

The knots in my belly tightened and pulled and pressed.

Every part of me felt needy and achy.

Bigger than normal.

Denser.

As if I were missing something and everything I needed was right there, begging me to reach out and take it.

His breaths tickled through his beard and breezed into my hair.

I kept trying to keep my breaths as even as his, but my pulse stuttered and sped.

Mostly because that spot between my thighs throbbed just as fiercely as my heart.

Somewhere in the abyss of sleep, Rhys Manning rubbed himself against my thigh.

I nearly came undone right then, a gasp raking up my throat and my entire body pitching in his direction.

He groaned a sound that shuddered through me like greed. "Goddess Girl," he muttered.

I gave into the ache that was taking me over, and I rubbed myself against him in return.

A kick of pleasure hit me.

Not nearly enough but the best thing I'd ever felt. In response, those massive arms tightened and tucked me closer to that magnificent body.

It made me bold.

Like a new dichotomy had been written on my consciousness.

Brazen and shaky.

Courageous and apprehensive.

This time when I rubbed against him, almost every part of me was involved.

My breasts sliding against the delicious hardness of his chest and that ache between my legs seeking release against his massive, muscular thigh.

Sparks lit.

A rush of severity.

A flood of desire.

A shallow, needy breath escaped my throat.

Rhys rocked against me, moaning low. The sound of him tumbled down my spine like a straight shot of need.

It was me who made the move. I was the one who shifted us until he was on his back and I was straddling him.

The sheets fell around my waist, and I stared down at the ruggedly gorgeous man who blinked up at me through the glittering streaks of daybreak that broke into his room.

Blue, blue eyes concerned but dimmed with desire. Darkened with lust.

Shivers of it trembled through the air.

Like glittering strokes of ecstasy that teased at the fringes of our sight.

His powerful chest was bare, covered in designs that I wanted to explore. My fingers itched to trace over the tattoos.

To understand this man.

To give in.

Beneath the Stars

To jump.

I felt myself right there, teetering on that precipice.

I rolled over him, his penis pressed hard against me. I gasped, wanting to do it again and again.

"Fuck, Mags. What are you doin'?"

It was a rumble of warning in the air.

A plea of need.

My answer was rocking against him again.

Huge hands flew to my waist, gripping on, so big I thought he could circle me all the way around.

Tied and bound.

That was just fine because I would happily become a prisoner to every pleasure he had to offer.

No fear left because I'd found myself in the storm. And I thought...maybe...maybe I'd found the one who'd been purposed to meet me in the middle of it. The one who could hold me in the darkness and stand with me in the light.

"Rhys." His name left me on my own question.

My eyes dragged down the burly, brawny expanse of him, from those eyes that saw so deep, across his chest, over his rippling abdomen, and down to his waist.

To where his cock pressed fat and full at his underwear. The fabric strained under the pressure.

Desire tumbled down my spine and dumped into my belly and sent a roll of shivers racing beneath my skin.

Hands shaking out of control, I set them on the cut, defined lines of his stomach, and I gave myself over to whatever he would give.

Angled myself so I could writhe against him a little better.

A groan rolled up his thick throat, those blue eyes close to midnight, the hands on my waist cinching down tighter.

"Sweet Thing...we shouldn't do this," he grated through clenched teeth, though he had hold of my waist, guiding me in the tiniest of brushes and rocks.

It didn't matter.

It was enough friction to light a wildfire.

For him to show me that we should.

"Please, Rhys. I want to experience this with you. I've…"

I trailed off. Not wanting to say it aloud. Knowing he got it, anyway.

That this was the first time I'd ever felt safe with a man.

That being with him made me feel like I was treasured. Like I could trust.

My tongue darted out to swipe across my bottom lip, the words a rasp, "Would you want it, Rhys? Would you want me if there was no one around to tell us we shouldn't? If we had no pasts holding us back? If it were pretend? Would you want it? Would you want me then?"

I wondered how I was even getting the words loose of my tongue. The way my mouth was dry from the blaze that consumed every inch. The way my heart tremored and sped because I couldn't believe this was happening to me.

That he was touching me, and I was touching him, and I wanted it.

God, I wanted it.

Rhys shot upright, one hand twisting in my hair, both desperately and gently, the other arm banding around my waist like he was going to be the one to hold me up.

"Would I want you? Fuck, Maggie. Don't think I've ever wanted anyone in my life. Not the way I want you."

We were rocking. Rubbing against each other with way too many clothes separating us.

I wanted no barriers.

No obstacles.

"Pretend with me."

He gave a harsh shake of his head. "No, Sweet Thing, no pretending with you. Please don't ask that of me."

Sorrow passed through his features when he begged it. Blurred by the haze of lust that billowed through the room on dense, sagging clouds.

Mist that obscured and danced with the shadows.

"I can't pretend, either. Can't pretend that you don't make me want this."

My fingertips scraped his chest. Trembles followed along

behind my touch, and his breaths turned ragged as he sucked for air the farther I went. I made it all the way to the elastic band of his underwear.

I pressed up on my knees so I could whisper in his ear, "You make me feel alive. You make me feel right. You make me believe."

I brushed my fingertips over the straining length of him.

He twitched.

Nerves shocked between us.

Sparks and flames.

His hand shot to my wrist. "Goddess Girl. No. We can't go there. Told you, only thing I'm good for is a good time. Not gonna muck you up like that. Wait for someone who can love you right. Wholly. Fully. Way you deserve to be."

We were still rocking, though.

The slightest movements.

His knuckles brushing my shorts between my trembling thighs.

I wanted to beg him to explore if maybe that could be him. Tell him we'd both been broken, and maybe we could find a way to hold the fractured pieces for the other.

Promise I wanted to heal him, too.

But I could see the grief stricken in the depths of his eyes. His fear greater than mine.

We kept moving.

Our gasps whispered in the air.

The desire for each other refusing to give up.

Those heavy, throbbing places growing in their need.

I knew he felt it.

My breaths and my heart and my desperation.

The way I whimpered and tried to get closer to him.

"Shit. Baby," he grunted, and those blue eyes were on my face when I whispered, "Please."

Needing his relief.

To sate this fire that burned and flamed.

"Want to break every rule for you." His words were a grunt, and instinctively, I was pushing up higher on my knees.

I had one arm looped around his neck, the other still trapped by his hand between us.

"Break this one. Touch me," I said at his ear before I moved so I could look down at him.

Our noses brushing, our gazes locked.

And I knew right then, this man was becoming what I shouldn't let him.

Everything.

Everything.

Every word between us was a pant. A scrape of breaths. A whisper of desire.

Our bodies rocked in time. In sync. Already way out ahead of his reservations.

With him, I wanted to chase down that beautiful something that I'd never before felt.

"Maggie," he murmured, and he shifted our hands so his knuckles brushed against my center.

Electricity cracked.

A shudder ripped through me. Head to toe.

"Please."

He released my wrist and shifted so he was rubbing me on the outside of my shorts.

I pitched and ground over his touch.

Wanting more.

Desperate to find it.

A buzz.

A blaze.

Tiny fireworks that promised to go boom.

His mouth was at my throat, his beard tickling against my skin, his words tumbling into my spirit, "Mags. Sweet Thing. So beautiful. What are you doin' to me?"

My fingertips sank into his flesh.

Hanging on.

Never wanting to let go.

"Want to break all my rules for you," he grumbled again, right into my pulse point that thundered and drummed. "How's that, Goddess Girl, that you got me tied?"

A tremble rolled through his being when I raked my nails down his back.

"And I want to give everything to you. Be there for you the same way you are for me," I managed to pant.

A thousand things flashed through his expression.

Sadness.

Greed.

Reservation.

The belief that he wasn't good enough.

My heart just about split.

Tore right in two.

One half of it given to him.

And maybe he had it right. Maybe this really was wrong, a terrible idea, because I could already feel the fractures forming. The attachment growing.

Tendrils that grew up from the sweetest, most sacred place inside me, spread and curled and looked for a place to take root.

And I was right there.

Riding this edge that stole my breath.

Made me writhe.

Made me beg.

"Please, Rhys. I need…"

His hand shifted so his fingertips were just under the edge of the leg of my shorts.

Worry filled those soulful eyes when he edged back enough to meet my gaze.

Nothing but care and desperation in his. "Yeah?"

"Yes."

A million times yes.

He nudged the fabric aside, still watching me.

My thighs trembled, nerves rattling.

But it wasn't in fear.

It was in anticipation.

In experiencing this by my choosing.

With him.

With him.

He brushed his fingertips through me.

I jolted.

Whimpered.

"You good?" The words were shards.

The man slipping.

Barely hanging onto his own raveling thread.

"More," was the only thing I could get out.

He slowly eased two big fingers inside me.

My mouth dropped open at the feel of it. At the need that flared.

"Oh, God, Rhys. Please. I need you."

I could tell I was wet and slippery when I started rocking over him, begging him for more.

"Fuck, baby. What are you trying to do to me? Gonna ruin me. Gonna ruin it all."

Every word dripped with affection as he started dragging those fingers in and out, stroking deep inside.

My walls clenched around the perfect intrusion, and my breaths turned ragged and my nails sank deeper into his shoulders and this feeling swept over me.

A storm.

So intense.

So right.

So perfect.

"Rhys." I rasped it, riding his hand, wanting to hold onto this feeling forever while I raced for a high.

The boiling that was coming to a head.

His free hand slipped around to one side of my bottom, covering the cheek and guiding me over the other.

His fingers felt big and massive inside me but barely enough.

The greed inside my belly urged me to drag his underwear free and take all of him inside.

I thought maybe he knew.

That he could taste it, the way his tongue darted out to lick across his lips, the way he started to drive faster and his thumb was suddenly rubbing at that swollen, achy spot and his ragged words were promising, "I've got you. I've got you. Trust me, baby. I've got you."

I was gasping, pressing myself harder, deeper, faster on his hand.

Everything glowed and gathered and threatened to burst. He swirled his thumb.

"You feel it, Goddess Girl?"

I nodded frantically.

Racing, racing.

"It's yours. Take it."

A second later, I split.

Felt myself splinter in his hands.

Pleasure tore through me like a bomb.

A detonation.

An explosion.

Rupturing.

Rendering.

Bliss sped through my veins and took over every cell.

Ecstasy.

I shook in it.

An earthquake.

I pressed my mouth to his neck to keep from pressing it to his mouth, burying the cries there. "Rhys. Oh. It's so good. It feels so good."

He grunted, and he was making these little movements that was drawing it out.

Paradise.

I wanted to stay there forever.

Tiny shocks kept firing, prickles and zings, shivers following in their wake until it finally faded.

I slumped against him, and he slipped his fingers out and curled me tight in both of his arms, the same way I did with mine around his neck.

Our hearts were a thunder in the middle of us.

Stampeding and raging and somehow quieted to a satisfied thrum.

"You good?"

Blinking through the thick cloud of emotion, I fought the urge to cry. "I don't think I've ever been better."

He edged back so he could look at me, ran his fingers through the disaster that was my hair. So tenderly. Almost as tender as when he murmured, "Goddess Girl."

Affection pulsed.

A ripple in the air.

It tweaked the edge of my mouth into a soft smile. I reached out and touched his cheek, scratched my fingers through his beard. "I thought I told you that you needed to stop calling me that or I might get the idea that I have a chance with you?"

The roughest chuckle rolled up his throat. "And I thought I said we can't do this?"

I kept scratching my fingers through his beard the way I'd been dying to do. "Maybe we should do this."

He forced a grin. "And maybe I should know my place."

"And maybe your place is right here." I pressed myself against his cock that was still painfully erect and trapped between us.

Maybe I wasn't fighting fair.

I couldn't help it.

Rhys growled a rumbly sound, though he was grinning wide, struggling for a way to turn the mood to light.

I guessed he faltered, couldn't find it, because he was back to twisting a lock of my hair around his finger and looking at me like I was the sun breaking after the darkest, longest night. "Don't ever wanna hurt you. Can't believe I let myself get carried away like that."

My fingertips brushed across his plush lips. "You just made me feel the best I've ever felt. The most beautiful I've ever felt. Please don't take that from me."

His thick throat bobbed as he swallowed. "Okay. Okay." Then his smile turned grim. "But this can't happen again, Maggie. I—"

Guilt covered his face.

Gushed from his being.

This time I swallowed, biting back the disappointment. The urge to argue that he was all wrong about us.

That he didn't need to protect me from what he had to give.

At the same time, I understood.

I nodded, suddenly feeling awkward.

What was the protocol after a man just gave you your first

orgasm and then told you it couldn't happen again?

I was thinking begging him to change his mind was probably the correct answer.

But there was a part of me that warned me to be cautious.

That he needed to be handled with care, too.

Rhys was at his limit.

His body still stretched taut. Rigid with need but his joy held by unseen chains.

I slipped off his lap and looked to where the man still sat up on his bed, the bulk of him taking up almost the whole thing.

Hair a mess, longer pieces sticking up, chest bare and heaving with jagged breaths.

The man so gorgeous and rugged and somehow so incredibly sweet.

His head tipped my way, and a ray of light spiked in through the drapes and lit his face.

Beautiful.

Raw, wild beauty.

He cracked a grin and gestured at himself where he was still pressing at his underwear. "Seems someone caused me a bit of a problem that needs to be taken care of this mornin'. Mind if I hit the shower first?"

My teeth clamped down on my bottom lip, redness streaking. Part of me wanted to go for him, beg him to let me do the honors.

On a groan, he shook his head, like he'd seen the whole reel of images flit through my mind. "Thought we established we're not goin' there, Sweet Thing?"

I gave him the slightest nod. "Shower is all yours."

I started to leave when I thought better of it and looked back at him just as he was rising from his bed. "I wish you saw yourself the way I do."

His expression turned grave. "And I'd be horrified for you to see who I really am."

Saddened confusion bound my forehead, and I gave him the gentlest smile I could find, and I started back toward the bathroom.

"Maggie."

Hope slicked down my spine, and I slowly turned when I felt him come up behind me. I frowned when he took my hand and pressed something to my palm.

"Thinkin' you might want this."

He said it with more understanding than I could fathom as he curled my fingers around the folded duck that I'd been clutching in my bed last night when I'd been drifting in and out of a torturous sleep.

When I'd felt the demons spinning through the darkness.

Catching up to me once again.

When I'd chanted over and over that I was in control. That I got to shape my life. I guessed I'd been realizing the shape I was forming it into was dangerous.

That I might not make it through to the other side.

Still knowing it would be worth it.

I swallowed around the rock lodged at the base of my throat. "Thank you."

I turned and started into the bathroom.

The man shuffled in behind me. I shifted a bit to the right toward the vanity on the far side where I kept my toiletries, while he went left toward the enormous shower at the far end of the bathroom.

Before I had the chance to grab my things, he turned on the showerhead.

The patter of the water falling to the marble filled the room, and I looked up and caught his reflection in the vanity mirror just as he was shrugging out of his underwear.

His ass bare.

Round and perfect and *oh my god*.

I froze for a beat. Jaw coming unhinged.

From over his shoulder, Rhys tossed me a grin and then he stepped inside.

It took me a second to gather my senses off the floor. To remember what I was doing.

Hands shaking, I grabbed my toothbrush and toothpaste from the vanity and went flying into my room.

I shut the door behind me and leaned back against the wall.

Heart a battering ram at my ribs.

My mind was still trying to catch up to what had transpired during the breaking day. It took a second to realize the biggest smile split my face.

Holy crap.

Rhys had touched me.

For a moment, I relished in it.

In the memory that I would take with me forever.

In the burn of his fingers still singeing my flesh.

Finally, I pushed off the wall and moved for my door so I could slip into the powder room at the end of the hall and brush my teeth.

I yelped when I flew out into the hall and ran smack into a hard body.

Royce.

Royce who was still spun up over my *fall* a couple days ago.

Royce who'd been flitting all around me. Worried. Watching me in a way he shouldn't.

Royce who was looking at me like he had been one hot second away from kicking in my door.

Stumbling back, I pinned a smile on my face. "Oh…hey, hi, Royce. Good morning."

Smooth.

Real smooth.

A frown furrowed his brow, and he looked to the open door behind me. "Where were you? I've been knocking for like ten minutes. Was gettin' worried about you."

Of course, he was.

My mind raced through what to say. What to offer. It wasn't like I was a child and couldn't make my own decisions.

But I could still hear his plea of a demand from the day we'd first gotten here. When he'd asked me point-blank to stay away from Rhys.

When he'd warned I didn't need the kind of trouble that boy would bring.

Disquiet and a newfound desperation wound through my spirit.

Undoubtedly, my brother was right.

Rhys was trouble.

He was probably going to hurt me.

I heard the faint sound of the shower echoing through the walls.

My heart twisted.

And I knew that man was worth the pain. Even if I only got to experience him for a short time.

I pinned a smile on my face because the last thing we needed was Royce getting suspicious.

Not when I had no idea where we stood.

If there was any way to move on from here.

"I must have been in the bathroom and didn't hear you knocking."

Royce's entire demeanor twisted in a frown, and he tipped his head toward my toothbrush and toothpaste clutched to my chest. "Then what are you doing?"

"Oh…well…Rhys is in the shower, so I was just going to brush my teeth down the hall."

Speculation jumped through his expression.

You know, considering I'd just told him I'd been in the bathroom.

Clearly, I was the worst liar in the world.

Awkwardly, I gestured behind me. "I…uh…had a *girl thing* and figured I'd better get out since I was taking the bathroom up for so long."

Wow.

Playing the period card.

Royce huffed out in uneasy annoyance, roughing a tatted hand over his pitch-black hair. "You shouldn't have to do that. You never should have agreed to share a bathroom, especially with Rhys. You deserve your privacy."

Another tremor ripped through me when I thought back to the way that bathroom had come to feel like a passageway into another world. Another realm. "I assure you that I have plenty of privacy, Royce. It's fine."

I sent all the disbelieving skepticism in my brother's direction.

"I mean, come on, Royce. I asked to come with you guys, and now I'm staying at a mansion on the beach for free. I think I can share a bathroom. You act like I'm some kind of spoiled-brat princess."

Royce grunted. "So what if I want the best for my baby sister."

"Your baby sister is being drowned in luxury as it is. Now, if you'll excuse me…"

I waved the toothbrush and toothpaste in his face.

He sighed. "Fine…just…keep your phone handy, would you? Don't like not being able to get ahold of you."

I released a small huff and gestured at myself again. "Not a child, remember?"

His grin was only half amused. "But you're still my baby sister."

"Royce." I almost whined it.

"Mag Pie," he whined right back, mocking me.

I sighed. "Fine. But it's charging right now, so you're just going to have to be satisfied that I'm in the powder room brushing my teeth and that I'm not in there bleeding and in need of rescue. Sound good?"

He scowled at my sarcasm.

I actually laughed and then mouthed, *love you*, before I dipped away from him and made a beeline for the small powder room at the end of the hall. I shut the door behind me, leaned against it, and tried to catch my breath.

I caught my reflection in the mirror.

My skin flushed.

My eyes wide.

And I knew I'd never felt so alive.

Maggie

*A*bout thirty minutes later, I slipped down the small stairway to the sound of chaos echoing from the kitchen.

Voices shouted and dishes clattered.

Taking a deep breath and smoothing out the printed floral sundress I'd slipped into, I did my best to compose myself as I hit the landing and moved down the hall, worried someone might be able to read what I was putting off.

What I was pretty sure was written all over me.

I just had my first orgasm, and it was freaking spectacular.

Was it wrong what I really wanted to do was walk into the kitchen and throw a fist of victory in the air? Or maybe start tossing out fist bumps? Pop a bottle of champagne?

Because this was undoubtedly cause for celebration.

It felt as if it needed to be recognized.

The way my smile seemed different.

The way my body glowed.

The way trembles kept ripping down my spine every time my mind drifted back to the place that was just for Rhys and me.

Chills lifted as I remembered the way he'd looked at me. At the feelings that had gushed from his spirit. At the connection we'd shared.

No question, I was wound up in the beauty of what had just happened.

The problem was, I doubted very much anyone else would see it the same.

It sucked because I felt like singing it from the rooftops. The way he made me feel. The goodness I saw in a man that I was sure was so misunderstood he didn't even recognize himself.

And after him?

I wasn't sure I fully recognized myself, either.

Or maybe I finally did.

Either way, I felt changed.

Like a dial inside me had shifted. Something intrinsic rearranged. A piece of me coming to fruition.

I hooked a left at the end of the hall and stepped into the circus that I'd heard from upstairs.

I smiled when I took in the mayhem that was going down in the main rooms.

At the gathering of family and friends. Old faces and new. People coming together to become something important to the other.

It was funny because if I told someone I was spending the summer in a mansion with a bunch of musicians, this was probably not the scene they would be expecting.

They'd be looking for a crew of wrung-out bad boys, passed out, face down in their own puke and still clinging to a bottle of Jack.

Most likely buck and tangled with a groupie or two.

At least that was a scene I'd witnessed plenty of times throughout the years, and I was getting the sense that might be the case when the rest of my brother's band, A Riot of Roses, arrived next week.

But here and now?

With Carolina George taking up the space?

Not so much.

Leif was at the island, chopping onions and tomatoes, while Mia and Violet were at the counter near the stove cracking eggs into a big bowl for omelets.

A swarm of children buzzed at their feet, taking the island like a racetrack, sliding on their socks around the corners on the marble floors.

"You can't get me!" Greyson had his hands thrown in the air as he blew around his daddy's legs.

Greyson was Leif and Mia's middle son. A handful. Adorable as could be. Dark hair and grins and sweetness for miles.

"Whoa there, little bud," Leif called as the toddler skidded around his legs. "You better watch yourself or you're gonna fall on your noggin."

Case in point about these rockstars?

Noggin.

I hadn't known Leif all that long, but I'd heard it said the hardened man had gone soft.

From where I stood at the entryway to the kitchen, affection bloomed. A rush of energy wrapping me in their comfort. This overwhelming feeling pulsing and crashing.

Love.

Devotion.

Loyalty.

I could feel each riding the air in the room.

So full.

So bright.

"I not gonna go crackin' up my noggin, Daddy-O. I gotsta get away from Brendon because he's so, so, so big."

Greyson stopped long enough to jump as high as his three-year-old legs could get him each time he emphasized how big Brendon was, as if he were aspiring to be just as tall.

The most adorable part?

Watching Brendon who was all tussled black hair and teenage

swagger, playing with his little cousin.

Brendon was Lyrik West's son. Mia, who'd gotten married to Leif a couple years ago, was Lyrik's sister.

That made Brendon their nephew. So, the kid was not only Sunder royalty, he was now a part of the Carolina George family.

The families of those two bands merging together.

So easily becoming one.

"You's fast!" Greyson pointed a finger at Brendon from over the island before the little thing cracked a grin. "But not fasts enough."

"Oh yeah, little man? I think you're just askin' for it," Brendon taunted, puffing out his chest before he took two stomping steps to the left.

Greyson shot into action, his squeal echoing across the floors as he darted around the island with Brendon chasing after him. Except Brendon slowed to give Greyson a head start.

So sweet.

Greyson's big sister, Penny, stretched out her hand. "Come on, Greyson, don't let him get you!"

Greyson grabbed her hand, and Kallie took his other.

Kallie was Sebastian and Shea Stone's daughter. Penny's best friend. The two young teenagers were inseparable, and Kallie had been here most every day since we'd arrived. They were always sharing secret giggles and sweet, hushed conversations.

Penny, Kallie, and Greyson went skidding around the island with Brendon hot on their heels.

"Holy camoly, you alls are nothin' but hooligans!" Daisy piped up. Violet and Richard's little girl was all black-hair and pigtails.

So cute and wild and always with something to say.

She stood on a step stool next to her mama, helping to prepare breakfast. "Dontcha know you are supposed to take the roughhousin' outside where it belongs?"

Violet grinned, sheer joy, the profile of her protruding belly becoming more apparent when she shifted to look at her daughter. "Well, aren't you a little miss bossy pants." She tugged at one of Daisy's black pigtails.

Daisy shrugged. "Well, someone arounds here has to do the

dirty works, and my papa isn't here to do it."

Shaking her head in amusement, Violet turned to get something out of the refrigerator. A warm smile covered her entire face when she saw me standing there on the fray.

"Hey, you, good mornin'," she said. "You're awake. I was just gettin' ready to send my wild child up to see if you wanted breakfast."

Oh, was I ever awake.

"Good morning," I peeped, my voice two octaves too high. Moving over to Violet, I gave her a quick hug, that buzz still blazing through my body.

I had to wonder if the energy running a circuit through my veins would be a palpable thing.

When Violet pulled back, she kept hold of the outside of my arms and searched my face. Curiosity and questions traipsed across her pretty features.

I guessed I had my answer.

I gave her a look of indifference.

She returned one that told me we were going to talk about this later.

I just grinned the most innocent grin I could find, cleared my throat, and let my gaze roam over everyone in the room. "Morning."

Richard lifted his coffee cup from where he sat on one of the short stools on one side of the island. "Mornin', Mags."

"Good morning," Leif said, still chopping the veggies with a slow smile on his face.

"Hey there." Mia's was wide and welcoming, tossing it over her shoulder at me while she balanced her youngest, Carson, in her arms while she continued whipping the eggs in the bowl.

"Smells good in here," I said as I walked deeper into the kitchen.

Correction.

Floated into the kitchen.

That's what it felt like.

Walking on air.

Yeah, I was going to need to come back down from whatever

cloud I'd hopped on if I thought I didn't want anyone to notice.

I moved over to Mia and pecked a kiss to her cheek and another to the top of Carson's head. The six-month-old boy tipped his head back, his gummy, two-toothed smile doing the craziest things to me.

Chest pulsing full.

I ran my hand over the infant's head as he continued to smile up at me. I whispered to his mama, "Wonder Woman."

Mia huffed out a laugh. "Hardly. I'm pretty sure with the way I passed out at eight last night and slept like the dead for ten hours straight, I did not earn that title."

Leif shifted around and wrapped his arms around her from behind, setting his chin on her shoulder as he hugged her tight. "You deserved that sleep. The kids have been running you ragged."

"See! Hooligans!" Daisy was grinning her adorable, dimpled grin when she shouted it.

Laughing, I moved over to hug her tight where she stood on the stool, lifting her feet just off the step.

God.

This child had owned me from day one. I'd had no defense against the onslaught of her wild, kind, curious spirit.

"And what would that make you?" I teased her as I set her down.

She tipped her head back to look at me, all her little teeth gleaming in a row.

"Um…I think I still got the tomfooleries, Auntie Maggie Pies. Papa said those ones are the worst." Her voice dropped to a secreted whisper. "Way worse than the hooligans."

I smiled down at her, my heart in her little hand.

Affection fierce and firm.

My own loyalty and devotion to this family overpowering.

Rushing my veins and whispering in my soul.

Then all of it went soaring when I felt the shift in the atmosphere.

A thrill sped through the air. Shockwaves of intensity. Blasts of light.

175

I barely held it together when I looked over my shoulder to find Rhys coming down the sweeping, curved main staircase. He bounded down the steps, larger than life, the longer pieces of his hair still damp and a tight tee hugging that magnificent body.

My chest squeezed, and I thought there was a chance my lungs might fail right there.

God, I had no idea how in the world I was supposed to handle this. How I was supposed to pretend like I wasn't drawn to this man in a way that was unstoppable.

Unfathomable.

"Did I hear somethin' about tomfooleries?" he shouted.

This morning, his grin was wide, that carefree cowboy back in full play.

It was crazy how much I liked it. How I felt relief in seeing him this way. Those blue eyes clear. The storm clouds nowhere to be found.

Daisy tossed her hands in the air. "Uncle Rhys! You finally wakes it up. I thought you were gonna sleep all day."

There went my blush.

My flush growing hotter.

"What? And not spend the mornin' with you? Heck no." He came striding our way, mirth and lightheartedness painted in bold stripes through his being.

Penny and Kallie blew passed with Greyson in tow, cutting across his path.

The man tossed a playful swat in the direction of a smirking Brendon who was *right behind* them, not quite catching the group.

"Whoa, there. Seems like I'm late to the rodeo this mornin'."

"That's because you're old," Brendon shouted, cracking a grin.

"Wow, dude, wow. Way to bust someone's balls before they've even had their first cup of coffee."

"Like I said…old." Brendon delivered the razzing, all kinds of smug.

Mia tsked with a smile. "Don't make me tell your dad about that sass you're tossing around, Brendon."

Brendon lifted his palms with a shrug. "Uh…newsflash, my dad knows full well I'm nothin' but a badass."

Wow.

Right.

I giggled, and Mia arched a brow. "Well, I guess I'll have to tell Tamar, then."

Dark eyes going wide, Brendon shifted his hands around so his palms were held in surrender. "Hey, now, hey, now! Don't go manipulatin' me, Aunt Mia. That's just cruel. You know the last thing I want to do is disappoint my Mama Blue."

"Then watch yourself," she teased.

"Watch myself? Pssh…have you seen me? I can't look away."

I tried to hide my amused smile at this kid who was so close to becoming a man. Cocky and sly. Way too handsome for his own good. Written in mischief and havoc.

Mia shook her head, all kinds of affectionate. "Good lord, you are your father's son, aren't you?"

Rhys chuckled low.

The sound rippled through the air and raked across my flesh.

He rubbed at his beard as he rounded the island, and he cut me a glance as he passed.

Blue eyes fierce and soft and knowing and flirty, and oh lord, my knees were knocking all over again. I had to dip my head to keep that flush hidden, the one that burned like fiery embers.

I shifted on my feet, backing away another inch as he invaded my space. As his energy sizzled and surged and made me feel like I was never going to get a full breath again.

I could almost feel time slow around us.

Like we were locked. Frozen in a second that lasted for eternity as he slowly edged by. Only when he jerked his attention away did time start moving again, jolting me free of the binds that I wasn't sure I wanted to get loose of.

He went right for Daisy and threw her into the air.

She squealed and laughed and flailed to get her arms around his massive neck. "Uncle Rhys! Whatcha doin'? Did you get hungry? Me and my mommy and everybodies are making breakfast."

He tossed her a little higher, his words a rough grumble of a tease, "I just so happened to have worked up quite the appetite

177

already this fine mornin'. Hungry as all get out."

Oh.

Um.

Okay.

Was that an innuendo? A message to me?

I blinked a thousand times, trying to process.

The ground unstable.

Shaking beneath my feet.

With it came a warning that blared from the depths of my mind.

The truth that I was getting in deep.

That my battered heart might not be able to handle it.

But I wanted it—whatever fragments of himself he might offer.

I craved his touch.

More than anything, I wanted him to look at me the same way as he had this morning.

When I peeked back that way, Rhys was tossing Daisy onto his back.

Shrieking, she curled her arms around his neck. "Giddy up, horsey!" She knocked his sides with her heels.

Without hesitation, Rhys reared up and whinnied. He launched into a gallop, scooting around the island and toward the main living room where the children had run. He clamored around the huge couch as if it were a barrel, gaining on the kids who'd decided they'd be better off if they became a team. "Faster, horsey, faster!" Daisy shouted. "We gots to get 'em."

"Y'all better not go tearing this house down," Violet called, laughing under her breath.

"Hecks no. Got it handled, don't we, Daisy?" Rhys shouted.

"Yep!"

It didn't matter if I tried to protect myself against it.

The assault of emotion.

The crash of need.

The truth of what I felt.

It was there.

Seeping into my bloodstream and sinking into every cell.

I couldn't look away as they frolicked and played and caused a commotion.

My insides twisted up tight in the sensation that swept the atmosphere.

Joy.

Like a tangible thing I could hold in my hand.

Rhys kept galloping, whinnying and bucking and making the kids howl with laughter.

Rhys and Daisy caught up to Brendon, and Rhys gave him a little tap with his hip, knocking Brendon off to the side. "Outta our way."

Brendon stumbled a bit as Rhys blazed passed, the kid laughing hard.

"We are the champions! Kentucky Derby, here we come. Tell me you've got one of those fancy hats, Miss Daisy," Rhys shouted.

"I gots a hat!"

"Dude...no fair...you're like a bull," Brendon hollered. He was bent in two and trying to catch his breath.

Rhys whirled around, one arm still securing Daisy to his back. "A bull? Bulls have no class. No smarts. No beauty. I'm a stallion, baby! I'm seeeeeexy!" He drew it like a clown, tossing his hair around as he reared back.

Daisy clung tight, giggling and laughing and hanging onto the crazy ride she was getting.

Giddiness welled.

Hope rising fast.

Just...this...feeling.

The feeling that I'd stumbled onto someone who was truly good. Onto someone who was kind to the core. One who didn't mind being a bit goofy. One who brought more joy to the room just by the fact he was in it.

The way he wanted to do.

I just wondered if he knew the whole of it. If he understood what he really meant. The way everyone was drawn to the joy he offered.

"Okay, Donkayyyyyyyyyyyyyy!" Brendon taunted back, catching up and tossing a playful fist into Rhys' shoulder.

Rhys put on the brakes and whirled around, the feigned horror on his face making me bite back laughter.

"Ouch, man, that was just a dagger straight to my heart. Heck, right to the soul. I'm a stallion. A stallion." He moaned the last and clutched his chest with one hand as if he were succumbing. His big body slowly crumpled to the floor, tumbling while he made sure to keep Daisy safe as they slumped in a withering heap to the marble.

"Oh, Lord, he's already at it? I'm going back to bed." The voice cut into the mayhem, and my attention whipped to the side to find a sleep-rumpled Melanie standing in the same spot where I'd been earlier.

I thought for the first time since I'd known her, her brown hair was a wild mess, bags under her eyes, her clothes disheveled.

Rhys hopped back to his feet, and he swept Daisy up as he went. He carried her into the kitchen and set her on the island as if she were two and not six. "Ahh, Mells Bells. Morning, sugar lumps. Why you lookin' so sour? Someone in need of a little lovin'?"

Daisy hopped to her feet and spun in the middle of the island. "Yes! Amor, amor, amor!" She sang the words while she twirled and lifted her arms over her head. "We all need loves and deserve it the most."

"That's right, Daisy Mae. Everyone deserves a little lovin', don't they? All the amor."

The glance he stole at me was so fast I wasn't sure if I imagined it before he swept Daisy back into those strong arms and hugged her tight, just as quickly as he swung her down onto her feet.

Goodness.

My heart was going to explode from my chest. A puddle right in the middle of the floor.

Decimated.

Daisy went racing back for the stool and clamored up beside her mom.

Melanie rolled her eyes, but she was smiling a soft smile when she rambled the rest of the way in, heading directly for the coffee pot like it was a lifeline. "The only lovin' I need in my life is from this baby right here."

She caressed the industrial coffee machine as if it could whisper sweet nothings in her ear.

Rhys shook his head and cracked a grin. "Now that's just sad. Seems to me you might wanna find someone who actually knows what they're doing if that's the most pleasure you've ever had."

He stole a covert glance at me when he said it. That time, I was certain of it.

A cocky edge ran the delicious rim of his mouth.

I was going to incinerate right there.

Spontaneously combust.

Poof.

I shifted on my feet as that achy spot reignited between my thighs.

The man was going to do me in.

"See, that's the thing, most devices are plenty good companions," Mel tossed back with a grin, still caressing the coffee pot.

Rhys cracked up. Rough and rambunctious, slapping his hand on the island.

Violet clapped her hands over Daisy's ears.

Mel's eyes went wide. "Well, crap. There goes my filter again."

Violet kept her hands over Daisy's ears, talking over her head, "And for the record, I feel it's my duty as a friend to tell you that is nothin' but a sorry, sad state of affairs."

Richard lifted his cup in a salute to his wife. "Couldn't agree more."

"True story." Mia nodded emphatically.

"Better be," Leif grumbled.

I fought mine, my teeth clamping down on my bottom lip, finally getting it.

Melanie poured coffee into a giant mug. She lifted it in front of her like a prize.

"Beats the alternative." She took a long gulp. "Mmm. See. Delicious."

"But the sad thing is, then you get no cream. That coffee's gonna start to taste really bitter and fast."

Everyone's attention jerked to Emily who had slipped in behind her best friend with my sweet baby niece squirming in her arms. Emily's voice was all kinds of wry and sarcastic.

Busting up, Melanie spewed the gulp of coffee she'd just taken from her mouth. She wiped the dribble from her chin with the back of her hand and whirled around. "Ah, there's my bestie…one who clearly likes her cup overflowin' with cream."

She gestured to Amelia who had her little fists waving in the air.

"Where *is* Royce on this fine mornin'?" Leif asked, grinning as he leaned up against the island.

Rhys laughed like it was the funniest thing he'd ever heard, all while those eyes seemed to seek me out in the middle of it, as if he were searching for me through the lightness that held fast to the air. This calm and peace that had infiltrated.

The true care that weaved these souls together, even when they did it with constant teasing of the other.

My chest tightened and my lungs squeezed, and I really hoped the breath that I attempted to suck into them didn't wheeze when I inhaled.

Shit.

I didn't know how to handle this.

I jerked my attention away only to find Violet's dark, intuitive eyes trained on me.

Double shit.

I ducked my head and went for a diversion, dashing for the refrigerator from across the room.

Awesome.

I opened the door and nearly crawled inside to douse the heat eating me alive.

"So, what else do we need for the omelets?" I asked, my voice so perky it squeaked.

I rummaged around like I was on the hunt for a life-saving ingredient.

"Apparently, the only thing we need around here is cream," Mel hollered.

I whirled back around, producing a nice hazelnut and waving

it in front of her. "Here we go."

She snatched it. "Fine. I'll find myself a little cream. But it better be sugar-free and fat-free and really freaking sweet because I don't need to be carryin' around any extra weight."

Rhys pounded a fist on the island, cracking up. "Standards are high there, Mells Bells."

"You know it."

"I mean, he's gotta check off all the boxes on your ridiculous list, and then the poor bastard has to pass the prick test on top of it."

Rhys shook his head in feigned sadness as he glanced between Richard and Leif.

"Yup. No dickwads. No druggies. No douches." Richard lifted his fingers as he counted them off.

Wow. Apparently, my brother wasn't the only overbearing one around here.

Mel rolled her eyes, and she pointed between all three guys. "Pssh...you think I need any of y'all's approval? Apparently, you haven't been payin' close enough attention because I'm the one who makes the rules around here."

Emily giggled, kissing the back of her daughter's head as Amelia cooed and kicked. "I think we've been on break too long and have forgotten who's the boss."

"That you have, and the boss wants to be fed." Mel smirked as she went ahead and doused her coffee with creamer.

"Well, then. The boss has spoken." Mia grinned at her before she passed Carson off to Leif. The man hugged and bounced his son as he paced with him around the kitchen.

Mia poured the mixture she'd made into a giant skillet, and I moved over to help, working quietly and steadily while they all chatted.

The kids remained rambunctious.

Voices full of teasing while running with an undercurrent of loyalty.

Peace filled me as the sun climbed higher into the sky and stole in golden streaks through the wall of windows that took up the east side of the house.

The ocean lapped gently at the shore in the distance.

Still, my skin tingled with flashes of heat as I moved around the kitchen, trying to both ignore and savor the rough scrape of his eyes when he'd furtively glance my way.

Stealthy and sly.

Worried and with all his care.

It didn't matter if he was trying to be sneaky or not.

It still felt like he was looking at me as if I were the only thing he could see. As if he couldn't look away any more than I could force myself to do.

When the omelets and bacon were ready, everyone filled their plates, and we gathered around the long table set up beneath the windows with a view of the ocean outside.

My brother was the last to join us, the man shooting me a smile when he sat next to Emily, taking Amelia from her so she could eat.

Everyone talked, conversations light.

The kids goofed and laughed and played. Through it all, I tried to pretend like I wasn't affected.

As if I wasn't painfully aware that Rhys sat directly across from me.

The table was large, and it might have seemed accidental, as if we really weren't that close.

But he was there. Invading my space. Stealing my breath.

Watching.

He tried to play it off, his voice loud as he sparred and volleyed good-natured insults with Leif and Richard.

A couple at my brother.

But I could still feel him sneaking peeks.

Aware even though he was distanced.

I jolted when he stretched out a leg and nudged mine with his foot under the table. My eyes darted up to find him staring at me. He let his calf press against mine, the man so huge that he managed to hold me from clear across the massive table.

Sparks flashed.

A sizzle.

You good? he mouthed.

Emotion welled.

So fast.

So overwhelming.

I wanted to ask him the same. To beg him not to let his mind go where I knew it had gone.

Thinking he'd hurt me. That in some way, he'd done me wrong.

Perfect, I mouthed back, only omitting the truth that I wanted more.

That I wanted to experience life in every way because we never knew how long we'd have it.

To cherish every single day.

"Oh my god."

I startled with the hand that grabbed me by the elbow just as I was making my getaway from the kitchen. Breakfast finished and the dishes cleaned, everyone was dispersing to get ready for the day.

Practice was at ten.

Which meant I had an hour to shower and get ready for work. *Work.*

Considering watching Amelia this summer was nothing less than a precious gift, I was having a hard time considering this a *job*.

Ill-at-ease, I shifted around, already feeling her distress.

Violet's eyes were wide with speculation…and worry.

"What?" I asked her. I gave her all the nonchalance and innocence I could front.

"Don't what me. Do you think I didn't notice whatever just went down back there?" She waved an errant hand behind her.

So, I wasn't such a great actress.

My brows lifted for the sky. "Breakfast?"

Still, I tried.

Rhys was worth it.

185

A scowl pulled across her pretty face. "And here I thought we were friends?"

Friends. My mind was instantly back on Rhys. Apparently, my definition of friends was getting skewed.

"Of course, we're friends."

"And friends don't lie to each other."

I started to argue, and she cut me off, "Or hide things."

I sighed.

Crap.

"I knew somethin' was different about you the last few days." Her voice turned soft, her expression caring.

Violet tipped her head to the side like she was getting a read on me. "Do you have somethin' goin' on with Rhys?"

My lips pressed together.

Mine and Violet's relationship verged somewhere between friendship and her viewing me like a little sister.

I thought right then it was more the latter because there was no missing the concern woven into every line of her expression.

When I didn't answer, she gave my arm another tug. "Out with it, woman."

I took a furtive glance around the room.

Mia and Leif were the only ones remaining in the big, open living space, but they were all the way across the room, snuggled up and hugging on each other. I was fairly certain they didn't even notice anyone else was there.

Rhys had taken all his rugged, irresistible energy upstairs.

"There's nothing to tell."

Her brows rose.

"We're just friends."

Her brows lifted higher.

I sighed in surrender. "I have no idea what's going on, okay?"

"It sure felt like *somethin'* was going on to me. I could barely breathe through breakfast, all of the air sucked up by the gravity pulling between you two."

Hope blazed. I couldn't help it. Because I felt it—felt that pull—the draw—and I wanted it. Needed it, even. And still, I knew if I fully gave into it, it was going to destroy me in the end.

The man so sweet and unruly and gorgeous that just looking at him felt like heartbreak.

"I…like him." I shrugged it.

"Obviously," Violet said. "And?"

My head shook. "I have no idea. He totally friend-zoned me, but every time we're in each other's space, that feels like a lie."

I left off the part where he'd blown my mind with that *friendly* orgasm he'd given me this morning.

"Well, I'd say that's plain as day to anyone."

Great.

Not what I wanted to hear.

But like I'd told Rhys, I wasn't sure how to pretend, either. How to act like he didn't make me come alive every time he stepped into the room.

My tongue swept across my bottom lip, and I struggled to find an explanation. "I know what everyone thinks about him, Vi. I know his reputation. I know he's known to burn through women so fast he doesn't even slow down long enough to catch their names. I know he's thought to be irresponsible and reckless and wild."

The jokester.

The player.

Emotion trembled at the corner of my mouth. Overcome with the truth of it.

"But I look at him and…and I see more."

Helplessly, I shrugged.

I guessed that was the whole of it.

I saw more.

I saw brilliance.

I saw goodness.

I saw a glowing, beautiful soul.

Beyond that, I saw the demons.

The pain.

The regret that he thought he kept shrouded behind all those wayward, affable grins.

And I wanted to be a part of them all.

A soft smile graced Violet's mouth. "There is definitely more to him than he lets everyone see."

She reached out and took me by both hands. She squeezed tight, and that was when the worry billowed through her expression.

When I felt it burn up my arms and take root in my chest.

I could hardly breathe around the weight.

"You think he's wrong for me."

Here was this man, a superstar in his own right, a man who splashed his conquests all over social media.

And then there was me, my experiences skewed and slowed and years behind most others my own age because of the fears that I refused to continue to allow to hold me down.

"There are some years separating y'all."

"Age doesn't matter."

Her head shook. "No. It's the needs and the goals and the hearts that do."

"So, you are worried?"

She huffed out a disbelieving laugh. "Have you met the man? Of course, I'm worried."

A slight giggle slipped free, though it was filled with sorrow. "I swear, I feel like I go after the most complicated things." The words were whispered, the knot in my throat making it difficult to speak.

Smiling, Violet reached out and brushed back a lock of my hair, tucking it behind my ear and tipping up my chin.

All her care pouring free.

"That's because you *feel* the most complicated things. I'm not sure someone like you can go for easy or light."

"Then you understand why I can't look away from him."

Her smile was sad. "You *feel* him."

I fought the tears that gathered when I nodded. "In a way I've never felt anyone. And…and I'm not afraid, and somehow I'm still terrified." I choked around the words, half laughter and half pain.

Violet exhaled, and she kept fiddling with my hair. "I love Rhys, Maggie. So much. He's such a good man. Kind and generous and playful. He loves his mama. This family."

She waved around the room.

"Even though he pretends like he's not, he's crazy smart. Talented far beyond being only a show cow the way he acts."

She swallowed hard. "But it's abundantly clear there are ghosts there, too, and I know you see them. I think you have to ask yourself if you're willing to tackle them with him. If you're ready for that."

Concern slipped out with her words.

Pain for me.

Knowing what I'd been through at the hands of the wicked.

The same as Emily.

The same as her sister—Lily.

My heart clutched thinking about her. The trauma she'd endured and how she was handling the aftermath now. Her courage. I was beyond thankful to have her on my side.

Evil had knitted us together.

Ruined us and made us stronger.

A tear slipped down my cheek. "I think we're getting way ahead of ourselves, don't you? Rhys and I are just friends."

She rubbed the tear away with her thumb. "And you both are liars."

My stomach tumbled and my heart sped, and I looked away for a beat to clear my head before I found the courage to return my attention to her. "For the first time, he makes me feel like I'm ready to try."

She nodded slowly. "Just…be careful, Maggie. I'd never tell you to guard your heart because we have to live wide open. Ready for what life has to offer. Willin' to take chances because love is always worth the risk."

She raked her teeth over her bottom lip, giving me a second to process. "Don't ever forget what my daughter said…we all deserve love. Find it. Cherish it. And know, beyond all else, that you deserve a love that makes you feel like you're flying. One that lifts you up rather than drags you down. Don't ever settle for less than that."

Thumb tapping my chin, she forced a grin. "And you are young, so it doesn't hurt to play a little, either. Figure out what you really want."

"And what if I already know what that is?"

"Then you fight for it. You listen to it. You nurture it. But you never let it rip you apart."

Her warning was thick.

Clotting the air.

Stifling my senses.

Sadness tightened my throat. "I won't."

She nodded and let her hands glide back down to mine, and she threaded our fingers together as she started to step back. She gave us a squeeze, her voice a song, "Amor, amor, amor."

My heart nearly splintered with the magnitude of it. "Love you," I whispered.

She released me and stepped away, leaving me with the softest smile. "I know."

She started to leave, and I whispered, "And please don't say anything to Emily or my brother, okay? This is between me and Rhys."

Violet laughed a tinkling sound. "Oh, Maggie. Believe me...I've seen enough bloodshed. I think we can do without any more."

Rhys

"Woooooweee! Sure feels good to be on the wide open road again, don't it?" I basically shouted it over the roarin' of the engine of my car as we sped down the highway back toward Tybee. Richard and I had been in Savannah at a music store picking up a new amp he'd had on order.

I'd been quick to offer to drive considering I had to get out of that house before I lost my mind.

The girl was everywhere.

Too close and too far away, and it was gettin' harder and harder pulling off that whole friend thing. Three days had passed since I'd woken up with her in my arms. Since she'd pushed me over an edge I'd promised myself we wouldn't go.

The sweet, sweet siren having no fuckin' clue what she was doing to me.

Even though it was hot as balls, we had the windows down, lettin' the wind whip the air into disorder while one of the country songs Richard and I had grown up on blared from the speakers.

Dude cut me a glare.

Clutching the *oh shit* handle in one hand and the other to the side of the seat.

"Sure, if I was in the mood to die, which I am not. Might like to get back to my wife, thank you very much."

Cracking up, I reached over and patted his cheek. "Always so dramatic, Richey-Poo."

He gave me a look that promised he was half a second from ripping off my hand.

I laughed harder.

So, I loved to fuck with the dude. Guy was as serious as they came. Best around, too.

Still, I couldn't let him get away with acting like a puss. "You hang on any tighter, you're gonna rip the leather. She might like to be ridden hard, but she doesn't want to be torn apart while you're at it. Show a little respect, man. She's a *lady*."

I said it as somberly as I could.

Disbelief shook his head. "How about we start by respectin' the speed limit?"

I scoffed. "Uh…because that'd be boring? Besides, I'm *barely* over."

That was as I went flying by a car that might as well have been standing still.

"What you are is *barely* sane."

He was right.

But this? This was how I managed. How I got through the day.

Laughing. Playing. Teasing. Doin' the best that I could. Bringing a little light into all the dark.

Except I could feel myself fuckin' that up, too. Allowing my darkness to invade. Ghosts to infiltrate.

Giving pieces of it to her, but I didn't know how to stop from wanting to take some of hers.

Problem was, I didn't know how to stand for her when the girl had a way of seeing straight through me. Knocking me down at the heart and dropping me to my knees.

Richard just chuckled before he got all serious again. "Practice has been good the last couple days, yeah?"

"Stellar." It was the truth. "Best songs we've written."

"Yeah…just feels…different this time. Like we've all figured it out. Except for you, of course." Dude tossed me a wink at that.

I rumbled a laugh. "You just wish I wasn't gonna show your ass up on this album."

He grinned. "How is that song comin'?"

Slowly.

Painfully.

Erratically.

"Gonna kill it."

"Know you will." He didn't even hesitate when he said it, then he glanced at me with a smirk. "Even though I'd love to see that godawful hashtag put out of its misery."

"No misery to it." I waggled my brows.

Crazy how that now felt like a straight-up lie. Fact that all of it was feelin' more and more like *misery* because I was havin' a hard time even contemplating going back to those ways.

Misery in the fact I hadn't been able to since I'd been back in Dalton more than six months ago.

Since Maggie. Since that prick had been up front and center, makin' threats again.

So I'd laid low. Kept my dick in my pants and my face out of the tabloids.

Of course, that *misery* had reached an all-time high when the girl had been in my bed, offering me something I knew she would one day regret.

Touching her and not really being able to touch her.

Not in the way we were dyin' to do.

My poor, destitute dick was half inclined to stage a revolt. Problem was, he was so not interested in anything or anyone except for the one who was makin' me lose my mind.

My control.

My sanity.

I zipped around a car, slowing quick as I came into the small beachside town that was nothing but quaint and quiet and peace.

"Thank fuck," Richard mumbled under his breath.

"See, you lived. When are you gonna learn to trust me, man?" I said it like I was all broken up about it.

"Uh, when you get your license permanently revoked?"

"Rude. And here I was nice enough to haul your sorry ass all the way into Savannah." I tsked.

Richard's brow twisted up in disbelief. "You practically begged me."

"Semantics."

"Whatever, man. You sure you're okay?" This time he really was frowning, shifting in his seat to get a better look at me as I came to a stop at a red light.

"I'm great. Why wouldn't I be?" I shrugged it.

"Because you haven't been fully *great* in a lot of years." Worry filled his voice.

My head shook. "All in the past." I said it with as much conviction as I could.

My oldest friend looked at me harder. "That's such bullshit, man. Can see it written all over you, and the older you get, the clearer it becomes. How long are you gonna drag that guilt around?"

Was he serious?

Forever.

"Was my fault."

All of it.

Both of them.

"No, man."

My teeth ground. "Let's not do this, yeah?"

"Funny how you had your obnoxious ass all up in my shit when I wanted to ignore it," he pushed. "Rubbing my nose in what I didn't want to acknowledge and forcing me to face it. And thank God you did."

I shot him a glare as I accelerated through the intersection. "And there was somethin' you could do to fix it. A way to change it. And you know I can't."

No way to unwrite what had been written.

"Wasn't your fault, man." His voice twisted in some kind of plea.

I just nodded in hopes it would make him drop the bullshit.

We'd gotten into the main area of town that was filled with little shops and cafés, touristy as all get out. Richard pointed at one of the shops on the corner. "There's that place Shea recommended, Calypso's. Let's grab some coffees and donuts for the crew before we head back."

"Winnin' points with the wifey."

Richard cracked a grin. "Always."

Good with me. I was basically game for any distraction.

I made a left and slipped into one of the angled spots that ran along the narrow street.

Here, the sidewalks were filled with people roaming in their beach attire. Not a whole lot of cares for the day except for relaxing and laying in the sand.

We climbed out and headed for the small coffee shop on the corner. A few bistro tables were set up outside, situated under colorful umbrellas.

I followed Richard inside, the bell jingling as the door swooped open. Instantly, I was struck with the smell of coffee and freshly baked pastries.

But it was the girl who overwhelmed my senses.

The girl who was at the counter smiling at the barista as she took an iced coffee topped with whipped cream.

"Maggie," Richard said, all warm and affable. He loped toward her. "What are you doing here?"

He didn't make it all the way to her before the girl welcomed me with the tracing of those charcoal eyes. Like she was drawing me in picture. Writing me in want.

Heat tracing my flesh like the images she was weavin' in her mind.

Shit.

She had my knees knocking all over again.

I stood there awkwardly while Richard hugged her tight.

Maggie giggled in that sweet, deep way. Like even though the conversation was casual, she saw into the fullness of it, experienced all the layers. And she had a way of takin' me there, too.

"Well, I had the whole afternoon off, so I thought I would do a little exploring. Shea has been gushing about these, so I had to see for myself."

She waved the cup in the air.

I had to restrain myself from going caveman. No different than her freaking brother when I wanted to tell her it wasn't safe. That she shouldn't be out here roamin' on her own.

Not when that day was still so vivid in my mind.

Her fear.

This feeling that there was something going on way deeper than she was lettin' on.

I guessed I told her anyway with the way I angled around Richard, acting like I was doing the same as him, making this girl feel welcome and a part of our Carolina George family when I hugged her.

Except I held tight.

Inhaling her deeper.

Jasmine and vanilla.

Sweet. Sweet. Sweet.

My arms constricted around her as I dealt with the rush of worry. This urge to wrap her up and hold her forever.

Fuck.

I didn't know how the hell to do this right.

Not when my hands were tied and I had nothing to give, yet I still didn't know how to let go.

For a beat, she melted in my arms.

Like she'd missed them.

Like she was aching to be there, too, same as I was aching to keep her there.

Her breath was a whimper when I squeezed her tiny body against the enormity of mine. Like I could swallow her up.

Finally, I released her when I felt Richard's eyes burning up the back of my head.

Reluctantly, though.

Like a physical rendering when she peeled herself away.

Those eyes were soft fire.

Soft enough that it might be easy to convince myself neither of us would get burned if we gave in.

"So, uh, how is it?" Richard asked.

Shocked out of our trance, she took a long drink from her straw, her voice all kinds of chipper. "Oh…um…unbelievable. Shea was not exaggerating. And have you smelled these?" She lifted a little paper sack that held a muffin to her nose and inhaled. "Delicious."

My mouth watered.

Yeah. I knew what would be delicious.

"Good. Glad we stopped then."

He cut me a glance before he moved to the counter and put in a big order of basically everything. While I stood there staring at the girl like doing it might change our circumstances. Her smile tender and mine hungry.

My fingers still tingled with the memory of touching her while my tongue wanted to lick her up and down.

"Yo, Rhys. What do you want?"

I jerked my attention his direction. Feeling stunned and out of sorts. "Coffee's good."

The clerk put in the order while another was running around filling the rest. I grabbed a bag that was stuffed with pastries and a tray of drinks.

"Here, let me help." Maggie sidled up beside me and took another tray of drinks while Richard paid and grabbed the last bag.

We all headed out into the blazing heat.

"You drive?" I asked, eyes running the row of cars parked at the sidewalk.

"Nope. I walked."

My heart basically dropped so low it smashed against the concrete.

"Really?"

Guessed it was an accusation. My eyes narrowed. I blamed it on the force of the sun.

"Really. I needed some air."

"Why don't we give you a ride back?"

I mean, unless she wanted me to trail her back to the house in my car because there was no fuckin' way I was just gonna leave her there.

God. This really was fucked.

Maggie gave a slight nod. A slight smile tipping her mouth. Knowing in her way. "Okay."

We walked the rest of the way to my car, and she followed me around to the driver's side.

"You can ride in the front, Maggie," Richard offered from over the top.

"I'm pretty sure I'll fit in the back better than you. My brother rode back here the other day, and I thought he might be stuck forever."

"Here, let me take that," I told her.

I set everything I was holding on the roof then took her tray of drinks.

Pulling the seat up, I set my hand on the small of her back.

You know, like the gentleman I was taught to be except I doubted very much my mama would approve of the thoughts currently racing through my mind.

Maggie shifted to the side to angle in, and I let my hand glide around to her waist as she slipped into the back. Girl fully capable, but I couldn't do anything but take the opportunity to touch.

She breathed out a throaty sigh.

Slowing for a beat.

Wanting it, too.

Fuck.

She was wrecking me, bit by bit.

She buckled, then let those eyes meet mine. For a second, I just looked at her sitting there so pretty in my backseat.

Hoping she knew.

That she got it.

Certain she did.

I straightened then stilled when awareness prickled at my senses. I turned to look behind me, eyes huntin' the street when I got an unsettled feeling that someone was watching us.

Discomfort and dread curled in my stomach.

When I didn't see anything, I gathered everything back up and passed it to Richard so I could drive.

He cut me a look when I slipped into my seat.

I ignored him, turned over the engine, and took the short drive the rest of the way to the house.

Did my best at playing it cool when I helped Maggie back out.

Pretended like I didn't notice her tight ass swaying in her black cut-off shorts as she bounded up the steps with the drinks.

I wound around to Richard's side to help him get the rest.

He started to hand me a bag then jerked it out of my reach, his voice a low growl. "The fuck are you doin', man?"

A frown pinched between my brow while my heart shifted into overdrive. "Taking in the coffees you wanted to get?"

"Don't bullshit me. Know you."

"Do you?" I challenged.

"Yeah. And I've only seen you look at one other girl like that before. Ever." This time, his voice was sympathy laced in a warning.

Grief nearly dropped me to my knees, and my words were seething out between clenched teeth, "You're seein' things."

"No, man, I'm not."

His gaze swept to the house, in worry, in contemplation, before he shifted it back to me. "It's time, man. Like I said, it's been written all over you, and I might have missed its true meanin' a minute back, but now it's plain as day."

"It's nothing."

The lie just spewed out.

"Yeah? Well it sure as hell looks like somethin' to me," he hissed, jabbing a finger at my chest, "and you'd be wise to check what you're gettin' in, *who* you're affecting, before you start fuckin' around. She's not some groupie."

"Would never look at her like that."

Richard nodded hard. "Exactly." He blew the air from his nose. "Just…be sure what you're runnin' toward, man. That you're doin' it right, before someone gets hurt."

Resolution bound with the fear. "Last thing I want to do is hurt her."

His lips pressed together as he pushed the bag into my hold and took a step backward. "Looks to me like she's not the only one at risk of it." He took two more steps backward, talking while he did, "You deserve to be happy, Rhys. But until you stop condemning yourself? You're going to take everyone you care about down with you. Don't take her down, too."

Without saying anything else, he swiveled back around and jogged up the steps, disappearing inside.

"Fuck," I grated, nearly bendin' in two with the impact of what he implied. I struggled to get it together, to pin on a smile when the door blew back open and Daisy came rushing out.

Shit.

"Oh, Uncle Rhys, did you brings me something goods to eat?"

She was already halfway to me by the time I took in a shattered breath and gathered myself enough to keep from tumbling when she slammed into my legs.

Full force.

All light.

She wrapped her arms as far as she could around my knees and grinned up at me.

Love burst.

So intense it hurt.

All that I was missin'.

All that I was never gonna have.

"Course, I brought you somethin'."

"'Cause you loves me?"

I swallowed hard. "Yeah, Daisy Mae. Because I love you."

seventeen

Rhys

I plucked at my bass where the four of us had gathered in the studio practice room in the basement.

Band doing our thing.

Richard strummed through the chords, Emily hummed low in her sultry way, and Leif thumped lightly at his drums as he vibed on what we were offering. Softly banging out the beat and adding his own unique style.

Same as me where I had my head rocked back on the chair and my fingers pluckin' along the thick strings. As I twisted that heavy thrum into the backdrop. As I gave the song something for our listeners to bob their heads along to.

Emily had been leaned over the table, scratching lyrics onto a pad, before she suddenly broke out in song.

Miles away
Years apart
How many days
'til you unbreak this heart
Till this weakened spirit
Stops fallin' apart

"Like it, Ems. Think you should dig deeper. Make it raspier. Not so much melody," Richard told her as he continued strumming chords on his acoustic guitar.

"Yeah," she agreed, still bobbing her head as she leaned over and made more notes.

I followed suit, shifting the style of my playing to accent the sensuous threads of Emily's voice.

The rhythm Leif had been drumming at became slower and harder.

A dusky throb.

Something sexy and unforgettable.

I think we all knew it right then. That we were creatin' magic. That as we knitted each intrinsic piece, we were weaving something spectacular.

We knew it in the way a power took over the room. A connection strung between each of us that bound and tightened and grew.

Becoming something big and profound.

Our music was just that way. Different in all the right ways. Country at its roots, but compelling enough that it crossed genres.

Without a doubt, it's what had gotten us to this place and what was gonna set us apart as we hit the airwaves in a big, big way with this album.

Even if I didn't get my song on the album?

Didn't matter.

I was a part of *this*.

This moment in time.

Felt the eyes on me, and I opened mine to catch Richard looking at me like he was feeling the exact same way. Like what he'd said yesterday had been pure truth—it was like we just got it.

Like we'd all perfectly meshed.

We trailed off when the clapping went up from the other side of the room.

Sebastian Stone pushed off the wall. "Now that is nothin' but brilliance." He pointed at each of us. "Brilliant. Don't stop. Keep it flowing."

Grinning, Richard jutted his chin. "Plan to."

"Good. I'll be back at the end of the week to start fleshing some of this out. Thinking this song right here is going to be our lead single. It's..." Baz shook his head like he was unable to put words to it.

"Agreed." This from Royce who'd been standing against the wall beside him. Royce had just about as much experience in producing as he did with playing. Dude had an ear for raw talent, and it meant something that he saw it in us.

Baz's head bobbed. "Yup. This is it. You guys work on nailing down this song by the end of the week, and we'll run through the rest of the material you've been working on this Friday. Focus on what we want to keep and weed out the rest. Will give us plenty of time to work on the collab with A Riot of Roses when they arrive next week. Two weeks from now, I want you in the booth." He pointed at the row of isolation booths at the back that faced the control room. "Sound good?"

He glanced at everyone.

"Sounds perfect to me. We've got a ton of material. It's actually gonna be hard to let some of it go," Emily said, flipping through her notes.

"That is a good problem to have." Baz chuckled. "All right, I've got to roll. Let me know if anyone has any questions or issues."

"We've got this. Don't worry," I told him.

"After that? Not worried at all." He sent a parting smile before he turned to whip open the door just as Mel came fumbling through. Girl with her face buried in her tablet the way she always did.

Frazzled and disoriented and so organized I was pretty sure she kept a record of every time we pissed. "I know we weren't exactly hidin' out or anything, but our whereabouts have definitely been discovered."

She shifted her screen around to the online gossip site that was basically responsible for my fame. Their favorite thing to talk about was my bad reputation, but I'd always used it to my benefit, to the band's benefit, just goin' with the flow.

But the images they had smeared on their front page had my heart plummeting to the floor.

I went scrambling for my phone.

Normally didn't mind being photographed with a woman or two. Hell, I hadn't even minded it all that much when they'd printed about my arrest for assault back in Dalton since I'd gladly go back and beat that motherfucker's face into the ground all over again.

Jailtime be damned.

But I sure as hell didn't relish in the feelin' of this. There were a slew of pictures of Richard and me walking out of that café with Maggie. Our faces had been focused in on a couple of times. But where it got carried away with the implication was when the lens had zoomed in on my hand on Maggie when I'd helped her into the car.

They made it look like it was some kind of *thing*.

And shit, it was basically the first real *thing* I'd had in so long and looking at it through their greedy eyes soured my stomach and left dread dripping into the vat of darkness that festered deep inside.

Knew it was bullshit. They bit onto any morsel that could be chewed.

But they'd taken a moment that'd felt private and twisted it into something salacious.

Which maybe it was, but they were so off base that it made my vision turn red. Hazy with rage.

Headline read: **Look who's #gettingwetwithrhys!**

I scanned the article used to incite scandal. Typical of the site but, for the first time, it made me want to throw a fist through the wall. I scanned over the crap about my upcoming trial because I didn't give a shit about that, getting to the part I knew would be there.

The Carolina George bassist was seen yesterday afternoon cavorting in the small town of Tybee Island, Georgia with the daughter of late record mogul, Karl Fitzgerald. The country-rocker couldn't seem to keep his hands off the young rock 'n' roll heiress.

Maggie Fitzgerald had been embroiled in the criminal trial against her late father as well as Cory Douglas, the former lead of A Riot of Roses, who'd stolen that head spot from none other than Maggie Fitzgerald's older brother, Royce Reed.

Royce is currently married to Carolina George's lead, Emily Ramsey, and it's been rumored the band is currently recording at the Stone Industries mansion located on the small island.

Manning is no stranger to being photographed with gorgeous women, but we've never seen him look quite so enamored. But is it dollar signs he has in his eyes or has this young girl stolen the heart of country music's most infamous cowboy?

I couldn't even keep reading when it went on to imply I was robbing the cradle. That I might be using her in some way. Nothin' but a sad, sick cliché.

Anger rippled beneath my flesh and nausea swirled in my stomach.

Hot and sticky.

My hand curled around my phone as Melanie continued to ramble about making an official statement, like this was just any other day or any other article.

Took me a second to realize it wasn't my own growl hitting the air when the sound ripped through the room.

I looked up just in time to see Royce's mouth curl in fury.

Richard scoffed.

Super loud.

"What bullshit. Rhys and I ran into Maggie at the coffee shop yesterday. I was the one who convinced him to stop by, and Maggie was already there. We offered her a ride and Rhys helped her into the car. Simple as that. Gettin' sick of the fabricated stories to make a buck. That shit should be illegal."

He stole a glance at me as he said it.

Dude had my back.

While I sat there feeling like I was gonna come out of my skin.

"As long as there are people hungry for that garbage, they're gonna continue feedin' it to them," Mel said, nonchalant. "Besides, I doubt y'all would have that much use for me if I didn't have to fend off these stories, anyway. But I know now that you have families, you want to keep things a little more private. I'll try to temper this so people won't come sniffin' around. Now, about tomorrow's practice..."

They continued on like nothing had happened.

Like Royce wasn't looking at me like he was figuring out exactly where he was going to bury my body.

Rest of practice passed in a painful, awkward way. I couldn't tap back into the vibe. My heart wasn't in it. I wasn't sure if I wanted to go to the girl and apologize for what they'd said or stay far, far away.

Far, far away would be the correct answer.

What I needed to do was take away the opportunity to even look at her because even that was leadin' to all sorts of indecent things.

Then that disquiet became fucking unbearable when my phone blipped with a message.

This feeling takin' me over before I even looked at it.

The dread that had been drip, drip, dripping into my bloodstream suddenly gathered to a flashflood.

Warily, I clicked into it, just knowing, anxiety so heavy and dense that I knew it couldn't be anything else.

It was the same picture as the article, the one where I had my hand on Maggie's waist. But what was most noticeable was the

expression I was sporting that had gone missin' a long, long time ago.

The message behind it was simple.

Nothing but pure hate.

Knew she had a name. Maggie Fitzgerald.

All it took was the same accusation he'd made at the bar back in Dalton to send rage blistering through my body. It blew and battered against the fear until it became a burning ball inside me.

Tight. Wicked. Abhorrent. Ripping up and down my spine like a lion pacing its cage.

Threatening to get loose.

My breaths came in ragged heaves.

I itched.

Wanting to stand up and run out.

Fucking fight but knowing I had nothing to offer.

No right.

Just like I'd told Maggie, no matter how badly I wished it was different, I didn't have anything to offer her.

Just because she has a name doesn't mean she matters. She's no different than all the rest. She's no one. She means nothing. She's just another fuck.

Wanted to puke when I tapped out the vile words. Of course, she was different. But my hands were tied. Nothing I could do. It was the only way to protect the girl from the wrath I could feel gathering. Getting stronger.

My debts finally coming due.

It didn't take all that long for him to respond.

You think I don't see it? Don't play me for a fool.

My teeth ground as I tapped out a warning around the terror.

Have given you everything I have. What more do you

want from me?

A second later, the response blipped through.

You think you've atoned for what you did? I warned you. For years. Now, it's time to pay.

Thought I was probably gasping out my rage and fear when I typed the next text.

This is my debt to pay. No one else's. Stay the fuck away from her and stay the fuck away from my mama, or you're going to discover what pain really means. Now tell me what you want so we can end this.

It blipped through with another message a second later.

It's not over. Not as long as you're still breathing.

Grief stormed through my being.
It clashed with the guilt.
Dark and sinister.
Stealing joy.
Stealing power.
As much as I hated the prick, as much of a psycho as he was, he was right in one regard: I didn't get this—didn't get to find joy when I'd stolen *hers*.
Genny.
Her face flashed.
Smiles.
Kisses.
Hope.
Horror.
Agony speared through me.
Dull, rusted blades that cut me in two.
Maybe I should have stayed away. Taken the warnings as true threats. But I hadn't known how to let it go. How to give up that

guilt or give up on her.

Not when my one job had been setting her free.

Maggie infiltrated the blur of thoughts racing through my mind.

Her grace. Her intelligence. Those eyes that saw through everything.

My chest squeezed like a bitch, and I couldn't fuckin' breathe.

That was the danger of hoping. Of letting the girl invade.

I knew better.

Knew I'd only wreck her in the end. But I craved it.

Craved her.

This girl who somehow managed to calm a storm that had been raging for years. Like she could dip her fingers into the toiling waters and coax the agitation into tranquility.

But if I let her, I'd only bring my destruction on her.

All kinds of frantic, I pushed to my feet and set my bass aside. "Gonna call it."

"Need to work on that song before Baz is back on Friday?" Leif cracked. "Better get on it."

"Good as done," I told him through clenched teeth.

Trying to keep my cool.

To keep from losing it.

From cracking from the weight and the pressure I could feel gathering. Because no matter how fast or how hard I ran, I'd never outrun this.

I was stuck.

Frozen.

A prisoner to this past that would forever haunt my future.

I ducked out the door and started up the steps to the main floor.

Shouldn't have been surprised in the least when I felt the presence emerge from behind.

"Thought I told you to stay away from my sister." Venom oozed out in his voice.

I scoffed out a manic sound. Barely hanging onto sanity when I whirled back around. "Gave her a fuckin' ride, man."

Yeah, I left out the one she'd taken on my hand. And as much as I'd love to throw it in his face that I'd never fuckin' touched her, that'd be a lie.

His throat bobbed. "Don't want her face splashed in the tabloids."

Disbelief shook my head. "Are you serious right now? You're every bit as famous as the rest of us. Probably more. This is our world. You brought her here. And if she wants to be a part of it, let her, or let her go. You know she'd be better off."

I didn't know if I was talking to him or to myself.

I roughed an agitated hand through my hair. "I get it, Royce. You want to protect her. And so do I."

From me.

From whatever I could feel coming at us full force.

His head shook, and he spat the words at the floor, "I just...fuck. She's not telling me something, and I feel like I'm going to lose my goddamn mind."

That dread filled my throat to bursting.

I struggled to swallow it down.

"She's a grown woman, Royce. She's not gonna tell you everything."

Pushing out a sigh, he shoved his hands in his pockets. "She used to. I was the one she came to when she was scared. I was the one who watched over her. The one who fought for her."

My hand curled around the railing that ran the narrow staircase. "And maybe because of that, she's now able to live her life. Way she wants to."

His nod was tight, and he scrubbed a palm over his face. "Sorry I was being a dick. I saw those pictures and..." He blew out a strained sigh, looking up to meet my eye. "Know you and Richard were only watching out for her. I appreciate that. I just..."

"I know, man." Guilt constricted, and I felt like a complete bastard. Standing there actin' innocent when I could feel the blame streaking through my veins. "Gossip sites are gonna talk. It's just what they do."

He nodded again.

"All right then." I curled my hand into a fist and gave a soft pound to the railing with the heel of it, turning to leave.

"Rhys," he called behind me.

I paused, worry clenching every cell.

"If you knew something was goin' on with her, if she told you, would you tell me?"

Warily, I shifted to look at him, my voice somber. "In confidence? No, man, I wouldn't."

Maggie

*I*t radiated through the walls.

Torment.

It felt like tendrils of it were seeping through the cracks and crawling across the floor, finding their way to me where they curled around my ankles and clawed up my legs.

Vapors that wrapped me in his spirit and dragged me into his sphere.

Willingly or as a prisoner, I wasn't sure.

All I knew was my ear was pressed to the bathroom door that separated us before I even knew what I was doing.

It was obvious Rhys had been trying to keep his distance, and I was pretty sure it stemmed from the article that had been published earlier today.

I'd seen it.

Had seen his hand holding so firm to my waist. But what had stricken me was the expression that had been on his face.

Something unmistakable even though the tabloid had tried to make it out as something lewd and obscene.

I'd also seen his expression tonight during dinner when he'd looked like a different man. When he looked like something new had been wrecked inside him.

I could feel it now.

Seeping from his spirit and saturating the atmosphere.

Agony and shame and the deepest, starkest kind of grief.

I didn't knock.

I just twisted the handle and pushed open the door to the chaotic darkness that echoed back. The man the storm in the middle of it.

I found him across the room. His shape nothing but a massive silhouette where he sat in an oversized chair in the corner. The hulking outline of him slung back in the plush fabric.

I took a step inside.

The air shivered and rushed.

I squinted through the darkness, allowing my sight to adjust. For all the lines and curves and angles that made him up to reveal themselves.

His hair was untamed and wild, his beard thick, his arms rested on either side of the chair. A beer bottle dangled from the fingers of his left hand.

The lines on his rugged face were carved into something vicious and desolate.

Right then, he looked like a Viking who'd conquered all his enemies but had been left with the burden of their blood on his hands.

Terrifying.

Fascinating.

Easing into the room, I snapped the door shut behind me.

At the click of the lock, a grunt hit the air.

A bluster through the oxygen.

"Shouldn't be in here, Maggie."

In the disquiet, my teeth raked my bottom lip, and my knees

wobbled as I took another step his direction. I did my best to keep my voice light. "Judging by the look of you, I think this is exactly where I'm needed."

It didn't work. Not when the words quivered with my worry for him.

Another grunt, and he took a long pull of his beer, eyeing me with those blue eyes through the clouds that rumbled, his voice a roll of low thunder. "You think you know me? Think you know what I need?"

It was a challenge.

A warning.

I took another step closer.

"Yes. Maybe not all the details, but yes."

He scoffed a self-deprecating laugh and rubbed a flustered hand over his face.

I took no offense because it was clear all the hostility vibrating from him was directed at himself.

He took another long pull of his drink. "Well, I'd like to spare you those details, Sweet Thing."

Bitterness poured out with the words.

"And what if I offered to hold them?"

He watched me, that hard gaze getting softer with each step that I took his direction. "Then I'd say you should stop bein' a masochist."

"I don't think that would be possible with you."

A rough scrape of affection climbed his throat.

I felt it like a caress across my skin.

I ran my palms up my arms to chase the chill it lifted, trying to stop from completely losing myself to him.

But I thought it was stupid to think I wasn't already there.

Foolish to think there was any stopping what I felt when I eased down onto the soft, thick carpet of his room. Like I needed to get down on his level. Or maybe the man just had me on my knees.

"And how's that?" Rhys asked.

I shifted around onto my bottom and wound my arms around my knees to give me something to do with my shaking hands.

Especially when the only thing they wanted to do was run over his body. Brush across his face. Take away some of his pain.

Squeezing my legs, I contemplated for a second because it was something I was just coming to understand myself. "I guess I was probably eleven or so when I started to realize I was different. That I experienced people differently than they experienced me. That I felt what they did, and it affected how I felt, too. Their moods catching. Their smiles and their tears. Their fears and their worries and their joy."

The smile I cast him was wistful.

Sadness blew through his expression, though he cracked the words like a joke. "That sounds horrible."

Rocking a bit, I watched the way his expression danced and played.

Dark and light.

Heavy and soft.

Everything itched and pulled.

It was painful trying to sit still with him so close.

"Sometimes it is. But sometimes…" I hiked a shoulder. "Most of the time…it feels like it's my purpose. Like I'd be missing something if I wasn't experiencing it. It feels right."

"A blessing and a curse," he quietly mused.

"Yeah." I nodded, hugging my knees tighter. "But with you…" I swallowed around the lump lodged in my throat, and my brow squeezed as I tried to make sense of it. "It's different."

Blue eyes sought me in the darkness, tracing me like he was chasing down a dream. "How?"

It was no longer a challenge.

It was a plea.

"I can feel you feeling me, and I think maybe you can feel me feeling you. And it feels like…it feels like a communion. Like an actual connection. Like we're bound in some essential way."

Air huffed from his nose. "Last person you want to be *communin'* with is me."

It was all flirty playfulness underscored by self-loathing.

"That picture was nothing, Rhys. There's no reason for you to feel guilty over it."

Okay. Maybe the picture meant something. But the article surrounding it? Total B.S. I'd rolled my eyes when Royce had asked me about it. He'd been worried I'd be upset or harmed by it in some way, which was ridiculous.

The only thing I worried about right then was Rhys.

"Don't want to drag you into my mess, Maggie."

"Life is messy, Rhys. It doesn't matter who I'm with or who I care about. They are going to have messy bits. Just like I have mine."

"I just wish mine weren't so ugly." Pain infiltrated his words, and he blew out a sigh.

"I think it's safe to say we all do. And all of us make mistakes."

Except he no longer felt like one.

His head shook in soft disbelief, in slow affection, in the warmest kind of greed.

I struggled to breathe around it.

His need and intensity and the sadness that continued to ooze from his spirit.

"I just want to be here for you, Rhys. In any way that you'll let me."

He rubbed a hand over his face, and I shifted a bit, drawn to the man who writhed in turmoil even though he was sitting still.

"What happened today that dimmed your light? That picture couldn't have bothered you that much. You've been photographed with women a million times."

His smile was grim. "Yeah. But none of those women were you." He edged forward a fraction, the man towering over me in the chair.

Big and bold and brutal.

He peered at me through the shadows. Desperately. Like he was trying to sear his truth into my psyche. "There are people who don't care for me much, Maggie. People who look for any reason to make my life hell. People who don't mind hurtin' the ones I care about to get to me."

Shock reared me back. "Someone's after you?"

Surrender shook his head. "No, Sweet Thing. Not after me. They already have me."

I'm standing still.

What he'd said the other day suddenly made sense.

Unable to stop myself, I shifted onto my hands and knees. Needing to get closer. Like the man had caught me by the soul.

"Why?"

Like he felt the same, he moved, too, sliding down the front of the chair until he was sitting on the floor.

His booted feet were planted on the carpet, his knees spread wide as he rested his arms on top of them.

Three feet separated us.

A world. A chasm.

A breath. A whisper. The simplest, sweetest kiss.

My stomach tightened, and I tried to rein the thoughts that stampeded. Urges that pounded through the atmosphere and became something palpable.

Swirling and spinning.

A call I wanted to heed.

"Already told you, I have a tendency to hurt the ones I love most."

Agony twisted through his features, and then he drove his fingers through his hair. He yanked at the longer pieces, and anguished laughter ripped up his throat. "Growing up, only thing I ever wanted was to be the good guy. Decent. Make the world a better place than it was. Make my parents proud."

Grief covered him when he lifted his face to look at me. I crawled toward him. Just an inch. Carefully. Recklessly.

"I'm sure your dad was proud of you, and I know your mom is. I've seen her look at you, Rhys. How could she not be proud of you? Look at you. Look at who you've become. Look at all you've achieved."

He choked over his misery. "I tried to, Maggie. Tried to make them proud. My daddy…he always told me how proud he was of me."

Sorrow twisted his mouth, though a grieved smile made its way to it. His stare went far away.

Like he was back in that time. His words came like a quieted confession. "He used to tell me I was strong as a horse. That I

217

could stand up and fight for anyone who needed it."

I moved for him. Unwilling and unable to keep the distance. I was on my knees between his legs when my fingertips grazed over the raging beat of his heart from over the flannel button-down he wore.

It ran wild.

Unhinged.

Untamed.

"Stallion." The full meaning of it came as a whisper from my tongue.

God.

The weight of it was brutal.

How he tossed it around like banter.

Like a joke.

I knew then he really meant it as an insult.

I felt the mockery of what he'd made of his father's love in a way that might destroy me. But like I'd realized before, Rhys Manning was worth the pain.

We met each other's gazes, and I nearly crumbled when a tear slipped from his eye and streaked for his beard.

This unruly, savage beast with the softest, kindest heart. A heart that was so broken I wasn't sure how to hold all the fractured pieces.

I let my thumb trace the moisture, riding up until I was cupping his rugged, gorgeous face. He curled his hand around my wrist. Like he didn't know whether he wanted to shove me off or hold me closer. "I tried, Maggie. Tried to protect them all. Tried, and I failed, and there's this hole…"

He rammed his fingers against his chest. "This hole that I can't fill, and I won't pull you down into it with me."

"Rhys."

His thick throat trembled as he smiled. "Goddess Girl. I'm no good. I mess it all up, even when I don't mean to."

"You're wrong."

Sadness tweaked the corner of his mouth. "Wish I was. Wish I was good enough. Wish my luggage wasn't so heavy that it can't even be moved. Most of all, right now, I wish I didn't want you so damned bad." With the last, a smirk pulled to the side, though it was sober and soft and filled with regret.

I touched him there, brushed my fingers over that sweet spot. The air thinned and the heat amped and my poor heart bolted and hurtled in an attempt to catch up to his.

"And I wish you'd give in." I edged in farther so I could whisper in his ear. "I want to jump."

I wanted to find this boy in his brokenness the same way as he found me in my dreams.

Edging back a fraction, I stared at him, our faces an inch apart.

Lips parted and breaths heaving from our lungs.

Need gathered in that bare space.

Dense. Intense. Desperate.

Rhys reached out and ran his fingertips down the angle of my cheek. "I'd be the luckiest damned bastard alive."

We rocked. Hesitated. Warred.

Those blue eyes flitted over my face the whole time. Searching. Learning.

"Sweet Siren," he murmured. "What are you doin' to me?"

"Begging you for my first kiss."

I guessed it was the wrong thing to say.

Because those big hands moved to my shoulders and he crushed me against him, only he didn't kiss me, he held my cheek against his chest. His arms fierce as he hugged me and muttered to the top of my head, "I refuse to steal from you somethin' you should cherish. Refuse to steal from your beauty. Refuse to steal from your grace. Refuse to *hurt* you."

"It's just a kiss."

"No, it's not."

I let him hold me for a long time because he was right—it wouldn't be just a kiss.

It would be me and him.

He hugged me.

Fiercely.

Frantically.

When I couldn't take it any longer, I peeled myself from his body, my smile knowing and sad when I climbed to my feet.

His was an apology.

I couldn't say anything else as I forced myself to turn and walk out of his room. I moved into the desolate vacancy of mine.

I thought maybe it was the first time I truly felt as if I were missing a part of myself. Like something had gotten lost. Because I'd found a piece that matched, and now that I knew the distinct shape of it, where it fit, I felt the void of it like a wound.

I climbed into bed.

Only I tossed.

Tossed and turned while the hours passed.

Tonight, the nightmares eluded me. I guessed it was because I'd become a prisoner to Rhys'. The man's spirit groaning from the depths of sleep from the room next door.

Torment.

Misery.

Finally, when the pressure became too great, I climbed from bed and padded over to my desk where I flipped on the small lamp. I dug into the drawer and found a piece of plain white paper, and I began to fold and fashion. The same way as I'd done with that duck. The tiny shape was crude and choppy, but I didn't care, and when I had it finished, I flipped it over and printed the words in tiny letters.

Then I stole into the darkness of his room.

To where he writhed and moaned on his bed.

For a moment, I stared down at him, unsure how to reach him, but knowing for certain that in some way, I was already touching him.

That there was something between us.

I tucked the small design into his hand, pressed my mouth to his sweaty temple, and I breathed out my peace.

My wishes.

My love.

Then I forced myself to leave.

Rhys
Nine Years Old

"Now you be careful, and don't touch anythin' up there," Rhys' daddy rumbled where he was focused on working on the front axle, barely payin' Rhys any mind.

"I know, I know," Rhys told him, climbing up the big tractor and into the cab, wishing his daddy would hurry up and get done so he could go over to Richard's.

It was summer, and they had no school, and since it was super hot, Richard's mama was gonna take 'em to the pool over by the library once Rhys got back.

Rhys couldn't wait.

Inside the cab, there were all kinds of buttons and knobs. A spot for a drink since the workers had to be in the field all day.

Rhys plopped down onto the cracked seat, kinda bouncing on

it, glancing around at all the knobs and dials and wondering if some day he would drive one or if maybe he'd work on it like his daddy.

He started making a rumbling noise deep in his throat as he imagined which one seemed like the most fun, and he grabbed the steering wheel, rocking it back and forth as he pretended like he was plowing up one of the fields. Then the rumbly noise grew high and faster, and Rhys shifted back in the seat as he hung onto the steering wheel, pretending he was sliding around a sharp curve, thinking he just might want to be a racecar driver instead.

"Vroooooooooooooooom," he hollered. He could almost feel the racetrack rumbling beneath him.

He rammed at the pedal with his foot, going faster and faster, pretending like he was shifting the engine as he yanked and pushed at the stick that came up from the floor close to the seat.

In his mind, he went whizzin' by two Indy cars like they were standin' still.

No one could catch him.

"Vroom vroom vrooooooooooooooooom!" he shouted louder, grinning as he shifted harder.

The tractor suddenly jolted forward. His eyes went wide with fear and his heart stopped workin' in his chest when he realized the tractor had actually moved.

But it was only an inch.

Whew.

But he was bettin' his daddy still noticed, especially when his daddy started yelling.

He was gonna be in big trouble because he'd been messin' around the way he wasn't supposed to do.

His daddy was shoutin', "Rhys! Rhys!"

The worry that he was gonna get grounded shifted and changed and became something ugly that filled up his chest.

Because his daddy's voice sounded different.

Hard and high and…and…and afraid.

Rhys shoved at the door. It banged open, and he scrambled out, taking the side like a jungle gym.

His breaths were harsh and short.

Then they went missin' altogether when he saw his daddy's legs where they came out from under the tractor.

He was moving them all weird. The heels of his work boots digging into the dirt but goin' nowhere.

"Rhys!"

Rhys jumped the rest of the way down. Fear covered him as he rushed to peer underneath.

His daddy's arm was pinned under the metal.

And there was blood.

Rhys gulped, and his head got dizzy, and he was sure he was gonna pass out.

"Oh, no, Daddy. I didn't mean to."

"Rhys, I'm pinned. I need help."

Rhys jumped up, and he grabbed the front of the tractor and yanked at it with all his might.

Straining and heaving and not makin' a budge.

"I'm not strong enough. I'm not strong enough." He shouted it, tryin' harder. Tears blurred his eyes, and he felt like he was in a fog.

"Rhys." His daddy was forcin' the words. "Rhys, look at me. Need you to listen and listen good."

Rhys dropped to his knees so he could see his daddy where he was under the tractor.

He got dizzy again.

Like he was sick in his whole body and it made him feel like he couldn't move his arms or his legs.

"I'm sorry." Rhys didn't mean to snivel and whine, but he couldn't stop it, the way everything burned and hurt and he felt so scared. "I'm so sorry, Daddy. I didn't mean to."

"It's okay," his daddy told him, his face twisted up in pain. "It's okay. I just need you to pay close attention. You remember where Mr. Crenshaw's house is?"

Rhys nodded, barely able to see through the tears that streamed in hot tracks down his face.

"Need you to go get him. Tell him your daddy is stuck and hurt and needs help. Need you to run real fast. Like a stallion. Remember?"

This time Rhys' nod was frantic.

"Now go."

Rhys flew to his feet, and he raked his forearm over his face so he could see the trail that led to Mr. Crenshaw's place.

Rhys ran.

Ran so fast that the dirt kicked up behind him.

So fast his chest burned so bad and he couldn't find his breath.

But he just kept going anyway.

Over the fields that seemed to go on forever. Whipping through the trees. Then he was screaming when he broke through the grove into another field and the house over on the other side of it came into view. "Mr. Crenshaw. Help! Help! My daddy needs help!"

Rhys sat on the hard plastic chair, his legs swinging back and forth.

Back and forth.

With his head dropped down, he watched where the tips of his old worn shoes barely scraped the linoleum.

His heart slugged hard and slow. The sound of it in his ears made his whole body hurt.

Tears just ran and ran.

Forever and ever, and he didn't think he was ever gonna be able to make 'em stop.

His mama was suddenly there, kneeling in front of him, her hand squeezing his knee. "Hey, you."

He dropped his head down lower because he didn't want his mama to see his face. Not how sad he was or how bad he was.

"You can see him now."

Rhys shook his head. "He's gonna be mad."

"It was an accident, Rhys. It's okay."

"It's not." The snivels were back, and he rubbed his nose with his arm again. "He's gonna hate me. I didn't listen. I wasn't supposed to touch nothin'," he cried. "He's not gonna love me no more."

His mama tipped up his chin, and then his heart was hurt all over again when he saw the way she looked.

Her eyes so red and swollen and the smile on her face more sad than it was happy. "Hey, don't ever think that. Remember what I've always told you…our home is built on love, love, love. It's the foundation of who we are. And that isn't ever gonna change."

Rhys blinked and nodded.

His mama tipped up his chin farther. "Now, I need you to be my strong boy when we go in there, okay?"

He nodded again, and he pushed off the chair, and he held his mama's hand real tight as they moved through two big doors and down a long hall and to a door where the room was kinda dark inside.

His mama held it open for him.

Rhys choked over the big fat ball of sorrow that closed off his throat.

His daddy looked different where he laid in the hospital bed. Smaller than Rhys remembered. Hooked up to a bunch of beeping machines.

All covered up where his left arm was gone.

Tears burst this time, and Rhys rushed for him and buried his face in his chest.

His daddy wrapped his only arm around him.

"I'm sorry, Daddy." He sniffled and tried to bury the cries into his daddy's chest, but he was wailing it, anyway. "I'm so sorry. I didn't mean to."

Rhys had never felt so bad in his whole life. So sick or scared or hurt or sad, and he thought for a second that maybe he was gonna die.

"Not your fault," his daddy rumbled. "I knew better than to let you go climbing up on that tractor. Wasn't payin' close enough attention."

Rhys knew he was lying. Knew it was all his fault.

"I'll take care of you, Daddy. I'll take care of you and Mama. I promise."

His daddy ran his fingers through his hair. "You're a good boy, Rhys. A good, good boy."

Rhys

*D*isoriented, I blinked into the murky darkness of my room.

Drawn from the depths of sleep that had tormented and slayed. Where the demons gathered and hunted and plotted to go in for the kill.

It was like I'd been called out of it. Offered a sanctuary. Reprieve. Like this girl was lurin' me into a different sort of dream.

Sitting up on the edge of the bed, I scrubbed a palm over my face to break me out of the trance.

Only I realized I wasn't empty-handed the way I'd been when I'd fallen asleep. There was something pressed to my palm that I was clutchin' like a lifeline. Like I'd found a buoy in the night.

Guessed it was almost in fear that I uncurled my fingers, my heart locked up in my throat where it beat a vicious chord.

Racing for a melody that had no place in my ear.

But it was there, strummin' louder when I peered through the wispy darkness at what I held.

My chest seized by the gesture.

It made me want to weep all over again, which was straight bullshit, but this girl had a way of pulling the darkness to the surface. Of making me feel things I shouldn't be feeling.

I brushed my fingers over the crude shape made from a plain piece of paper.

A horse.

A *stallion.*

Warmth spread beneath the surface of my skin. Like the blooming of somethin' that couldn't be.

Because I knew better. I fuckin' knew better...

I flipped the horse over with my fingers, squinting more in the bare light when I saw the lettering on the back.

I'm already yours.

My mind spiraled back to the last thing I'd said to her. When I told her I couldn't steal the good parts of her. Taint the pieces that should be cherished.

Last thing I wanted was to be a regret.

Didn't want to hurt her.

How the fuck could I offer her something when I knew I didn't have all myself to give? When I knew I was forever gonna be stuck? Fact there'd always be a part of me that belonged to the past?

In the middle of all that, energy flashed, and I struggled to maintain my footing around it.

Stand ground when I could feel it crumbling out from under.

Could feel myself dancing into treachery. Treading into perilous waters. The power of whatever the fuck she conjured hoverin' somewhere in the fringes of who I was.

I didn't know how to ignore it.

This *thing.*

The lure that bound and trapped and most assuredly was gonna turn up a blade in our backs in the end. One that had me on my feet and moving to my balcony doors like that was what I'd been called to do. My spirit was already there, taken to the place where she had gone. She was out on the beach where the full moon shone bright, the girl dancing in the waves.

She wore a sundress that struck in the night with that stunning face tipped up to the heavens. Like she was seeking its wisdom.

Offering it her prayers and her hopes and her fears.

A goddess beneath the stars.

It was no secret I wasn't exactly the type who got an A+ for good behavior.

But I was pretty sure I was scraping the bottom of the barrel on this one. Tossing all good intention out the window.

Because I was moving.

Drawn.

Overpowered.

Overcome.

I was out my door and down the stairs and stealing into the night before my brain could catch up to my spirit that had met her somewhere in our dreams.

She dipped her toes in the rushing waves.

That energy crackled and lashed.

Zapped all logic and rationale.

Because I was standing twenty feet behind her, and the girl froze in awareness before she looked at me from over her delicate shoulder. Black hair whipping around her gorgeous face.

Charcoal eyes doing that mesmerizing thing.

A lightning storm that coaxed me right into tranquility.

Tracing me in chaos and comfort.

Like I was at peace with the coming destruction.

Her need was palpable.

Her adoration real and unfounded and the best thing I'd felt in all my life.

"Maggie." I said her name like greed.

For two beats, we stared.

And then she was runnin' toward me.

Just as I was moving for her.

In a flash, she was in my arms and off her feet.

And I didn't know if she was kissing me or I was kissing her.
Only thing I knew?
It was pure fuckin' ecstasy.

Maggie

*W*e crashed.

No hesitation.

No reserve.

Rhys lifted me into the strength of those arms just as his mouth crushed against mine.

Warmth and blinding light.

Like all the stars that glittered in the sky flashed and gleamed. Filled the air with a blast of intensity.

A shockwave of electricity that streaked through the night.

His mouth moved in a desperate bid to claim, his lips covering mine as they pressed and pulled and gave.

Gentle plucks and hungry nips and, oh my god, Rhys Manning was kissing me.

My head spun and my pulse raced as I turned myself over to

the moment.

It wasn't even close to being awkward or tentative.

It was power. It was purpose. It was the most decadent sort of persuasion.

He rode a hand up my back and fisted it in my hair, while the other arm locked around my waist to keep me held firm against the rigid expanse of muscles that flexed and bowed across his massive body.

My arms curled around his neck as he hoisted me higher, and I offered him all I had to give.

In a single kiss, the man cut my heart wide open. Or I guessed it'd already been. Cracked and fractured and splintering into his big, capable hands.

Now he was there to allow me to pour it all into him.

Fingers gripping his hair like I needed something to keep me grounded, to keep me from floating away, I let the tip of my tongue sneak out to taste his mouth.

It was the barest touch.

It didn't matter.

It was bliss. So much bliss.

It rocketed and shook and spun us into a frenzy.

Rhys moaned my name. "Maggie." The sound was a needy reverberation against my lips as his moved over mine. Brushing and caressing and almost terrified to take more. "Maggie. Sweet Siren. Fuck, baby. What have you done? What have you done?"

An earthquake of emotion sheared through me.

It slicked down my spine and quivered through my being.

Shattering.

Shifting.

Like all the missing pieces were righting themselves.

His arms tightened, and my legs constricted around his waist, and I was rubbing myself over the taut planes of his ripped abdomen.

"Maggie. Sweet Thing. Goddess Girl." He whispered the words like praise. Like a warning as his kiss became more urgent.

As his hands became needier in their search and the air began to pant from his lungs.

And I got the sense that we'd been written in the heavens. That this moment had already been written in time. That it'd been coming for an eternity.

I ground against him.

Sparks lit.

A tremble between my thighs.

No shyness or fear to be found.

My lips parted with the greed that flash-fired through every cell.

"Rhys."

He took it as a plea for more. The hand in my hair tightened, and a growl rumbled up his thick throat. Angling his head, he licked across my lips.

Heat raced, overwhelming, consuming, and I welcomed it. I opened to him so his tongue could slant against mine in a tangle of greed.

Fire.

Flames.

Everything. Everything.

I gasped and whimpered and struggled to get closer.

I swore I could feel his spirit trying to crawl inside me. That he felt me the way I felt him.

That he knew I could sense his fear. His dread. The guilt he carried like stones.

I wanted to hold each one.

Find a way to his innermost secrets.

Whisper his doubts away so I could show him the man I saw.

"I feel you. In my dreams. I feel you." Like he was thinking the same thing, his words came as a low rumble against my mouth as he kissed me into a state of delirium.

It was confusion.

It was need.

For both of us, it was the terror of stepping into the unknown. Into the uncharted where we would discover where we had always belonged, or where we would lose ourselves along the way.

But I knew, without a shadow of a doubt, this man was worth that risk.

Besides, what life was worth living without risking your heart?

"And I feel you in mine. Meet me there, Rhys. Meet me in this place that belongs to us."

He groaned. "Don't want to hurt you."

Our bodies rocked and pitched. I climbed higher and higher like I was going to find a way to crawl inside him.

"You won't."

His spirit shook. His devastating fear that he would.

But still, his hands explored. They ran my back and gripped me by the bottom as he rocked me against him.

I struggled to get closer. My dress was wrapped around my waist, and my panties were rubbing all over the bulge in his jeans.

Need twisted me in two.

And I ached.

Ached in an acute way that I refused to ignore.

My nails dug into his shoulders, and I gave into frantically begging for all that I'd been missing. As I rushed for a new freedom I knew I would find in him. "Take me inside, Rhys. I want to feel you. All of you." I demanded it between our kiss.

"Maggie." I thought he was going to argue but instead he started to carry me toward the house, kissing me wild as he trudged through the sands up onto the boardwalk.

Holding me in the promise of those massive arms. Drowning me in the sea of his reckless kisses. Owning me with the whisper of his breath and the shout of his soul. "Maggie. Want to break every rule for you. How's it possible, Sweet Thing? How?"

He was pleading it as we hit the elevated patio. He headed around the side of the house and angled enough to open the side door. The second we were inside, he pressed me to the wall, kissing me harder as he rocked against me. "How?"

He didn't wait for an answer before he had me scooped up higher in his arms and was climbing the narrow second staircase.

Kissing me and kissing me as we went.

At the landing, he paused to peek out into the darkened hall and check that it was clear.

The only sound was the lapping of the waves against the beach and the sleeping house that echoed back.

Then Rhys was looking at me like I was a secret.

A treasured, bittersweet secret.

And I was touching his face, scratching my nails through his full beard.

"Stallion." I said it so softly, and he dipped his chin to kiss the tips of my fingers that whispered across his lips.

"You make me remember what it feels like to want to be the good guy." Blue eyes swam with regret and swirled with a current of hope.

"You are a good guy, Rhys. More than a good guy. I feel it…" I leaned in so I was whispering at his ear and still far enough back that I could meet his eye, my touch tracing over the wide expanse of his chest. "This beautiful, beautiful spirit."

He stared up at me as he carried me down the hall. The air both thinned and dense.

Energy crackled.

A thrill in the atmosphere.

Wrapping and holding and coaxing us to the destination I thought we'd been purposed. Because I'd never been so sure of anything in all my life.

This man. This man.

He entered through my door, and he snapped and locked it behind us, kissing me again as he moved through the bathroom and into the dusky haze of his bedroom.

Though his kiss had turned tender.

Reverent and adoring and careful.

Because we both knew where we were headed.

At the end of his bed, he settled me onto my shaky feet.

The enormous room felt smaller. The walls closed in. So close to this man that I felt myself moving through him.

With him.

So slowly, he climbed down onto his knees in front of me, though he sat up high on them, holding me by the outside of my trembling thighs. The fabric of my dress was bunched in the press of his hot, hot hands.

My heart sped out of time.

Nerves and anticipation and a newfound greed.

My stomach was in knots and my skin alight.

Rhys looked up at me.

This savage beast with the sweetest soul.

His fingers trembled against my flesh.

"You sure we're doin' this?" His voice was gruff. Lust coated the words while his care slipped out on his tongue.

"Yes," I promised.

"Don't wanna hurt you," he said again.

"I'm not afraid."

Groaning, he pressed his nose into my dress right over my quaking belly.

Need rushed, and my hands found his hair, and he was nuzzling his face into the fabric of my dress, kissing me over the top of it and muttering, "Luckiest bastard alive. Maggie. Fuck. What are we doin'?"

A whimper left me, and he was peering up at me as he let his hands slide under the skirt of my dress.

I jolted when he hooked his fingers in the edges of my underwear, and my hands shot to his shoulders to keep myself standing.

To keep my knees from buckling.

Rocked by the moment. That I was going to share it with this man.

Worry filled his expression. "You say, and we stop."

"I'm not afraid," I vowed again, my fingers brushing across his plush lips.

They parted, kissed the tips, and then he was peeling the lace down my legs and winding them free of my ankles.

And I was shaking and shaking, all while drawing him closer, my hands at the back of his head as he glided his palms up the outside of my legs. He kept kissing over my dress, nudging it up as he went, before he was laying soft kisses to the bare skin at the top of my right thigh, then moving to the left.

His hands moved higher.

The same as his kisses.

And I couldn't breathe.

Couldn't see.

Beneath the Stars

All I could feel was the rush of sensation when he nudged me apart the barest fraction and licked me.

Kissed me deep and slow and carefully.

My hands tightened in his hair and the air jutted from my lungs.

Pleasure lit.

A spark.

A match.

A whimper fell from my mouth. "Rhys."

"I know, baby. I know."

It was affection.

Devotion.

The impact of it profound. Banging against the walls.

True and real, even if he didn't have the capacity to acknowledge it.

Pulling back an inch, he started to ride my dress up over my hips, the man slowly standing as he went.

The fabric lifted over my abdomen.

My breasts.

Until he was towering over me when he peeled it over my head.

Cool air caressed my heated flesh.

I lost a breath.

Standing there bare and vulnerable in front of him.

Cut open.

Willingly.

Wholly.

With trembling hands, I started to work through the buttons of his flannel, my lungs squeezing when I finally got the last freed and pushed the shirt over his wide shoulders.

He shrugged the rest of the way out of it, the man standing there in nothing but his jeans with his gorgeous chest heaving.

Every inch of him miraculous.

Covered in ink.

Like he wanted to cover everything written underneath.

I traced them with my fingertips, and the man shuddered, his stomach flexing and bowing with need.

"Wish I could give you everything," he rumbled.

I pressed a kiss over his battering heart. "Just give me this."

I crawled backward up onto his bed.

Naked.

Exposed.

Shivers ran rampant.

Need blistered.

Thrilling around us.

Like vapor that bound.

Rhys watched me carefully. All the playful mischief he wore in front of others gone.

"You just say." It was a grunt, and I was inhaling, trying to see through the desire that ricocheted against the walls when he ticked the button of his jeans, unzipped his fly, and pushed them down his thighs.

I nearly passed out when I saw the magnitude of him.

My chest squeezed and butterflies flew and oh my god...

"Baby."

My heels pressed to the bed. "Please."

He shrugged the rest of the way out of his jeans, and then he was gone for a beat, his round, firm ass bending over when he dug a condom from a drawer. Then he was on his knees on the bed, climbing up to hover over me, breathing my breaths as he prepared to take the last bit of me.

And I knew it was right.

That I already belonged to him in every other way. Even if I couldn't keep him, this moment had been written somewhere in the stars. Destined.

I knew it completely when he covered himself and then wound himself between my legs that wouldn't stop shaking.

When he brought us nose to nose.

When he whispered my name when he splayed his big hand over the mark above my breast.

Like he could hold it.

Heal it.

I wrapped both arms around his neck, and I let our mouths barely brush when I whispered, "I'll hold yours, too."

Pain lanced through his rugged face, and he brushed back a lock of hair stuck to my jaw, and he smiled a wistful smile. "You already are."

He held me close.

Chest to chest.

Breath to breath.

I shook.

And I wanted to tell him that he didn't have to be careful with me. But the man could already see all my broken parts the same way as I could see his.

So he held them.

Gently.

Watched down over me with his arms wrapped tight around my shoulders as he slowly nudged himself into my body.

Old fear fluttered for the barest beat.

Fear he washed away with those kind, knowing eyes.

As he made me feel cherished and safe.

As he filled me and filled me until there was no air, and I was only breathing him. Until he was grunting low and every muscle in his magnificent body tensed with restraint.

Until I whispered my praise. "Rhys."

Emotion swarmed us.

A hazy, glorious dream.

And he smiled. Smiled softly. "Yeah?"

"So much yes."

I clawed my nails into his shoulders when he started to move because god, everything about him was big and overwhelming.

His hips started to rock and jut. Tiny movements at first, the man keeping watch on all the pieces he was holding in fear one might get loose.

But the truth was, I'd never felt as whole as I did right then.

So right with his massive body covering mine, as he filled me again and again, as our bodies picked up a perfect rhythm.

His breaths turned shallow and he worked me into a needy, whimpering puddle of greed.

Pinpricks of pleasure licked across my flesh.

I was sure I was going to catch fire.

The way my belly tightened and everything throbbed. As I raced for that beautiful destination, Rhys leading the way.

Setting both hands on either side of my head, he pushed his weight onto them.

So glorious where he gazed down on me.

The longer pieces of his hair fell around his striking, powerful face. Sweat beaded at his temples, and his tongue raked over his lips as he grunted, "Goddess Girl. Fuck. So good."

My head rocked back on his pillow, and my hips met his thrust for thrust. "More. Please. I need you."

"I know, baby. I've got you. I've got you."

Everything grew frantic.

Faster.

Needier.

Grittier.

The intensity we shared burning us up.

Eating us alive.

He dropped to his elbows and angled a different way. "Sweet Siren. Shit."

He hit me in a spot that made me gasp and writhe and beg him for more. "Rhys...you...need you."

And he gave it.

Took me harder and deeper because he knew those pieces were safe with him. And he was spreading me by the knees and driving me into oblivion.

To where it was only music and song.

Stars and the deepest night.

Rhys and me.

Rhys and me.

And there, with him, I splintered apart. Pleasure burst. Erupted. Laid every inch of me to waste. Gasping, my hips came from the bed, desperate to get closer to him.

To get lost in this perfection forever. To meet him there.

And I was suddenly gathered back up, my back barely touching the bed, the man taking me with him as he rocked and thrust.

"Maggie." He choked and lifted me by the waist. "Fuck, Maggie."

And then he was with me.

That ecstasy offered to me as he surrendered to it. Every

muscle in his body tensed and pulsed as he came.

We floated together.

In a place we needed no words to understand. Where it was real and right and there were no lies or secrets or pasts standing between us.

Where it was us.

We stayed there forever. For not nearly long enough.

Before we slowly drifted down.

Still, he held me, his mouth at my temple. "Maggie. Sweet Thing. Tell me you're okay. That I didn't hurt you."

Dread filled his voice.

His regret trying to stage an assault.

I hugged him fiercely. "I've never felt safer, more beautiful, freer, than I do right now."

Relief left him on a breath, and he curled his arms tighter and nodded against my head.

Clinging to me the same way I clung to him.

After a long time, our holds loosened, and he let my weight fall back to the mattress. Though he didn't go far. He propped himself up on his elbows, the man still pinning me to the bed.

He brushed back my hair as our breaths evened.

That same energy lapped, but it'd been lulled into a quieted peace.

Then Rhys grinned. This sweet, wicked smirk that made me weak all over again. "Must've died and went to heaven. Goddess Girl." He traced his finger along the angle of my chin.

My teeth raked my bottom lip, like maybe it stood a chance of holding back the affection that bled free.

Impossible.

"I thought I told you to stop calling me that or else I might get the idea that I have a chance with you?"

Sadness drifted through his smile. "Clearly it's me who doesn't stand a chance."

twenty-two

Rhys

I stared down at the girl who gazed up at me. Two of us locked.

A tangle of limbs and erratically beatin' hearts.

It was certified.

A little checkmark next to my name.

I had officially lost it.

Gone so reckless that I could feel the devastation simmerin' at the edges of my sight. Collecting at the farthest edge of the ocean. Coming like a tsunami. Gathering strength as it rushed forward with the full intention to annihilate.

Just loved to play with fire, didn't I?

But I wasn't sure I could stomp out these flames if I tried.

No way to turn from the one who made it feel like something bigger might be possible.

A way out.

An escape.

Like she might see all I was responsible for and still find something worthy to keep around, anyway.

Swore to God, there was a sanctuary in those charcoal eyes.

Understanding and goodness and all the things I knew better than hopin' for.

This girl who'd swooped in without warnin' and ensnared me.

Her kiss motherfuckin' bliss.

Don't fall. Don't fall. Don't fall.

Was chanting it. Searching for a way to resurrect a wall. Maybe put up a steel barrier or two. Somethin' to keep me from heading in the direction of a place I couldn't go.

I edged off her so I could ditch the condom in the wastebasket next to my bed, hoping it might put a little space between us when I did.

Only thing it achieved was me rushing back for her. Needing her warmth. Though this time when I wrapped her in my arms, I shifted us a fraction so we were lying on our sides.

Just…looking at each other through the languid darkness. Memorizing a moment that meant more than it should.

With a trembling hand, Maggie reached out and ran her fingers through my beard.

Softly.

Reverently.

Adoration I didn't know how to stand beneath rolled off her in waves.

"You keep doin' that." My smile was slow. Voice soft.

She almost giggled. "What's that?"

"Pettin' me." I let the tease wind with the murmured words.

Maggie grinned. "Well, you are a stallion. What do you expect me to do?"

My chest squeezed. So tight. Didn't know if it was in pain or affection. I fiddled with a lock of her hair. "You regrettin' taking that ride, yet?"

I went for light.

Playful.

Didn't come close to pulling it off considerin' I choked over the words.

Fact that earlier I'd been faced with the truth that I had to ignore this. Turn my back on this connection. It wasn't safe. That bastard would do whatever he could to ruin me. Destroy everyone around me if they got too close just for the sake of causing me pain.

And all it'd taken was her care for us to end up here.

Her fingers scratched deeper into my beard before she caressed them along my lips. "I could never regret a second spent with you."

Shame clawed through me and closed off my throat. "Wish I could be worthy of that statement."

"And I wish you saw yourself the way that I do."

Grief flashed, old wounds ripping wide open.

Screams.

Shouts.

Blood.

Loss.

I couldn't stop it. I couldn't stop it.

Didn't have time to brace myself against them. To keep it from flashing across my face. But I should have known better, anyway, known she could feel each of them like she was experiencing them herself.

"Rhys. My wild boy with the biggest, most beautiful heart." She set her hand over the hammering it was currently doing against my ribs.

"It's all fucked up, Maggie." I murmured the confession. Praying she'd get it. "Not mine to give."

And the problem was, it was reaching for her, anyway. Communin', the way she'd said. Like this was where I belonged.

Guilt invaded.

The promise I had made that I didn't have a single fuckin' clue how to keep.

"You're thinking about her? The one you fell in love with?" There was no judgement there. No hurt except for the hurt she was feelin' for me.

God.

This woman.

So genuine.

So real.

So fuckin' right.

I took the fingers she kept running over my face and twisted them with mine. "Yeah."

Wistfulness danced around that mouth. "What was she like?"

My lips tweaked with the sadness. "Sweet. Kinda like someone else I know."

I went to brushing back a lock of her hair, needing to do something with my hands before I had them running over her body again. Fingers itching to get lost in all that bare, gorgeous flesh.

Then Maggie had to go and press even closer.

Right there, ready to hold my words.

Maybe I shouldn't have been bein' so upfront and honest. Just…laying it out like this. Another girl would slap me across the face. Rightly so. But I didn't know how to be any other way with Maggie. Not with this girl who got me in a way that no one else could or ever had.

Even her.

Genny.

All blonde hair and shy smiles.

"She was young. So young. Barely eighteen." I blinked through the memory. "It was years ago. Carolina George was just makin' a name for itself. We were in this spec of a town in Tennessee, the bar nothing but a dive, but the crowd ate us up like we were the best thing they'd ever experienced. We were all soarin' that night. Might have been the first time we all knew we were on to something. Like we could feel the promise of success trembling around us. And there she was, out in the crowd, off to the side, hovering in the fringes. Nothin' but nerves. Wide eyed. Like she hadn't even known a place like that existed."

Truth be told, she hadn't really. She'd snuck out with her best friend since she hadn't been allowed to leave the house unsupervised. Her family so fuckin' twisted.

Not allowed to make her own decisions.

Kept under lock and key.

And I'd been ignorant enough to think for a second that I'd been purposed to be there with her that night. That it hadn't been an accidental encounter.

That maybe I could make a difference.

"So of course, I'd gone for her. Always after what I shouldn't want." I shifted our twined hands and ran my knuckles up the angle of Maggie's jaw.

"It's hardly a crime to love someone, Rhys."

"But sometimes you commit one crime, and it trickles down through your entire life, destroying everything you touch."

So you spent your life dabblin' in the insignificant. Never dippin' your fingers deep enough to make an impact. Making sure you never connected on a level that mattered.

Shiny on the surface, your life appearing nothing but fun and games.

Easy smiles and passing, forgettable faces.

Then someone slammed you from out of nowhere.

Unanticipated.

Their very existence threatening that precarious balance.

"And I'm terrified of doin' the same to you."

Those eyes traced me in the night. Sketchin' a picture. Like she somehow found beauty in my ugliness.

"What happened to her?"

"I set out to rescue her from her chains, and instead, I dragged her straight into mine."

A frown pinched between Maggie's eyes, and I knew more questions were coming, questions I couldn't face or answer, so I scooped her into my hold and climbed to my feet.

She looped those sweet arms around my neck. "Where are we going?"

"Shower."

Had the sudden urge to clean myself off this girl before it seeped in and I poisoned her more.

I carried her into the bathroom and turned on the shower. I held her against me while the water heated and steam filled the room.

Vapors.

Mist.

A hazy dream that I wanted to step into and never reemerge from.

When I was sure the water was warm enough, I eased us into the massive shower. "Good?"

"Perfect."

Carefully, I set her on her feet, though I kept a hand on her. Truth was, it didn't matter how much I'd fucked up, taking her when I shouldn't have, I didn't know how to let go.

I nudged her chin back so I could wet the long length of her hair.

Maggie sighed, watched me with those eyes.

I squirted a gob of shampoo into my hand, that shampoo that smelled exactly like her and almost sucked me straight into a trance.

I shifted her around so I could massage it into those locks.

Girl bare and so damned beautiful.

My teeth clenched.

Fuck.

"What?" she whispered, sensing my hesitation.

"Your ass is spectacular."

She giggled a slight sound, rocking said ass into my dick that'd gone hard as stone.

A tease.

A treat.

My fingers tangled up in her hair, massaging the locks, her scalp, her neck.

She moaned and leaned into my touch.

I rinsed her hair, then I grabbed her sponge and lathered it up so I could wash her back.

She leaned against me.

Her hair in my face.

Jasmine and vanilla.

Sweet, sweet, sweet.

"Maggie." Might have been a problem that I literally groaned her name. Bigger problem when I burrowed my nose in her hair and inhaled. Then I got really greedy with pressin' my lips to her shoulder. I ran them across the delicate, delicious length. Wanted to devour every inch.

She angled farther, twisting her head to look back at me.

That was all it took, and we collided.

Because fuck, now that I'd kissed her, I didn't know how to stop.

My left hand fisted up in the wet mass of her hair, while the other wrapped around to take her by the chin so I could control the kiss.

This one fierce.

Scorching.

Red hot.

Any trepidation the girl'd felt before obliterated in my touch.

I didn't know how I was supposed to make it through this without losing my cool. Without crossing another line there would be no returning from.

Before I fuckin' slipped and fell right over the side.

Because she was my perfection.

Knew it.

Wanted to run from it almost as much as I wanted to hold it and cherish it.

Like I felt the fullness of all I was supposed to be starin' back at me.

This connection I couldn't quite make sense of. That didn't matter in the least because she still held me in the palm of her gentle, lust-inducing hand.

She was a spark in my spirit that I needed to stamp out before it set fire to my entire world.

Could feel myself getting burned, anyway.

Incinerated.

Done for.

She shifted around, and the girl was kissing me like it was the only way she could breathe.

"I'll hold you, too," she promised into the kiss that she dragged over my beard and down my chest.

Her whisper moving to my heart.

Her tongue licked out.

Stroked my flesh.

"Sweet Siren."

That's what she was.

A song in the storm.

Lulling me into peace when it was gonna be my demise.

Wanted to find her in it, anyway.

Need stampeded through my body when she kept kissing over my pecs and back up my throat.

"Maggie," I growled out.

"I'm not afraid," she murmured again. Girl giving no heed to a single one of my warnings.

Her fingers dug into my shoulders, and I was hoisting her into my arms at the same second she was wrapping those legs around my waist.

Instinct.

Two of us moving on intuition. Like there was something instilled in us that predestined exactly where we were gonna go.

From zero to one hundred in a second flat.

"Shit," I hissed.

I was just beggin' for the pain, wasn't I? Running straight for it.

But with her, I wasn't sure there was any turning back.

"Rhys," she rasped, rubbing her bare pussy against my cock.

"Want me again, Sweet Thing?" My voice grew rough.

Gritty and raw as I pressed her against the shower wall and rocked against her like a fiend.

Water rained over us.

Steam coating the air.

Girl ruining me.

Second by second.

"I've wanted you since the second I saw you."

A grunt escaped my throat, and she was suddenly stroking me between us, her hot little hand pumping my cock.

Holy shit.

Energy flashed. A flicker of light that burst in the air.

"Lookin' for trouble." Didn't know which of us I was talking to.

"No, Rhys, I was looking for you."

My mouth dove for peace. For this feeling that there might be something better. Bigger.

I kissed her in a way I was pretty sure I'd never kissed anyone before as she kept stroking me.

Passion burned on our lips and our bodies writhed in the fire.

An imprint.

A score.

A scar.

I didn't know.

Only thing I knew was we both wanted to be marked. Tattooed in this moment as she fisted me, shifted me so my engorged, aching head was running through her pussy, as I gathered her up closer and let my mouth worship this girl.

Lips and tongues and teeth.

Like any caution we'd had, had been tossed into the sea.

Our tongues were chaos.

Every touch insanity.

When I couldn't take it a second longer, I drove home.

Filling her full.

Maggie gasped, her back arching from the wall, her small breasts that were sexy as all fuck pressing into my chest.

Taking her by the outside of the thighs, I began to rock.

Hard and rigid and fast.

Maggie just urged me faster.

Like the girl had made the choice to take a dive into the disorder.

Like she craved it.

Her hands in my hair and her kiss trashing any reservation.

I let my mouth wander. Over her jaw and down her neck. Maggie lifted her chin to grant me access, and she held me by the back of the head as I let my tongue slip-slide along the delicate slope of her throat. I took a quick path south until I had the rosy, hardened tip of her nipple in my mouth. I nibbled it with my teeth.

"Rhys," she whimpered. "Oh, God."

"Am I hurtin' you?"

"No. I want you. All of you. In any way. In every way. If you only knew the fantasies I've had about you. All the ways I imagined you taking me."

She said it while she used my hair for leverage, rocking that tight body over my dick, riding me hard.

"Baby."

I used the word like a caution sign because she sure as shit shouldn't be talking to me like that.

All she said was, "Please."

I shifted her so I was holding her with one arm around the waist, the other twisting between us so I could rub her throbbing clit.

Girl writhing. Begging.

So gorgeous.

Need screamed across her shimmery flesh.

This girl who the only thing I wanted was for her to spread her wings and fly.

"Look at you, Goddess Girl. Don't know how it's possible. Touchin' you like this. Feel so good. You have any idea? Best fuckin' thing I've ever felt."

"I'd never dared to hope that someone could make me feel like this." It was more praise falling from her tongue. "Don't stop. Never stop."

Pleasure raced my spine.

Prickles and sparks.

Coming in waves.

I rolled my thumb over her clit while my hips thrust erratically.

Girl met me stroke for stroke.

Driving me to a bliss I'd never known.

"You feel it?"

Frantically, she nodded her head, girl bouncing all over me like the best kind of wet dream. "I feel you."

"Let go, Sweet Thing."

I gave in, too. Taking her hard and deep.

Nails scratched into my shoulders.

"Yes. Rhys."

Her words were choppy, and I could feel every molecule in her wind tight.

Pleas dropping as whispers from her lips. Growing thicker. Needier. Deeper.

Swore, I could see it gather in the space.

Way the mist swirled and glowed.

Something brilliant.

Something blinding.

Something I didn't deserve but couldn't stop from taking, anyway.

Felt it the second she split.

When her walls clutched my dick.

When her head rocked back against the shower wall and she moaned so deep.

And I held her there as she flew. While she mumbled incoherently.

While my hips jerked and snapped and this girl dragged me with her.

I pulled out a second before I lost it, scrambling to set her on her feet while I went to rubbing myself all over her belly like a desperate, needy fuck.

I came all over her stomach.

Thought for a minute she would be horrified, but I should've known this girl would take it as something cherished, too.

Way she was still rocking, her hands on my ass, pulling me closer as she shot me to the stars.

Took me to a place where nothin' made sense because we were the only thing there.

Together and real and whole, and fuck, it was probably the single most dangerous thought I'd ever had.

I gasped as I shook, my body trembling, hers matching mine with the aftershocks.

That energy buzzed.

Like now that it'd had a taste, it would never be sated. Instead, that shit had only grown.

Force coming fuller.

Hungry for more.

I dropped my forehead against hers.

And shit.

I grinned as I sucked for a breath, and Maggie was grinning back.

"Sorry. Didn't bring you in here for that."

Turning around, she grabbed the sponge I'd had and squirted more soap on it. She shot me a playful, tempting glance over her shoulder. "You sure about that, Cowboy?"

I growled. Laughter in my throat. I pressed myself against her bottom.

Shit.

Wrong move.

She nudged back.

"My intention had been to take care of you."

She turned around, smiling slow. "Believe me, you did."

Emotion crested, and I tipped up her chin. "Maggie." Was a whisper from the vacancy that howled from the depths of me.

Like my spirit recognized that she was the only one who could fill it.

Then she was lathering me up, running that sponge over my body, those eyes tracing every inch as she went.

Tenderness and care. Shit, how could something feel so good and hurt like a bitch at the same damned time?

I returned the favor, washing her, rinsing her, adoring her.

This goddess who had me on my knees.

Turning off the shower, I grabbed one of the huge plush towels and wrapped it around her body, tucking it up close to her chin.

"Thank you," she said.

I tapped her nose.

Playfully.

"Darlin', clearly it's me who's reapin' all the benefits."

I repeated what I'd told her that first night because even getting a minute with her felt like the greatest gift.

A reprieve.

Gettin' lost in the sanctuary of those eyes.

I grabbed a towel for myself, and Maggie moved over to her vanity while I moved for mine, two of us brushing our teeth, taking peeks at each other through the mirrors.

My smile felt impossible.

So big.

So wide.

While hers had grown sweet and shy and ripe with the questions I didn't have the answers for.

What does this mean?

Where do we go from here?

Then she ducked into her bedroom, while I stalled, waited. Finally, I moved to her door and nudged it open an inch when I couldn't sit still for a second longer.

She was sitting in the middle of her bed, wearing a tank and some of those ridiculously short sleep bottoms that made my mouth water all over again.

I leaned against the jamb. "Now what exactly do you think you're doin', Sweet Thing?"

A frown pulled across her brow, the words leaving her like playful confusion. "Getting into bed?"

"That so?"

Her teeth raked her bottom lip, and she gave a quick nod. "Yeah."

Then I was smirking, stalking her way, and the girl was shrieking when I swung her up and tossed her over my shoulder.

Joy.

Felt the fullness of it pulse through the air.

I struggled to breathe around it, to tamp the fear it elicited, and just be fucking happy that I got this.

Even if it were only for a minute.

Even when I knew full well I couldn't keep her.

When that dark place kept screaming at me to be careful or I was gonna fall.

"What are you doing, Rhys?" she whisper-hissed, holding back the giggles that were floodin' from her mouth.

"Uh…takin' you to my bed. Where you belong." I squeezed one of her butt cheeks in my hand.

She gasped. "Rhys."

A low chuckle rumbled out, and I carried her back through the bathroom and into my room and I tossed her into the middle of my bed.

She bounced on it.

Laughed.

Her sweet heart overflowed the space.

She smiled up at me.

Softly this time, while I stood at the side gazing down at the beauty of who she was.

"Play me your song," she whispered.

And I doubted there was anything I wouldn't do for her, so I sank down onto the floor and rested my back on the bed, grabbed my guitar where it was propped beside it, and cradled it on my lap.

I strummed the chords.

Let the melody wind into the space. It was supposed to be an upbeat song, but it came like a whisper into the night.

Mesmerizing.

Dragging both of us into a trance.

I could feel her shift, sit up on the bed behind me, this girl who held me in the palm of her delicate, caring hand.

I let my voice unfurl with the truth of who we were.

Didn't know what was comin'
Didn't know where I was goin'
Fallin' faster
Comin' slower
Lookin' for a lover
To get lost under covers
In my whispers
In my ear
Wishing on a star
Hoping on a heart
And then you were there
You caught me in a dream

I think I heard you in my sleep
I think I found you in my dreams
I think I felt you in the daylight
Give me one minute, sweetheart

And I'll ruin everything

Thought I was a stranger
A man without shelter
A wanderer
Until I heard you whisper
And I knew that I was home

I think I heard you in my sleep
I think I found you in my dreams
I think I felt you in the daylight
Give me one minute, sweetheart
And I'll ruin everything

My fingers stilled on the frets.
How did I keep from ruinin' everything?
Maggie was there, hovering above me, those hands taking me by the outside of the head. I followed her lead and rolled my head back on the edge of the mattress.

The girl stared down at me.

Watching me with charcoal eyes.

She leaned in and pressed the softest kiss to my forehead.

But where she was really touching me was in the empty spot that would forever groan in the middle of my soul.

Rhys
Ten Years Old

*R*hys pushed his key into the lock and twisted the knob, so slow and quiet as he edged open the door. He poked his head inside.

"Daddy?" he called, though his voice was hushed.

Fear clamored up and down his throat. It filled his whole body when he swallowed.

His heart beat hard. So hard it hurt his ears and made his stomach twist in knots.

Same way as it always did when he came home.

When he opened the door to the house that was too quiet.

His mama was at work, down at the diner.

They'd fought about that, too.

Her gettin' a job. His daddy so mad but his mama saying it was what she had to do to pay the bills.

She'd said she'd do anything to make it work.

That she'd fight for their family.

Love, love, love.

She'd said it again and again.

But Rhys knew it was his job to fight for them. He was supposed to be the one takin' care of them, the way he'd promised. Especially when it was his fault to begin with.

Sticky silence echoed from the house, the sun blazing in through the windows but the air so thick it might as well have been pitch black.

He softly clicked the door shut behind him and let his backpack slip off his shoulder and onto the floor.

Rhys went straight into the kitchen and to the refrigerator, already knowing his job. What his daddy would want. It was the only thing Rhys could do.

He grabbed the four beers left on a six-pack, and then he tiptoed down the hall, pressing his ear to his daddy's door that was open an inch.

The sound of the television droned, so low you could barely tell what was bein' said, everything else just as thick and sticky as the rest of the house.

Rhys gave a little push to the door. It drifted farther, yawning open to the room.

His daddy sat in the chair where he always sat. The one that looked out over the backyard at the fields that went on forever behind their house. Where he stared blankly for hours and hours.

All his daddy's stuff was on a messy table beside him, pill bottles that were tipped over, some empty, some full.

A bunch of empty beer cans littered the space.

Today his daddy had one of the tall clear bottles, too, and half the alcohol inside was already gone.

"Daddy?" His voice trembled.

His dad barely moved.

Carefully, Rhys inched into the room, carrying the beers like an offering. He slowed even farther as he rounded the bed and moved into his daddy's space, his eyes squeezing shut when he pushed the beers onto the table.

"There you go, Daddy. Anything else I can do?"

"Leave."

Rhys' ugly heart got twisted up in the knots in his stomach. He nodded quickly, started to leave, before he stopped by the bed. "I'm sorry, Daddy."

His daddy flinched. "Just go, Rhys. Don't like you seein' me like this."

Rhys slinked back out, nearly tripping when his daddy's voice hit him when he got to the door. "You're a good boy, Rhys. A good, good boy."

Rhys couldn't answer. He just dropped his head and slunk out the door. His feet feeling like they weighed five million pounds. Because he wasn't close to being good or strong. He was supposed to take care of his daddy. Make it better. But he didn't know how.

Rhys' mama kept brushing the hair back from his face where she was on her knees next to his bed. "Don't cry, my sweet boy."

"I wasn't strong enough, Mama."

"You're so strong. So strong. Look at you, so brave every day, bein' the man of the house."

Her smile tipped at the edge of her mouth, and Rhys knew she was tryin' not to cry.

"Daddy's so mad at me."

Her head shook, and she kept running her hands through his hair. "He's just sad, Rhys. Real, real sad. We just have to keep loving him hard and strong until he's able to smile again."

Rhys nodded, and he swiped the tears staining his face with the back of his hands. "Okay. I'll love him hard and strong and forever. Take care of him and you. I promise."

His mama squeezed his knee. "That's your daddy's little stallion. So strong and brave."

Her lips trembled, same way as Rhys' heart.

And he remembered what his daddy said. That some people

were made extra special and needed extra care. For people to stand up for them.

He knew that was his daddy now.

"Now, you get some sleep. You've got school in the mornin'."

"Yes, ma'am."

He crawled under his covers, and he smiled up at his mama who smiled down at him.

His mama kissed his temple then moved out of his room, clicking off the light and casting his room in shadows.

He tossed in the heaviness of them. Like he no longer fit in his bed. Like the air was wrong.

From the weight in his chest? He guessed he should have known his daddy was never gonna smile again.

twenty-four

Maggie

Blinking into the dull morning light, my chest cracked wide open when I saw the blue eyes gazing back at me.

No defense, considering every guard I'd ever possessed had been obliterated last night. Laid at his feet.

"Hi." His grumbly, raw voice welcomed me from the best sleep I'd ever had.

My teeth clamped down on my bottom lip. "Hi," I whispered.

My insides shivered.

I'd slept with Rhys.

Twice.

Redness raced. Streaking my skin. It wasn't in shyness. It had everything to do with the way he was watching me from where he lay on his side about two feet away.

I got the sense that maybe he'd been doing it for a while.

Looking at me like he had woken to find a treasure he hadn't expected in his bed.

Except I felt like the one who'd stumbled upon something spectacular.

Untouchable because he was so damn extraordinary.

His chest and shoulders bare.

His hair a mess.

Those blue, blue eyes so soft.

But it was that mouth wearing that smile that nearly did me in.

A smirk ticked up at the corner of it. "How'd you sleep?"

I moaned a little moan and snuggled deeper into the plush pillow. "Like a dream."

His smirk widened. "Huh. Wonder why that could be?"

Joy crawled over me, filling my chest.

A lightness fell over us this morning that had never been there before.

"Hmm. I don't know," I mused playfully under my breath. "It might have something to do with this really hot guy who blew my mind last night."

He quirked a teasing brow. "Hot guy, huh?"

"Really hot guy." I laid it on thick, not even fighting the well of giddiness that bubbled inside.

"And who might this really hot guy be?"

"Oh…no one you'd know."

"Don't know him? Weird. I could have sworn it was my name you were screaming last night."

"Oh, that's right. I guess I was just blinded by the hotness and I forgot it was actually you."

I squealed when Rhys suddenly reached out and grabbed me, rolling us until I was on top of him.

Without giving me a chance to orient to the new blissful sensation, he started tickling my sides.

My squeals turned to shrieking laughter, and there was no keeping quiet.

That well erupted.

Overflowed.

Happiness and hope.

"Forget me? Oh darlin', you're in trouble. Tell me you don't just want me for this body." He kept tickling me, and I was squirming all over, laughing and whining and trying to get away and not wanting to go anywhere. "I mean, I know I'm somethin' to look at, but that's just outright mean."

Except he wasn't upset at all.

Delight radiated from him. From his expression and those eyes and his beautiful spirit that consumed the space in the most magnificent way.

"I don't know. It's awfully distracting."

He tickled me harder.

I squealed loudly.

And then we were both slowing, and I was gazing down at him and he was threading his fingers into my hair.

Gently.

Tenderly.

This good, good man.

"Last night was amazing, Rhys. The best night of my life. And I'm *never* going to forget it."

His thumb traced my chin. "And I'm the luckiest bastard alive that I got to share it with you."

"I think I'm pretty lucky, too."

I didn't wait for his face to blanch. For his self-reproach to take over.

I dropped a kiss to his mouth.

A little peck.

Still, he moaned, and the man was hard, and my stomach got all twisty and achy with need again.

I groaned in frustration. "I need to get up. Practice starts in thirty minutes, and Emily's going to be wondering where I am."

Rhys bucked up. "I can think of better ways to spend the day."

Those hands splayed across my back before he spread them across my bottom, holding me tight.

This time I whimpered. "Rhys."

He chuckled. "Get out of here before I keep you tied to my bed all day."

Oh, I would be one happy prisoner.

Safe and freed.

I rolled off him and started to climb from the bed.

Rhys caught me by the back of the neck, and he brought me down for a searing kiss.

Deep and long and so thorough I felt it to the tips of my toes.

To think I was begging him for my first kiss yesterday and now we'd *done this*.

Had somehow ended up in this moment.

And I had no idea where it would lead, but I was going to relish in being here.

With him.

I fell into that kiss.

My hands on his face.

My heart in his hands.

I whispered against his mouth, "I'll be thinking about you."

He pulled back. Blue eyes danced. "Believe me, Sweet Thing, I'll be thinking about you."

My teeth clamped my bottom lip as I smiled, like it might hold the avalanche of feeling inside.

This thing that bound us.

Beckoned us.

This bright, glowing beacon that gleamed and glittered. Begging for our surrender.

There was no doubt in my mind acknowledging it would send this broken boy running, so I did my best to keep it contained, and I turned from him, shuffling on bare feet across the floor and pausing to give him a small wave at the door.

He was leaned up on an elbow, that hulking body so gorgeous beneath the rays of morning light.

My stomach lodged itself in my throat.

"Have a great day, Sweet Thing."

"Hope yours is even better, my stallion."

His smile turned wistful, and I held onto the flash of his pain. Promised to hold it tight. Carry it until it didn't weigh so much.

Then I ducked out, trying to clear the spinning in my head because oh my god…

I'd had sex.

And it was beautiful and perfect and more than I ever could have hoped.

That giddiness leapt, and I pressed both hands to my face and squealed my excitement into my palms, and then I caught my reflection in my vanity mirror as I was passing through for my room.

My cheeks pink and my eyes wide.

Every inch of me aglow.

I was pretty sure the grin I was wearing was going to be permanently carved there.

That was until I stumbled when I moved into my room, a gasp raking up my throat and punching the air. I clung to the bathroom door handle for support and tried not to let the panic get away from me.

I forced a light smile back to my face. "Oh, goodness, Emily, you scared me."

She sat on the end of my bed with Amelia sleeping in her arms.

I waved a flustered hand behind me. "I was just in the bathroom."

A frown formed between her eyes. "Maggie…that bathroom has been empty for the last thirty minutes that I've been sittin' here."

"Oh…I…" I scrambled for an explanation, rubbing my hand on the back of my neck as I looked into the bathroom, my heart running just about as fast as Rhys drove his flashy car.

"I…"

I looked back at her, and the smile that took to her face was almost sad.

Worried and knowing and full of care. Everything that was my sister-in-law. "I heard you. With him."

Horror took to my face, and she rushed to clarify, "No. Not that." For a second, she looked horrified, too. Then she tilted her head to the side and widened her eyes, like the gesture would convey a secret. "But you clearly were wakin' up next to him."

I blew out a sigh, contemplated, glancing behind me once more before I snapped the door shut and edged into my room. I got down onto the floor in front of her, sitting crisscrossed with my hands clasped in my lap.

Amelia squirmed as she woke, and Emily shushed and bounced her, holding her close. "So...did you and he...?" she asked cautiously.

I nodded. "Yeah. We did."

My whole being quivered with the thrill.

We did.

She almost shook her head, though there was affection riding out with her words. "That cowboy. Swear I knew it, the way he's been lookin' at you."

"I guess I've been looking at him the same way."

Nervously, Emily roughed her teeth over her bottom lip, looking at me with all that care. "I think it's safe to say you have." She paused, watching me with those intense green eyes. The love she held for me washed over me in waves. "How long?"

Air huffed from my nose. "Just last night. But I think...I think it's been coming for a long time."

Probably since the moment I met him.

Emily climbed down onto the floor to bring us eye-to-eye. Without a doubt, this wonderful woman was compelled to share my secret. With my sweet niece tucked to her chest, she exhaled, both worried and supportive. Making a clear statement that she was there for me, no matter what. "Wow...so last night was the first time? That's...how do you feel?" she settled on, watching me for any sign that I might fall apart.

"Do you really want to know?"

She quirked an annoyed big-sister brow, somehow both nosy and filled with compassion. "Obviously. And don't you dare lie to me."

Hugging my knees to my chest, I rocked back, feeling the heat rush to my cheeks. Still, the truth was tumbling from my tongue, "Amazing."

There was no hesitation. In fact, my voice had gone dreamy.

I couldn't help it.

Her expression turned soft. "So that's how it is."

Affection quivered on my chin, and I fiddled with a string that was coming loose on my shirt, not quite sure what to do with myself. "Yeah. It's like that. At least for me."

Except that felt like a lie.

I knew there was something there when Rhys looked at me. Knew it for sure when he touched me. It was big and beautiful for him, too. But where I wanted to run straight toward it, he wanted to run from it.

A tender smile pulled at the edge of her mouth, and she glanced at the closed door. "I've seen him with women after a lot of shows—"

I cringed.

Sympathy lined her features, and she probably wanted to take back what she'd said, but instead, she waited, like she was giving me time. She laid Amelia on her blanket on the floor between us while I wrestled with the picture of the man I knew and the one that belonged to the rest of the world.

Emily and I scooted up to the edges of the blanket, and I slipped my finger into Amelia's tiny hand. She cooed and kicked and made my spirit bubble over with love.

I sat staring down at her, adoring her while I dealt with how thinking about Rhys with those women made me feel. This crushing feeling that I wasn't sure where it came from.

Emily's voice grew quiet, "And I've also seen him with you, Maggie, and I'm pretty sure *it's like that* for him, too. That he's feeling the same thing you are."

"I'm not jealous…I'm just…" I toyed with how to answer, knowing I didn't quite have the words.

She reached out and touched my knee. "You want more."

More.

I wanted more joy.

More hope.

More peace.

And I wanted us to find it together.

I swallowed around the lump in my throat. "So much more. Does that make me foolish?"

Just a naïve girl who'd fallen for her first, magical kiss?

Emily released a soft puff of laughter. "No, Maggie. It makes you a believer. A believer in something inside of someone else

267

when no one else might see it."

"Or maybe I'm just infatuated. Have you seen the man?" I attempted a joke because seriously, Rhys Manning was gorgeous. But I saw how beautiful he was underneath that skin, too.

"Is it? Infatuation?" she goaded through the tease. "Nothin' but an obsession over all that ridiculous muscle and that obscenely handsome face?"

"No," I whispered.

"Then what is it?" she pressed.

And I knew she already knew, you know, considering I was pretty sure my chest was actually screaming it.

Still, I uttered it like a secret. "It's love."

Her nod was slow. "I've been seein' it in your eyes every time the two of you get in the same room. I was wonderin' when one of you were gonna recognize it."

She inhaled deeply and slowly blew it out. "But that man…he's complicated." There was the warning.

I nodded. "I know. He has walls built so high, I'm not sure how he's even let me peek over the top of them."

Stalling, she glanced over my shoulder before she looked back at me with sorrow coating her being. "Has he told you about his daddy?"

That lump grew into a knot. Thickened and tightened and constricted airflow. "No. I mean, he told me that he's gone, and he's implied some stuff, but he hasn't given me any details."

I only knew whatever it was, it was dark.

Ugly and harmful and oppressive.

That it was what dimmed those blue eyes into misery.

Emily swallowed over her own emotion. "I won't tell you what happened, Maggie, and I know you wouldn't want me to. That's between you and him. But he lost two of the people he loved most in one devastatin' moment…and I'm not sure he knows how to come back from that."

"I have a tendency to hurt the ones I love most."

Torment blistered and blew.

His poor, beautiful, broken heart.

Emily reached over and gathered up my hand. "He's an

incredible man. One of the best. But he has demons that have been hauntin' him for a long, long time."

"And he's terrified I'm going to become another one of them."

The dip of her chin was grim. "I love him like a brother, Maggie. So much. But you are *my sister*, and I need to make sure you know what you're gettin' yourself into."

"I'm not sure I could get myself out of it even if I wanted to."

And I didn't.

God, I didn't.

Her smile was slow, and she squeezed my hand. "I know that, and I wouldn't ask you to turn your back on him. It's the ones who've been hurt the deepest who need the most care. The most love. They need someone strong and fierce to believe in them, to show them lovin' someone is worth the risk."

"He could ruin a piece of my heart, Em, but I've always known he was worth that risk." Emotion crested, and the words began to flood, "Every day of our lives is a risk, but I want to live each of them without being disabled by fear. In the best way that I can. I did it for so long, and I can't any longer. And that doesn't mean I'm not scared...it just means it's worth it."

All of it.

Rhys.

Helping those women.

Living my life to its full extent.

Heart first.

"And I know it might cause me more pain in my life, that I'm cutting myself wide open and making myself vulnerable," I continued, "but without it, I'd miss out on so much joy."

Had I hidden away from Rhys? From that connection? I would have missed out on *this*.

The corner of her mouth trembled. "And that's the only thing we want—for you to experience every joy."

I tossed her a quirk of my brow. "Even Royce?"

She giggled a little, then she went somber. "I know he drives you crazy. Heck, he's been frettin' so much over you since your fall, he's kinda drivin' me batty for you, too. But your brother...he's terrified of the *joy* slippin' away, and he thinks he has to constantly be fighting against the possibility of that."

"He's not going to be happy," I muttered.

She ran her thumb over the back of Amelia's hand, the two of us holding onto the tiny infant who was a representation of all that joy. "Maybe not at first, but that's all he wants for you, Maggie. Give him a little bit of time."

I glanced back at the closed door, captured by the sound of the water running on the other side. There was no stopping the vision of Rhys standing in front of his vanity. His rugged face in the mirror. His hulking body in those underwear.

Gulping, I forced myself to look back at Emily. "I don't want him to know. For now. At least until I give this thing a fighting chance with Rhys."

"I'd never tell him. That's gonna be a conversation the two of you are goin' to need to have. When you're ready."

Love poured out. "Thank you."

Her head tipped to the side. "For what? Gettin' to spend time like this with the sister I'd never had? Believe me, this is my *joy*, too, Maggie."

"I love you. Thank you for being here for me. For listening and understanding and not casting judgments."

She leaned over Amelia and cupped my cheek. "My only job is to listen. To be here for you, in whatever capacity you need. You can trust that. You don't have to keep things a secret from me, but I also won't force things out of you if you're not ready to share them."

I pressed her hand closer. "I do trust you."

On a slight nod, she leaned farther forward to press a kiss to my forehead. Then she leaned back with a smirk. "And you better make sure that man is takin' good care of you or else I'm gonna have somethin' to say about it."

How she could pack so much innuendo into a few words, I didn't know.

I grinned through my flush. "I think it's safe to say Rhys knows what he's doing."

She softened, and she touched my chin. "And I hope he takes care of your kind heart, too."

I didn't answer.

It wasn't needed.

She just gathered up her daughter and pushed to standing. As she bounced her, she looked down at me. "I love you."

I smiled up at her. "I love you. So much. I'll be into your room in a few."

She started out the door. "Sounds good. I mean…unless you get sidetracked." The last wafted through the room on her tinkling laughter.

I bit my lip to keep myself from shouting back, *I like the way you think.*

It was just after four in the afternoon when I was sitting in the parking lot of the small grocery store clutching my phone in my hand and staring at the text that had come through right as I'd turned off the ignition.

I sat frozen, horrified and fighting a rush of fear. That feeling I'd been trying to ignore coming at me full force.

The warning that I'd gotten myself so much deeper than I'd ever imagined I could.

Amelia was almost out of diapers, so I'd offered to run to the store since Royce had been downstairs with the band and Emily was feeding her up in their room. It was an errand that I hadn't given a second thought to at the time.

Except now, distress coated my spirit, and a sheen of sweat covered my flesh, even though cold air was blowing from the vents.

I stared at my phone with a shroud of sorrow blanketing my spirit.

This hurt that resonated inside me was expected, wasn't it? But it didn't matter how many times I'd attempted to convince myself that I'd accepted it. That it was okay. My mother's disregard, her cruelty, continued to demolish me.

I'm finished playing nice with you, Maggie Penelope. Come back home. Immediately. Before we both regret the consequences of your actions. I know you took it, and you won't get away with it. There are some things that cannot be stopped once they're set in motion. I trust you will stop being spiteful and make the right decision.

I guessed in her desperation, she'd resorted to outright threats. No longer trying to pretend she didn't know.

I swallowed down the terror that threatened to take me under.

I'd made the decision that I would no longer be paralyzed by fear.

Lifting my chin, I clung to it then. I would no longer let my insecurities hold me back. I would no longer cower in the back of a closet hidden by my clothes the way I'd done for years, frozen in terror that someone would come for me.

No.

I would stand.

I would fight.

I would give what little I could back and pray that it made a difference.

A well of emotion slammed me.

I'd been lucky that I'd had my brother to stand with me. One who'd fought for me. And I had the rest of this amazing family, not born of blood, but who'd become a part of me. People who'd come along beside me while I found my feet. While I discovered who I was and what I wanted.

As I'd grown and changed and tapped into a strength that, for many years, I'd been too brutalized to realize existed.

Not everyone was so fortunate.

It was just a reaffirmation that this needed to happen.

And soon.

I could feel my mother losing her cool.

The fine strands of her patience unraveling and fast. I lifted my phone, glancing around at the few sparse cars in the parking lot as I made the call.

Lily answered on the first ring.

"Maggie. Hi."

Lily was Violet's sister. Her sister who'd been held captive for years by my father. Unbeknownst to her family. Missing for years until the day Richard had stumbled upon her and found a way to set her free.

I'd met her right after my father had been killed. I'd bonded with her quickly. Fiercely. But once I'd gotten her involved in my plan, we'd decided it would be safer to pretend as if we hadn't connected. As if we never spoke.

My brother would lose it if he knew what I was up to.

Forbid me, which was the reason I hadn't told him or involved him. Besides, the sacrifices he had made were already too great.

This one—this one was on me.

With her voice, relief thrummed through my spirit. "Hey, you. How are you?"

"I'm good. Really good," she promised, and I could feel her truth.

Hope blustered. As fierce as the gust of wind that rushed over the waves.

"That makes me happy," I told her.

In that moment, I felt a crush of her happiness. Shimmers of joy that bled from her wounded spirit.

There was so much this woman had to offer.

Kindness and decency and light.

Cruelness and vileness had kept it trapped for so many years. Had shackled her by their greed and debauchery.

This.

This was why I would risk everything.

"You sound happy," she returned, almost like she recognized something new in me.

I guess I shouldn't be surprised it was that obvious.

Affection curled my lips into a wistful smile. "I am."

"That is wonderful." When she cleared the easiness away, worry replaced it. "So, what's going on?"

My spirit sank back to the unanswered text left sitting on my phone. "I don't think we can wait until next month. My mother is certain I have it."

And it wasn't like it wasn't the truth.

"I can feel her patience has hit a dead end. I can't keep playing it off that I don't have it, and I'm not sure the lengths she will go to get it back. It needs to be distributed."

Placed safely in the hands of the ones to whom it was owed.

Dread banged through the line. "Are you sure this is a good idea?"

She'd been questioning me since I'd contacted her about it. When I'd uncovered that stash and knew it was my responsibility to get it where it belonged.

"It's the only thing I can do."

"Okay then." She cleared her throat. "Kade was able to help me track down seven more women. He's goin' to help us get it to them."

Kade's own daughter had fallen victim to my father's heinous crimes. He'd been intrinsic in getting so many out of that house and giving them shelter until it'd been safe for them to go free.

Now, he was right back in the middle of it again.

But I trusted him...trusted him implicitly.

Then she started to rush, her voice lowered with emphasis, "And all of them need it, Maggie. This will give them the fightin' chance they've been missing."

My chest squeezed. "Everyone deserves that."

A fighting chance.

She sniffled a little. "I still can't believe you're doin' this."

"I just wish I could do more."

She scoffed a disbelieving sound. "This is major, Maggie. More than anyone would ask of you."

"You know there's no way I could leave that money sitting there. It's not right."

"Just...be safe, okay?" she whispered.

"I will."

"I'll let Kade know it needs to happen next week. I'll text you the details as soon as I have them."

"Okay. I'll see you soon."

"Bye."

I ended the call, and my arm dropped with my phone to my

lap. I stared out the windshield.

Gathering myself.

Refusing the paranoia that lifted the fine hairs at the nape of my neck.

I blew out a sigh and flung open the door, grabbing my purse and rushing into the store. I grabbed the diapers, paid, and was rushing back out less than five minutes later. I moved right for the car, my hand on the doorlatch.

I guessed I'd been too focused on getting in and out quickly that I hadn't slowed down long enough to listen to what was really happening around me.

To allow myself to process it.

No time to sense the vileness in the air.

The evil.

The greed.

It hit me so fast it nearly dropped me to my knees.

Terror raced my spine.

Wild and suffocating.

Trying to breathe around it, I fumbled to get the door open. To hurry. To get away. Praying all the while that I really was being paranoid, and somehow knowing this was real.

It'd barely unlatched when I felt the presence emerge from behind me, trapping me against the metal before I could swing it open and get inside.

A scream warbled in my throat, but the sharp blade of a knife against my throat froze everything. My knees wobbled when the disgusting voice seethed its venom against my ear, "It's about to end, and there is no place you can run."

Then his arm swiped away, and I rocked forward.

Shocked.

Confused.

His footsteps disappeared behind me, taken by the wind, while I tried to remain standing.

My world spinning from the disturbance.

Unable to believe that my mother would actually take it to this extreme. The threat of her words manifesting to the physical.

That confusion only took new shape when I registered the pain across my chest. When I gasped and stumbled back to see the blood that seeped into my shirt.

Dizziness whooshed. Horror raced.

Oh my god.

Oh my god.

The diapers slipped from my hold, and I clutched the fabric like it would take it away while I blinked and tried to process what had happened.

Then I stumbled to the side, the world spinning faster and faster.

I hardly made out the shouts and screams coming from a woman. A woman who had been across the lot and came running toward me in the same second that I pitched to the side and tumbled for the pitted, hard ground.

A second before I made contact, I was swallowed by the darkness.

Rhys

"*G*iddy-up, horsey!" Daisy knocked her heels into my flank, and her little arms were wrapped tight around my neck where I had her slung on my back.

I whinnied like the showman I was because obviously the kid was in need of a little entertainment. I reared back, making her clamor and squeal with all that sweet joy and hold on tighter.

Securing her by the legs, I galloped down the cavernous hall of the second floor.

Her laughter spurred me on.

My mangled heart got all twisted in her fist. Same way as it was threatenin' to get twisted up in Maggie.

Maggie, that girl who'd wrecked me last night.

Girl who was way too good to be givin' herself to the likes of me.

But fuck.

I wanted to take her, anyway. Get lost in that sweet body and those soulful eyes and the kindness of her heart.

This girl who could make me question everything.

My chest tightened in hope and fear. The terror of doing it again.

Ruinin' another life.

Daisy jerked her arms to the left like my neck were her reins.

"Down the stairs because we gots to eat!" she shouted, cracking up when I took a sharp turn like I'd almost missed it and sent her bouncing all over the place as I bucked and bounded like a wild animal downstairs.

"You is the craziest horse in all the land." It came out in little choked giggles since she was gettin' jostled like a ragdoll.

"Stallion, little Miss Daisy."

She giggled harder, but then I was slowing and slipping to a stop when I saw Royce's expression where he stood just outside the hallway.

Like he'd gotten frozen to the spot with his phone pressed to his ear.

My insides clutched with the way the color drained from his face and his entire being rocked like he'd been slammed by a boulder. "What? Okay... Okay... Yes... I'll be there as fast as I can."

Daisy jerked at my neck and kicked me in the sides while I tried not to drop to my knees.

Because I just knew.

Could feel it like the cuttin' away of flesh.

Still, I forced out, "What is it?"

Royce blinked through his shock. "Maggie was attacked."

Didn't matter that I'd already known that somethin' was bad. Agony ripped through me. Razor-sharp talons. Clawing me into pieces. "What?"

He blinked again before the fury overtook the shock he'd been hit with. "Fuck. Fuck." He ripped at his hair, and he moved for the little high wall table that was littered with everyone's keys and shit. He dug through the little dish.

"Shit. She has the car. She went to the store. She was just supposed to be going to the store." He rumbled the words under his breath, the guy tryin' not to lose his mind.

Wasn't so sure that I was doing such a bang-up job of not losin' mine. I eased Daisy down my back and onto her feet and shoved my hand into my pocket. "I'll drive. Where is she?"

Tried to keep the trembling out of the words. But I was pretty sure they were jagged. As jagged as this horror that crawled through my being. Laying siege. Devastating.

This girl.

This girl.

My Sweet, Sweet Thing.

I swallowed around the ball of broken glass that had gathered at the base of my throat.

Royce choked out a breath that might have been a sob. "Ambulance took her to Memorial in Savannah."

My knees rocked.

Every muscle in my body went weak.

I scrubbed an anxious palm over my face.

Didn't think I could take it if…

Couldn't even think it.

Process it.

She had to be okay. She had to be.

Daisy wrapped her arms around one of my legs. Just hanging on. The child not immune to the instant apprehension that curled through the air.

Emily came rushing down the stairs. "What happened?"

"Maggie was assaulted." Royce's words were clogged.

Emily gasped and she started to rush faster. "Oh my god. Is she okay? What happened?"

"Don't know. Need to get there."

Dread fired like a shotgun through my senses.

Scattering and ripping and tearing through my psyche.

Suddenly so much of it makin' sense.

The inclination I'd had that something was up, which I'd chalked up to family shit, but it was becoming clear it was so much bigger than I'd given credence to.

Fact she'd been acting so sketchy when she'd told her brother she'd fallen.

Her answer to my question when I'd confronted her on it.

"Have you ever been willing to do something right for someone else, so desperately, that you were willing to risk it all? Whatever the cost?"

Fear pumped into my bloodstream.

What was she involved in?

Why would she put herself in this position?

Fuck. Why hadn't she confided it in me? Trusted me to hold it? What if it was too late?

Sickness tumbled in my guts.

Royce hugged his wife fiercely when she hit the landing. Emily's expression was nothing but the panic and desperation I was feeling. "Okay. Let me know as soon as you know anything."

"I will."

He started to walk, and she grabbed him by the hand, gave it a squeeze as he looked back at her. "Love you."

"Love you. So much." He shifted to look at me. "Let's go."

I ran my fingers through Daisy's hair, hoping it might comfort her since I could feel the anxiety oozing from her. She just squeezed tighter. "Please tell my auntie Maggie to be okay, and that she's gots all the amors, and I need to give her more."

I could barely nod. "She'll be okay. She'll be okay."

I refused to believe anything else.

A second later, I was out the door and runnin' to my car. Royce and I were both inside and on the road in less than a blink.

Problem was, that's all it took for a tragedy.

A blink.

One second the world was at your feet and the next it was crumbling around you.

I knew it firsthand.

I blazed through town as carefully as I could, and then we were flying when I hit the highway that led between the island and Savannah.

That lump in my throat was so thick I kept strugglin' to breathe around it, only growing thicker as Royce's apprehension and anger and worry seeped from his pores.

So intense it was sure to drown us both.

Anxiously, he rubbed his thighs with his sweaty palms. "Can't believe this. Can't believe I let someone get to her. Fuck." He gave a harsh shake of his head. "Why? Who the fuck is after her? Knew it, though. Just had this feeling."

I nodded.

Guilt sucked me even deeper considering how deep I'd been in his baby sister last night. Especially after I'd promised him I would stay away from her.

For her safety.

For her well-being.

Because she deserved so much more than the trouble I would bring.

But this was different, wasn't it? Didn't have a thing to do with me.

My hands tightened on the steering wheel.

Maybe...maybe she needed me. Maybe for once, I could make a difference.

"She's goin' to be okay, man."

His head shook again. Agony flooded out with it. "Couldn't handle it if she wasn't. Don't know what I would do. Fuck...she's been through enough, hasn't she? And then what, she goes looking for trouble?"

"Let's not jump to conclusions. We don't know what's goin' on yet."

He nodded hard even though neither of us accepted it.

Both of us sure there was something sinister at hand.

Could just...feel it.

Sense it in the air.

I rammed the accelerator to the floor.

Needing to get there.

To see her face.

To touch her skin.

To find that she was safe and whole.

For someone to tell me this was all one big fuckin'

misunderstanding.

I barely slowed as I got into town, zipping by cars and screaming around corners. The tires squealed as I skidded into the hospital parking lot. Royce and I were both jumping out before I fully had it in park.

Manic.

Frantic.

Every step of our thudding feet only incited a whole new dread.

He blew through the double-sliding-glass doors. I was right behind him, antsy as hell when he asked the man behind the counter for Maggie.

Royce mumbled, "Thank you," when the guy buzzed him through the huge swinging door to the back.

And maybe there was some relief in that. Relief in the fact they didn't give us some bullshit that someone would be out to talk to us while we realized we were about to get the worst news of our lives.

That tiny stake of consolation released some of the pressure.

I trailed him through the door.

Maybe he'd thought I was just his ride, but there was no way I could sit out there and wait.

I was on his heels, and he was cuttin' me a questioning glare, and I was deciding I really didn't give a fuck.

I didn't know if it was rage or relief that I was feeling when we got close to her room and there was an officer slipping out.

Only thing that really mattered was Maggie was sitting up in the bed.

Whole and real and alive.

A burst of air left Royce like a punch.

While I pushed both palms to my face like it might cover the magnitude of what slammed me.

Overwhelming.

Overpowering.

Terrifying.

The rush of comfort and devotion that gushed.

Shit.

I needed to check this bullshit before it was too late.

The officer shot us a look as he angled passed. Royce just ignored him, ripped open the door, and rushed to her side.

He pulled her into his arms in the same second that I slipped into the room. I made the prudent choice of hanging by the wall like I was completely cool and wasn't about to get charred to ash.

Worked for all of a flash before I saw the way she flinched. The way she tried to pretend like she wasn't in pain, playing it off like this was no big thing.

Rage spiraled all over again.

Consuming.

Raw and deep and horrible.

Pulling away, Royce took her by the outside of her shoulders. "What happened?"

Maggie forced a shaky smile, all that black hair matted and littered with little pieces of dirt and debris, her spirit in turmoil.

Knocking against the walls while she did her best to keep it contained. "I'm okay."

The shake of Royce's head was harsh. He was most definitely not gonna let that fly.

"What happened, Maggie? Are you hurt?"

Those lips trembled. Maybe he didn't notice it, but I saw the way she curled in on herself a fraction. Like she could guard herself from the danger. "I'm barely injured, Royce. I promise. But someone...cut me."

She whispered the last like a secret.

"Cut you?" Royce almost shouted it. "What the hell does that mean?"

I itched where I stood at the wall, trying to hook myself to it rather than give into the urges that were hammering me like a drum.

Part of me felt like a stranger. Like someone who didn't belong. All while trying to fight the feelin' that I'd never been so sure of where I belonged in all my days.

That it should be me, right there by her side.

Reckless.

Dangerous.

Which was the absolute truth, but I didn't know how to shuck the sensation.

The demand.

Charcoal eyes traced me for a beat.

A welcome and her own relief.

Drawing me into her intricate story.

Fuck. I had no idea how to pull this off when what I really wanted to do was push Royce out of the way and take this girl into my arms.

Run my hands over her to ensure she was safe.

Hold her and promise I'd never let anyone get to her.

Kiss the hell out of her, too.

Yeah.

I was about to lose it.

Like I was going to crumble into those sweet hands.

It'd probably been less than a beat that she'd been staring at me, but it felt like a physical rendering when she tore her attention away and returned it to her brother. She lifted an innocent shoulder that even Daisy would be able to tell was a total sham.

"I don't even know, Royce. It happened so fast. I went inside to get diapers..."

Her throat trembled when she swallowed. "I came back out and went to climb back into my car and...and..."

Her head shook and she blinked like she was trying to make sense of what happened.

Now that I believed.

The girl had been blindsided.

"Someone just...came up behind me and slashed me."

Her hand went to her chest that was covered by the dressing gown.

Shit.

I staked the fingers of both hands through my hair and held on to keep from going to her.

"Someone cut you? Out of the blue?" Royce growled it.

"Yeah."

He wasn't buying that, either.

"What did this person say?"

"Nothing. I think...I think maybe he thought I was someone

else or something. I don't know. It was a blur and happened so fast. He was already gone before I'd even realized he'd cut me."

Uneasily, I shifted on my feet.

Left in the chains of her fear. The stark terror I could feel coming off her, even though she was doin' her best to play it off.

But I knew, it was a big freakin' thing.

Maggie was scared and lying and clinging to some sort of resolution that I saw shining in the depths of her eyes.

And I'd do whatever it took to protect her from whatever she was hiding from.

Dinner had been a somber affair.

Everyone had fretted over Maggie when we'd first walked through the door after she'd been discharged, while the girl had faked the fakest smile ever faked and tried to play it off like it was just another day.

Conversation had been stilted.

Forced.

Awkward as all hell.

I'd twitched, knee bobbing at warp speed under the table while I'd picked at the pizza we'd ordered since it'd been so late when we'd gotten home.

Whole time, Royce had silently raged.

Dude a fuckin' monstrous dark cloud that had gathered at the horizon.

His landfall promised the obliteration of anything that got in his way.

Or maybe what had really been goin' down was the guy had just been feeding off mine.

This fury I could feel growing in strength.

Taking over.

This girl who was wrecking everything I thought I knew.

Everything I'd held fast to for so long.

About thirty minutes before, Maggie had excused herself,

claiming she was tired and wanted to get some rest, while Leif and his family packed up to go to their house outside the city for the night.

Violet and Richard took Daisy to their room, same as Royce and Emily took Amelia to theirs.

Mel hovered.

Shootin' daggers at me like maybe I was the one who was responsible for this.

For the first time ever, I wasn't.

Trying to divert the coming questions, I moved into the kitchen to clean up. Mel backed me into the corner the second we were alone.

"What the hell do you think you're doin', Rhys?"

"Nothing."

"That girl—"

I flew into her face.

I loved Mel. Respected the hell out of her. Appreciated every-fucking-thing she'd done for me.

But she needed to know this was different.

"That girl is special. I know. I fucking know. But please, stay out of it."

"Rhys."

"Please."

I didn't confess that I'd been with Maggie last night.

Figured Mel knew me well enough to see through any bullshit I'd feed her anyway.

What I wanted to confess was that I cherished Maggie.

That I would take care of her.

Protect her.

That I'd give anything to be able to keep her when I knew that was an impossibility.

Instead, I simply asked Mel for space. "Just drop it. Not tonight."

"Rhys," she protested.

"Serious."

Warily, she backed away, seeing that I was close to my end. My nerves frazzled.

I finished cleaning up and then climbed the stairs.

Both anxious and drained.

Needing to get to the girl.

I was turning the knob to my bedroom door, the hushed sounds behind closed doors echoing like omens, not one of us immune to it, when I felt that dark cloud descend.

Royce was there.

His black eyes flares in the shadows that crawled the hallway walls.

Stilling, I shifted to look back at him.

The tat on his throat bobbed when he swallowed. "Need you to do me a favor."

My chin lifted in question. "What's that?"

"See if you can find out what's going on with her. Know you two are friends, and whatever it is, she doesn't trust me with it."

Guilt blazed. Thing was, the protectiveness and care I felt for this girl doused it to ash. More powerful than anything. "If she won't tell you somethin', I hardly think she'll confide in me."

He roughed a hand through his hair. "Just try, Rhys. For me. For her. Know she's lying, and I can't stand aside and pretend like this isn't happening."

"Yeah. Sure. Of course. Anything." This time it was my turn to lie. "Not hopeful, though."

"All I'm asking is for you to listen out for anything that might be amiss. If she says something or you hear anything."

"Of course, man." I turned the knob to my door. "Try to get some rest, yeah?"

He scoffed out a laugh. "Doubtful."

"I'll check on her."

Fuck, I was really laying it on. Doubling down on the lies. Acting like I was nothin' but good intentions.

"Thanks, man. I appreciate all you've done," he said.

"No problem."

Without saying anything else, I slipped into my room and shut the door behind me. I dropped my head and tried to get my wits. To pull it together.

I felt like a total piece of shit for touching his sister. Maybe more so for being desperate to do it again. For lying to him.

For feeling this need to hold somethin' beautiful when I didn't have the right.

But the call she had on me was a powerful one, that was for damn sure.

The way I was already movin' through that bathroom and nudging open her door that was cracked an inch.

An open invitation.

The girl sat on her bed looking at the door. Waiting for me.

Feeling me, too.

I stopped in the doorway. "Hey there, Sweet Thing."

Her mouth trembled, and a tear streaked her cheek, and I saw that folded duck she clutched in her fist. I rushed for her, swooped her into my arms, and took her to my room. I carried her to the chair in the far corner, and I shifted around and eased onto the chair with her cradled on my lap.

She hung on tight.

I held on tighter. "Scared the piss outta me today, Sweet Thing."

She almost smiled, her laugh a whimper. "Got the piss scared out of me, too."

My hand rubbed along her hip, trying to soothe her, soothe myself.

"What really happened out there?"

She flinched.

"Don't pretend with me, Maggie. Know you're in somethin', and I can't sit aside and act like this isn't happenin'. Someone *attacked* you."

Horror scraped my throat when I forced it out.

She exhaled and sagged in my hold, and her fingers started playing across the fabric of my shirt that covered my chest. "My father was responsible for hurting a lot of people."

My murmur was slight. "Yeah."

Old agony curled up from her spirit. Unmistakable hurt but there was this quiet ferocity at the center. Like this girl had found her strength in the middle of it. "He kept women and men prisoners, Rhys. Tricked them into slavery. Used them for their bodies like they were possessions."

I think Maggie was just needin' to say it aloud since all of that was well known. Splashed all over the airwaves.

When Royce had exposed his stepfather's seedy empire, some of the captives had escaped. Others had been moved before the Feds had descended on the compound. I think it was safe to say we still didn't know how deep it went or how many had been affected.

Dude was a fucking monster.

Fact he'd let one of his artists do the same to his own daughter and then covered it up? Doubted much the man even had a soul, though I hoped he did. Hoped even though he'd gotten off easy here, paying with his pathetic, disgusting life, he was receiving justice somewhere in the afterlife.

"I just want to make a difference in their lives. Help the only way I can." She said the last so quietly that I wasn't sure I'd heard her right.

Her confession.

Because that's what it was.

My arms tightened around her as dread marched across my flesh. "What did you do, Maggie? Tell me what you did, and who hurt you. I'll end it."

Tonight.

I'd hunt down any fucker who would dare harm this girl.

Her head shook. "There wasn't a lot of money left once his accounts were seized."

"I heard that."

Mylton Records had been dismantled.

That article a few days ago had talked like Maggie was some rich, spoiled heiress. I knew better. There'd been very little left. Not for her or her mother.

"But he was smart, Rhys. He kept enough hidden so no matter what, he could make his way back to his fortune."

My blood sloshed. Heavy with dread. Not liking where she was going with this.

"I found it." Her voice was a breath of fear and hope.

Shit, this girl had my heart thuddin' in her fist. "What did you do?"

"I took it. And I'm going to use it for good."

"Maggie."

Her head shook. "Don't try to talk me out of it or tell me it's dangerous. I know the risk, and it's worth it."

"Someone hurt you," I argued, words nothin' but a plea when I shifted her on my lap so she was straddling me. Hand shaking, I carefully reached up and dragged down the loose tee she wore, exposing the bandage taped on her chest.

Right over the scar she already had.

I barely brushed my fingertips over it, pain leaching into my words when I looked from my fingers to her eyes.

"Someone hurt you." My teeth ground when I reiterated the truth.

She gathered up my hand. "It was a threat. A warning. Nothing more. And I refuse to cower or give in. I…it's my mother, Rhys."

Anger squeezed my chest.

That crusty, nasty bitch.

"She's trying to scare me into doing what she wants me to do," Maggie rushed. "She did it for years, twisted everything about me into a lie. And I believed it, Rhys. I believed it. But no more. For the first time in my life, I'm taking a stand. I'm doing what's right. And there is no one who can stop me. And I'm asking you…begging you…to stand by my side while I do it."

Charcoal eyes filled with moisture.

With determination.

This sweet, amazing, beautiful girl.

"Baby." It was a whisper. "Of course, I will stand with you. Fuck…not gonna let you out of my sight."

The most tentative smile played across her delicate mouth, and she reached out and traced mine, those fingertips dancing across my lips. "Thank you."

My nod was slight, and then I inhaled and pushed ahead.

"How much?" I dreaded asking it.

"Five million."

"What the hell? Maggie." I blinked through the outright shock. "Where is it?"

Guilt raced across her features. "Under my bed. In duffle bags."

My mind raced back to the day I'd helped her bring in her things. She'd almost come out of her skin when I'd tried to take them from her.

"Maggie…that's fucking…crazy."

It was.

Reckless and foolish and the bravest thing I'd ever heard.

"Maybe, but it's the right thing to do."

"What are you doing with it?"

"Lily…Violet's sister. She's helping me find the women who need it most. So they can restart their lives. Their lives my father stole from them. This is owed to them, Rhys, and no, money can't cover it or erase what's been done, but it can give them something to rebuild on. Hope that's been missing."

"And you're not telling your brother…"

"You know why, Rhys. You know he'd stop me. Intervene. And he's already given too much. I can't ask this of him, too."

Overcome, I wound my arms around her and hugged her hard. Probably too hard.

But she was hugging me just as tight.

And there was nothing between us.

No barriers.

No space.

All except for the glaring hole that roared inside. A violent echo that rang in my ear, reminding me that I couldn't have this.

My debt was too great.

My life too wrong.

Her words were suddenly rasping at my ear as she clung to me, "Be with me for now, Rhys. Tell me that right now, I belong to you and you belong to me. I feel your burden, I feel your heart, and I know you'll never love me, and I know we're not supposed to pretend, but I need it, Rhys. I need to feel this for a little bit. We never know how long we have, and this is the first true, real thing I've ever had."

My soul shook with her statement.

Hitting me like stones.

This precious girl.

My arms curled tighter, and I breathed out the agony, the need and the devotion and that feelin' that I couldn't acknowledge. I edged her back so I could meet her eye, and I brushed away the wispy locks of black waves that stuck to the side of her face where the tears had fallen. "This is real, Maggie. Whatever you're feeling. But you deserve to be loved with every fuckin' part of someone. Completely and without a lick of reservation. Want to be him. Fuck, I do. But I'm not."

"Be him now. Just for a few days. Until I have to go."

I nodded at her, but then I was making my own demand. "As long as you promise to let me be the one to do it. Whatever shady as shit plans you have, they just got shadier, you got me? You're not doin' this. If someone wants that money? They're gonna have to go through me to get it. You don't leave my side until it's done. Deal?"

Maggie swallowed, and her nod was small. "Okay."

"Okay." Relief slammed me, and then that relief was transforming.

Growing bigger.

Stronger.

Fiercer.

Because Maggie was kissing me, and I was kissing her, and I was carrying her to my bed.

And I was terrified that whatever she was feeling, I was feeling it, too.

Maggie

"Auntie Mag Pies!! Happy birthday! Oh, it's gonna be the best day in the whole wide world because guess what? We're makin' pancakes." Daisy was pure excitement from where she stood on the stool at the kitchen counter in front of a whipping bowl.

The softest smile pulled to my mouth while my heart threatened to explode.

I hovered at the edge of the kitchen while Emily and Violet bustled around.

"Happy birthday," they said almost in unison when they could get in a word with Daisy's exuberance.

Warmth radiated from them. A blanket of welcome and love.

"Thank you," I replied, shuffling a little deeper into the kitchen.

I was still wearing sleepy eyes, sleep pants and a tank, and probably a loved-up glow that I really should try to cover.

But right then, I couldn't bring myself to be concerned.

Daisy was right. Today was going to be the best day in the whole wide world.

Today, I was twenty-one. Not that years mattered much. But tonight, we celebrated. My brother's band, A Riot of Roses, would be arriving, and there was always a kick-off party.

Since it was also my birthday, Shea Stone had suggested we have it at the bar she'd inherited from her uncle when he'd retired, a place called Charlie's over on the Riverwalk in Savannah.

Royce had immediately objected. The last place he wanted me at was a bar after what had happened last week.

I'd gladly accepted. Royce had finally come around when I'd pointed out I'd be surrounded by a ton of people who cared about me the entire time. After I told him I'd only turn twenty-one once, and I wanted this experience.

Truth was, my excitement was probably just as big as Daisy's. I'd chosen to live in the moment, and I refused to take for granted even a single one of them. Refused to hide because of the threats my mother issued.

What really spurred the feeling was I'd woken to a text from Lily with a time and place to meet Kade this coming week. The transfer would happen three nights from now. I'd received it with a dose of anxiety and a shock of hope—hope to finally end this.

To put an end to my father's name. To cap off his wickedness with something good. With the smallest measure of justice.

Then I would move on. Move on to the rest of my days.

The icing on my birthday cake? Rhys still belonged to me.

At least for now.

Maybe I was a fool to hope for more. To hope that things might change. To hope that someday he might trust me enough to let me hold him the way I'd allowed him to hold me.

But sometimes brokenness went so deep it was hard to reach the bottom of it, and I was sure Rhys was terrified to dig around in the gaping ravine of his past.

"Guess what, Auntie! These pancakes are a special, special kind. They are goin's to be your favorite in all the favorites. Just you wait."

"And what if I can't wait? It smells too good in here. I might just have to come in here and gobble them up," I teased the little pumpkin pie as I went clomping into the kitchen like I was going to make good on my threat.

Daisy giggled and squealed and tried to hide whatever she was making in the bowl. "No. No way, Auntie. You can't looks yet. It's a secret special present."

Laughing low, I dropped a kiss to the top of her head. "Oh, okay, fine. I guess I'll have to wait then."

She looked up at me with one of her grins. "Dontcha know the best things in life are worth the waitin' for?"

My chest squeezed.

"Yeah. You're right, Daisy. The best things in life are worth waiting for."

And mine came sauntering down the sweeping main staircase.

All unruly hair and rumpled grins and this tee that stretched across his massive shoulders and hugged his narrow waist.

Fingers running down his beard in the sexiest way.

Cocky and wild.

My mouth went dry.

God. I loved it when he was like this. When all he had to offer outshined the demons that dimmed his eyes.

Violet was suddenly sing-songing in my ear, "I think it's pretty clear what Maggie wants for her birthday."

I swatted at her, sent her a glare, and hissed, "Shh. Would you stop it?"

So, two days ago she'd backed me into a corner and demanded the truth out of me, too.

Apparently, I wasn't so great at hiding my emotions.

Violet giggled.

Tinkling and light.

Then she sobered and reached out to squeeze my hand, her voice held so only I could hear. "It just makes me really happy to see you this way."

"It's always been there. I just had to find a way to set it free."

Her nod was knowing. Soft and sure and filled with her

sincerity. "Love you."

"Love you, too."

"Hey now, I'm gettin' jealous over here." Emily was all smiles when we looked at her. "It is *my* sister's birthday and Violet's over there hoggin' her. Whisperin' secrets that I can't hear. That's just rude."

A giggle worked its way free. "We were just saying how lucky we are to have you."

Scoffing, she glared at us with mischief dancing in her eyes. "Liars."

My giggle deepened, and I glanced at Rhys whose grin was twitching into some kind of lusty possession as he hit the landing. I figured I needed to duck out from under his pull, so I moved over to my sister-in-law and gave her a tight hug. "I love you. And I am *so* lucky to have you. This will be the best birthday of my life…because of you. Because of this family."

With dough all over her fingers, she awkwardly wrapped her arms around me, trying to keep from rubbing it on my shirt while still swallowing me in the comfort of her arms. "I love you. So much. It's me who's grateful. Me who received the gift."

"I think we're all on the receiving end of that."

Pulling back, she smiled, soft and adoring, and then she was letting her gaze move over to Rhys who wound around the island.

Coming closer.

Clearly on a mission.

"There's the birthday girl."

His hulking body filled up the space, and the air squeezed from my lungs, and then my knees were straight giving out when he wrapped me up in all that bristling strength and hauled me against his body.

Oh my goodness.

His heart thundered. Maybe as hard as mine.

It wasn't like I hadn't spent the last five nights in these arms. It wasn't like we hadn't lost ourselves in each other again and again. It wasn't like I hadn't explored every inch of this body the same as he'd been exploring mine.

But he'd never touched me like this in front of the family.

Never had he made such a claim.

And at first it seemed almost playful.

Normal with the way he hugged me and kind of whipped me around.

But there was no missing the way the air changed. Zapping with an electric charge as he continued to hold me. As our movements slowed. As he buried his nose in my hair and his hands splayed out over my back.

I fell into it.

Just gave myself over. Because I refused to be afraid. This man might demolish me in the end, but I was taking that chance.

And then that crackling turned to a thunder, and I pulled back to find my brother glaring daggers at us from the other side of the island.

So much for happy birthdays.

Rhys set me back onto my feet while discomfort spiraled through the room.

"Happy birthday, Mags. It's a big day." Rhys said it as casual as could be as he ambled toward the coffee pot.

"Thanks. It should be fun," I peeped, way too high, all kinds of flustered as I smoothed out my shirt.

This was stupid.

My brother didn't get to be mad.

But I also had no right to put Rhys on the spot when he'd made it clear this was only temporary. No reason to burn the bridge between the two of them when they had to be together for the rest of their lives.

They'd seemed halfway friendly as of late.

I shook myself out of it the best I could.

Out of the wash of need.

Royce glowered, his dark, dark eyes flitting between Rhys and me.

"Hey you. I was just comin' to find you. Is Amelia still asleep?" Emily broke into the discomfort.

"Yeah. Just checked on her," he grumbled.

Emily wove her way to him like she could cut through the uneasiness. Disperse it into nothingness.

She popped up on her toes and kissed him.

He rumbled something against her mouth before he pulled back.

He smiled at me. Worried and soft. "Happy birthday, Mag Pie."

"Thank you."

Emily spun away, all sways and swishes of her hips as she sashayed back to what she'd been preparing. If anyone could distract my brother, it was her. "Breakfast is almost ready. And like our Daisy said, it's gonna be somethin' special."

"Yups. It's my nana's specialist birthday recipe."

Violet tried to hide it, but I felt her flinch. Felt the gush of her pain.

It crested through my body, and I eased that way, and from behind, I hugged my friend tight where she stood at the stove flipping pancakes. "You miss her."

Violet glanced back at me with tears in her eyes. "So much. But I know she's here." She waved a hand around the room. "And I know she's here," she said as she touched her heart.

"She is."

She swallowed it down, and then she and Daisy were shooing me away so I wouldn't ruin the surprise.

They were a mess of clanking dishes and whipping metal bowls and laughter. I watched the scene with so much joy from the edge of the room, while Rhys watched it from the opposite side. And I couldn't help but wonder what it might be like. How good it could actually be if we somehow truly found our way to each other. If we could meet in the middle.

Daisy hopped down and clapped her hands with a squeal. "It's ready!"

Racing for me, she grabbed my hand and gave it a tug. "Come on. You have to sit down in your special spot."

She led me to the head of the table just as Leif and his family came bustling in through the front door.

Melanie came jogging downstairs, too, and Richard joined the mayhem a second later.

I sat down at the head of the table.

Surrounded by these amazing people.

I'd thought for so long I'd never really have it. That it would forever be Royce and me against the world, him with his fierce sword drawn and his armor shielding me.

And it was. My amazing brother who would give anything to give me a good life.

His sacrifices great.

Now we were both surrounded.

Loved.

Leif dropped a kiss to my head with a rumbled, "Happy birthday, Mags," before he took a seat. His kids hugged me tight, and Mia squeezed my hand and told me how excited she was for me to embark on this new era of my life.

Everyone clamored into chairs, the legs screeching as the children found their places, the adults taking theirs.

Rhys slipped into the one right next to me.

And that's what this was—a new era.

Not because of a birthday, but because of the *home* that I had found. The place where I belonged. Where I belonged to these people and they belonged to me.

A family.

Daisy helped her mom slide a tray in front of me. "Look it, look it, Auntie Mag Pies! Isn't it the prettiest in the whole wide world?"

On the tray was an overflowing pile of pancakes covered in pastel icing and sprinkles and twenty-one candles. Candy letters spelled out *Happy Birthday*.

There was a handmade card from Daisy.

All glitter and cutouts and the front claiming, *Amor, Amor, Amor.*

Love. Love. Love.

So much love.

So much that it crashed and broke and spilled all over the place.

A flood where I'd be happy to drown.

Then Rhys took my hand under the table and threaded his fingers with mine.

Tears pricked my eyes.

"Make a wish, Auntie!" Daisy squealed.
And I did.
I made the most important wish of all.

twenty-seven

Rhys

*C*harlie's was this awesome bar down on the Riverwalk in Savannah.

Housed in a cotton warehouse from way back in the day, the rafters soared in the rambling building, so high the ceiling basically disappeared into the darkened nothingness. Aged wood made up the walls, blackened with time. The lights swinging on chains from that swellin' abyss cast a dingy glow across the even dingier floors.

Place was this cross between dive and luxury. The booths were plush and a bit ostentatious where they rested in a secluded row along the far wall that ran up to the stage at the very back. A bunch of high-top tables surrounded by stools filled the space next to them, right up to the dance floor situated below the elevated stage.

On the opposite side of the massive building were a slew of pool tables lit by traditional billiard lights.

A huge bar floated in the middle of it all. Wood this gleaming, intricately carved mahogany. The barback was glass and metal, all the bottles illuminated in colorful lights.

It emitted a vibe of urban antique.

Carolina George had played here a ton of times through the years. Its original owner, Charlie? He was this cool as fuck old guy who'd welcomed us with open arms. By the second time we'd rolled through, he'd treated us like family.

Felt good to be back.

But what felt really good?

It was sitting in that private booth at the very back where a few other tables had been drawn up close so we could celebrate Maggie's twenty-first.

Maggie who kept laughing loud and smiling big and having the time of her life.

Maggie who was wreckin' me.

She sent me a sly grin where I sat three people down from her in the booth while the server rolled a cart for bottle service over to our spot.

This was a party, after all.

That glance, though?

It punched me in the guts.

Got me all twisted up in her pretty little fist.

I tried not to act affected. Tried to pretend like I was just another of the crew there to celebrate a friend.

Pretend like my dick wasn't perkin' up at the gorgeous sight of her.

But that was the problem. Every time I looked at her, I wanted more. That body and that sweet, sweet soul.

Knew I was gettin' lost. In so deep I didn't recognize myself any longer. With Maggie, it was easy to forget the lines that had to be drawn. Easy to get to thinkin' that I might have the right to stand at her side.

Easy to break every fuckin' rule. But those rules had been written for a reason, and I'd do well not to forget them.

"Now, now, everyone out of the way. I've got this. I'm an old pro." Shea Stone popped up from where she sat at a table and moved for the cart. She was all country smirks and sass as she started pouring clear liquid into the shot glasses that had been left for our party. "Watch how it's done."

She started passing out the tiny, glittering glasses to everyone there.

This mish-mashed Carolina George family.

Most of Sunder and their wives.

The rest of Royce's band. Van, Arson, and Hunter. All nicknames they'd earned back runnin' the streets of Hollywood. Thought the dudes might have the whole sex, drugs & rock 'n' roll vibe trademarked, right down to the T.

"You sure you want one of those?" Royce shouted at Maggie over the clamor. Dude was watchin' his sister like a hawk, though he had his own smile pulling at the edge of his mouth as he looked at her from where he sat on the opposite end of the booth.

Guy was nothin' but devote adoration.

Had more respect for that than I could express. Which was an entirely separate reason guilt kept slogging through my bloodstream. My loyalties muddled.

Slowing my pulse before it went racin' again when the girl would glance my way. When she'd sneak a brush of those fingers through my beard or devour me with those eyes.

"I think I can handle it," Maggie shouted back, lifting the glass in his direction.

"Question is if you can handle the hangover come tomorrow?" His expression was soft and playful.

"Don't worry, Tamar here has me covered."

"You know I do," Tamar said.

Tamar's present to Maggie had been a basket filled with a bunch of aftercare shit, Advil and Alka-Seltzer and Gatorade, not to mention this silky pajama set that I couldn't wait to peel off her body.

Those eyes found me then, like she'd felt what I'd been thinking, and she started imagining the same damned thing.

That charcoal bright and glowing. Sketching a different story than the one I knew we were destined for.

My stomach fisted in want as I gazed at that angled, soft face.

Lips plush.

Chin firm and determined because this girl had her whole life waiting ahead of her and there was no question that she was going to tackle it with all the fierce kindness she had to offer.

She had those black locks curled into these gentle waves that spilled over her bare, seductive shoulders, the strappy blouse she wore coming up a little higher on her neck, no doubt to cover the wound that was hidden underneath.

Just thinking about it had a hidden geyser of protectiveness eruptin' from within.

I didn't bother to swallow it down. I let it fester around my heart and my fists because if I could give this girl one thing, it'd be her peace.

Stepping into the fray to stand for her.

Would take the brunt. Any fucking danger her bitch of a mother thought to send her way.

Fuck.

It made me irate.

Fact a woman could be so callous. Money the prize and not the fucking amazing daughter she'd been given.

But it was that cunt who was missin' out. Missin' out on this girl who sent me a secret smile.

Arm slung on the back of the booth, I smiled back.

Slow and casual while my insides shook.

My teeth gritted while I silently chanted, *Don't fall. Don't fall.*

Because I could feel myself teetering at the edge.

Ground crumbling.

Weak, weak, weak.

Thank God Royce stood and cleared his throat, giving me a reason to look at him and not his sister.

All the laughter and conversations died out around us, though the music still thundered from the speakers. He lifted his voice to shout over it as he turned his full attention to his sister. "Got a couple things I'd like to say on Maggie's birthday."

A round of shouts went up. "Whoop…Maggie!"

She grinned and blushed, and fuck, there she went, stealing another slice of me.

"I remember the day I got to meet you." Emotion clotted Royce's voice, and I could feel the love rushing out of Maggie.

A river that raged.

Was funny considering Royce was basically this scary motherfucker. Wearin' a suit to a dive bar with all his tats leaking out from underneath. Though affection tweaked at his mouth and tenderness filled his gaze.

Was crazy how love could melt us into a puddle no matter how damned hard we were on the outside.

"You were this tiny little thing wrapped in pink blankets. I was jealous at first, when I snuck into your nursery and found our nanny, Maude, rocking you while she fed you a bottle. But then she called me over, and she let me get close so I could look at your face. I climbed up on the edge of the chair with my heart in my throat. I was kinda scared to even look at you. But then you opened your eyes and blinked up at me like you already knew me. I remember being startled because your eyes were the exact same color as mine. All it took was that one second to realize I'd never loved anything as much as I loved this little thing wrapped up in that pink blanket."

Royce's voice grew thick.

Maggie's eyes filled with moisture.

Everyone *oohed* and *awed* and lifted their glasses while I struggled to breathe.

"I told Maude right then and there that you were mine, and that I would always take care of you."

Maggie's chin trembled while she tried to keep her emotions in check. "And you always have."

He nodded hard. "And it's been the biggest honor getting to be that person in your life, Maggie. Getting to watch you grow into a beautiful woman. Inside and out. And I always thought it was on me to teach you what life was all about. But it's the other way around. You taught me what it means to love. To believe in possibility. To forgive. To chase down our dreams."

Her head shook. "Only because you showed me first."

His throat bobbed, and the air was this bottled, boiling thing. He lifted his glass. "Nah, Maggie. It was you. You who shined goodness. May you show it to the rest of the world. All you are. And may it return every joy back to you because God knows, you gave it to me."

Royce glanced at Emily.

Love spilled out.

Hunter and Van pounded on the table. "Here, here!"

Tamar stood to lift her glass, and everyone followed suit except for us who were tucked in the booth and unable to stand.

But my heart was already there.

Lifting.

Standing.

I raised my glass.

"To Maggie, to a life of happiness, joy, and many, many orgasms," Tamar shouted with a smirk.

Royce grunted.

I tried not to chuckle with the way Maggie tried not to look at me.

"To Maggie!" everyone agreed as they lifted their glasses and clinked them together and threw the alcohol back.

"To Maggie," I said, voice low. But still, she heard me.

Our gazes tangled for the longest beat, and I lifted mine a little higher.

To Maggie.

And we both tossed our shots back.

To Maggie.

The night grew rowdy. Alcohol flowin' free, though I was sure to keep mine in check because there was no chance I'd let down my guard when it came to Maggie. She was out on the dance floor surrounded by the girls.

Emily, Violet, Mia, and Mel.

Shea, Tamar, and Willow.

They danced and danced while the country band played.

Maggie kept tossing her head back and laughing. Letting her

friends spin her as they took turns two stepping to the upbeat rhythm. Girl wore this shimmering sequined skirt and sky-high heels, those legs sleek and toned and making my teeth clench with the onslaught of fantasies that kept invadin' my mind.

I couldn't look away.

Neither could about half the bar, either.

I stood on the sidelines nursing a beer and trying not to lose my cool while the vultures buzzed and hovered and measured how to dive into all the gorgeousness goin' down in that tight-knit group.

Since most of the women touted rocks the size of Texas on their ring-fingers, it was a dangerous, dangerous endeavor.

But I got the sense they were thinking Maggie and Mel might be free game. I might not have the right to make the claim but considering Maggie had asked me to be hers for as long as this charade could last, I was having a hard time tamping down the possession that streaked.

Didn't help that Maggie kept shooting me these sly glances.

Like the girl was dancin' for me.

Ripples of lust rode on the air.

Her need real and potent.

Intoxicating.

From where Royce stood on the other side of Richard, he scowled at whatever text lit up his phone. "Shit," he grumbled.

"What's up?" Richard shouted over the din.

"Sitter. Amelia won't stop crying."

He contemplated for a beat before he weaved into the throbbing mess on the dance floor. Emily beamed when she saw him coming, then her expression fell when he leaned in and gave her the news.

Party was about to be shot.

That was my cue.

Another bit I could rescue. It was my Maggie's twenty-first, after all.

I wound my way over to them. We'd all ridden over in the party bus Emily had hired, and it was currently idling in an alley waiting to take the crew back to Tybee.

"Sorry to bust up the party so early, Mag Pie." Royce's voice was all apology.

Maggie wiped the sheen of sweat from her brow and sent him one of her understanding smiles. "It's fine. Amelia always comes first."

"Tonight was supposed to be special, though."

"It's been more than special," she assured him, but I figured we ought to keep it rolling that way.

"Why don't you two call it, and I can hang back with anyone who wants to stay?" I shrugged it just as casual as could be as I strode up to them.

No big deal.

Like I wasn't dyin' to get a minute alone with Maggie.

All this pretending was downright painful.

"Really?" Maggie asked, far too excited by the prospect.

I hid my smile.

Royce scowled. "Not sure—"

"Won't let her out of my sight," I promised. Hell, if she went into the restroom to pee, I'd probably follow her in there, too.

"Sounds good to me." This from Van, Riot's guitarist. He'd made his way over to where everyone had gathered off to the side of the dance floor. "It's early. Not sure when you turned into a pussy, man, but this shit is embarrassing."

He made a show of looking at his watch that didn't exist.

Dude had better duck because Royce sent him a look that promised he was about to get his teeth knocked from his mockin' mouth. "Since I found something more important than pissing my nights away on shit that doesn't matter."

Van cracked up and lifted his glass in Emily's direction. "Sure, man, sure. Guess I'd be eager to head home, too, if I had a woman that looked like that."

Emily wrapped herself around Royce and tossed a wry smile in Van's direction. "And a cryin' baby. Don't forget the cryin' baby."

Van held his tattooed arms up in surrender, his drink sloshing over the side of his glass. "Now that would be a hard pass."

Emily gasped like she was offended. "That is my daughter you're talkin' about."

Van grinned. "Hey, as long as it's yours and not mine, we're good. I'll chill here while you go handle that, yeah?"

"Gladly," Royce said, though his attention was skating back to his sister who'd started dancing with Tamar again.

Anxiety oozed from his flesh.

I took a swig of my beer, stuffing down the guilt that flashed. "I've got her, man. Let her dance. Won't let her out of my sight. Promise I'll get her home safe. Go take care of your family."

While I take care of mine.

The words supplied themselves in my mind before I had the chance to squelch them.

What the ever lovin' fuck?

There I went.

Gettin' reckless. Wishing for things that could never be. Letting reality skate out from under me. Losing sight and feelin' like I was seeing for the first time.

Royce contemplated for a beat and then stretched out his hand. "All right."

When I shook it, he squeezed hard and leaned in to mutter where only I could hear, "Trusting you. Take care of her. Don't let anyone near her. Got me?"

Clearly, I was included in those numbers.

I squeezed back, not sure if it was in annoyance or agreement. Because anything Royce was thinking right then was spot-on.

He was thinkin' he couldn't trust my greedy ass as far as a bull could toss me, but he knew, too, that I would guard Maggie with my life.

That whoever that bastard was who'd gotten to her last week wasn't gonna get through me.

Was also clear in his eyes that he'd seen what'd gone down in that kitchen this morning, and he was speculatin' on all kinds of salacious things while trying not to believe them, either.

This thing that I didn't know how to fight any longer.

Pulling away, he went over to his sister, held her tight and told her a bunch of stuff in her ear that she nodded along to as she hugged him hard.

Then he peeled away and took Emily's hand, and Ems was

giving me a small, knowing wave as they wound the rest of the way through the fray.

While I tried to settle my nerves that instantly took on an edge. Protectiveness and greed.

Maggie, Tamar, and Shea got right back to the party while half our group left to return to their families on the bus.

I remained on the fringes like I wasn't a partner to it.

But that didn't mean I wasn't feeling it.

Didn't mean I wasn't gettin' hammered with every tidal wave of joy that crashed from her.

She was havin' a blast, and it was the damned best thing to see.

This girl so close to free besides for the bullshit she'd gone and gotten herself wrapped up in. Bullshit that made me so fuckin' proud that I thought my spirit would bust right outta my chest, all while wanting to hedge this girl in a forcefield of protection.

The thought of it had my attention skating the crowd again, ensuring no strangers got close.

Wasn't the strangers who were the problem, though.

It was that fucker Van who thought it was the opportune time to sidle up to Maggie. He took her hand and spun her like the girls had been doing. But he had that look in his eye.

Lust.

Maggie remained light. Laughing as he spun her, and then he was tugging her back to him and looping an arm around her waist and tucking her firm against his seedy body.

Red flashed through my sight.

Fucking fury.

I itched, trying to stand still.

Which was straight bullshit, but it didn't matter a thing because I couldn't breathe. Air squeezed from my lungs, and my spirit screamed in possession.

Lyrik West scraped a chuckle at my side, knocking me out of the fog. "You're fucked, man."

I grunted as I took a swig of my beer. "That obvious?"

He lifted a disbelieving brow. "You might as well hoist a Maggie flag in the air."

"Shit," I grumbled.

"Question is, what are you gonna do about it? Seems to me, you're the one who's been skating tonight, and that girl's been silently beggin' you to show her what she means to you. Or are you gonna let that sleaze Van show her what he can offer, instead?"

Last was a taunt, and there was no sitting still any longer. I drained my beer, slammed the empty on the table, and pushed my way into the crowd.

Music unruly and a bit wild. As wild as the crush that danced and laughed and gave themselves over to the revelry.

Maggie must have felt me coming because those eyes snapped my way, and my heart rate amped. Need twitched my fingers.

She smiled a coy smile from over Van's shoulder, and shit, she knew exactly what she was doing to me.

Van tossed his gaze my direction when he realized Maggie was no longer paying him any attention. A glower dented his forehead.

"Excuse me for a minute, man."

I slipped between them without giving him a chance to respond, jostling the asshole aside.

Maggie bit that lip and tried to hide her giggle.

"Wow, dude," Van objected.

"Royce's orders," I clipped. Not that I needed Royce's input, but I figured mentioning his name would be a sure-fire way to get rid of the prick without making a scene.

And I was about zero-point-five seconds from making a damn scene.

Dude was cool and all until he'd turned his sights on my girl.

My girl.

She grinned up at me after I'd twirled her and hauled her up close, trying to play the embrace off like we were just *friends*.

Think that idea had been bullshit since the moment we'd claimed it all those months ago.

Her nearness filled my senses with her sweetness.

Jasmine and vanilla and a touch of that spice.

That mouth nothin' but wry and overwhelming temptation.

Playful and genuine.

My chest clutched.

"Someone's jealous," she sang over the roar, her words a tiny bit slurred.

I grunted at her while a smile tugged at the corner of my mouth.

"You got a problem with that, little miss drunkey drunk?"

Her giggle deepened, and a flush splashed her cheeks, and heat lifted in the bare space between us.

One touch from this girl and I caught fire.

"And how do you think I felt with all those women flocking around you?"

My eyebrow arched. "What women?"

Scoffing a soft sound, Maggie shook her head and tried to keep her voice light like it didn't bother her all that much. "Are you serious right now? There was a whole herd over there salivating at the mouth to get a taste of you."

"Didn't notice."

She frowned like I was full of it.

"Mean it." It was a low rumble. A promise. An oath.

Getting gutsy, I reached out and ran my thumb along the curve of her top lip. "How could I notice anyone else when the only one I see is you?"

"Rhys." She whispered it as her fingers curled into my shirt.

"Goddess Girl."

There wasn't a thing I could do but wrap her up, sliding an arm around her waist and bringing her flush. The other went way up high on her back, fingers tangling a bit in that hair.

Her heart beat manic against mine.

Drawing mine closer.

Closer and closer.

Right up to that edge where I could feel myself slipping off the side.

"Maggie." My mouth was at her temple, and my stomach was in these fucked-up, twisted knots.

No longer sure exactly where my heart belonged.

We danced like that for what seemed like hours, me spinning her then bringing her in to sway, our bodies and minds and spirits in sync. She'd smile, and I'd do the same, and I'd murmur the words to the Carolina George cover the band played.

She'd laugh and her fingers would tease, and the night moved on in a magical sort of way.

Like we'd been given a reprieve. A moment for us. Couple by couple, our friends left for the night, while we danced and pretended like we weren't so wrapped up in each other that not a soul noticed.

Like Lyrik had said, I was completely fucked.

So entirely fucked when Maggie got gutsy, too, and she let those hands wander.

Gliding up my chest and down my back and spreading over my ass.

I rubbed my hard dick against her belly.

Maggie moaned and clutched me tighter.

Two of us dancing in the flames.

Greed and gluttony.

Then I dipped her low, and she laughed, and her fingers drove into my hair.

I hauled her back up, and we swayed again, and she whispered, "My Stallion," as she peered up at me with those eyes. "Ask me what I want right now."

Need filled her voice.

Every cell in my body fisted.

My palm spread across her cheek. "What do you want, Sweet Thing?"

She swallowed hard. "You. I want you, Rhys."

"Well, since it is your birthday, darlin', what kind of gentleman would I be if I didn't give you what you wanted?" I let the tease wind into the words, but there was no keeping the tenderness out.

Her eyes flashed with softness and affection and everything I'd been fighting.

Energy sparked.

A crack in the air.

That pull that whipped and whirred.

A low hum that drowned out everything except for that call that shouted between us.

And I realized we were just standing still in the middle of the crush. Nothin' else existing but the two of us. One hot flaming second from devouring this girl in front of her brother's band.

"Need to get you out of here. Right now." It was a growl of desperation.

She nodded hard, and I peeled myself away so I could grab her by the hand, and I was marching through the crowd with the girl fumbling and giggling behind me as we made a beeline for the door.

Shouldering through the mass that had grown thick.

Lyrik, Tamar, and the guys from Riot were the last ones standing. I barely gave them a jut of my chin as a parting good-bye as I dragged Maggie along behind me. I hoped on all the hopes that they'd buy into the idea that I'd been charged with getting her home safely, and not that my actual intentions were gettin' her out of these clothes so I could get into her tight, sweet body.

None of them were really paying us that much mind, anyway, but Lyrik looked up from where he had his face buried in his wife's neck long enough to shoot me a smirk.

Right.

Not obvious at all.

I hauled her out the door and into the humid night. The night sky drooped low, and the streetlamps lining the walk cast a blurry glow into the stagnant, steamy darkness. The door closed behind us, cutting the uproar to a muffled drone, two of us alone for the first time tonight.

I took full advantage of it.

I no longer recognized when I was delving into dangerous behavior. A fell swoop of bad marks that had started to blur since touching this girl felt far too right to be wrong.

In an instant, I had her pinned against the wall. Kissing her hard. My hands in her hair and hers fisted in my shirt while she struggled to get closer to me.

Her tongue stroked me into delirium, and her hands drove me to madness.

I dug in my pocket to get my phone, and I barely even broke the kiss while I fumbled into the app to call a ride. Somehow, I managed to press confirm with hardly looking at it, accepting the two-minute wait, and got right back to kissing the hell out of my girl.

Our mouths were a collision of tongues and lips and nippin' teeth.

Nothing else mattered but this.

My hands got lost in her hair, and my tongue was dead set on taking all I could get. Relishing the moment. This *chance*. Knowing full well the end would come but unable to stand the thought of it.

Our hearts raced, and I got that same high sensation I got when I was flying down an open road in my car. No boundaries. No limits.

That desire screamed. Begging for surrender.

For me to finally just let go.

"Rhys," she whimpered, grinding against me right on the wall, half giggling, half moaning against my mouth.

I smiled beneath our kiss. "Ruinin' me, Sweet Thing."

"Already ruined. So ruined…" she slurred as her nails dug deeper. Should have been worried. But I just smiled wider and hoisted her up into my arms when the car pulled to a stop at the curb behind us.

"Since we're goin' down, at least we're goin' down together," I told her.

Could feel her grin.

Her joy.

My heart raced faster.

"Take me home, Rhys."

"Gladly, baby." I didn't set her down as I spun us around and carried her to the car. I leaned into the front window that the dude rolled down as Maggie clung to me from the front, giggling and burying her face in my shoulder.

"R. Manning?"

"That's me."

He gave a jerk of his chin, and I opened the back door with one hand.

Maggie slipped a little, and she yelped, and I was laughing as I held her tighter. "Got you."

"Don't let go," she breathed.

"Never." Fuck, what I wouldn't give for that not to be a lie.

I slipped us into the backseat with the girl straddlin' my lap.

Neither of us were willing to break the connection.

She dove right back into kissing me while the car pulled from the curb and took to the street, zipping through the night while the intensity between Maggie and I grew.

Red hot.

Desperate in a way it hadn't been before.

No longer tentative.

Like our bodies weren't hoping for something to happen but rather that it would never end.

"You are somethin', Maggie."

She grinned, edging back to look down at me. All that hair rained around her face, and those eyes watched me in the flashes of light that stroked down from the streetlights we passed under.

"Something, huh?" It was pure playfulness.

I held her by the outside of the hips and rocked her against my aching dick. "Yeah, somethin'. Thought I was gonna die tonight. Not gettin' to reach out and touch you. Tell the whole damned world that you're mine."

That sweet gentleness fluttered through her expression. Though mixed with it tonight was a temptress.

"I am yours, Rhys. Yours for the taking. Anything you want."

My sweet siren played her siren's song.

Entrancing.

Mesmerizing.

Sucking me in and taking me under.

Spellbound.

Wishing for every impossible thing she offered.

"Goddess Girl," I murmured up at her. One of my hands wound in that lush hair while the other locked around her waist.

Girl had on that skirt, and it was bunched around her thighs, her pussy barely covered by a slip of fabric.

Heat burned.

An inferno set to ten.

Her fingers were scratching into my beard as she took over the mind-bendin' kiss.

Wrecked.

Fuckin' wrecked.

Because she was whispering at my lips, "My sweet stallion. I feel you. I see you through all of it. I *know* you."

She said it like her own confession, and our movements grew frantic.

Intensity rising.

Felt the eyes on us from the rearview. "You two fuck in my car, I at least get to watch."

Gasping, Maggie buried her laugh in my shoulder. Embarrassment billowed from her. I chuckled low and dug my fingers into her bare thighs while I met the driver's gaze through the mirror. "Sorry, dude. Not into sharin' my girl."

She laughed deeper.

This sexy, needy sound, and I was thanking God when we finally made it across the highway and onto the island. He made the few short turns, and we were finally pulling into the round drive.

Maggie jerked back and peered through the window. Stillness echoed from the house.

Just in case, I slipped her off my lap, gave the guy a quick, "Thank you," before I opened the door. I took a furtive glance around to make sure we were in the clear before I pulled Maggie from the backseat.

Grabbing her hand, we started slinking under the cover of night toward the side door.

Quiet as we could though our hearts were beating so loud I was pretty sure it might wake the entire town.

Maggie held onto my hand with both of hers, her high, high heels clicking on the walk.

I tossed her a look over my shoulder and put a finger to my lips. "Shh."

"Bossy," she mocked just below her breath.

I edged her against the side wall where we were completely hidden by the tall trees and shrubs. "I'll show you bossy."

She reached out and squeezed my dick.

Holy fuck.

Choking, my hands shot out to the wall on either side of her head, and she grinned up at me.

"Fuck. Baby."

"Shh." She grinned. All kinds of sly.

A low rumble of greed and laughter rolled up my throat. "Sweet Siren. And here I thought it was me who was the trouble."

And then I was scooping her up and into my arms, and the girl was squealing not so quietly, and I was carrying her through the door and up the stairs. I paused only for a second at the top to make sure it was empty before I raced the rest of the way into my room.

I set her on her feet and clicked the lock behind us.

Shutting us in our haven.

Where it was just me and Maggie and no one else on this earth had a fuckin' say.

She swayed softly, like she heard our own beat.

A song weaving through the night.

I took a step forward.

Energy snapped.

A shockwave.

She stepped backward, running her hands over the front of her silky tank.

A lure.

A trap.

One I didn't ever wanna get free of.

I went to ticking through the buttons of my shirt, winding it off my shoulders and dropping it to the floor as I took another step her direction.

She rasped a needy sound, those eyes raking me in the night. "You're so beautiful, Rhys. I look at you, and I shake. And then I feel you…" She touched her heart, right up close to the scar. "And I know where I belong."

"Maggie." It was a warning. Desperation. "Make me wanna break every rule for you."

She stared at me through the shadows. "Let's make our own. Let's show them we aren't a mistake."

A growl reverberated through the room.

Self-control fracturing.

World breaking away.

Nothin' left but me and this girl.

Me and this girl.

She took another step back as I took one forward, and she was hiking up that skirt. Dragging it up her toned thighs.

Teasin' me.

A smirk ticked up.

"Ah, you wanna play?"

My insides twisted in a clutch, my poor cock hard and hungry. I went for her, gripping her sweet face as I took her mouth.

This kiss wasn't soft.

It was raw.

Potent.

Rough.

"You taste like a dream, baby."

Like a fantasy. An impossibility.

"And you taste like everything I've been missing. Like I've been starving for my whole life, and now I finally understand what it means to be satisfied. Filled. And still, I know I'll always want more," she said almost frantically.

Those hands went to work on the buckle of my pants, and she was unzipping them and pushing them down my thighs. This time when she took my cock in her hand, it wasn't because she was playing.

She stroked me, long and purposed.

I shuddered in her fist. "Damn, baby. You know how to wreck a man."

"You deserve it," she rumbled at my mouth. "Doing what you do to me."

"You like it?"

It was only half a tease.

That protectiveness rising up to make its mark. Telling me I always had to take caution with this girl. Make sure I wasn't pushing her toward something she wasn't ready for.

"Do I like it?" She leaned in closer, her words a breath of desire across my face. "I love it. Let go, Rhys. You'd never hurt me."

I dragged that shirt up over her head. She wasn't wearing a bra, and I tried to mask the rage that surged to life when I saw the little butterfly stitches that covered the spot exactly over the spot where that fucker had cut her before.

Wasn't right.

It was sick and twisted.

And I wanted to make someone pay for what they'd done.

"Let go," she begged again, the words wisps of that spell she kept luring me under. "Right now, it's only you and me. Let go."

Maggie stroked me harder.

Girl whimpered as she did, her head rocking back when I went to kissing a path up and down the slender column of her neck. My hands slipped from her jaw, all the way down until I was cupping her tiny, perfect tits in my hands.

She arched into my hold.

"You got any idea how fuckin' gorgeous you are? How I was hard all night, watchin' you on that dance floor? Thought I was gonna claim you right in front of your brother."

She gave a quick nod, her words thick. "I felt you. How badly you wanted me. Almost as badly as I wanted you. And I wanted you to. Claim me. Just like I'm begging you to do now."

"Maggie. Baby." I touched her face.

Her lips parted, and she blinked up at me through the darkness.

Vulnerable.

Open.

Fierce.

Every fucking thing I hadn't known I'd been missing. That vacant spot that howled from within closing in.

Clotting up.

Our tongues tangled in a clash of need.

Flames lapped.

Energy singed.

Our lips greedy and desperate.

And I doubted there was any stopping it.

This girl taking me right up to the edge.

Lust thundered against the walls.

Ricocheting.

Gaining strength with each bounding pass.

A fever pitch that screamed.

And she was raking her nails up and down my back as I pressed my dick to her belly.

Our bodies were frantic.

Banging together.

Spinning.

Turning and pressing and begging against every solid surface I could find to pin her against. The walls. The high footboard of the bed. The balcony window where the waves beat against the shore beneath the stars.

I spun her around.

Maggie gasped and splayed her hands against the glass.

She still had on her heels, her back bare and lush, her shoulders so fucking sexy I wanted to sink in my teeth. That scrap of a skirt covered her ass, and I gathered it up so I could palm her cheeks.

She pushed back into my hold. "Rhys."

I kicked off my shoes and shrugged the rest of the way out of my pants, taking my briefs with them as I shoved them down.

My cock pointed for the sky, and I nestled it against her crease, molding myself to her from behind.

Spreading my hands around to her belly, I leaned in and kissed along the delicate curve of her shoulder.

Wanted to devour every inch of this girl.

Worship her.

Give it all.

"Rhys." She leaned farther back, rubbing her ass against my dick.

I groaned. "Baby. So fuckin' sexy wrapped up in all this sweet. Not even fair. Wasn't prepared for you. Tell me what you want."

Her hands pressed harder to the window, and she was grinding herself against me. This girl never hesitating to demand what she needed. "You. Always, you."

I groaned again, and I dropped to my knees behind her. I reached underneath the fabric of her skirt so I could grab the edges of her panties and drag them down the length of her lust-inducing legs.

Girl had my head spinning as I peeled them down.

Rushing me with a type of lightheadedness I didn't expect.

Dizziness blistering.

My chest both heavy and light.

I twisted her underwear free of her ankles, and I kissed back up her calves, savoring every inch that was this girl. "Baby," I murmured as I went.

Chills lifted on her flesh, and she was whimpering by the time I made it up the back of her thighs.

Then I was gripping her cheeks again, nudging her legs apart, and dragging my tongue from her clit to her ass.

Her knees buckled. "Rhys."

"You good, Sweet Thing?"

"More," was all she said.

"Turn around," I told her, and those eyes met mine where I was kneeling in front of her.

Girl's back hooked to the window, her knees rocking and her soul quaking.

I reached up and dragged a finger through her slit before I slipped two fingers in real deep.

She moaned. "More."

I shifted her so one of her legs rested on my shoulder, opening her up wide so I could give her what she was asking for.

I curled my fingers in the spot that made her shake while I suckled at her throbbing clit.

Lapped and laved and licked her into a puddle.

All it took was a few deep drives for the girl to go off like a rocket.

Her hands dove into my hair and ripped hard, spurring me deeper and faster while she writhed.

Her legs gave way as pleasure shot through her being. She sank to the carpet and crawled back for me. Climbing up to straddle my waist, taking me in her hand to position me at her tight, sweet cunt before she sank down deep.

"Fuuccccccccccccck." The moan was out. Reverberating the space. "So good. How's it possible you feel so good?"

Her arms curled around my neck, and her fingers clawed into my skin. "You are the best thing I've ever felt. The best thing I've ever had. Nothing compares to this, Rhys. Nothing. No matter what happens, I need you to know that. I will never regret a second I've spent with you."

My arms curled around her waist as she started to ride me. All that hair raining down around her shoulders. Girl the most gorgeous thing I'd ever seen.

"My stallion."

And her callin' me that almost hurt and felt so perfectly right because not a soul in this world knew me the way she did.

So we clutched and murmured and let our mouths race over each other's flesh.

Touched and adored.

Moaned and whispered.

"Nothing, Rhys. Nothing in this world."

She gazed down at me while I stared up at her, our bodies gripping and pitching and rocking.

I knew what she meant. What she was saying.

Didn't need the words when I'd never felt anything so intense.

I knew tumblin' usually resulted in broken bones and bloodied knees.

But still I was saying, "Nothin' in this world, Maggie. Never. Not in all my life."

And it felt like a betrayal, but not admittin' it felt like a betrayal, too.

So I let this girl carry me to ecstasy.

Let her fingers play and her body hypnotize.

She dragged almost all the way up, watching between us as she did, my cock soaked and glistening with the girl.

Everything shimmered.

She slammed back down.

Everything glowed.

And I no longer knew anything but Maggie and me. Our bodies that lurched and quickened. Our energy that zapped and whipped and bound us in a way I'd never been bound.

My soul shook, and I murmured her name. "Maggie." My

thumb found her clit. "Come with me, baby."

Come with me.

Stay with me.

Find a way with me.

But I didn't know how to make the words come out.

So, she fell with me instead.

Bliss breaking us together.

Sending us over that edge.

Spilling us over the side.

She gasped and writhed, and I came and came, this girl's body hugging me tight as she pulled the greatest pleasure out of me.

Our bodies shivered and twitched, and we relished in the afterglow. She hugged me for what felt like forever, her face up high on my neck, girl wrapped around me where we sat on the floor.

My arms refused to let her go.

Because I knew I would never get to experience a moment greater than this.

Knew I could never feel anything bigger than this.

And I was sure, right then, that I would give her my all.

Willingly.

Wholly.

All the while praying that I wouldn't fuck it up all over again. That for once, maybe…just maybe I could be right.

Finally, I stood with her still in my arms, and she held on tighter as I took her into the bathroom to clean us up.

Then I carried her into my room and helped her into her panties, and then I grabbed a clean tee of mine and pulled it over her head.

A blush filled her cheeks, and she let her gaze wander down my shirt. "It's different, isn't it?"

I moved into her space, my hand on her cheek. "Yeah, Maggie, it's different. It's everything."

Then I scooped her up and tucked her into my bed. I nestled in at her side.

Maggie sighed.

I kissed her forehead. "Happy birthday, baby."

"Best birthday ever," she whispered.

"I'm so glad I got to share it with you."

She nodded, and I heard her silent prayer. That we'd get the chance to spend a hundred more together. And I guessed I was the fool to pray for it, too.

Rhys

*S*hock slammed me into consciousness when I was ripped from the most blissful-sort of sleep by two hands that grabbed me by the shoulders and tore me from bed. Still half asleep, I flew across the room.

An explosion of rage blasted the space.

The force of it bashed the walls and rumbled across the floor like an earthquake that was picking up speed.

I hit the carpet with a tumble, trying to orient myself, to get a hold on the threat, while Maggie screeched.

My attention darted for the girl considerin' she was the only thing that mattered. She'd scrambled to her knees on my bed with the sheets we'd been tangled in bunched at her chest.

Charcoal eyes were wide and terrified.

First instinct was to rush for her. Throw myself over her and promise her I'd take any harm coming her way.

Only thing that managed to keep me from doin' it was the tablet that was tossed to the bed like a barrier between us. Maggie's attention was instantly drawn there, too.

Took me a second to process the bullshit I was seeing. To let the bleariness clear so I could make out what was on the screen.

Shouldn't have been a shocker that it was that motherfuckin' site that sought to ruin my already ruined life.

My heart seized in my chest, alarm squeezing my ribs so tight I thought they were gonna collapse.

This mornin's story told a very raunchy tale of Maggie and me. There were a bunch of pictures of us out on that darkened street like what we'd been engaged in was some sort of lewd act.

Maggie pressed to the building, skirt bunched up around her thighs with my hips wedged between hers. Another of her straddling me as we'd slipped into the backseat of the car.

My mouth and hands all over her sweet body.

Shit.

Fuck.

Hell.

Not smart on my part.

Gettin' distracted like that.

Not last night or right then.

Because a fist landed at the side of my face without me even preparing myself for the blow. A burst of pain splintered through my brain, so extreme I was a second from losin' coherency.

Lights out.

Rocking to the side on my hands and knees, I blinked hard, trying to keep it together while I shook off the shock.

All while the dread I'd been feeling for weeks careened through my bloodstream, recognizing the fury that stormed the room like an army.

Only this was a one-man battalion.

A ragin', furious man who came for me again. "You piece of shit. I knew it. Knew it."

Another fist landed on the other side of my face. This time I was almost prepared for the knuckles that cracked against my jaw and sent a string of bright lights flashing behind my eyes.

Maggie screamed. "Royce. No. Stop."

Her voice hittin' the air only fueled his anger, and Royce was unlocking and jerking open my door. "You fucked my sister? I trusted you."

It was pure disgust.

Horror dripped like venom from his mouth.

The sound of the door banging against the wall added to the riot.

To the roaring in my ears.

To the pain that throbbed my face.

I barely looked up when Royce came stalking for me, dude that dark storm that had made landfall. He hauled me up by the arm while I was wearin' nothing but my underwear and tossed me out into the hall.

Barely kept my footing as I slipped out onto the hard marble floor. Somehow, I righted myself, then I was reeling again when another blow slammed my face.

I let him.

Took it.

Hell, I basically begged for it since I'd been asking for trouble from the start.

I bottled the violence that nearly burst every capillary in my system as he came at me again.

Cracking and fracturing and splitting me apart.

The instinct to stand and fight back.

Thing was, a brawl between Royce and I wouldn't end pretty for either of us.

And this was on me.

I deserved whatever penalty I had coming my way.

Stealing from the pure.

Taking from the good.

"Sick motherfucker." The words grated from Royce's mouth, dude not even pretending like he hadn't come unhinged.

No doubt, the fear and protection he felt for his sister, all the years he'd spent trying to make sure she had a fighting chance—the time he'd sacrificed behind bars so she could fly—had hit a boilin' point.

I'd been the dumbfuck to turn the burner to high.

But I couldn't regret it.

Couldn't regret a thing when I let him back me down the sweeping staircase and across the ramblin' main floor, knowing we needed to get out of this house before we woke everyone up. We both knew full well no one else needed to witness this.

Because the guy had death on his face and mayhem in his body.

I'd take it.

All of it.

For Maggie.

Maggie.

Maggie who was right behind him, whimpering and trying to get ahold of him by the shirt. "Royce. Stop it. Listen to me. You don't understand."

"I understand perfectly."

It was menace.

Hate.

"Asked you to watch over her. Take care of her. And you took advantage of her." His voice curled in revulsion.

Couldn't deny a single one of those things except for the fact I didn't know how to accept what Maggie and I had shared as wrong.

Our time precious.

Treasured.

And I knew…knew my girl wouldn't regret it, either.

Didn't mean this wasn't comin', anyway.

Truth that I could never keep her. Truth I would never be good enough. Truth that my past would always catch up to me.

"No, Royce. Stop. I'm not a child. You don't get to decide who I'm with," she rushed as she fumbled across the floor, grabbing at her brother like she might be able to make a dent in his rage.

Walking backward with my riotin' heart in my throat, I groped behind me to open the back door, glancing once at Maggie in an appeal.

Stay inside. Please. Goddess Girl. This is on me.

The door banged open, and I edged out onto the porch.

The heated planks were hot against my bare feet, sun beltin' down on my skin that was already covered in sweat.

The ocean pattered on the shore behind us, but it didn't do anything to give a semblance of peace.

Because my girl followed us out anyway.

Her panic this bubbling, boilin' thing.

"Stay inside, Maggie." The words left me on a low plea.

Royce growled.

Maggie whimpered and followed us out.

"Please, baby," I begged. Last thing I wanted was for her to feel guilty for this. For her to witness this.

Apparently, it was the wrong damned thing to say.

Because Royce was coming for me, and I was backing out farther, and a sob was eruptin' from Maggie when Royce punched me again.

This one was a hook that got me under the chin.

Fuck, he had a fist.

I floundered backward, stumbling, losing footing and falling off the edge of the elevated deck.

I took it.

Fell to the sand below.

Misery seared through every inch of me.

Face on fire.

But I guessed it was my heart that was gettin' charred to ash.

I managed to get up to my hands and knees, pushing up to kneeling in time for Royce to clamor down and bust me with those knuckles again.

My head whipped to the side.

Blood gushed from my nose and splattered on the sand.

Maggie wept, and all I wanted to do was go to her. Arms this wild ache to hold her. Promise her none of this shit was her fault. Couldn't stand the sound of her torment.

But it kept coming. "Oh god. Please, stop."

Could barely sense that we'd gotten an audience. Emily and Mel burst through the door. Two of them gasped and cried out with what was going down. "Oh my god. What is going on? Royce. No!"

Whole time, Royce glowered down at me, old pain leaking out of him like a broken main. "Get up, you piece of shit. Stop being a pussy and fight like a man."

The words were shards of razor-sharp glass.

My head barely shook. "No, man."

I'd take it. I'd take it.

Maggie tried to scramble for us. Emily held her back while she shouted at her husband, "Royce, stop it. Please. Don't do this."

"Rhys," Maggie cried from where Emily hugged her to her chest.

Energy crashed.

My girl.

My girl.

I barely chanced a glance at her, knowin' my face was all busted up. Last thing I wanted was for her to have to see any more. "Baby…please go back inside."

"I can't."

Another blow, this one to my temple.

Darkness clawed at my consciousness.

So close to gettin' knocked clean out.

My chest clutched, and I fought to keep the madness from getting free.

"Get up!" Royce's shout trembled. Rocked and pitched with his agony. Dude thinkin' he'd failed when that was on me.

I dropped my head.

Preparing for the next blow.

"Get up." This time he begged it, and the breath was heaving from him, and he was ripping at his hair. "Get up. Get up, you piece of shit."

His voice had grown thin, sounding of disbelief.

I waited for another blow.

"Jesus Christ." Royce stumbled to the side in some kind of shock. "Tell me you're not in love with her?"

My spirit screamed, and I croaked over the truth of what I couldn't deny any longer. I slumped forward and let it consume me.

Overwhelm me.

Overpower me.

That feelin' that I'd been fighting for so long.

And I wasn't looking at Royce when I lifted my head.

I was looking at Maggie.

Our gazes tangled and that energy slashed.

A second later, Maggie broke free of Emily's hold and came running for me. Missing two steps and jumping off the boardwalk, feet flingin' sand as she flailed in my direction wearing my shirt. She was on her knees three feet away, frantically crawling the rest of the way until she was throwing herself at me.

My arms encircled her.

Finally accepting their place.

Tears stained that stunnin' face. I reached up and cupped her cheeks, trying to brush away the tears.

"Do you feel it?" she barely managed to ask through the sobs coating her voice, those eyes all over me, taking in everything.

"Do I feel it? Sweet Thing… How could I not? Don't think there's a way not to love you. God, I love you. Know I don't deserve it, but I do. So much. So damn much." The confession poured out.

I didn't even try to stop it.

More tears streaked down her cheeks, but it was different, that joy gushing free, and she was mumbling, "I love you. I love you, Rhys. More than anything."

In a frenzy, the girl was kissing me, and I didn't care that it hurt—that we were probably smearing blood all over the place—I was kissing her back, my arms wrapped around her waist as she pressed her sweet heart against the thunder raging in mine.

"Died and went to heaven," I rumbled.

Maggie sighed and dropped her forehead to mine. "No, Rhys. It's time to live."

twenty-nine

Maggie

I dabbed at the cut on the corner of Rhys' mouth, eyeing the giant of a man who leaned against the vanity gazing down at me.

My insides twisted in love.

Love and hurt and hope.

God, he looked like a beautiful mess.

He'd pulled on some jeans, though his hair was tousled, and his face was littered with cuts and scrapes.

But what held me rapt was that ocean of blue that roiled and churned.

His severity a blaze in the air though he remained almost frozen while I patched him up.

I kept vacillating between anger and ecstasy, and I swallowed the clot of it as I cleaned the largest cut that was at the top of his cheek. "I can't believe he did this to you."

I stood wedged between his thick thighs. He reached out and squeezed my hip. "Believe me, Sweet Thing, if I thought someone was hurtin' you? I'd do the same."

My head shook. "But he should have known—"

He squeezed a little harder. "Mags...your brother loves you. Would do anythin' for you. You're gonna come first, no matter what. And I let those pictures happen. Deserve to get my ass kicked for that alone, not to mention the rest of it."

Blue eyes dimmed with anger and remorse.

"I don't care what the world says about us, Rhys. Let them talk all they want. What matters is how the two of us feel."

His expression was grim while that love poured out from a reservoir deep within him. His emotions ablaze. At odds yet somehow twining with mine. It was difficult for either of us to find air under the pressure of it.

"Wish that was the only thing that mattered," he finally admitted.

"Isn't it?" I asked, trying to ignore the way my heart rate slugged and slowed with the way he said it.

Something cold rushed across my flesh.

"Maggie, I..." Rhys hesitated. Warred. I could feel the old grief that had kept trying to get free pushing at the surface of his spirit.

And I was terrified of it and wanted to hold it all the same.

A flop of hair fell over his eye, and I carefully reached up and brushed it out of his face.

Tenderly.

"Need to tell you somethin'." Misery filled his words.

"I know."

His face pinched in agony.

Setting the cloth aside, I reached up and cupped his jaw, his beard rough against my palm. "There is nothing you could tell me that would make me love you any less."

The promise rasped from my mouth, and I prayed he felt me the same way as I felt him.

That he would know my sincerity the way I was sure of his.

Anguish crested from his being. "Wish that was the truth, Maggie." He gathered up my hand and pressed it to his mouth almost frantically. "Warned you that I'm really good at ruinin' the things I love most. And I don't want to mess this up, but I'm afraid I'm not strong enough."

Torment lashed.

A torrent of it.

Rising fast and sucking him under.

I edged closer, erasing the barest inch that separated us, staring up at this man who was still clinging to my hand. "You are the strongest person I know, Rhys." I took our entwined hands and pressed them to my chest. "Do you think I can't feel it? Your strength? Your goodness? The fierceness that radiates from you? My stallion."

He flinched and my name broke on his tongue. "Maggie."

We both froze with the knock that sounded on the bathroom door.

I eased back, but only an inch because I couldn't handle any space between us. "Come in."

Emily poked her head through. Her expression was cautious, her voice an apology. "Hey, you two."

"Hi." I forced a weary smile.

Sympathy and remorse coated hers.

"Em-Girl," Rhys muttered, going for a smirk that fell flat.

She blew out a sigh as she stepped the rest of the way into the bathroom. "I'm so sorry this spiraled out of control. I should have—" Helplessly, she gestured at the open door.

"Nothin' you could do." Rhys cut her off with a shake of his head. "Knew it was comin'. All's good."

"Is it?" She frowned her disagreement. "I should have kept a closer eye. Closer tabs. Made sure I could intervene before my husband became a ravin' lunatic."

Her disappointment in my brother was patent.

Rhys looked at me, and one of those soft twitches tweaked under his beard. It had a tumble of that need flapping in my belly. "Yeah. Everything is good. Really damned good."

Tenderness filled that blue gaze.

My heart nearly burst.

Love. Love. Love.

He was right.

So right.

Everything was good and right.

We might have a few things to sort out, but we had each other, and that was the only thing that mattered.

Emily cleared her throat. "I'm glad you feel that way, but it doesn't make it right." Emily swiveled her attention to me. "Your brother is hoping you'd be willing to talk to him, though, Maggie. I can finish patchin' Rhys up for you if you're willing to hear him out."

I glanced at Rhys who watched me with all that care and affection. He lifted his chin. "Go on, Sweet Thing."

"But we need to talk."

"Think you'd better clear the air with your brother before we clear up anythin' else."

I hesitated.

"We'll talk later," he rumbled. "Promise."

"Okay."

I started to walk away, but he snatched me by the wrist and swung me back around.

A giggle busted out on its own accord.

Thanks to my brother, this wasn't exactly a happy moment, but still, I felt like flying.

Caught between joy and the injustice of what Royce had done.

Rhys dipped down for a swift kiss that stole my breath. When he pulled back, he was grinning one of those grins and ruining me all over again. "Now that I can kiss you any time I want, not gonna be the fool who squanders it. Now don't be too hard on your brother. Thanks to this mornin', I get to be kissin' on my girl any time I want. And I *want*."

He waggled his brows.

Pure teasing.

Giddiness leapt.

I popped up on my toes and gave him the peck of another.

"Promise?" Lightness wound its way into my tone.

His hand framed my face, running down to tip up my chin. Affection rippled through his expression. "All the time, Sweet

Thing."

I stared for a beat.

Locked.

Held.

Happy.

"Now go on before I carry you back to my bed and your brother doesn't see you for the next three days."

He winked.

And I finally understood what it meant to swoon.

My heart fluttery and my body flustered.

Slowly, I forced myself to pull away. I ran my fingers through my hair, trying to straighten myself out as I thought about facing down my brother.

I was incredibly angry, but I guessed there was a part of me that understood, too.

I'd kept my brother in the dark. Made him question. Made him paranoid. Made him worry. Not that it was an excuse since I hadn't told him in the first place because I'd worried he'd pull something like this.

"He's in our room," Emily said like encouragement.

I nodded as I passed by her, and she reached out and squeezed my hand. "He really feels awful, Maggie. I'm not makin' excuses for him because that was unwarranted and irrational, and I'm really pissed off, too. But I know him, and I know when he's hurtin'. And he's hurtin' bad."

She glanced at Rhys with a playful grin. "Maybe not hurtin' as bad as your boyfriend here, though."

Boyfriend.

A blaze of giddiness had me clamping my teeth down on my bottom lip, and I tossed my attention to Rhys who chuckled low.

"Nah, I let him get at me. Dude's lucky. Would've gotten his ass handed to him had I let go."

Rolling her eyes, Emily started for him, her country drawl thick with her annoyance. "You both would have had your asses handed to you. At least you had some wits about you. Who knows what would have happened if the two of you had really gotten into it." She went to the cabinet where the medical supplies were stored.

"Now I'm gonna need you to put on a shirt if you expect me to doctor you up because…" She curled her nose. "Gross."

"Ah, come now, Em-Girl. You're just sad your man doesn't look like all of this." He puffed out his glorious chest, and his chuckle grew easier.

With that, I forced myself out because a girl could really get distracted.

I took in a couple cleansing breaths. Trying to exhale the anger that wanted to fester and take root. When I felt calm enough, I left my room and headed down the hall to the opposite wing. I gave a soft knock to the partially cracked door before I nudged it open.

Royce sat on the end of their bed, bent over with his face buried in his hands.

Torment and regret blistered from his being.

I stepped in and snapped the door shut behind me.

"Hey," I murmured, cautiously edging his direction. I dragged the footstool from the lounger up closer to him and settled on it a few feet away.

For a long time, we sat in silence. No doubt, my brother was dwelling in his self-imposed misery. I would have rubbed it in except for the fact I could feel his sorrow. The truth of his regret.

Finally, he looked up at me.

A part of him crushed.

"I'm sorry." He heaved it out like a load that crashed to the ground, clanking and battering on the hardwood floors.

"That wasn't right."

He rubbed his hand over his mouth. "I know that, Maggie. I know. But I…I woke up to those pictures…" He swallowed like the thought of them were still bitter. "I lost it, Maggie. Fucking lost it."

I gave him a slight nod. "You did. You didn't even give us a chance to explain."

"Because I never want anything to harm or hurt you, and I just reacted."

"You think I don't know that? That's the only reason I'm sitting here right now. But you can't decide what makes me happy. You can't decide my path. You can't take *my* choice away."

He laughed out a dark sound of self-reproach, and he looked to the ceiling as if he were searching for an answer before he dropped his head back between his shoulders, talking to his feet. "Every intention I've ever had was to take care of you, Maggie."

Warily, he lifted his gaze to mine. "Like I told you last night, since the second I met you, I knew you were my responsibility. Even then, before all the bad shit went down, I knew. I see it now, Maggie. I get it. I fought for your happiness so hard that I didn't give you a chance to fight for it, too. And I'm so damned sorry for that."

I touched his knee. Caught in his sincerity. My brother who had sacrificed everything for me. "Because you love me."

"Yeah, because I love you." His nod was almost grim, and he was shaking his head in disbelief. "Rhys?"

Just his name had butterflies fluttering.

"I know he doesn't exactly check off all your boxes." I cracked the joke as best as I could, trying to keep the trembling out.

Royce leaned his forearms on his thighs.

Looking at the floor. Processing.

"No, he doesn't." He tipped his attention back to me, a single brow quirked. "But does he check off all of yours?"

My chest squeezed.

Happiness and faith flitted and danced.

"All of them, Royce. Ones I'd always hoped for and ones I didn't know existed."

Royce groaned. "Don't need those details, Maggie."

It was almost playful, then his tone turned pensive. "He's different than what I imagined for you."

He didn't need to declare every detriment that clearly went through his mind.

He was too old for me.

He had a reputation.

He was trouble.

He had something dark inside him that he still hadn't shared with me, though I doubted Royce knew anything about that.

"Yeah, he's different than what I imagined, too. Different and better. We might look like we don't match, but he perfectly fills the voids inside me, the same way as I do for him."

"He treats you right?" Royce's pained expression told me he desperately needed the confirmation.

Wistfulness played across my soft smile. "You know, when I saw you with Emily, when I felt you with her…"

I splayed my hands over my chest.

Not holding back.

Deciding for once I wouldn't downplay the way I experienced those around me.

"I thought I would never meet a man who would love me the way you love her. Would never have a man who looked at me that way. It was so beautiful and real…and I was so happy for you two. So happy. And I thought that would be impossible for me because it's so rare to find something so true." Overwhelmed with the intensity of it, moisture filled my eyes. "And I feel that when he touches me. When he looks at me. With everything that comes from his mouth."

Royce's lids dropped closed. Then he nodded. "I'm happy for you, Mag Pie." His one-sided smile was sad. "Terrified, but happy."

"I know that." I pushed to my feet. When he dropped his head, I leaned over and pressed a kiss to his crown and whispered the words, "Thank you for always worrying about me. For taking care of me. For fighting for me. Because of it, I'm here, with this chance. The chance to experience. The chance to make my own mistakes and to claim my own victories. The chance to *love*."

I could hear his hard swallow. "Love you."

"Love you, too."

I started to walk out, and I stalled when his voice hit me from behind. "Just…be careful, Mags. Please. Don't wanna see you get crushed."

I tossed the most confident smile I could find over my shoulder while a bolt of foreboding slammed me. The fact that Rhys had been keeping something from me. The fact I still had all that money sitting under my bed. The fact I'd kept the real danger I was in from my brother.

I guessed in some way, all along, I'd been protecting him, too.

"As long as you promise to stop beating up my boyfriend." I forced as much playfulness into it as I could find.

This time he cracked a smirk. "Now what kind of brother would I be if I promised that?"

I scowled. "Most likely a lying one."

He laughed, then his smirk softened. "I'll try." He fiddled anxiously with his fingers. "It's hard for me to let go."

"I'm not asking you to let go. I'm asking you to stand beside the choices I make."

No matter how reckless they might be.

I guessed both Rhys and I were exhausted because we spent the rest of the day lazing around.

Content.

Comfortable.

Rhys was tough, but I was positive his head had to feel like he was carrying around a boulder. Throbbing and swollen and aching like crazy.

On beach towels, we rested by the shoreline beneath the gleaming rays of the sun with our fingers twined and our souls tangled.

Quietly.

No words needed for this day. Just the satisfaction that we got to have *this*.

Us.

We needed to talk. We could feel the weight of it pressing down. A menacing, murky overcast.

But I think we both needed the reprieve. A moment to just be.

The drop was coming up fast. So far, I'd gotten no further threats, and I'd started to hope that my mother had given up. Maybe there was a tiny spec of a conscience in her, after all. Maybe she regretted what she'd had done to me last week and had decided to let it go.

Slim.

I knew.

More than that, Rhys had seemed wary when I'd returned to the room after I'd spoken with Royce.

Somber and scared, the dread he'd sank into dragging me to the darkest depths of those blue, fathomless eyes.

So instead of pushing, I'd held him quietly.

Surely.

Resolutely.

After our afternoon on the beach, we ate dinner with the family. Daisy continually made us laugh and giggle and sigh, and I wondered if Rhys might be imagining the same thing as me.

A brood of little boys and girls with their daddy's southern accent, playing on the lawn out in front of that old rambling house that would always need work, a stable full of our horses out back.

Me on the porch watching over them with Rhys wrapped around me.

Not a cowboy in sight.

Just my stallion and the family I'd been aching for since I was little.

A place to set free this wealth of love that had been searching for a home.

He squeezed my hand on the table and glanced at me, and I thought maybe...maybe we could be.

Our hearts and bellies full, we dragged our drained bodies upstairs and curled on Rhys' bed just as the sun was sagging in the sky.

"Tired?" he rumbled sleepily where he was propped against the headboard, my cheek on his chest where his heart thudded at a calmed, peaceful beat. He fiddled with my hair as he asked it.

"Exhausted."

"Wore you out last night, huh?" Playfulness wound into his tone.

I peeked up at his beautifully rugged face that was swollen and starting to bruise. "Are you thinking about wearing me out again?"

"Definitely. But after we sleep. Don't think I can move." He groaned with a smile.

"Some kind of stallion you are." I wasn't scared to let go of the tease.

No longer tiptoeing around this man.

A low chuckle rumbled from his chest. "I'll show you stallion. But later. Stallion. Must. Rest," he grumbled, and then he scooted down until his head was on the pillow and we were staring at each other through the bare space.

His face had really started to swell in a bad way. I ached with the strains of fury that wafted like loose threads around my being.

"I'm sorry."

"Come now, Sweet Thing. You think you aren't worth a couple weak punches?"

He winked with a swollen, black and blue eye.

Even though he was being playful, there was no missing the devotion that came on a roar from his being, transferred to me on a whisper that shouted, *I'll never let you go.*

He draped an arm around me and tugged me closer.

I let my fingertips flutter through his beard. The way I'd been longing to do for so long. The action no longer illicit. No longer a secret. The truth of the feeling I'd been holding gliding free of my tongue. "I love you."

He leaned in and kissed my nose. "I love you."

"This feels like a dream," I whispered into the lapping shadows that had begun to fill his room, all mixed with the golden streaks of light that blazed through the drapes.

Serenity.

He hugged me tighter. "No pretendin' with us, remember?"

My spirit squeezed with affection. "No pretending."

He heaved out a sigh, and he snuggled in closer, and I traced my fingers along the contours of his face.

His eyebrows.

His nose.

His lips.

"I couldn't begin to fake this," I murmured.

Massive arms curled so tight. I melted into them.

"No, Goddess Girl. There's no fakin' this."

And like that, we let the world fade away.

My nightmares quieted in his arms, this man who heard me in

my dreams.

I jerked awake. My heart was a thunder that boomed in my ears and pulsed like lead through my veins.

Rhys' heavy arm was still draped over my chest, his breaths deep and long where he was lost to sleep.

I blinked through the thick darkness of his room. Trying to orient myself. To figure out what had knocked me from the peace.

My phone vibrated from his nightstand, the light breaking through the night.

Carefully, I peeled Rhys' arm off me and gently laid it beside him.

He grunted and moaned before he turned fully onto his stomach.

Trying to slough the apprehension, I quietly climbed over him and out of bed, telling myself to stop overreacting about a text.

But there was just something in the air that wouldn't let me settle.

As if everything I'd once thought paranoia, what I'd tried to quell and outrun, had manifested as real.

I grabbed my phone and tiptoed out of his room and into the bathroom so I could see who was trying to get ahold of me.

I craned my ear to the sleeping house. My phone told me it was just after midnight, and Rhys and I had been asleep for more than four hours.

I skimmed my thumb over the faceplate and entered my code, frowning when I saw the texts from the unknown number.

I squinted as I stared at the first. It was a picture from last night that had been in the tabloid.

The one where I'd been on Rhys' lap in the back of the car.

An intimate moment that had been stolen for gain.

But this?

I could feel the intent.

Something sinister and cruel as the image stared back at me, lit

up like an omen in the darkness.

Unease churned in my stomach.

Fingers starting to shake, I scrolled to whatever words had been texted below it.

Did you know you're sleeping with the devil?

Sickness surged. Anxiety and apprehension.

Even though part of me wanted to shut down my phone, bury whatever maliciousness this person wanted to convey, I warily began to scan through the pictures that had been sent to my number, unable to stop myself from taking in the scene.

One I'd known full well existed.

The pictures were of Rhys from throughout the years, and he wasn't alone in any of them. He was with woman after woman, each of them wearing one of his shirts.

That sickness coiled in gripping pain as I stared at the images.

Not in jealousy, but in the knowledge that this man was harboring something so deep. Something no one else had taken the time to recognize.

In almost every one, the man sported that sexy grin that held the power to bring an entire nation to its knees, an arm slung casually over the women's shoulders or wrapped around their waists, but I knew him well enough to see the vacancy that glazed over his eyes.

The detachment.

Another text blipped through.

Did you fall for it? Like they all do?

Anger slammed me, this protectiveness that rose and grew fierce. I shouldn't even respond, but I couldn't help but want to stick up for him. I typed out a response and hit send.

Obviously, you have no idea who he is.

Then, I hesitated, my thumbs hovering over the plate, my

tongue swiping over my dried lips before I started to frantically type again. Not sure I should be asking for the answer but unable to stop myself from doing it, anyway.

Who is this?

I swore, I could almost hear the malignant laughter in the air. Whipping and stirring our world into disorder. I could feel it…sense it…this person had intimate knowledge of whatever stole the joy from Rhys' brilliant blue eyes.

It doesn't matter who I am, now does it, but rather who your boyfriend is? What would the world think of him if they found out who he really is? What he's done? What would you think of him?

Nausea caught fire, rolling up and down my throat. I fought to swallow it down. To keep from losing it. Because the truth was, I didn't know what he'd done. What had happened or what he'd gone through. What ghosts stalked the man in the night. I only knew whatever it was caused him horrible grief.

When another text blipped through, there was no stopping the bile that climbed my throat and sent dizziness bounding through my brain.

It was a picture of Rhys with another woman. Only in this one, Rhys was on his knees at her feet. One side of her face and neck were completely covered in scars from a burn.

And it was guilt that marred Rhys' face.

Around them, I could almost see the remnants of a raging fire that had long since been extinguished but still charred their lives. But it was the words that came in behind them that had me on my knees.

Look what he did to his wife.

Rhys' torment came at me full force. The burden of what he wore. The devastation in his eyes.

His wife. His wife. His wife.

Memories of his confession banged through my mind.

"Someone's after you?"

Surrender shook his head. "No, Sweet Thing. Not after me. They already have me."

He'd tried to push me away. He'd warned me his heart wasn't fully his to give.

But I knew Rhys. Knew him deeply even without having an idea of the details. He would never turn his back on her. Would never step out. There was more to this. So much I didn't know, but I knew enough.

Knew enough to read between the lines.

Whoever this asshole was…he'd been blackmailing Rhys. Manipulating him. Holding him under his thumb.

I knew it in an instant.

My teeth clenched as a riot of anger swarmed my being. I was shaking with anger as I tapped out the text.

Bullshit.

Three more pictures blipped through. They were segmented pieces of a news article from Rhys' hometown.

Dalton, South Carolina.

It was dated seven years ago.

The horror of it nearly knocked me from my feet, my eyes wide and anguish cutting my heart wide open as I scanned the words.

I wanted to refuse them. To reject this story. Chalk it to fiction but instantly knowing it was Rhys' truth.

The article spoke of the suicide of a forty-five-year-old Keaton Manning.

My soul cried as I heard the torment that had groaned from Rhys' voice.

Seven years gone.

This article was talking about Rhys' father.

I kept reading the words again and again. The fiery crash that had happened at the end of their lane on the same night, a woman who'd been rushed to the hospital with severe burns.

Genny Manning.

Oh god.

I blinked and struggled and fought to process what it all meant. I hadn't come close to making sense of it before another text came through.

It's interesting if you search for that article, you won't find it. I think it's plenty clear why Rhys had it suppressed, isn't it? Why he's hiding? Unwilling to accept fault? How sad it'll destroy his career when everyone finds out what I know. What he was responsible for.

Rage blustered through me when I read the disgusting words.

Money.

I knew it.

Knew that's what this was about. It was what it was always about. What drove people to depravity. Greed the dictator of the cruelness that raged through the world.

I fought the sting of tears as I tapped out the message.

What is it you want? Money? Just say it and quit playing these games. How much?

It took all of five seconds for a response to come through.

What is he worth to you? What are you willing to pay to cover his sins?

A slimy stickiness drenched my flesh. I didn't need to hear the tone of this monster's voice to recognize the wickedness. The malignant evil that festered and bubbled.

This person who'd been exploiting Rhys' pain...his grief...for God knew how long.

I glanced at the door that separated me and Rhys. To his spirit that finally drifted in peace.

My sweet, sweet stallion.

I didn't have to pause or contemplate my own truth.

I was willing to give anything for him.
Everything.
I'd give it all.

Just tell me where and when and how much. I'll be there. But if I pay you, you end this. You forget you know Rhys Manning.

It only took a second for his response to come through.

Ah, I see he really has gotten to you. $100,000 and all that I know will be buried forever. Tomorrow at 3:00 p.m. Tell Rhys, and the deal is off.

It was followed by an address in Tennessee.
Tennessee.
Where *she* was from. I remembered it from the night Rhys had told me a little about the woman he'd fallen in love with. When his words had been soaked in regret and shame.

Darkness clouded the edges of my sight.

It wafted in like an omen.

A specter.

I looked around the bathroom like the walls might hold an answer. Like they might take away the fear that suddenly saturated my being. Like they might shout that what I was doing was right.

Because it only took a moment for me to realize I might be getting in over my head. Terrified I was making a mistake. Doing it wrong, giving in to this extortion when I had no real assurance that this would actually bring it to an end.

But I'd always known Rhys was worth the risk, and this wasn't any different.

I'd do this.

Take a chance on giving him this freedom.

Then I'd come back and ask him to tell me.

Beg him to let me in.

To make me understand what all of this meant. Tell me about his daddy. About Genny.

I choked over the misery of it, feeling as if I were slipping through the man's pain, the burden he'd tried to keep concealed suddenly fully feeling like my own.

And I'd carry it.

I'd carry it.

Just like I'd promised.

Before I could change my mind, I shot into motion, quickly formulating a plan.

No doubt, Rhys would try to stop me if he knew, so I quieted my frantic feet as I moved into my room.

The most glaring of it all was I could put no trust in any deal I made with this jerk. This man who seemed to have zero issue blackmailing Rhys and manipulating me.

I could only do the best that I could.

Spread my intentions into the world and pray they were good. That they would come back to Rhys in a positive way.

As much as I hated to turn it over to the asshole, the money wasn't really an issue. I'd inherited enough to cover it, and I'd gladly go penniless to set Rhys free of these chains. I'd have to take it from the stash, but I'd replenish it.

I wouldn't make the mistake of not safeguarding the rest.

I edged into the closet, crouching down, thinking of how many times I'd done it in the years I'd lived in my mother's and father's house. I'd done it out of fear. Because of the scars and the timidity.

Tonight, I did it out of ferocity.

I dialed Lily's number, hating to wake her in the middle of the night, but I didn't have another choice.

She answered on the second ring, her voice groggy but immediately on edge. "Maggie. Are you okay? What's wrong?"

I kept the words as quiet as I could. "Lily. Hi. Nothing's wrong." Saying it felt like a lie. "But, um, something came up, and I need to get this money to you. Ensure it's safe. I'm going to bring it to you tonight."

The trip had already been calculated in my mind. I'd have plenty of time to get to Dalton tonight, sleep for a bit, and then make the trip to Tennessee tomorrow. By then, Rhys and Royce would be frantic.

The thought of it riddled me with guilt. I shook myself free of the onslaught.

It was worth it. He was worth it.

I could hear the rustling of her covers, and I could tell Lily had sat up in bed. "What? What's happening? Did someone threaten you again?"

"No. It's Rhys. He's…I have to take care of something for him."

"Uh, you're goin' to have to elaborate." Clearly, her own senses were kicking in. Sure that I was evading.

I swallowed down the worry. "Someone's holding some things that happened to him over his head. Bad things. I'm going to meet them tomorrow to try to put an end to it, but not before I know this money is safe."

She blew out the strain. "Oh, Maggie…this is…someone's blackmailin' him? Over what?"

My mind raced with that article, moisture clouding my eyes. I shoved it down for later. "It doesn't matter. I just…I'm going to pay him, okay, but not before I know the rest is safe."

"God, Maggie. I don't think… Does Rhys know?"

"Of course not." The man would literally make good on the threat to tie me to his bed if he even caught a whiff of it. I pushed the heel of my hand to my forehead. "Listen, I know it's not the best of situations, but I have to do this. For him. Please don't try to talk me out of it."

I already knew it was probably useless.

Foolhardy.

This guy would most likely turn around and ask for more.

But I had to try. Had to fight for Rhys the way he was fighting for me.

She hesitated. "I don't trust this, Maggie. You don't know his intentions."

I almost scoffed. "His intentions are clear, Lily. He wants money."

She sighed heavily. "Fine. But no matter what, Kade is going with you to make sure you're safe."

I could feel her care from across the states.

A.L. Jackson

"Okay." I wouldn't argue. She was right. Kade was ex-military and had kept Lily and the rest of the women protected until it was safe for them to come out of hiding. He was well-equipped.

My spirit trembled in a warning that this might be dangerous. I'd be a fool not to take every precaution.

"What's going on, baby?" The rumbly, gruff voice caught through the line, and I knew Kade was waking up at Lily's side. An unlikely pair, but so often the greatest connections were forged during the most excruciating trials.

"I'll explain as soon as I'm off," she murmured to him.

For a beat, I got locked in her joy. My chest stretched tight with hope against all the dread that was stretching me thin.

"I'll be there in a couple hours," I told her.

"Are you sure you want to do this?"

"Yes."

She exhaled. "Okay. Drive safe and keep me updated along the way. We'll be waiting."

"I will. Thank you."

A storm of emotions whipped through me the second I ended the call.

Rhys' suffering my own. And I prayed...I prayed that he wouldn't break me the way I'd been so sure that he would. Prayed that our connection was bigger—stronger—than whatever this was.

I edged from the closet and over to the desk in my room. I pulled out a plain white piece of paper, and I wrote a quick letter, hoping he would understand, that he wouldn't take this as another burden on his shoulders.

Then I folded it, molded it into us, the crude star left on my bed with all my love, sure he would find it.

Then I started to rush, shrugging on jeans and a tee and stuffing a few things into an overnight bag.

I dropped to my knees and dragged the duffle bags from under my bed. I loaded two on my shoulders, and then peered out my door into the stillness. When I found it clear, I slipped out and raced for the stairs as silently as I could.

I loaded them in Royce's rental.

God, he was going to be pissed. Angry and worried and pissed.

And I felt bad, but not bad enough to change my mind.

I rushed back upstairs and got the rest of my things and then darted back out.

Down the stairs and out into the slumbering night.

I had to refuse the urge to slow down because if I did, I'd have to give in to the call I could feel radiating from Rhys' room.

The sudden torment I felt oozing from him.

As if he'd begun to toss in those terrible dreams.

Maybe…just maybe I could finally help him mend it.

His beautifully broken soul.

I fumbled to get my seat belt locked, and then I pushed the ignition and drove away from the house. Hands sweaty, skin slick, heart shuddering.

My nerves raced out of control.

I could do this.

It was no big deal.

I was just…anxious. There was no real danger. Kade would be coming with me. He wouldn't allow anything to happen to me.

Resolved, I took the few turns through town and hit the main highway into Savannah.

Darkness filled the night.

The sky full of stars and silence.

With it came a slow foreboding.

That paranoia building.

But somehow…somehow, I knew the paranoia hadn't been paranoia at all.

But rather a warning.

I guessed in all my staunch determination I hadn't allowed myself to register what it was.

What that black omen had meant back at the house.

No time to process the wickedness that rode through the air.

No time to change course or turn around.

Because the headlights that had been way far back since I'd left Tybee came up so fast I didn't have time to prepare myself.

No time to do anything about the fact that I'd been lured out with all that money. No time to accept that I'd been a fool, after all.

No safeguards.

No defense before I was rear-ended, slammed from out of nowhere.

Metal crunched in the same second I jolted forward, and the car swerved to the left, tires screeching as loud as the scream that ripped from my throat.

Struggling, I tried to correct it, jerking the steering wheel to the right.

But I did it too sharp, and I was going too fast, and the back tires began to skid.

Then it caught, and I flipped.

Rhys
Seven Years Ago

*R*hys saw her from the stage. She was loiterin' off to the far side of the crowd where the strobing lights barely reached her shy, curious, stunning face.

For one wayward beat, his mangled, hollow heart thudded.

This girl with the golden blonde hair and curvy hips and jittering hands.

She looked out of place.

Nervous and excited and maybe the best thing he'd seen in a long, long time.

She looked up through the flashing lights. Green eyes bright and shining.

Snagging him from where he stood finishing out the last song on Carolina George's set list where they played at a small bar in an even smaller town in Tennessee.

Rhys was all about having a good time. Giving over to the greed. It was the only reprieve he ever got from what he'd done.

But right then, he thought he might like what he saw in her eyes better.

Innocence.

Naivety.

Blamelessness.

Maybe having a little bit of it would take away some of his.

The blame.

The guilt that constricted so tight he couldn't sleep at night.

His *daddy* ruined.

Rhys had been the one responsible for stamping out his father's spirit beneath that tractor all those years ago. He might as well have finished him that day with all the livin' that he'd done since.

Grief crested in a giant swell when he thought of it. What he'd put his parents through.

Turned out, he hadn't been close to bein' strong enough. Nothing but powerless to put a dent in his father's depression.

His fault.

He knew it.

Owned it.

He scrounged up every last penny he earned to send to them. Trying to do his best to make a difference. To take care of them the way he'd promised, but it wasn't enough.

Worst part?

He was the pathetic bastard who tried to run as far and as fast away from it as he could.

A coward who could barely face what he'd done. Staying away for longer and longer stints like it might eventually blot out the guilt and grief while the years only proved how much it'd grown.

Before he allowed himself to spiral, he sucked it down and pinned a booming smile on his face and climbed off the stage. He went saunterin' her way.

She averted her gaze as he approached, her fidgeting getting greater, those eyes even more timid when she finally looked up at him.

"Hey, there, gorgeous. What are you doin' out here by yourself?"

Shyness blazed from her body, and still, she said, "I guess I must have been lookin' for you."

"I shouldn't be out here with you," she whispered where they were hidden out behind the bar while the next band played. The energy emitted from the music seemed alive, thrashing around them, though theirs had been subdued a fraction by the brick walls that served as a barricade.

He was leaned against an old crate that had been tipped upside down with his legs stretched out long, sipping from a beer while he kept watching her, thinkin' something this good had to be a hallucination.

Genny stood between his thighs. Close, but not quite close enough.

He eyed her from over the bottle. "Yeah. And why's that? Tell me you don't have a boyfriend."

He meant it as a tease because there wasn't a chance in the world this girl would be stepping out on her man.

He had a knack for readin' people.

Knowing who was out for pleasure and who was out for gain. This girl?

She was as blameless as they came.

Except a blush raced across her face. Hot and heated and ashamed. He eyed her harder when he saw her reaction. "Tell me you don't actually have a boyfriend."

He almost choked on it because shit…he was gonna be struck dumb if he'd pegged her wrong.

She laughed a hard, bitter sound, and she dropped her face.

Heart stretching his chest tight, he reached out and tucked his knuckle under her chin, lifting it to him.

He had the overwhelming urge to wrap her up tight when he

saw a single tear slip down her face. Hold her and promise her he'd fix it, whatever it was.

"No, Rhys. I don't have a boyfriend."

A frown dented his brow. "Then what?"

She wavered and warred, and then she was spitting the words like they were poison. "I have a fiancé."

What the actual lovin' fuck?

She cringed again and swayed in some kinda dismay that had him drawing her closer rather than pushing her away like he should have been doing.

"He's…he's my father's best friend's son. It's been assumed since we were babies that we were gonna get married. It's been planned forever that I would marry Noah and he would take over my father's company. The wedding is in three months, but I don't…" Her face lit in that shyness. "I haven't even…."

The girl couldn't even say it.

"That's ridiculous."

"It's still what's required of me."

"Tell me you're jokin'," he demanded. Anger rose in the middle of him. This protectiveness for a girl who clearly was being forced into something she hadn't agreed to.

"Not jokin'. It's what's expected of me." That time, she laughed, but it was dire and hollow.

She lifted her arms out to the sides. "For the first time in my life, I got brave and fought with my mama about it today. Told her she couldn't make me. She told me to stop bein' silly and to accept what I was born to do. That our family legacy was riding on us merging our families. The women in my family don't step out or go chasin' after dreams, Rhys. But tonight, I did. I chased a single dream. I snuck out with my friend so I could get the taste of freedom. Just for one night. For one moment."

Then she flinched. "I know it's gonna cost me when I get home. I'll be punished, but it will be worth it."

This was the most fucked-up shit that Rhys had ever heard, and he was having a hard time processing. Making sense of it.

"What are you sayin'? Someone's goin' to lay a hand on you when you get home?"

Redness flushed her face, and he could taste her terror.

"Shit." He blinked a bunch of times. "Then why don't you leave? Get away from there?"

She ran her hands up her bare arms like she was chasing away a flash of chills. "I wish it were that easy. They'll find me. Noah and my father…they are…" She flinched.

Motherfucker.

Rhys suddenly felt like going on a murder spree.

"It'll be bad enough if they discover I sneaked out tonight." Then she smiled. Smiled an awed smiled that made his chest ache. "But it'll be worth it. Just for a second of this."

She tipped her face to the sky like she was relishing the moment. Imprinting it into her being. Writing it forever on her memories.

Rhys choked over the intensity of what she was feeling right then, scrambling to find a solution. Half wantin' to pull out his hair and the other wanting to go on a manhunt.

Because this was straight bullshit.

"This is insane. Come on, Genny, stuff like that doesn't happen anymore. They can't make you."

She blanched. "Look around you, Rhys. You're not exactly standin' on modern ground. I've known since I was little that I was supposed to marry Noah. My daddy…he owns this whole town, and because of me, Noah is next in line."

She trailed off with the misery.

Rhys' heart started to beat in real time. A flicker of somethin' he hadn't felt since he'd been a boy.

"And then every once in a while, God makes someone extra special. Someone who is more vulnerable than others, and it's our job to protect them. To take care of them. Even when it ain't pretty."

His dad's words flooded him from that spot that had been vacant since his hope had been ripped away. Since the day he'd stolen his daddy's.

Maybe…maybe this was what he'd meant.

And Rhys knew it was crazy. He didn't even know this girl. But

359

he knew she needed help. That she was gonna waste away her life, probably be used and abused on top of it, too, if he didn't do something about it.

So he was going to.

He was gonna stand for someone else.

He pushed to standing, and she gasped a little sound and stumbled back when he cast her in the shadow of his towering frame.

Caught off guard and frightened by the sudden movement.

And he was sure of it then.

That she needed someone to be that person for her.

"Fuck Noah," he said.

She blinked and he stretched out his hand. "You wanna run, Genny? How about you run away with me?"

"Rhys...I...I'm not sure. Noah will kill you."

Rhys cracked a smirk. "Let him."

They did. They ran. Hopped on Rhys' bus with his band and toured around the country. And this girl he didn't know—he loved her.

But it was different.

It was slow and sweet.

Devoted.

He made her happy and, for the first time since he was nine, he felt happy, too. And when they got to Vegas, they snuck away and got hitched at one of those chapels because it felt like the right thing to do, forged the papers and their names.

Once he somehow found a way to get her birth certificate, they'd do it for real.

He just hoped he could love her right.

Be all she needed him to be.

And maybe...maybe it might make his father a little bit proud, too. Maybe spark some of that joy that had been missing forever.

His chest tightened.

God, he wanted it something fierce. He'd give anything, do anything, to see his father smile.

Most of all, he prayed for once he'd do it right.

That he'd be strong enough.

That he wouldn't fail her, too.

Rhys pulled their hands that were twined and resting on the console of the truck to his mouth. "Can't wait for you to meet Mama. She's gonna lose her mind when we tell her."

Genny beamed at him, though there was no missing her nerves, seein' as how they'd done it in secret, and now that they were finally back in South Carolina, they were gonna surprise his parents with the announcement.

"What is she gonna lose her mind about? That her wild boy finally got reined?"

He smiled, too. "That's exactly why she's gonna lose her mind. She woulda thought it'd be impossible."

A wry smile ticked up at the corner of her pouty mouth. "Hmm…didn't seem all that hard to me."

"That's because it took a special girl to make it possible."

She blushed, and Rhys tried to ignore the flashes of anxiety that kept lighting up inside him.

The dread he felt every time he came face-to-face with his father. The man barely grunting. Barely eating. Barely breathing. While Rhys' guilt had built exponentially.

Coming home only amplified the feeling.

The memories of those walls.

The ghost of that day that he was sure was going to haunt him his entire life.

His mama had tried to convince him it wasn't his fault, but Rhys knew. If he had just listened, minded what his dad had instructed, it wouldn't have happened.

They drove through his small hometown while Genny peppered him with a thousand questions about what it'd been like when he was growing up. He told her stories about the way he and Richard had run that town as teenagers, earning their reputations.

He also did his best to prepare her to meet his father, his voice rough and thick as he explained more about what to expect.

That his father might not even acknowledge them.

Or he might scream at them to get out of his room.

Maybe throw a bottle against the wall.

Wasn't the most ideal of circumstances to bring his new bride home to, but that was his dad. Rhys might be ashamed of himself, but he wasn't ashamed of his father.

But he guessed he hadn't prepared her at all when they finally made it to the other side of town and hit the two-lane road.

He saw his childhood house in the distance up ahead.

Red and blue lights flashed through the night.

He rammed the accelerator to the floor, flying up the road and skidding as he cut a left into the bumpy dirt drive.

Dust billowed like the scream of demons as he flew up that tiny lane toward the circus of ambulances and police cars, and he was out the door and running for his mama who was running for him.

His guts coiled and sickness had already taken him hostage by the time she threw herself in his arms and buried her face in his chest. "He's gone, Rhys. He's gone."

A roar of agony tore from his spirit.

"What happened? What happened?" He tried to break away from his mama and run for the house. "Oh god. What happened? Dad!" He screamed it and started for the house. "Dad!"

Tears blurred his eyes and streamed hot down his face as he struggled to push through the officer who tried to hold him. His mama jumped on him from behind. Her torment making her stronger than he ever knew she could be. "Stop, Rhys. Stop. You can't go in there. Please. Stop. Listen to me."

And Rhys knew.

He knew what he'd done all those years ago had finally ended his daddy.

Had destroyed their family.

He roared and his knees quaked. He wasn't even *strong* enough to stand.

He dropped to the ground.

Love, love, love.

He'd crushed the truth of it beneath his feet.

Then he felt her behind him, her panic, her disgust, Genny shaking her head frantically as she backed away. "No. No, no, no."

She kept shaking her head, stumbling as she floundered backward, before she turned and ran back for the idling truck.

He could feel her horror as she jumped in the front seat, though Rhys wasn't sure he could process it through his grief.

Through the pain.

The sickness.

The truth of who he was.

He should have known he'd never be enough.

That Genny would see right through to the ugliness of him, too.

He moaned, torn between running for her and running into the house like he could stop it from happening.

Change it.

Fix it.

Maybe he could run so fast that he could get back to the time before it had begun. To the time when he was just a child and he'd believed he could save a small piece of the world.

Back to before he'd made the biggest mistake of his life. When his daddy was whole and right and the strongest man he knew. Back to when his daddy believed in him.

Instead, he remained on his knees.

Frozen.

Locked in his horror.

Locked in his shame.

Watching as Genny shifted the truck into reverse and flew backward, skidding and weaving as she threw it in drive. She tore down the lane.

When she got to the main road, she gave no heed to the headlights coming up the bend, her need to get away from him greater than anything else.

And there was nothing he could do.

Nothing he could do but scream and watch as the rest of himself went up in flames.

Rhys

*P*anic knocked my ribs into havoc and my heart clawed out of my chest as I was jolted awake to the chasm of darkness. The memories consumed. That fuckin' nightmare haunting my dreams. The truth of what I'd done. Of what I'd caused.

For years, my mama had done her best to convince me it wasn't my fault. Through tears, she'd say she knew it hurt, but that I was holding onto a burden that wasn't my own.

She'd promise again and again that I'd been just a little boy, like that made a lick of difference.

Because it was that little boy who'd had to carry the knowledge of what he'd done to his daddy into his days of bein' a man.

A man who'd had to stand aside, helpless, watchin' his father wither away until there'd been nothing left. No reason to stay. So broken that he'd taken his life.

Then Genny…

Guessed it was karma responsible for that. The fact that what I'd done to my father had ruined her on the very same night.

It'd always felt like a message being sent.

The truth that I wasn't allowed joy when I'd stolen his, and just for the fact that I'd tried to take a little of it, anyway, Genny'd been the one who'd had to pay.

I'd never known it so true than when I'd started to race down the driveway to where she'd pulled out in front of another pickup truck on the main road. Would never be about to forget the sound of the sheering and twisting and groaning of metal. The splintering of glass. It'd all happened two seconds before the trailer the other driver had been hauling had burst into flames.

I had never felt the true impact of it until I'd pulled her from the fiery wreckage.

That was the night my fractured, mangled heart had completely collapsed.

Only saving grace had been that the paramedics had already been on site. They'd saved Genny and the other driver…my daddy was already gone.

Gone.

I choked over the swell of agony.

On some kind of twisted instinct, I reached for the one who'd come to hold the power to fill that void.

My Sweet, Sweet Thing.

Fear slicked like ice down my spine when my hand hit the spot on the mattress where she'd fallen asleep curled in my arms. It was as cold and vacant as the warning I could hear howlin' from within.

"Maggie," I wheezed it, fighting the instant fear that rushed through my veins.

I scrubbed a palm over my face like it might put a crack in the chaos.

God. I was probably overreactin'. That was the problem when you got paranoid. When you worried night and day that your past was finally going to devour you. You were constantly jumping to conclusions.

"Maggie?" That time, I barely managed to keep it below a

shout. My eyes swept every corner of the darkened room. When it came up bare, I tossed off the covers and slipped from the bed.

I stole across the room to the bathroom door, tryin' to ignore the shock of distress that impaled my senses.

Sticky and hot.

A tingling sense that this one good thing I'd been given had gone bad.

Just like I knew it would.

I flipped on the bathroom light, blinking against the starkness of it.

The AC droned, pumping cool air into the space.

"Maggie?" Croaked it that time, this feeling coming on that I refused to perceive. I crossed the bathroom, nudged open her door, and peered into the darkness of her room.

A void radiated back. A vacuum that stirred the emotions into disorder.

My chest tightened, heart instantly dippin' into a mad, violent rage.

"Maggie, where are you baby?" It was a rumble of that dread.

I had the fleetin' thought that she could have just gone downstairs to grab a bite to eat, and I wasn't doing anything but being crazed and overbearing.

Or maybe she'd slipped out back to get some air.

Wanted to picture her there. A goddess beneath the stars.

A siren.

My Sweet, Sweet Thing.

But that energy that had connected us from the get-go had me standing at the edge of her bed. Staring at the shape of a star that I immediately recognized she'd fashioned with her hand. I reached for it, entire being shaking like an uncaged beast as I flipped it around in my fingers. Then I was tearing into it when I realized there was something written inside.

Rhys.

My stallion.

Please, don't be angry, but it's time someone stepped in and offered something to you. Don't worry. I'll be back soon.

I love you with every piece of me.
Maggie

What was she doin'? Fuck. What was she doin'?

Terror gripped me as I sank to my knees so I could peer under her bed. Some part of me already knew those duffles stuffed full of money were gonna be gone, but still I was crumbling in fear when I got confirmation.

"Maggie." It was a choked cry of desperation.

What was she thinkin'? Why would she do this without me? She was supposed to let me hold this for her. Shoulder this for her.

Confusion spun, so fast I couldn't see, so fast that I was stumbling to my feet and tearing out of her bedroom.

I raced for the bottom floor, praying to God maybe I'd catch her in time.

I whipped open the front door and flew out into the stagnant night.

Already knowing.

Already knowing.

Still, a fuckin' rock the size of the Titanic sank to the pit of my stomach when I saw that Royce's car was gone.

My mind reeled and my spirit wept.

What the hell had happened between when she'd fallen asleep nestled in my arms to right then? She'd promised that she would let me do the dirty work. Let me be the one to get in the line of her fire because I couldn't tolerate the idea of the girl getting mixed in even the suggestion of danger.

I balled the note in my hand. Every damned thought I could have bounced around inside me.

The message she'd left, trying to process what it meant.

That cut. That abhorrent attack.

The worry that I wouldn't put anything past her disgustin' excuse of a mother. She'd threaten her. Back her into a corner.

But this note…felt like it weighed fifteen-thousand tons.

That was the thing about this brilliant, kind, selfless, reckless girl.

She'd think she was doing this for me.

That's what it was, wasn't it?

She thought she was savin' me some kind of heartache by going herself when in truth something happening to her would be the one thing my heart couldn't take.

I roared back into the house, feet banging the floors as I pounded upstairs.

I needed to stop her before she got herself into trouble.

Trouble.

I'd always thought I'd be the one to bring it to her, and now I was praying I was worthy enough to be the one to get her out of it.

I hit the landing with panic lighting my feet, my rage so loud that it had a door crashing open on the opposite wing.

Royce.

He came storming down the hallway like I'd reached a hand into his room and plucked him from his bed.

Dude was pure darkness and hate.

I latched onto it. Let it feed me. This resolution to ensure my girl was safe.

"The fuck are you doing?" he hissed below his breath, even though he was lookin' around, searching for the danger, too.

"Maggie's gone."

He stumbled a step. "What?"

She'd trusted me with this, believed in me to hold her secret, but I didn't know how to keep it when doin' it would only be a disservice. An injustice to this girl who would give anything to make this world a better place.

I was determined to make it better for her.

Dude was gonna kick my ass all over again.

Anxiety skidded through my limbs. Words barely bitten out. "Royce...fuck, man, she got ahold of some money your stepfather had hidden. She's tryin' to get it to some of the women who were affected. She organized it through Lily and Kade. She was supposed to let me do it, but I woke up, and she was gone."

Confession came out haggard.

Knew my expression verged on grim when I looked up at him.

Only thing it did was send the color draining from his face.

"What?" he demanded. "What are you saying?"

"She brought it here with her. It's a fuck ton of cash, Royce. And Maggie thinks it's your mother who's been after her, tryin' to scare her into giving it back. She promised me…" I rammed a fist against my aching chest. "Promised she'd let me do it. That she'd let me keep her safe. We need to get to her before your mother does."

I started into my room with the intention of doin' just that. I went for my phone, hoping to God I could catch her. Talk some sense into this girl. Understand why she'd make such a rash decision.

"How much?" The question was a jagged spike that pierced me from behind.

"Five million," I mumbled.

Knew he was ripping at his hair when I told him.

"What the hell is she thinking?" His voice cracked on his worry.

On disbelief.

I flipped into my phone so I could call her. Tell her to pull into a public spot and I would be there just as fast as my car would carry me, which was pretty fuckin' fast.

In an instant, the dread switched.

Flipped.

Pitched me straight into a vat of horror.

Rage flash fired.

Strokes of hate and disgust and guilt and shame.

I stumbled back, holding my phone like it might burn right through skin and bone when I caught sight of the text.

I blinked through the haze of red and agony.

I should have known.

Should have known.

Only thing I was good at was ruinin' the ones I loved most.

I'd known this was coming from the beginning, hadn't I? Had I been such a fool to think a thing had changed? That I'd outrun what I'd done?

Because Noah had sent a picture, that sick, twisted

motherfucker who'd sought to crush me. It was clear he was finally dead set on finishing it.

Picture was this gutting portrayal of the two women I loved most.

My mama and my Maggie.

It was a dark, grainy image, night all around. Two of them were tied up somewhere in the forest. Tears streamed in dirty streaks from my mama's face, a gag in her mouth and her arms behind her back.

But Maggie's face—it was bloody. So fuckin' bloody. A gash was busted wide open on the side of her head. Clearly, it'd gushed, though it'd dried and matted, and a little still dripped from her chin.

The walls spun.

Spun and spun.

Faster and faster.

I couldn't breathe.

And I knew I was a beat from succumbin' to the pain that splintered through my body.

Rending me into a million fuckin' pieces.

"What's going on?" Royce rasped from behind, dude tapping into the illness that seethed.

This manic crux between crumbling and goin' on a rampage.

The urge for a rampage was definitely gonna win out.

"It's not your mom. She's not the one responsible for hurtin' Maggie."

Instantly, knew it as fact.

"What?" Confusion boomed from Royce.

"He has them," I croaked.

"Who?"

"Noah." I heaved it out like a stone.

"Who the fuck is Noah? What the hell is going on, man?"

He rushed me and grabbed my phone, a shout of fury coming from him when he saw the picture.

His sister bound and bloody.

"My past finally caught up to me, and I got your sister trapped in the middle of it."

371

I'd known better.

Known better.

After the crash, Genny had gone back to her parents'. She told me to stay away. That she didn't want me anymore. That, I got. Respected. But it was the stayin' away part that I couldn't do.

The promise I'd made her that I'd forever take care of her holding fast. So, I'd snuck there again and again, inevitably knowing I'd get a death threat from Noah when I did. All fuckin' talk because the only thing that bastard wanted was the money I sent on a monthly basis. More and more of it as the years went by. Genny'd beg me to stay away, all while relief would flood from her when she'd see me slink through her window.

Thing was, the guilt would never allow me to turn a blind eye. Could never end the worry I'd had for her. For her life I'd derailed. For the happiness I'd stolen. For the love we'd shared for a flash of time that'd been real.

Love that'd been crushed under my heel.

That shit had brought me back time and again. Just to check. To see that she was whole and fine.

But in the last year, something had changed. Noah going to Dalton and showing up at the bar. Then the pictures he sent of my mother right after I'd gone to visit Genny the last time. The texts he'd been sending that seemed unhinged.

Different.

And now…this.

This.

I cracked in two, body buckling at the middle. My hand shot out to the nightstand to keep me from falling.

Don't fall. Don't fall. Don't fall.

But I had.

I'd fallen hard and completely, and now I'd brought that destruction to Maggie.

To my mama.

My spirit moaned and the room swam.

A flood of torment.

But it was purpose that filled me when another text pinged through.

It was a dropped pin for the location.

A gauntlet thrown.

A call to war.

My past thirty miles away lurking in the desert converging with what I'd been fool enough to hope could be my future.

Let's finish this. Come alone, asshole. Maybe I'll let you decide which one it is going to be.

Which one it was going to be?

Cocksucker had it all wrong.

It was gonna be him.

We drove like a silent hurricane through the night. Spirits whipping and lashing and gaining in strength.

Deadly.

Lethal.

The threat of it emanated from our beings as we blazed through the deep, deep darkness from Tybee in the direction of where I'd been summoned to the feet of wickedness.

Fury hissed and crackled.

Every muscle in our bodies were rigid.

Taut.

Nerves set to high alert.

Our fists clenched and our hearts beating an erratic drum of vengeance.

Violence this palpable, acrid scent in the broiling air.

Richard hadn't hesitated when I'd knocked at his door and I'd told him I needed backup.

Dude my oldest, closest friend.

One who got it.

One who'd always stand at my side just the same as I'd always stand at his.

Now, where he sat in the backseat, viciousness seeped from his pores. "Funny how we seem to keep gettin' ourselves in these same situations," he rumbled, rushing an aggressive hand through his hair. "Wasn't but six months ago you two were climbin' in next to me so we could get to Violet. How's it trouble always finds us?"

I grunted. "Think it's because guys like us beg for it."

Royce seethed from the front seat. He kept rubbing his palms on his thighs, itchin' and antsy, like he was having a hard time remaining sitting, wishing he could throw himself out the door and be exactly where we needed to be.

"It's greed, man. Money." Royce spat each of them as an answer. "That's how. Wrong people get a taste of it, and it becomes a disease. That's what happened to my mother. The dollar signs in her eyes shined so much brighter than the face of her daughter."

Rage curled my hands tighter on the steering wheel, trees whipping by so fast that the landscape blurred in a whorl of thrumming disorder.

Refused to believe I was driving straight for tragedy.

Maggie and my mama. Maggie and my mama.

My heart stuttered and sped and made me feel like it was gettin' cleaved from the center of my chest.

Nothing was going to happen to them. Nothin'. I'd die first.

I made a sharp left, the tires squealing, our pulses thundering when we realized we were getting close.

So fucking close, and I had no idea what length this maniac would go.

Tension bound the cab of the car. Anxiety suffocating. Nothing but fuel to feed the fire that burned and ravaged and became this violent aggression that raged through our veins.

We were on this desolate two-lane road with nothing in sight but trees.

I slowed, my approach filled with caution, breaths turning ragged as I watched the map lead me to this destiny.

To my girl.

Girl who'd changed everything. Who'd made me want to believe.

Fuck. She had. Had made me believe that there might be

redemption for the damned.

Not a chance.

Only thing that mattered then was setting her and my mama free. Maybe Genny in the process.

My skin crawled with desperation. Shivers racin' my flesh like my cells couldn't sit still with the upheaval.

"Nothing is going to happen to them." Royce's voice was hard. Raw and cutting.

"No. Won't let it happen."

The fierce turmoil of it spun.

The promise that was made.

I slowed when I saw the small road I was supposed to take comin' up on the right.

Apprehension rolled. A tidal wave of it. So fast and huge that I felt like it was knockin' me from my feet. Catching me up in the undertow and suckin' me to the darkest depths. To the place where those demons lived. Where they'd cried out for years. Where I'd always known I'd destroy the good.

Never fuckin' strong enough.

"This is it," Royce grumbled.

The road was nothin' but a break in the trees. A dirt path carved out by old tire tracks. Grasses grew up in the middle, making the lane barely visible.

I slowed to a crawl as I made the turn, the low profile of my car scraping on the uneven terrain.

Aggression gathered. My chest squeezed around the ferocity of it.

Royce shifted uneasily.

I stopped the car as soon as I was clear of the main road. My headlights speared through the night, like silver blades that slashed through the vapors and revealed the true darkness lurkin' on the other side.

Royce's hand curled around the doorlatch, his throat bobbing as violence skated through his being. "We come out of this alive. All of us. Don't get stupid. Just roll with the plan. Sent the text to Baz so he can make the call for backup now. Closest station is seven miles away. If a cruiser is closer, they'll be here sooner. Stall him unless we get a good shot."

My nod was hard, and he was slippin' out the door and letting Richard out, and they were silently slinking into the shadows while I let off the brake and slowly wound my way up the uninhabited path.

Trees rose higher on each side. It ramped up my anxiety, stokin' the illness that had infested me since I was nine.

Ravaged my insides and infected my soul.

All the ugliness finally eruptin'.

No way left to beat it down. No fuckin' wayward smile to pin on my face, no hashtag or pictures to hide behind.

When I came to a stop, I was pared down to the raw, bleedin' skeleton of myself.

Anguished fury thrashed as I took in the scene where my headlights illuminated the small meadow where there was a break in the trees. A stream rolled through, and some rotted logs were toppled on their sides. A truck was parked off to the left.

But the only thing that mattered was what was to the right over by the brook.

My mama was on the ground and pushed against a toppled log, her arms tied behind her back and that gag still in her mouth.

Bile mauled my throat. I swallowed it down and forced myself to focus. This was the one thing in my life that I wasn't gonna wreck.

Problem was I felt my entire body rock with rage when my gaze traveled to Maggie.

I was struck with an overpowering urge to jump from the car, the riot itchin' at my fingers threatening to send me ballistic.

Because there was my Sweet, Sweet Thing.

She lay in a wretched ball on her side.

Tied up.

Broken and battered.

Felt it.

That crazed energy that whipped and whirred. A cyclone that spun mayhem into the air. Her spirit that whimpered and cried.

Agony and pain leeched from the well of her body.

She was hurt.

Really fuckin' hurt.

Wanted to rush for her. Drop to my knees and run my hands over every inch of her body. Find where she'd been injured. Promise I would fix it. Heal it.

But I knew this was the only thing I could do.

I snapped open the door, and I wrapped my other hand around the handle of the gun, felt the weight of its finality as I carefully slipped out of the car and into the swath of darkness that was only cut by the blindin' glare of the headlights.

You're a good boy, Rhys. A good, good boy.

I squeezed my eyes against my father's words. Against the praise I'd never deserved. Prayin' and prayin' that once—just once—I might find the fullness of that strength.

Take care of my mama the way I'd promised to do.

Get Maggie the hell out of here. Protect her from the shit that was my life.

Be good for someone else.

Those more vulnerable.

Malice jumped into my veins when I felt the movement off to the right. I squinted, trying not to lose my quickly raveling control when Noah came slippin' like a snake out from under the cover of the trees. A gun casually held at his side and a smirk on his face.

"Ah, he's here."

"Let them go. This is between you and me." Tried to keep the wobblin' out of my voice. Still could barely fathom the fact he'd done this. That he'd been huntin' Maggie all these weeks. That he'd taken both her and my mama. That we were standing here.

He just laughed a disbelieving sound. "Is that really what you think?"

My chest stretched tight and every muscle in my body flexed with the promise of retribution.

To end this motherfucker, once and for all.

Maggie's gaze found mine through the murky, disorientin' view of the headlights. But those charcoal eyes—they were clear—writing me in their story.

377

Sketchin' me in her belief.

Shockwaves of her relief banged into my spirit.

Coaxed me forward.

My sweet siren beneath the stars. Except this was a setting she never should have been victim to. She was supposed to fly. To soar. To chase down every good thing in this life.

I was never, ever supposed to hold her back.

Tightening my hold on the gun, I lifted my glare to Noah who stood ten feet behind them.

Hate on his face.

Different this time, though.

Murderous rage.

Or maybe I was just sensin' my own.

Way my blood curdled in contempt. Way my finger fluttered on the trigger, wondering if I could get to him faster than he could get to me.

"Told you to let them go." The words scraped the dense, heated air. "Not sure what you think you're doin', but this isn't gonna end pretty."

He cracked a grin. "Now that you are right about, Rhys Manning. See, you should have thought twice all those years ago before you went and played the cowboy. Jumping into business where you didn't belong. Playing a hero."

Agitation spun, and my world was gettin' rocked by the rustling that came from behind him as a figure stumbled out from the shadows.

Genny.

The air punched from my lungs.

Genny.

Genny who was holding a gun in her hand that trembled almost as ferociously as her chin, appearin' disoriented, lost, and absolutely traumatized.

What the fuck?

My mind was blown to nasty smithereens. Was that what this was? Some kinda ambush? Had I been playin' the fool all along?

"What are you doin', Genny?" It was a plea. Disbelief.

My attention darted to Maggie. To my mama. Wanting to run

for them. Throw myself on top of them.

"Genny." I said it again, like the sound of it might talk some sense into whatever insanity this was.

"Rhys, I'm so sorry. I never wanted this to happen."

Was she serious?

Blinking like crazy, I swung my attention to Noah. "What the hell is goin' on? This is bullshit. Just...let them go, and I'll give you whatever you want."

Maggie whimpered in protest. Her arms bound and her mouth gagged and her body bleeding. Her heels dug into the dirt, girl writhing in agony.

Fuck. I was gonna come out of my skin.

Noah laughed. Hard and malicious. "You still don't get it, do you?"

He cocked his head.

It was a taunt.

Asshole baitin' me.

Drawing me a step closer.

"This is between you and me," I rushed. "Isn't it me who stole your girl? Took what you thought belonged to you and you couldn't handle it?"

Noah laughed a mocking sound. "You have no clue what you stole."

Genny flinched at his side.

He took a step forward, and I had to internally scream at myself to keep my cool. To hold my ground.

This fucker had been driving me to breakin' for years. Luring me into his depravity. Driving me to snap.

This time I was sure it was the other way around.

"You had no clue what you did. What you stepped in on. Did you know we were married, Rhys, Genny and I? Did you know all those months, you were fucking my wife?"

I rocked back. Stunned by the blow. My breaths gone. Dizziness had me swaying to the left, and Genny whimpered, "I'm sorry. I didn't mean to hurt you."

What the fuck?

She was married?

Bile sloshed from my stomach and rose in my throat. I'd trusted her. Wanted to give her somethin' better.

"I warned you, Rhys," she started to stammer. "I warned you that night when you asked me to leave with you that Noah would want to kill you. I'm sorry. I'm sorry. I loved you. I did."

"Shut up, Genny," Noah hissed.

"Please, Noah," she begged, that gun still quivering at her side.

My brow twisted and my guts knotted.

A sense coming on that I didn't want to surrender to.

So dark. So vile. So disgustin'.

"Took me a few months to track her down, to figure out who she'd run off with. Wasn't about to let her get away with it. Stealing what was rightfully mine. My place in her family."

"She never loved you." Why I thought it prudent to drive that blade deeper, I didn't know. Probably because my mind was spinnin' so fast I was trying to play catch up, too. Tossin' out the facts that left my tongue like bitter barbs.

Hatred and rage twisted his mouth into a sneer. "You think this was about love? This was about my position. What you stole from me."

Confusion rocked me to the core.

"So, that's what all this is about?" I gestured at my mom and Maggie. "You want to pay me back for sleepin' with your wife when I didn't know she was married? All because you want to take over a fuckin' produce company?"

It left me like a question, and the second it was out, it crystalized. Think a part of me had always known it. Somethin' deep inside had warned Genny hadn't been straight. That things had gone way seedier than she'd ever admitted.

Noah scoffed a laugh. "Are you that stupid, Rhys?"

Was feeling it right about then.

He sneered. "All these years and you still don't know. Her father owned all of Tennessee. The underground parts." He angled forward, the man a squall of disjointed fury. "And you should have stayed out of it. Only meant to take back what was mine the night I went to your parents' place."

Dread slammed me, hard as a rock to the side of the head.

I struggled to keep my feet planted.

My mama whimpered and squirmed.

Wanted to go to her. Wrap her up. Promise I wouldn't ever let anythin' happen to her. That I would never fail her again.

One arm for her and one for my Maggie.

Still, I held fast. Sweat beaded on my temples as that confusion swarmed. Somethin' sinister coating my flesh with the way he dealt the words.

Noah had been there.

The bastard had been there.

Flashes of memories struck me. Genny's panic. The way she'd fled. Way I'd thought she'd been scared of me.

Fuck.

I nearly buckled in two when I realized she hadn't been runnin' from me at all.

"But your father…" He might as well have stabbed me in the gut with the way I lurched forward when he said it. His voice turned to feigned sympathy. He grinned, a fuckin' sadist feeding from the pain.

"Yeah," he taunted as I swallowed and twitched and struggled to keep from fracturing apart. "He didn't take too kindly of my being there. Not very welcoming, if you ask me."

Around her gag, my mama yelped, and Genny, she let go of a sob, the sludge of words comin' from her nothing but whimpers, "I'm sorry. I didn't mean for it to happen. I should have told you. I should have told you. I didn't mean for it to happen."

Sorrow pressed down.

That old agony so intense I couldn't see.

It got all mixed up with the rage.

Rage that gathered and grew.

Shivering as it came alive.

"I'm sorry, Rhys. When we got there…all the ambulances and police were there, and I knew. I knew it." Genny's words started to tumble, and she was stumbling forward. "I knew it…and…and I ran. At the hospital, Noah was there, and I made him promise, Rhys, made him promise that he wouldn't go after you, too. My father agreed he couldn't touch you." She started coming for me like what she was sayin' made up for it. "I made him promise."

But it was the despair that had me shaking. What had me stunned. Body just moving her direction, already sure doin' it would drag me to the deepest pit in Hell.

"What did you know?" Didn't give a fuck about the hospital. About any promise she had made. I wanted to know. Had to know.

My mama moaned from across the space, and Maggie's spirit wailed.

"What did you know?" I screamed it when she just fidgeted, her head shakin' as she wheezed, "I'm sorry."

"Shut up, Genny, and do what we came here to do. It's time to prove your loyalty. Take your rightful spot in this family."

"What did you know?" I screamed it that time, not even able to process the threats that Noah was tossing.

Fucker cocked a smirk, and I guessed it was that expression that finally sent my spirit crumblin' apart.

"What is it you want to know?" he goaded. "That I was the one who killed your father? That it was so easy to turn the gun he had on me on him? That I wrapped my hand around his and pulled the trigger? Is that what you want to know?"

A wail tore from my spirit.

My daddy.

My daddy.

Torment burned my throat and moisture filled my eyes.

I staggered forward.

Misplaced anger filled his face. "Only job I had was to get her back safe, and we could reclaim our spot in the family." He gestured a crazed hand at Genny, and I was seein' it then. That she'd run because she was actually truly terrified. That she'd been runnin' for her life. That again, she was being held against her will.

That this bastard destroyed and destroyed.

Fuck.

I couldn't see.

Couldn't see.

My daddy.

"Bitch ran and got into that accident. I was demoted like some kinda nobody, nothing but a fucking dog who got charged with watching over her. No longer her husband, my rank stripped, demoted to watching her night and day. You have any idea how much money that cost me? Your fault. Never would have happened had you not come riding in. A fool who had no idea what he was doing."

Genny whimpered. "Please, Noah. Let's just go. I'll stay with you. I'll stay. I promise."

He didn't spare her a glance when he took another step my direction. "Now, your time has finally come due. I've sat aside for seven fucking years, actin' as her glorified babysitter while you came time and again. Filling her head with all your make believe. Turning her against me. Begging her to leave and ruining my chances all over again. Warned you if you came again, it would be the last time. That I was going to destroy you."

His expression turned cruel. "Finally got rid of her daddy, so now Genny is going to prove her worth by getting rid of your mother and that whimpering bitch, and you're going to watch her do it. And I'm going to relish in every second of it. Then she's going to watch me end you...like I've been dying to do for seven years, or else she's gonna die, too. Her choice. Seven years you stole. Promised you, you'd only begun to pay."

His grin was smug derision. "Knew it was going to be a good night, but I have to admit, the money I found in the trunk of your girlfriend's car was a nice bonus."

Genny fumbled forward, beggin', "I'm sorry. I'm sorry, Rhys. I didn't mean to use you. I needed help. I needed you. I cared about you. So much. That's why I ended us. I was protectin' you."

"Shut up, Genny."

"Rhys, I'm sorry, please, you've got to understand. I won't do this, Noah. Please. We can't do this."

Before I could make sense of it, Noah whirled around. "Told you to shut the fuck up."

Then he pulled the trigger.

For a beat, I was stunned.

No ability to process.

To fathom.

Genny dropped to the ground.

My Maggie and my mama cried out beneath their gags.

That's all it took for me to snap.

I dropped my gun and charged him, roarin' as I went.

Eyes blurred and soul slayed and everything I'd thought I'd known gettin' torn to shreds.

My daddy.

Maggie.

Genny.

My mama.

He'd hurt every single person I loved.

I have a tendency to hurt the ones I love most.

It was him.

I was halfway to him when he spun back around and another gunshot rang out.

A shock through the night. And still I was running, and that was right when Royce and Richard busted out of the trees from behind. They tackled Noah before he got off another shot.

I didn't slow.

I dove right into that spiral.

Blinded by the fury that eclipsed all reason.

Blotted out coherency and all thoughts of what was right.

I tore into him.

Fist after fist.

"You killed him. You killed him." Haggard, rippin' words gasped and shook from my raw throat.

Crack, crack, crack.

Bone crunched and blood gushed and my spirit screamed.

Agony. Agony. Agony.

"You killed him."

My daddy.

My daddy.

You're a good boy, Rhys. A good, good boy.

My fist landed on his mouth, knockin' free teeth. I did it again and again. Unhinged. Unchained. Uncontrolled.

That sickness consuming. One I couldn't free myself of.

Because I knew nothing right then but hate.

This thirst for retribution more than I could bear.

"You killed him. You killed Genny. You hurt Maggie. You hurt my mama."

I wailed into him.

But he wasn't movin'.

Wasn't fightin'.

And I was bleedin'.

Bleedin' from the wound in my chest that I was pretty sure he'd inflicted that night seven years ago. Richard dragged me off him as I flailed and fought to bring down another blow.

"Stop, man. You've gotta stop. One more hit and you'll send him to the other side."

Vengeance cried out for it.

My daddy.

My daddy.

You're a good boy, Rhys. A good, good boy.

I slumped to the ground.

Unable to breathe.

Chest completely caving in.

Pain sheering and my mind reeling.

I'm so sorry, Daddy. I didn't mean to. I didn't mean to.

Maggie was suddenly screamin'. Her spirit tore through the air like a tempest.

Whipped the trees into a disorder.

The blackened sky was an endless abyss behind her.

I blinked as I looked up at her.

Her gorgeous, stunnin' face brutalized by my mistakes. Tears streamed from her eyes and those sweet hands were on my cheeks. Her fingers scratching into my beard.

"My stallion. My stallion. You came. You found me. I knew you would. You're okay. You're okay. We're going to be okay."

I reached up and fiddled with a piece of her black hair. "Look at that...a goddess beneath the stars lookin' down over me. Must've died and went to heaven."

And my daddy's voice filled my ears. Sank into my consciousness.

"And then every once in a while, God makes someone extra special. Someone who is more vulnerable than others, and it's our job to protect them. To take care of them. Even when it ain't pretty. You understand what I'm tellin' you?"

But it was her bravery that made her vulnerable. Her willingness to give and give. To sacrifice her safety for the benefit of someone else.

This sweet, good, beautiful girl.

And I prayed this was enough. That she would pass on that extraordinary belief. Live every single day to its fullest.

That she would spread those wings and fly.

Soar.

And if she ever found herself one of those cowboys, she wouldn't settle for bein' treated for anything less than the treasure she was.

For that, I would give it all.

Maggie

I was jarred up to sitting, gasping and shaken from the dream.

From the nightmare that had fear saturating every cell of my being.

Disoriented, I blinked through the disorder. Trying to see through the haze of pain laying siege to my body, to hear over the beeping of the machines, to find reality in the room cast in shadows, dark save for the small light above the hospital bed.

Hospital bed.

It only took a second for me to realize the visions in that nightmare were actually memories.

Being rammed from behind.

The car rolling.

The pain.

The pain.

That vicious, terrifying face, the same man from the bar all those months ago when I'd thought Rhys had lost it on a complete stranger, when it'd become clear that it had gone so much deeper than that when the monster dragged me from the wreckage of the car.

That tyrant who'd raged.

Torment clawed at my already aching chest.

Rhys had come. Had come to save me and his mama.

And he'd been…shot.

The air wheezed up my throat when the dream became a reality, and I flailed, the panic striking in a whole new way. I ripped and tore at the tubes and wires that I was hooked to so I could get up.

Find him.

Oh god.

No.

"No, no, no," I mumbled frantically.

Please.

A sob burst as I fought to get free.

As physical pain tore through my shoulder and splintered down my right side.

As I felt my entire world collapse.

Then I froze when I felt the shift.

When that energy thrashed.

A shockwave of intensity.

Bright and blinding and the most beautiful thing I'd ever felt.

My attention shot to the door of my hospital room.

I squinted, praying that I wasn't seeing things.

That a hallucination hadn't taken me over because that hulking, beast of a man was there in the doorway. He wore a hospital gown over his massive frame and a soft, wistful grin on his face. "Whoa, there, darlin'."

I choked over the sob, the sound shifting to a cry of deliverance. "Rhys. You're okay. You're here."

He was here. He was here.

"Shh…" He hushed me as he pushed the door open wider, and he angled in pulling a wheeled vital-sign monitor that was hooked to the wires that weaved under his gown.

"Rhys."

He lumbered across the room.

His pain palpable.

Slow and wounded but alive.

A whole, gorgeous, mesmerizing sight.

He wound around to the side of the small bed, and carefully, slowly, he crawled in beside me. Grunting and groaning as he went all while I couldn't contain the emotion that crashed.

It banged the walls and sank in the most astounding kind of comfort into my soul.

Moisture overflowed my eyes and dripped down my cheeks, and I didn't know whether to weep with relief or with the tragedy of it all.

"Rhys," I whimpered as he wound those arms around me.

The two of us were nothing but tangled wires and beeping monitors and frantically beating hearts.

He tugged me against his chest, and he pressed his lips to the top of my head as he murmured, "It's okay, Sweet Thing. I've got you. I heard you. I heard you in my dreams."

A sob broke free, and he tightened his hold. "I've got you."

"I'm so sorry I left. I should have known he was manipulating me."

"Don't apologize, Maggie. Know what you were doin'. Know you thought you were looking out for me. Protectin' me."

His arm curled fiercely around my body, and his words turned haggard, "That's supposed to be my job, baby. You should have trusted me to be the one to stand in the line of fire for you. Turns out, you were standin' in mine. Never wanted to put you in that position. Fuck...I—"

Determination shook my head, and I prayed that finally, finally he would understand. "No, Rhys...when two people love each other, they protect each other. They take care of each other. They are willing to sacrifice, and just like I know you'd willingly give your all for me, don't you get that I would do the same for you?"

A remorseful sigh heaved from his lips, and it sent wisps of my hair fluttering through the night. His spirit burdened.

Yet, I could feel it catching up.

Coming to certainty.

To a place where it would fully meet with mine.

My fingers softly traced over his sternum. "That's what you've always thought of yourself? As the one who was supposed to take care of everyone else? You thought it was your duty?"

A payment.

A penalty.

I still didn't have the whole story, but the pieces were building into something devastating.

Shame shivered through the dense air.

"I have a tendency to hurt the ones I love most."

His poor, beautiful, broken heart.

I didn't need there to be light in the room to read the anguish inscribed on Rhys' face. "I was nine when I caused an accident that made my father lose his arm." The confession left him on coarse, cragged words that he uttered to the crown of my head.

Agony and grief.

He struggled, the man at war with his past, but he managed to continue, "He lost so much more that day, Maggie. I didn't recognize it until I got a bit older, but I watched my family fall apart. He lost his job, of course, but as time went on, he lost his purpose. His will. He gave up, Maggie, and that was the worst thing I've ever had to bear."

"And you blamed yourself." It wasn't even a question. I could feel the guilt radiating from his bones.

"How could I not when I know full well it was my fault?"

"You were just a little boy."

"A little boy who destroyed his daddy's life."

Sorrow pulsed, and I burrowed deeper.

A promise that I would hold some of the weight.

Shoulder it.

Be there for him in every way.

Big or small.

In heartache and joy.

"I'm so sorry. I can't imagine what you've carried your whole life, Rhys."

Could feel the heavy bob of his throat when he swallowed. "Tried my best to be a man after that. To stand for my family. To take care of them both. Be strong enough. All I ever wanted, Maggie."

His words were gruff, the fractures in this man's heart finally breaking free.

"Stallion," I whispered.

Rhys trembled. "Wanted to be."

"You are. I know your father has to be looking down at you and see the man you've become. Your giving heart and your kind spirit. The sacrifice you're willing to make. The love you give."

Rhys choked back a sob. "Whole time, I'd thought he couldn't take it any longer. Thought I'd finally driven him to his end. Turns out I did, but in a different way."

My head shook with my cheek still pinned to his chest. "No, Rhys. You and your father were both standing for the people you loved. The ones you cared about. There is no blame in that. And I may never have gotten to meet him, but I promise you, your daddy loved you. There's no way he couldn't have."

"Just wish I could have done more. Stopped it. Changed it. Still can't believe..." He trailed off, stricken. "I can't believe Noah was responsible. That he got to my daddy when he'd been comin' for me. That it was him who hurt you. That he turned around and took Genny's life. God...that poor girl."

I refused the bolt of jealousy. Let the torment that had gushed from her fill me. Her fear. Her hurt. Her own ferocity. "It's absolutely horrible. I'm so sorry, Rhys. I know you loved her."

Rhys sighed. "I'm devastated for her, Maggie. That I couldn't change it or save her. All those years, I tried. And I did love her, but not in the way you're thinkin'. I would have done anythin' for her. Anything. At the time, I didn't know the difference. But I do now. I never burned for her. I was just in love with the idea of savin' her."

"When we were together..."

"Genny and I had been over for a long, long time." He shifted me so his hands were framing my face, forcing me to meet the intensity in his gaze. "Goddess Girl, would never do that to you.

391

Was just afraid I would fail you, too. Thought my life was nothing but bad marks."

Nodding, I sniffled. "I don't think you could fail me, Rhys." I cleared my throat, pushing on, feeling like the time I'd been sedated had been a decade.

Like a new history had been written and I'd missed it.

"What about Noah?"

Rhys' spirit thrashed. "His charges are long and deep. He was arrested for the murders of both Genny and her father. I've asked them to open a case for my father, too."

"Oh, Rhys. My sweet man."

I touched the edge of his mouth where it trembled.

"My daddy was a good man."

"No doubt," I whispered. "Look at the son he raised. Look at this good, good man."

Rhys kissed my fingertips that I ran across his lips.

I blinked. "I should have waited for you. The money..." I trailed off in a bit of misery. God. I'd thought I was protecting it, and all I'd done was turn it over to someone just as cruel and filled with greed as my father had been.

A glint instantly sparked in the depths of those blue, blue eyes. "Ah, no need to fret, my Sweet Thing. Your brother is a cunnin' devil. Seems he took off with the duffles into the woods before the cops showed. Dude thinks on his feet, that's for sure."

Relief rippled free on the softest giggle. "Of course, he did."

Rhys ran his thumb across the nape of my neck. Massaging. Comforting. "Another one of those good men."

"He is." I gulped around the lump that formed. "I can't believe I thought it was our mother this whole time."

I found solace in that. A spark of hope lighting that maybe...maybe she had a spec of a conscience, after all.

His lips shifted to grim. "I hate that I dragged you into my mess. Warned you I would."

"But we came out of it together."

Tenderness traipsed through his expression.

"What happens now?" That I whispered.

Those massive hands held tighter to my face. "We live, Maggie.

We live. As long as you still want me. As long as you're still feelin' this after everything I put you through."

"Do I feel it, Rhys? I felt it the day I met you. Something different. Something bigger." I rested my cheek back on the thundering of his chest. "And my heart—it got molded into a new shape. It got mended into the shape of you."

He chuckled low. "Huh. Seems mine got all mangled up in the shape of you, too."

Laughing, I swatted at him and edged back so I could see his smiling face.

One of those smiles that took my breath away and made me weak in the knees.

"Mangled, huh?" I demanded playfully.

He softened, his fingers gliding through my hair. "Yeah, Sweet Thing. So twisted up it no longer knows how to beat without yours."

My teeth clamped down on my bottom lip.

It was crazy how life could be.

How we could never anticipate the turns it would take.

How we could never predict the sharp curves in our paths or the direction each day might take.

How it only took a few months for our hearts that had been being sculpted for years to be forged into something brand new.

Something beautiful and right.

"I love you, Rhys Manning," I murmured.

Affection tugged his lips up at the sides. "Luckiest bastard alive."

I giggled, and he hugged me tight.

We both jerked when the door whipped open and a nurse rushed in. She stumbled a beat when she saw us then sent us a scowl. "There you are. You're not supposed to be in her bed. You're supposed to be in yours."

Rhys adjusted me so I was draped over the top of him, both of us wincing but knowing this kind of connection was worth a little pain. He was looking directly at me when he spoke. "Sorry, ma'am, I mean no disrespect, but no one gets to tell me whether it's right or wrong if I'm with my Maggie anymore."

Reaching up to cup my face, he chuckled. Low and rough. "Turns out, I'm good with breakin' all the rules for you."

Giddiness leapt.

"Let's break them together. Forever."

"Ahh, Goddess Girl, I like the way you think."

The nurse scowled, then Rhys shot her a smirk, and I was pretty sure she sighed. "Just for a bit. Then you need to get back to your room. You both need your rest."

She fiddled around us while Rhys held me tight, then she eased back out without saying anything else.

"Such a rebel," I teased.

"You always said you wanted a cowboy."

"No, Rhys…I want a stallion."

Love flashed across his face, and then he was tucking me against the safety of his humming heart again.

"Sing me that beautiful song you've been writing," I murmured.

And that gruff, rough voice billowed into the atmosphere.

Curling me in peace.

In hope.

In this faith.

Didn't know what was comin'
Didn't know where I was goin'
Fallin' faster
Comin' slower
Lookin' for a lover
To get lost under covers

In my whispers
In my ear
Wishing on a star
Hoping on a heart
And then you were there

I think I heard you in my sleep
I think I found you in my dreams

Beneath the Stars

I think I felt you in the daylight
Give me one minute, sweetheart
And I'll ruin everything

Thought I was a stranger
A man without shelter
A wanderer
Until I heard you whisper
And I knew that I was home

I think I heard you in my sleep
I think I found you in my dreams
I think I felt you in the daylight
I'm terrified, sweetheart
That I'm gonna ruin everything

Let's not pretend we're make believe
Let's just accept this destiny
You came and rearranged everything
This heart
This soul
This joy
Everything I'd thought I'd known
This man who'd forgotten to hope

I think you heard me in your sleep
I think you found me in your dreams
I think you felt me in the daylight
Now I'm going to give you everything
Oh, Sweet Thing, I'm gonna give you everything

epilogues

Maggie

I blazed down the two-lane road in my truck. The windows were rolled down and *Sweet Thing* blared from the speakers. A half-moon hovered just above the horizon where the mountains met the star-spattered sky, and the cool wind whipped my hair into chaos while my husband's voice whipped my heart into putty.

As he sang the love song he'd written for me when our lives had been in transition. As our crooked paths had intersected and brought us together.

Right where we belonged.

It was a song that had easily been added to their album that came out last year, although Rhys had put that hashtag to rest, anyway.

The man rewriting his story into what he wanted it to be.

I slowed as I came to the road to our property, turning right and slowly taking the dirt lane to our home where it sat in a valley in Rhys' hometown.

I was struck with a crest of energy.

My heart forever bottled in beautiful bliss.

It was a rambling old house that would forever need work, and ten horses were in the stables out back.

We were hard at work on the whole five-kid thing.

And when I pulled up to the rounded gravel lot there wasn't a cowboy in sight.

Just a stallion where he stood on the porch fronted by flowers waiting for me, all bristling, powerful muscle and that smirking smile where he leaned on the railing.

My spirit leapt.

Jumped and danced, and I was tossing open the door, smiling wide as I slid out of the driver's seat and grabbed my bag as I went.

"Look at that, a goddess under the stars," he called down to me.

It didn't matter how much time had passed. It still rushed heat across my flesh and splashed redness on my cheeks, my teeth clamping down on my bottom lip as I swayed my way up the walk.

"You must have hit your head," I teased him.

"If I did, no one better wake me."

I climbed the three steps to the porch, and he was pulling me into the warmth of those massive arms. He swooped in and planted a fierce kiss to my mouth. Those blue, blue eyes glowed their sweet severity when he pulled back. "How was the meeting?"

Lily and I had started an advocacy group here in Dalton for women who'd been through trauma of any kind.

A safe place.

Small, but needed.

I was still earning my counseling degree. Slowly but surely. But I knew this was what I'd been called to do.

That where my circumstances had shaped me, I had something to offer from those folds. Maybe—just maybe—I might be able to envelop myself around someone else to help them shape their own future.

"It was good. Really good."

His smile was adoring, and I couldn't do anything but scratch my fingers into his beard. "I missed you. How was your night?"

A smirk kicked up at the corner of his delicious mouth. "Um…went to Mama's for dinner. Couldn't be bad, now, could it?"

He'd wanted to level his mama's house and build something new. But after everything that had happened, she hadn't wanted that. She wanted those walls that swam with the memories.

The good and bad.

Of course, we'd settled right down the road because we didn't want to be far from her. She and Rhys were closer than ever, and we wanted to raise our family with her nearby.

We wanted her a staple in our lives. A fundamental piece.

It's what I'd always wanted.

A place to offer all this love that had been burning inside me.

Rhys and the band were still traveling. Touring. Their stardom had hit stratospheric levels.

Just like Sebastian Stone had been sure of, Carolina George had become a household name.

But all four of them knew what was important. Their families were their center. The grounding that drove everything else.

"I wish I could have been there."

He shook his head. "You had important things to do. I'm just glad you're back now. Been missin' the hell out of you."

"That so?"

We'd started to sway.

That energy spinning.

Drawing us closer and closer.

He rocked his hips forward, rubbing my belly with his hard cock.

Shivers raced but still I managed to tease, "Oh, guess someone did miss me."

He rumbled a chuckle, and then he was lifting me off my feet and into those arms.

Carrying me to our bed.

A place that was only ours.

A place where we met and loved.

Where he held me, and I held him.

Where we shared our dreams and held each other in our sorrows.

When life got heavy, and in the times when we felt like we were flying.

And he loved me there.

Wholly.

Easily.

Completely.

Those blue eyes gazing down as our bodies met in a tumble of need and devotion.

Giving.

Taking.

"Sweet Siren," he murmured through our kiss, his hands in my hair and my heart in his fist. "What are you doin' to me?"

"Loving you."

Eternally.

This beautiful man.

My stallion.

My forever.

Rhys

*W*ith our heartbeats thrumming their content, Maggie and I lie

staring at the ceiling, trying to catch our breaths while smiles rested on our faces.

"I guess someone really did miss me," she said, shifting a fraction so she could press a kiss to my pec where she curled up in the well of my arm.

Was pretty sure that arm had been made to hold the shape of her.

"Warned ya."

I glanced down and found those charcoal eyes tracing me. Writing me in her story. This girl with the greatest belief. One who I'd been terrified held the power to change everything.

Love nearly busted right through my chest.

Just lookin' at her.

The fact that she had.

Her truth that I was worth so much more than just a good time, though I was all too happy to give her a whole lot of that, too.

"Sweet Thing."

She sighed and kissed me in the same spot again, and then a tiny cry was coming from the monitor. "Sounds like someone else was missin' you, too," I told her. I dropped the peck of a kiss to her temple. "Why don't you get cleaned up, and I'll grab him."

"Thank you."

I slipped from the bed and into my underwear, then I crossed the creaking hall because when my girl said she wanted an old house, that's what I'd delivered.

Walls aged to a glowing, thrumming perfection.

But it was the love livin' here that did that.

I eased open Keaton's door, and I knew he felt me approach, way his little spirit shifted from his distressed cries to the sweet little grunts coming from his mouth.

A nightlight that cast stars across his walls and ceiling lit the space, and I crept over to his crib so I could gaze down at my little man.

My chest squeezed tight.

Fierce and swift and with the greatest amount of devotion.

Every once in a while, God makes someone extra special. Someone who is more vulnerable than others, and it's our job to protect them.

And I knew my daddy had meant his family then, too. That he'd passed that on to me. That it was our jobs to protect and teach and love somethin' mad.

Keaton saw me and cooed, staring up at me with his charcoal eyes that matched his mama's, his little feet kicking in excitement.

"Hey there, little man. You gettin' hungry?"

Another coo, and he went to shoving his tiny fist into his mouth.

Love stretched like a bow, and I reached up and twisted the dial to his mobile. The one thing that seemed to soothe him other than being in my or his mama's arms. The one that was made up of crudely folded horses and ducks and interspersed with a few misshapen stars and hearts.

His eyes bugged out when the melody of *Sweet Thing* filled his room, and he smiled around his fist.

My hand reached out and splayed across his whole abdomen.

Like I could shield the entirety of him with only my hand.

We stayed like that for a bit, just restin' in the peace that I never thought I'd be afforded.

Every day of my life, I would cherish this gift.

Standing there in the shadows of my son's room, I could see a vision of my daddy doin' the same. I could almost feel the presence of him standing over me when I'd been the same size. And I promised him all over again that I understood. That I got it now. And I knew, without question, he'd loved me to the end.

I shifted when I felt the energy emerge from behind.

Big and booming.

Stealing air and sanity.

My gaze skated that way.

She stood in the doorway with that smile on her face that made me weak in the knees, all that black hair in a messy twist on her head and wearing a set of those short sleep shorts that drove me insane. "There are my men."

My whole bein' shivered and thrashed.

"No matter what she looks like, once you feel it right here…" He tapped his fingers over the beatin' of Rhys' heart. *"She'll be the only thing you can see. Just like your mama always says…it'll be love, love, love."*

Love, love, love.

Yeah. It's what made up this house.

This family.

Luckiest. Bastard. Alive.

the end

Thank you for reading *Beneath the Stars!*

I hope that Rhys and Maggie's story gave you all the feels!

Want more from the Caroline George crew?

Start with their drummer, Leif, in *Kiss the Stars*

https://geni.us/KTSAmzn

Did you love the men and women of Sunder? Start where it all

began with Shea and Sebastian in *A Stone in the Sea*

https://geni.us/ASITSAmzn

New to me and want more? I recommend starting with my
favorite small town alphas!

Start with *Show Me the Way*

https://geni.us/SMTWAmzn

Text "aljackson" to 33222 to get your LIVE release mobile alert
(US Only)
or
Sign up for my newsletter
https://geni.us/NewsFromALJackson

More from A.L. Jackson

Redemption Hills
Give Me a Reason
Say It's Forever
Never Look Back
Promise Me Always

The Falling Stars Series
Kiss the Stars
Catch Me When I Fall
Falling into You
Beneath the Stars

Confessions of the Heart
More of You
All of Me
Pieces of Us

Fight for Me
Show Me the Way
Follow Me Back
Lead Me Home
Hold on to Hope

Bleeding Stars
A Stone in the Sea
Drowning to Breathe
Where Lightning Strikes
Wait
Stay
Stand

ABOUT THE AUTHOR

A.L. Jackson is the New York Times & USA Today Bestselling author of contemporary romance. She writes emotional, sexy, heart-filled stories about boys who usually like to be a little bit bad.

Her bestselling series include THE REGRET SERIES, CLOSER TO YOU, BLEEDING STARS, FIGHT FOR ME, CONFESSIONS OF THE HEART, FALLING STARS, and REDEMPTION HILLS.

If she's not writing, you can find her hanging out by the pool with her family, sipping cocktails with her friends, or of course with her nose buried in a book.

Be sure not to miss new releases and sales from A.L. Jackson - Sign up to receive her newsletter http://smarturl.it/NewsFromALJackson or text "aljackson" to 33222 to receive short but sweet updates on all the important news.

Connect with A.L. Jackson online:

FB Page **https://geni.us/ALJacksonFB**
Newsletter **https://geni.us/NewsFromALJackson**
Angels **https://geni.us/AmysAngels**
Amazon **https://geni.us/ALJacksonAmzn**
Book Bub **https://geni.us/ALJacksonBookbub**
Text "aljackson" to 33222 to receive short but sweet updates on all the important news.